The Broken River Tent

The Broken River Tent

Mphuthumi Ntabeni

BLACKBIRD
BOOKS

First published by BlackBird Books, an imprint of Jacana Media (Pty) Ltd, in 2018

10 Orange Street
Sunnyside
Auckland Park 2092
South Africa
+2711 628 3200
www.jacana.co.za

© Mphuthumi Ntabeni, 2018
©Author cover image: Helen Ntabeni

ISBN 978-1-928337-45-4

Cover design by Palesa Motsomi
Editing by Alison Lowry
Proofreading by Joey Kok
Set in Sabon 10/14pt
Job no. 003261

Printed by **novus** print, a Novus Holdings company

See a complete list of BlackBird Books titles at www.jacana.co.za

To my late father, Mzoli Ntabeni, who shadow-walks me

2017

The Gravediggers

THE ENTRANCE TO THE HANGBERG MULTIPURPOSE Sport Centre was unusually busy for a non-social grant payment day. Media cameras were everywhere. Their little village town had caught the attention of the nation, Phila thought, if not exactly the world.

"*Ngawethu!*"

The main speaker for the evening had entered the hall. While other speakers assembled on the podium Phila took a seat near the back. Although he regarded himself as part of this community, he felt somewhat out of place, as if he was faking his solidarity to leech onto the people's pain.

It was soon evident that the community meeting had been hijacked by politicians and Phila had difficulty holding his concentration. A guy from something to do with Social Justice was saying something about the government marginalising and criminalising the poor. "The lies of the city and provincial officials who call us drug lords when we demand our constitutional rights shall be exposed!" he cried, becoming very animated. He spoke for quite a long time, mixing English in Afrikaans. People clapped violently.

Next a Rastafarian took the microphone, first hailing Haile Selassie and Jah and then dissing the "Babylonian governments and their system of oppression. Dem tell us to reconcile, meantime dem serve us snake for fish, and rocks for bread. *Mandela se kak!*" The crowd went wild. "*Ons KhoiKhoi mense!* We demand our land back ..." There was something impressively radically anarchist about the Rasta.

As the meeting finally looked as if it was drawing to an end, after almost two hours, and the cameramen were packing up their equipment, Phila went outside to get some air and have a cigarette. He found himself reflecting on the reason for this meeting, the events of the past week which had culminated in what the media, with their flair for dramatic nostalgia, had called Black Tuesday. The police had come, around 2am, in what one of the speakers had termed 'apartheid style', to evict people who had illegally invaded land on the slopes of Hangberg. Phila wasn't totally clear about the details but the violence had started when residents resisted the police. On his walk back home earlier, after having fish and chips at Fish-On-The-Rocks as the sun went down, his route took him close to where the events of Black Tuesday had unfolded. The place had looked like an abandoned movie set for the apartheid era. On his way he had stooped to pick up a used teargas canister shell, obviously from a police shotgun, and he'd slipped it into his pocket without thinking.

That speaker was right. The events of the previous week had introduced a reminiscent order of apartheid days in the streets of their village town. Phila himself had been there, doing what he could to help. When a TV newsman at the riot scene had asked him to give his opinion, on camera, he had wanted to sound revolutionary, to send a clear message that the impoverished should not be pushed around and criminalised for being poor. Instead, dogged by his middle-class timidity, he'd come up with a cautious statement about "the irony of the fact that when developers for the rich want to push mountain firebreaks it is done at the stroke of a pen, but now that the poor have run out of living space they are treated like brigands who are illegally occupying land."

It irritated him that he was always so cautious, reasonable and unspontaneous. His mind was neither quick nor nimble; he lacked the gift of spontaneity, which was why he found it hard to improvise on the spot. At best he had keen powers of observation and some originality when given a moment to apply his mind, but his kind always got swallowed by the revolution.

He thought about how, a decade and a half ago, during the so-called rainbow era of Mandela, the country was full of hope and assertive belief in the renewal of its humanity. Now he saw the return of cynicism, suspicion, despair, and police terror, the suppression of freedom, with all the accompanying horrors. Community meetings with fired-up rhetoric. Loud-hailers on the streets, calling citizens to action – like the one on the red bakkie that had gone past his window and alerted him to this meeting tonight, urging residents to "do a postmodern on the BRUTALITY of the police last Tuesday, when they invaded our community APARTHEID style. Injury one! Injury all! The BOEREBOND is on the rise again!"

Outside he was joined by a podgy fellow who had been at the podium table and whom Phila was sure he'd seen somewhere else. Initially he couldn't place him but then he realised: he was the security guard at the local supermarket, who usually greeted him when he went there for supplies, who sometimes helped him with the groceries, very politely, to the car. Phila always made sure to tip.

"Nice of you to join us, sir," the fellow said with his usual politeness.

Phila was glad to recognise a face in that sea of strangers. The fellow swapped his cigarette to his left hand before extending his right, and they ended up shaking hands for a little too long and more vigorously than was necessary.

"I never figured you as the revolutionary type," Phila said, regretting the statement the moment it went out of his mouth. It turned out the fellow was a community leader of some kind. Inside, when people had kept referring to community leaders and shouting socialist slogans, they had been referring to him. An ironic twist surely – socialists guarding the doors of capitalism? Talk about capitalism producing its own grave-diggers, thought Phila.

He was still turning fiery phrases over in his mind, of the type he could have used in front of the TV camera when he'd had the chance. *The government is wiping our turned-up noses with the sword; our liberators have turned into our oppressors. A luta continua!* Deep down he knew there was no way he could have said all of that. Even in his head it all sounded fake. He was no revolutionary; neither did he want to be one. He believed more in the evolution of the mind, the gradual progress etcetera. The usual crap of weak characters who never want to be involved in the real struggles under the guise of being civilised. The irony was that he spent almost all his life trying to civilise his mind; now he was doing everything possible to escape the fate of Prufrock, the ineffectual, well-bred man during times of rising tensions and turbulences.

Irony struck him again as he said goodnight to the community leader and set off home. These riots, when it came down to it, were all about one thing. Land. The irony, in the twenty-first century, was that the players were still the same as before. You had the KhoiKhoi people on the slopes of Hangberg, and the Xhosas – mostly from the Eastern Cape, where their forefathers had fought the British colonial powers – on the slopes of Karbonkelberg where Imizamo Yethu informal settlement was situated. And then in the affluent valley down below were mostly the white people, progeny of the settlers from the 1800s.

Phila walked home under a maturing sheet of darkness. Moonlight cracked the sky with pale fissures of light.

2007

River People

THE DAY WAS WINDY AND COLD. Phila sat in the bright silence of Prospect Hill, against the stone walls of Fort Frederick, reading from the book *The Consolation of Philosophy* by the Ancient Roman philosopher Boethius. He had to hold tight with both hands to keep it steady against the wind. From a short distance, a racket of laughing-quarrelling homeless people broke the hum of the motorway traffic. Lately he had been feeling lethargic. The arrival of a luxury bus, carrying Chinese tourists, distracted his reading. Soon the tourists filed past him with their digital cameras and smartphones, taking panoramic pictures of the city below. Phila raised his eyes to meet smiling faces exposing bad teeth. Some rudely took pictures of him without the courtesy of asking. He felt insulted. Others came to sit next to him, making hand gestures indicating that he must keep reading while their friends took photographs. *"Nî hâo. Zuò! Bùyào zhànlì."*

Hemmed in and harried, he resented being made into an exotic object but, as usual, was too polite to protest. He distrusted their exaggerated laughter, as if they were trying to convince themselves and the world that they were free to do as they pleased. Their fake exuberance was instructive.

Eleven years bunkered in the city of Port Elizabeth had been, for Phila, more of a retreat from his failures than progress towards something. The city, with its sleepy aura and lost industry, felt like a place for quiet endings. It was easy to be indifferent within its village soul, stubborn colonial character and bland industry. Its pleasing forlornness was the natural habitat of his melancholic spirit. The city had achieved a spiritual victory over the crassness of urbanisation by expanding in interconnected village towns that conceal its industrial areas.

Often, when people asked what he did, Phila felt defeated. His explanations differed according to mood, but they all touched on his failed architectural firm and musings about collecting material to write the

11

history of the area. He tended to be vague with the specifics except that
it was historical, with an emphasis on Xhosa resistance against British
colonialism. Many were awed, others suspicious, but nobody disputed his
bona fides. In reality, he wandered about the city, like Mr Biswas, looking
for something to turn up and a place to call home. He visited museums
and art galleries when he got tired of reading in the library where hobos
bullied him with their intransigent attitudes. He frequented the nightlife
of Central, where the extorted comforts of social misfits and the excluded
flourished. He lived in the township, where residual anxieties threw sharp
light on the rising standards of revolt. In short, he was a dangling man.

Aeons ago, when apartheid was still in fashion, Phila had got a
scholarship to study architecture in Germany. Such ambitions were
still forbidden to black people in his country in the 1980s, but a way
was found for him to beat the system. He went overseas, did what was
expected of him, even managed to find his way around Deutsch. He never
anticipated he would feel *unheimlich* upon returning home. Nine years
in Europe had made him a stranger to his roots. He felt 'his people' – the
ones he shared culture with by birth, whom he had had to leave before he
could cognitively feel part of – did not share his ambitions or intellectual
torments. Before he'd left he'd presumed a superior destiny to them, even
disdain for what he thought to be their indolence because he felt spurred
by a sense of elevated sensitivity far above the typical township aspirations.
Hence it was not too difficult for him to leave, to expose himself to other
frontiers. Voluntary exile tested his salt, and taught him humility towards
'his people'.

When the Chinese tourists had filed inside the fort, Phila made to read
again. Distracted once more, this time by the sounds of construction work
from the City Hall down below in Main Street, he closed the book. He
recalled how his architectural firm had won the tender to refurbish that
historic building, and subsequently lost it when he'd refused to grease a
certain government official's hands. At the time the country had been under
the euphoric cloud, the new freedom of the Mandela years. It had been
waking up, if slowly and with a hangover, from the National Party era.
But Phila hadn't felt a part of anything. He'd found himself wandering the
streets, trying to be part of one thing or the other, but nothing had quite
fitted. His internal space was disconnected to the national jubilant echoes.
That was when he'd felt he needed time to rediscover home. By and by
he found himself searching for reasons behind the present situation in the
country. Most of the answers lay in history, so he started there. He never

thought whatever he needed to do would take more than a few years. Complications kept piling up, mostly driven by the need for a corrective catalogue of his shortcomings.

His cell phone vibrated in his pocket. The sounds of the tourists coming back to the revving noise of the tour bus made it impossible for Phila to hear properly. He moved away from the maddening crowd to the leeward side of the fort, regretting losing the faint heat from the sun, what the Xhosas called the baboon sun.

"Hello?" he answered, noticing on the screen that it was his home number. It could only be his sister Siya. After perfunctory greetings, she went straight to the point.

"We've just been informed that our father died from a peptic ulcer last night. I've been trying to get hold of you but your phone was off," she said, in her usual matter-of-fact way.

Phila felt there was something of a veiled insinuation in her brisk tone.

"Ja ... my phone loses signal sometimes ..."

Static silence ensued before Siya broke it with another tacit comment – "I guess you'll be coming home soon then?" – although this time it sounded as if she was retracting the insinuation.

"Yes, of course." He did not know what else to say.

Home was Queenstown, about four hundred kilometres from PE.

"Okay then, see you soon."

The phone went dead. Phila's ears transmitted very little beyond a grim tinnitus buzz. He faked a yawn to open them, but the trick failed.

He walked, with a lost stride, around the fort to the side facing the harbour where the slow-moving green Baakens River surrendered to the sea. The highway over the river, itself collapsing on entering the suburb of Humewood towards the more affluent Summerstrand, was a wonder to observe. His grandma used to call highways 'flying roads'. "White people can milk birds if you ask them to," was her leitmotif on such things. To Phila, this estuary area was where things came to a head. It was there – or thereabout – in 1820 that the British settlers had landed. Phila had read in the papers that they were planning to build a gigantic statue of Nelson Mandela, like the Statue of Liberty in New York, in the area. For what, he thought to himself. To counteract the colonial spirit?

Down below, huddled in the groove of the hill against the harsh wind that combed its crest, Phila recognised some of the homeless people who were always around here. He descended towards them. They were cooking in tin pots over an open fire. Secretly envying their carefree vagabond lives, he thought about the nobility of poverty. He didn't really believe in it, though. He was not a Franciscan in spirit; his tendencies were more epicurean. He liked clean clothes, the comfort of restful sleep on clean white sheets, hearty food properly prepared, and many other such pleasures. Among these friends he felt like an impostor, not really fitting in even if they let him laugh at their crude jokes. He knew the only thing he was good for with them was an occasional note to buy something to soften the harsh realities of passing time. They greeted him with welcoming familiarity. The lady with laughing eyes (he could never tell whose girlfriend she was) passed a bottle of vodka to him after swiping a pull from it. He politely declined and moved on a bit.

His sister's phone call managed to settle, in a less than a minute, a question he had been wrestling with for some time now. There was nothing for him in the city anymore. He thought about making a fresh start somewhere, even as he knew there were no fresh starts because we carry ourselves wherever we go. We bring our lares with us, the Romans, according to Boethius, would say. It worried and relieved him that he was not really part of anything: the dangling man. The Germans called it *Heimweh nach der Fremde.* Wanting to be where one is not, a continual process of deferral. His bane.

He trained his eyes back on the river, thinking he might learn something from the manner in which it gave itself to the vastness of the sea. Anything to take his mind off his father's death was preferable at that moment. The thing about nature, he thought to himself, is that it knows its part in the bigger picture, because it is driven by forces beyond its control. To Phila this was the meaning of fate. He took out his pencil, as was his habit, to scribble some of these thoughts down.

Rivers are instructive and fascinating. In a river stream there are levels of flow. Where inhibitions occur swirls develop. A swirl creates noise but does not run deep. If it tries to take short-cuts it often eddies, spins off and dies. This is due to lack of depth. Or else it scatters into a swamp that festers with either life or disease. If the eddy is lucky, it gets caught up again in the deeper current of the river to become part of the wider, silent stream.

No stream runs higher than its source.

Parents are natural banks and channels for the run of their children. Without banks, the water becomes a swamp that breeds infectious diseases. Channels that are too deep become choking dungeons where children can't breathe, or can't take a better view of the world. Channels of proper depth and right direction carry their children as tributaries to the fertile depths of the ocean, where life gestates life, and deep calls unto deep!

Phila's parents divorced when he was in his teens. He was now about to crown forty. He and his father had rarely seen each other, maybe once a year if they were lucky to bump into each other in town. Those accidental meetings were awkward, with both parties wishing to part as soon as possible after perfunctory greetings. But the harsh finality of his father's absence in death confused Phila.

Memories evoke a strong sense of incompleteness.

Phila's head felt clubbed as he walked to the bus stop, and his ears registered each step with a dull, dumb-dumb force against a water-filled tank. He didn't feel grief per se. Remorse, rather. Remorse for things left unsaid and undone. Remorse for running out of time.

Seated inside the bus, he opened his book where he had left off, the section about fate. What is fate, he thought to himself. A debunking of coincidences? The presence of driven circumstances beyond one's anticipation? He tried reading about it, but mental and emotional fatigue fractured his concentration. It was as though he was entering an airy lightness between consciousness and sub-consciousness as his mind hiccupped into a no man's land.

He was aware of someone standing before him. He saw a stocky, muscular, prune-faced man with a cadaverous visage, wearing traditional Xhosa clothes and a leopardskin blanket thrown over them. The man quietly sat down next to him but Phila didn't feel the seat give. Try as he did to move, Phila's body stayed motionless as a jug. He suspected things were not following their natural order. The man, now seated next to him, wore voetskoene on his feet – nobody wore those things anymore – with his gnarled toenails protruding. Phila gave the man a slide-along, bent-down look. Something about the stranger looked familiar.

'I came to this world when our nation was tottering towards serfdom.'

The man spoke with the heavy inflections of the rural Xhosa, to Phila slightly insular.

'I've asked myself, time and time again, how could a couple of scum from the ocean manage to defeat and reduce us in such a short period to being refugees and beggars in our own land?'

Phila was a little startled by the statement but he kept quiet. Possibly interpreting this as encouragement to continue with his speech, the man went on. 'My cradle was of eutectic execrations. Misfortune dogged me from the start. It bred murder in a gall of bitterness and a bond of wickedness in me.' Phila, whose Xhosa was demotic, found himself struggling to understand the old-fashioned construction, the unusual manner in which the man used words.

'If you don't mind, sir,' he interrupted, more bored than polite. 'I'm not having a good day myself. I have a lot of stuff occupying my head right now.'

But the man continued regardless. 'I was instructed to tell you about my life. To learn you the truth.'

'You mean to teach me the truth.'

'No – to learn you the truth,' the man repeated, unapologetic. 'The language of this world shall know and fall short to convey the meaning I am trying to impress on you. But we must both be patient. Everyone – children, especially – needs a secret world in which to live things that have not yet been. This is where the power of the imagination resides. This is what informs the character and personality.'

Phila looked out of the window at St George's Park, where the Nelson Mandela Museum had hung a banner advertising a George Pemba exhibition. Pemba had been born in Korsten, the Sophiatown of PE. The banner said the exhibition was in honour of his posthumous reception of the Order of Ikhamanga. Phila was trying to recall what type of flower ikhamanga was when the man interrupted his thoughts.

'Sometimes you need to be invisible for people to see you,' the man said. 'Like now you are beginning to see your father. When you have the strength you require, after I have departed from your vision, you must tell of things you heard from me. Of tales of the old country. Of things not of this world but living forever in the hearts of its people. You must tell of the River People. Of how they haunted the heart of our nation into self-destruction. Tell of the ocean's eye that opened to let in the people of wheat-coloured hair who brought a double-edged sword to our land. This is the only way you shall learn the truth of yourself. But you must first believe in your heart.'

Phila's mouth was salty from the anxiety and fear he tasted from the man's words. The calf of his left leg was shaking. He averted his eyes and looked out the window again, at the orange fuzz of street lights that were beginning to flicker outside. Two teenage boys, in cricket white attire, were racing across in a radius line by which the bus was circumferencing the park. They were obviously from Grey High School, the first black kids to attend such posh schools. They had the confidence to match it by the way they threw their bags behind the driver's seat after clipping their bus tokens. Panting, they continued with whatever it was they'd been talking about before they'd had to face the bus. They spoke with the nasal timbre termed the Model C accent in South Africa. Phila's interest in them faded with their voices. And with that grew his strange visitor's voice.

'Your side of life is to learn to control the use of your imagination to desire only goodness, which aligns you with the ultimate truth, the source of life, Dal'ubomi. When I was under the wheeling of time, like you, I was very unlucky. I was woken into maturity by thundering cannons and stuttering rifles. I spent my life writhing like a roped bull. That's the fate Dal'ubomi dished me with the coming of white people in our land. Now I carry within myself a place of my own exile.'

Phila looked around to see if any of the other passengers were privy to this Thespian performance. After he realised none could hear or see the old man he dropped his head on his lap. His first concern was that he might be losing his mind. Checking back with apprehension, he counselled himself into thinking straight. Tracing his mind back to the news of his father's death, he comforted himself with the notion that he was just under extreme stress. Try as he might to put a distance between himself and this, by trying to concentrate on what he would cook for supper, the voice of the old man came back.

'There were times in my life when everything that came to me was a source of misery. I was never given the opportunity to be my own self. Being born of royal blood in times of exceptional disquiet was my curse. I was groomed only to be a warrior. I knew very little beyond war. Its iron ate deeply into my spirit and flesh. In the end, what became more difficult for me was adjusting to peace; to fighting nothing. Outside war I was like an eagle without wings, clumsy with its awkward talons to scratch the itch. So I took a destructive path.'

'Oh, for crying out loud!' Phila threw his head on his knees again and tried to close his ears. But the old man continued narrating his story unabated.

He used to think, he told Phila, his eyes narrowing, that his latent defect was being born of a weakling father in internecine times. 'I was young then and ignorant of fate. Fate that pinned men to their doom. I had not properly learnt that we're all like worms on the hook. Age confers a spirit of wisdom on a man.'

The bus had now stopped outside the Greenacres Mall where the pollution of artifical light gave a mock festive mood with a garbage of screaming screens advertising electronic gadgets and women's shampoo.

When the white people first came, the old man continued, seemingly oblivious to everything around them, inside and outside the bus, they welcomed them, tried to learn their ways. He grew up under a person he called Khula, a white man who married his grandmother.

The verbosity of light and the old man's garrulousness were now getting Phila's goat, but something told him anger would make things worse, so he tried placating the old man.

'Look, this is really interesting, man, it really is,' said Phila. 'But I'm kind of in the middle of something right now. I've just learnt of my – '

'*The chief concern of mortal men is to keep their hold on life.*'

What the hell? The man was quoting Boethius?

'*As if this is the only life worth living.*' The old man finished the quote with an ease that went beyond disquieting Phila. This was freaking him out. They were now leaving Korsten, meaning next would be his own suburb.

'This is the only life we know,' Phila said, acting unconcerned.

'The truth is, when white people came they took us by surprise. We were loosely organised tribal confederations, given to too much quarrelling among ourselves and against one another, and riling under the blind bondage of superstition.'

'Amen to that.' Phila attempted to be frivolous. 'And since we're quoting Boethius – "*Luck is good luck to the man who bears it with equanimity.*" *Makawe amazulu ukuba ayasindwa yinyani!*'

He was preparing to leave, his attention on his stop coming up, but his joints were stiff and for some reason he struggled to get to his feet. The man jabbed him with a corner of his eye and Phila slumped back down again. Then the man did something even stranger. He translated what Phila had just said in Xhosa into German. '*Bitte um Gerechtigkeit auch beim schlechten Aussiecht.*' That sent shivers down his spine. This apparition and now this Tower of Babel clamouring in his head – obviously they were connected but what did they mean? Was he going mad? Madness had always been what Phila feared most.

If the man even noticed Phila's anxieties, he disregarded them.

'We had no precedent to follow in dealing with white people,' he continued, as if he hadn't been speaking German two minutes ago. 'Other nations we understood. Arabs were our ancient visitors. The Quena, whom the white people call Otentottu, constantly found a home with us, constantly joining our tribes, intermingling and marrying ...'

'I hear you treated the Bushmen like trash,' Phila succumbed.

'I suppose you mean the hunting people who call themselves Kung? You must disabuse yourself from the habit of calling people by derogative terms. I do not even know why you call yourselves Xhosas. That was the name the Kung called us in anger. We never adopted it.'

'I think it was the white people who adopted it for us. It has since stuck.'

'We treated the Kung like trash only when they stole our cattle, but integrated them when they respected our customs. I don't know if you've heard of Hermanus Matroos?'

'Can't say I have, and frankly I don't –' Phila tried to resume his aggressive sarcasm but got no chance as the man carried on.

'A brave man for a runaway slave. We shall talk about him later. We had nothing against foreigners who respected our ways and didn't just want to seize land from us. White people were different. They did not want to intermarry with us, they cheated us of our wealth, and generally held themselves with superior airs against our traditions. They found it beneath them to accept us as their equals.'

From the curling of the man's lip Phila spied reticent disillusionment.

'Well, at the risk of generalising, nothing much has changed since. Why return? Didn't find any tribes to lord in the netherland?'

'Even my father, Ngqika, with all his cunning, ended up on the losing side where white people were concerned. While most Xhosa chiefs were still confounded by the coming of whites, Ngqika saw a gap. He sought to make white people his allies in the wars he was engaged in with the likes of Ndlambe. And what did that gain him? An addiction to white man's liquor and an early grave, induced by a swollen liver. On top of that, he lost most of his land to the white men in any case. His friendship with them gained him no favours.'

'Sounds familiar. Yourselves, you had taken the land from the Kung. Whites took from you.' Phila had by now taken down his crock, as the Xhosas would say.

The man appeared unperturbed by his tone. 'Had we put aside our tribal differences,' he said, 'and recognised the common danger, stood together, we'd have stood a chance against the white people, no matter how many redcoats they brought from the sea. We knew the land better. We were beginning to exploit their greed by buying rifles and gunpowder from them, and we were generally numerous and agile.'

'Ja, right!'

The man seemed oblivious to Phila's sarcasm. 'In any case, no use crying over spilt milk. I've no need to justify myself. I'm done with prevarications and the elegant myths of historical lies. I had enough time to think when the white man incarcerated me in the wet limestone desert.'

'You mean Robben Island, hee? Man! Were you alive now, you'd be famous! You would become a president or something; or at least a minister of something. Ask Mandela.' Phila resumed a frivolous tone but the man didn't appreciate his humour.

'Mandela went there way after my time.'

'So I've heard. You guys were pioneers. Robben Island was the University of Life for recalcitrant kaffirs, hee?'

'You think?'

'That's what I've heard. If you don't mind my asking – what does an incarcerated person do on the island with his time? Speak to the wind? I mean, I've always wanted to ask you lot, Mandela, Napoleon, St John – at least we know what St John did, he jotted his visions down into becoming Revelations in the Bible.'

Clearly the man wasn't going to rise to any of the bait Phila was offering.

'With the wind the degrees of fellowship are levelled. All distinction is obliterated and things are naked as they should be. Your conscience becomes the only tribunal. The lesson I understood late in that miserable dungeon is that it is better to listen to the wind than to brave the storm.' He stopped to contemplate his point.

'Sorry I asked.' Phila reverted to sarcasm again.

'I, Maqoma, son of Ngqika, have seen and done horrid things, things that nearly broke my spirit. I've languished under a dark roof; talked to parliaments of owls in that dungeon; slept in the flummoxing environment of screeching bats. But ...'

Maqoma. So that's who he was. Phila had thought he looked familiar.

'That's the rod of Victoria for you,' Phila said. 'Mandela's spirit was still not broken, though, when he came out.'

'When I contemplate what I was, what I became as a result of white people, I tremble to the core of my being. I used to have the temper of a snarling dog. I would pass my days in planning their annihilation and nothing else. We softened the horror of murder by calling it war, or defending our motherland. But I learnt patience upon the rock. Dal'ubomi, Qamata kaTayi, is now my only quest.'

'They got you good, hee? The whites tended to have that effect on native warriors the world over. I guess you had your winter training?'

'I am gathering the wind from the four corners of the earth. Before my body became the property of maggots I had no wisdom in me. But when I joined the ancestors wisdom became my companion. I've come to you as a friend, and a guide for your thoughts. Far have I journeyed to share this year with you. My duty is to teach you the message I denied with my own life on this earth. I have been a man of misfortunes. Yet my heart is not bitter. And that I carry to Qamata as my prize.'

'You know what they say: no man is completely happy that something somewhere does not clash with his condition. It was nice meeting you. But I am in no mood to be a student, or an initiate of bygone wisdom ...'

'Human life can be a trivial illusion. Like a meteor, it fades away after momentary brightness.'

'Amen to that. Now you see why I don't have time for all of this.'

'I present my life story to the wind. Catch its meaning and learn from it if you want. One thing is certain – vanity is the commanding passion for your age. It is the weakness of mortal man and proud principalities. But it shall be your downfall if you don't change your ways.'

Something was happening. People were standing up. Jerking motion and the whoosh of electronic doors opening. Some women were talking, laughing, and a baby was crying somewhere behind him. Phila opened his eyes and realised the bus had stopped. He had cramped feet. The seat beside him was empty. He looked around but the man was nowhere to be seen. Only his body odour lingered in the air – smoke mingled with old sweat, sharp as the smell of aloe juice.

Waking up the following morning at his house Phila was troubled by yet another strange dream that felt more like a vision. He wondered if it was mental pressure from learning of his father's death causing all this, or whether there was something sinister at hand, more than mere psychological disturbance. He decided to research the phenomenon at the library.

The best he could find when he got there was a condition he decided to call 'triple N' – a combination of neurasthenia, narcolepsy and intellectual *ne plus ultra*. He received renewed energy from the diagnosis. The trick now was to manufacture the cure. The best way to deal with your fears is to face them directly, he told himself. After a few hours in the library he went back up to Prospect Hill and Fort Frederick. He sat in the same spot against the stone wall as he'd done the previous day, daring things to follow the same course to the phantom circuit again.

Nothing happened.

Looking down on the bay below, Phila tried to imagine the reaction of the Xhosas watching the first British ship dock at what was then known as Algoa Bay. What a strange phenomenon indeed it must have been to them: a house floating on water, then white people coming from it, with hair flowing like maize cobweb, whose ears 'lighted' when hit by sunlight. The Xhosas, as quintessential wanderers, hardly had any feelings of xenophobia then. In fact, like Abraham of the Jewish clan, they treated visitors like honoured guests, as sacred beings. They had a saying: *Isusu somhambi asingakanani, ngemva ngumhlonzo*. Its casual translation would be that sojourners don't have many demands a simple kindness cannot quench. This was probably the seed of their demise with the colonising people whose predominant attitude was one of gain. The colonists tended to interpret generosity as a sign of weakness.

Phila's train of thought was broken by the sudden recall of his father's death. He imagined his father's visage: the weary disposition of his weather-beaten face, the compassionate eyes, the kind withdrawing silences. This tenderness towards his deceased father felt insincere, even hypocritical, as if he was attempting to flatter his own vanity and ego. The realisation introduced a lingering sensation of having just been punched in the stomach. Why must our heroes always lie in graves, Phila asked himself as he watched the river, his eyes tearfully clouding. His grandma had another saying: "You cannot beat a river into submission." Phila grew to understand that this meant you must surrender to the power of nature if you want to use it. That we're driven by instincts that transcend our own volition and understanding. That an all-encompassing reality shapes our rough-hewn lives.

Enough philosophising for the day. Phila stood up. He decided to walk to the internet café on Russell Road. As always he admired the neat, stepped file houses of Donkin heritage. Say what you must about those colonialists, he thought to himself, they had some neat tricks and great building skills.

The internet café was clammy and stuffy as usual.

"What time?" shouted the Somali lady in the black burka. She was always in some contrived hurry.

"One hour internet," Phila answered back, feeling insulted without exactly knowing why. His peevishness had reached a stage where it concerned him, even if her lack of courtesy irritated him. Each time, he meant to call her aside, to find a way of correcting her, so as to break the paralysing mistrust. It was this sort of thing, he was certain, that developed into feelings of mutual resentment, festered, then turned into xenophobia. Now, though, since he had decided he was leaving PE, the time had run out to correct this. Things unsaid were again left to fester. He handed over his five rand coin with his irritation changing to empathy, because he, too, knew how it felt to be a migrant in a foreign land and not fit in. And the frantic expulsion that makes one break the ocean in half only to meet nothing that wants you – to paraphrase the African American poet Nayyirah Waheed.

"Number 8!" the lady shouted without even looking at him.

Phila proceeded to the cubicle he was pointed to.

The Tower of Babel in his head was complemented by that of the internet café's, a conglomeration of Somalis, Ghanaians, Nigerians, Congolese – sesquipedalian clamours, all competing in loud voices. Phila loved the cosmopolitan feel of the city here: the riot of colours in flummery dressing, the jingle of trinkets, the dance communication and the competing languages.

He started sweating profusely the moment he sat down in the cubicle. The emails were mostly spam and adverts, nothing from the international publications he had been sending articles to. The green architectural proposals and competitions were now his major source of income. One email caught his eye, from Nandi, his former girlfriend-cum-friend-with-benefits confidante, who lived in Grahamstown, a drive of about an hour and a half away. Phila visited her on weekends now and then for friendship and an occasional booty call. He had to first re-read what he had sent her the previous week before he could fully make out what she was trying to say.

She rambled and raved a lot, trying to explain herself. The gist of the matter was that she was becoming tired of waiting for him to "make something" of his life, and had decided to move on. "I cannot live my life permanently betrothed on hopes of fantasies." The simplified and abridged version was: I'm fucking my colleague, "who, though married, is soon to be separated. We're making plans to stay together next year." Phila was hurt and relieved at the same time. There was something to be said about never, ever again having to deal with that flibbertigibbet. While he felt he had dodged a bullet, his ego was shattered. The bombardment of loss in his life at that moment was getting ridiculous.

On the doorpost of the first building he passed as he left the café was written the single word *Resurgam*. It was an elegant building of ancient Greek composite architecture. Though the whitewashed walls had turned grey because of neglect, the simplicity and harmony of the structure was still intact, in fact even more pronounced now without the adorning colours. Phila walked with the acquired patience of the *flâneur*, feeling wide awake and seeing signs of rebirth everywhere. It felt as though he was emerging from himself into his real life. In this Bachelardian wonder he tried to conjure lyrical possibilities from reading the cultural memory from the building. You must always be able to find a metaphor for humans in a house or building. Until you do the scales will not fall from your eyes. He stopped to wonder if this, finally, was what Bachelard in his lectures, and Paul on regaining his sight meant about the scales falling from the eyes. Perhaps the scales are the unnecessary clutter we carry, the fingerprints of memory and imagination's dream shelters. Wishing to be wherever he wasn't, Phila walked on.

Fiat justitia ruat caelum!

The phrase smuggled itself into his mind. Indeed, let justice be done though heavens may fall! Though egos are shattered; though lives are disrupted; though brains misfire!

Flower Chambers

It was around ten in the evening when Phila made a stop in Grahamstown on his way home to Queenstown. He rang the buzzer at Nandi's flat with slight trepidation. Hesitantly, he announced himself on the intercom and waited for some form of reproach, but Nandi said nothing in buzzing him in. After fiddling with the latch for what felt like eternity, she opened the door. Phila missed his step on the threshold as he entered but managed to get hold of himself in time before falling. He scraped his feet on the doormat to allow for the awkward moment to pass. Nandi gave a fed-up snort before turning her back, leaving him to close and lock the door. The fluorescent light of the TV gave the lounge a soft ambience, its muted sound intensifying the church atmosphere.

Nandi and Phila grew up together during the tumultuous eighties, when the country was under the riotous fog of transformation. They had an affair that was truncated by Phila's leaving to study in Germany. When he came back they drifted into being friends, with benefits. Something about it always felt like it was done for old times' sake. They regarded themselves as moralists, just that their ethics were not derived from any particular religious code or ideology. With loss of innocence and, perhaps, the birth of deeper knowledge, the friends-with-benefits thing was also losing steam, leaving them stranded on the platform of nostalgia. Before Nandi's email they had not yet figured out what they wanted to do or not do with each other. Nandi, with an enduring quality of casting a bright light on the experience of others, was always a convenient candle to Phila's moth. He hadn't been surprised when she'd chosen psychology as a profession because she possessed all the capacious qualities of goodness: resilience, kindness, empathy and good listening skills. Phila, with the typical psychological cannibalistic character, often abused these qualities, with her tacit encouragement. She was strict with herself but condoning of weakness in others.

They sat on the sofa, each quiet for different reasons. Phila wished he could repair the shock of surprise, which in turn, he hoped, would bankrupt her growing asperity. Nandi, in her turn, was trying to control her annoyance.

"Phila! You can't keep showing up here during late hours; leaving with the crowing of the rooster when it pleases you."

Even her anger did not manage to suppress the kindness of her eyes. Phila knew he deserved the anger after the way he'd left the last time, without explanation.

"I'm sorry. It's late. I didn't know where else to go. I lost track of time wandering around Fingo township. I think there are more *shis'inyama* places than people in that place. Egazini River has dried into a dirty streamlet. What is happening to our rivers?" Phila wanted to direct the topic away to other things but Nandi was having none of it.

"You need to be more sensitive. What if I was with someone? I've a life too, you know. It might not be as carefree and rootless as yours, but you damn well will respect it."

"I'm sorry ..."

Silence.

"Would you like tea or something?" Nandi asked in a calmer voice after a few minutes.

"Something stronger preferably," Phila replied, feeling relief growing.

"The vodka you left in the cupboard is still here."

While Nandi disappeared into the kitchenette, Phila plugged his iPod into her music system and selected *Bright Eyes*. Momentarily the moaning depths of Conor Oberst came on. Hearing the clatter from the kitchenette, a little louder than necessary, he concluded Nandi was still angry. She came back with a half-full bottle of Absolut, a glass filled with ice and lime cordial on a tray.

"Otherwise, how have you been keeping?" she asked, sitting next to him, fitting her head under his chin after he finished pouring himself a drink.

"To tell you the truth, not too good." Phila was overwhelmed by her scent.

"I'm sorry about your father. I was not even aware he was sick," Nandi said, lifting her head to look him in the eyes. He tried to figure out how she knew about his father before remembering he'd answered her email with a sentence: "My father died yesterday." He almost feigned literal prowess by imitating Camus but reined himself back because it felt kitsch, like chasing down a shallow sort of mimesis.

"Most of us didn't know. He kept it to himself. It was a colon ulcer that perforated or something, doctors even suspect cancer; there's a family history of it."

"Didn't they do a post-mortem?"

"What would be the point? Ulcers are caused by stress, are they not?" Warm fuzz went through his head as the vodka settled in. The vodka, as usual, raised the intensity of his emotions, making him nostalgic and eager.

"Mostly, but not always. Some ulcers are hereditary."

"I'm prone to stress." He stopped talking. They looked at each other with loving familiarity before Phila wrestled her gaze to the ground. "I remember reading an article somewhere about some of the cruel things you people do in the name of science." He wanted to occupy his mind with something other than his father's death. "It said some psychologists in America put a mouse in a cage and gave it electric shocks. The poor thing became so stressed up with those shocks that at death it was found to have oversized adrenal glands and numerous stomach ulcers."

"I've heard of the experiment. It's redirecting aggression. They enclose a wooden stick with other mice, so that each time the shock is administered the mouse bites into the stick, to redirect its pain. After death it is found that the mice with sticks had smaller adrenal glands and fewer ulcers. The clincher is that if you put two mice in the same cage they become aggressive and fight each other each time the shocks are administered. In the end those mice were found to have normal glands and no ulcers."

"You see? It helps to redirect your anger and pain. Shall we fight more?"

They both chortled. Phila was relieved to feel Nandi's annoyance dissipating. He got up to fix himself another drink.

"The poor guy without a stick or someone to redirect his pain towards was found to have ... what's the word they use?" he asked, coming back to the sofa, feeling lighter.

"Autopsied!"

"Ja! Autopsied."

"I think I'm autopsied," Phila said after a couple of moments' silence between them.

"What do you mean?" Nandi cautiously enquired.

"I do not understand what's happening to me."

"How do you mean?" Nandi showed more concern.

"I hear and see things other people do not," Phila said. He glanced down to see if she thought him freakish.

"Like what?"

"Like people that are not there, or other people do not see."

"You mean you hear things in a schizophrenic way?"

"I wouldn't put it that way. Just visits from historical characters, mostly people I'm reading about. I think sometimes I cross the divide. I don't know how, it just happens. When I least expect it."

Nandi looked thoughtful. "Would you like to come to the office tomorrow?" she suggested. "I have class, but we can talk after, in a more professional manner?"

"I don't know. I mean, I have to go and bury my father. Besides, with all due respect, I know what your profession has to say about this sort of thing. I've read some stuff."

"Reading stuff does not beat the understanding ear of a professional, and a friend."

"We'll see."

"Are you hungry?"

"Famished."

"I have leftover pasta from my supper. You can help yourself while I take a shower."

Phila always thought there was something Quakerish about Nandi, the emphasis on integrity, quietness, peace and all. He had always felt protective when it came to her, more like a brother; well, a brother she sometimes fucked. He plotted ways to protect her against him, his ambiguous vanity, emotional opaqueness, cruel detachment ... His thoughts galloped to things he was not yet prepared to admit about himself.

To avoid the turn his thoughts were taking, he stood up to investigate the bookshelf. He looked through the books, hoping to spy on Nandi's reading habits. There was a lot of psychology material, Freud, Jung, Lacan, Marcel, and the rest of the brood from that nest and its academic work. She had some literature also, Penguin Classics mostly. He looked to see which book he could borrow. His eyes hesitated on Chinua Achebe's *Things Fall Apart* but passed when he recalled he had read it a couple of times, and rested on Tolstoy's *War and Peace*. He wondered if it was time he tackled the book again. The last time he'd tried he hadn't been able to get beyond the third chapter. In his deliberations his eyes wandered to another row of books, where his attention was caught by James Joyce's *Ulysses*. Tolstoy, in his view, was too intrusive as a narrator, and thus didn't fit with his current mood of looking to let things be in resigned ignorance. Joyce's *Ulysses*? All that topographic confusion would make him dizzy now, he thought, but he was enticed by the considered vividness and subtlety of Joyce he'd loved in *A Portrait of the Artist as a Young Man*. His eyes moved along the row. Proust, perhaps, something with memory as a neurological thread and parallel consciousness as an organising principle. But then his eye fell on Kafka's *The Castle*. He immediately knew it was the book most suitable for his current mood. He had been feeling strange and exotic to himself lately.

Nandi came back, smelling of womanly scents.

"Had a good shower?"

"Invigorating. Do you wanna watch a movie or something?"

"Too tired." He sat back down on the sofa, where Nandi was now applying nail polish to her toes. He held up the book. "May I borrow this?"

She looked up. "Sure, why not?"

"Remember that film we watched when I was here last, *The Sixth Sense*, I think it was called?"

"About the boy who saw dead people, and his psychologist? Great twist in the end?"

"Exactly!"

"What about it?" She handed the nail polish bottle to him to close while she carefully inserted the last of the cotton balls between her toes.

"I sometimes feel like him."

"You mean in your mind?"

"I mean – what the fuck is the difference if it's real or in my mind?"

"Calm down." She looked up, frowning.

"I'm sorry. I mean, if I cannot be sure of the reality of what my senses portray to me I have no claim over my sanity. I don't want to ..." He stood to walk towards the balcony in an attempt to bottle his temper.

"I'll get you something to calm you down."

"I don't want pills ..." He stopped in the middle of his sentence before continuing again, more calmly. "What I want is my freedom back, not serotonin drugs or tranquillisers. I want freedom from dependency. I want things to firmly establish their objective reality in my head, but I can't do that if the stuff of my imagination conscript themselves as objective reality in my mind. Surely this means something is clearly loose in my faculty of comprehension?"

"It's all right. You don't need to be melodramatic."

"I'm just trying to put this in a language you would understand. You don't seem to understand my plight. I feel I am soon gonna lose my capacity to distinguish between reality and fiction, memory and presence."

"I do understand," Nandi said. "But I can't help you when you erect a firewall between us."

"I have to deal with these things in my own way. I came here because

29

I feel calm around you." He fell quiet for a moment before saying, "May I take a shower too?"

"Of course."

Phila's bag was still lying in the passage. He picked it up and took it to the bathroom. Nandi went out onto the balcony to dry her nails. By the time she came back inside Phila was done with his shower and on his third vodka and a plate of warmed up pasta. The vodka was elevating his vitality and plumbing his vigour.

"So what about that session tomorrow?" Nandi asked.

"We'll see."

"Is that a yes?" She tickled him as she sat on the sofa next to him.

"Stop it. You know I don't like that. You people explain everything as neurosis; and you favour the descriptive over depth. I don't like it."

Nandi got up and went to the kitchenette. "I just want to establish the uniform modus of your symptoms, so as to outline the procedure, in order to give a diagnosis."

"In short, you want to fuck with my unconscious mind," Phila raised his voice to reach her. He could hear the kettle boiling.

She popped her head round the door. "If you wanna look at it that way."

"I don't think so."

"Just promise you'll try."

Nandi handed him a cup of rooibos tea. She sat down on the sofa and rested her head on his crotch. "If you decide to leave tomorrow, at least have the decency to say goodbye before you go. I can't stomach another of your disappearing acts." She spoke with force of feeling but kindness of tone.

"Perhaps I would like to stay?" Phila rested his arm on the shoulder of the sofa and clasped his chin. "Would there be a room for me?"

"Ja, right! I'm not hedging my bets on that."

Nandi knew Phila; she knew that he was a man who sometimes unwilled what he willed because of second, third or fourth thoughts.

"When I go, *if* I go, it'll be for the last time. Will you wait for me?"

"That'll be waiting for the coming of Nxele!"

"Come on. It's only been two centuries. The Christians have been waiting for their Messiah beyond two millennia now. And the Jews have been waiting forever."

"I'm not religious."

The music tempered the silence.

"Nandi?"

"Mhm?"

"Do you think when I come back we could, perhaps, live together or something?"

"What are you asking?"

"Only what is in my heart."

"When you get back, if you still feel the same, we'll discuss it. But I must warn you, there'll be conditions, expectations."

"I've been living without conditions for far too long. Perhaps it's time I learn to fulfil some expectations."

"Why now?"

"I've grown to believe the end of my journey is with you." Phila decided to grasp the nettle by swinging a blunt axe. "What about your professor?"

"What about him?" Nandi raised her head to meet Phila's gaze, which refused to meet hers. She continued without guilt. "It would have been nicer had you said you loved me. I guess you're right not to promise things you don't feel. Things have to be better than that between us."

Phila found himself awake at 3:40am. He lay for a while in the dark, listening to the morning sounds. Dawn was at the stage when darkness seemed to illuminate light. A distant rumble of a car engine approached in strain, climbing the steep hill before slowly fading as the headlights moved across the room, leaving behind a convergence of alienation and melancholia. Stasis. *Sich verfahren*. Losing his head to where, he wondered.

Beside him Nandi was snoring and emitting heat and occasional hypnic jerks. Something he had read somewhere came to mind, about the fundamental teachings of Mahayana Buddhism, the *kshanti paramita*, which is the capacity to receive, bear and transform the pain inflicted on you by your enemies; also by those who love you. The description seemed to fit Nandi. He had lost count of how many times he had left her for other women. He felt an urgent need to know if Nandi practised Buddhism, as if the answer to that question would collapse the gap between the experienced and the read. He elbowed her, lightly first, then a little harder the second time.

"Hmm ... What is it?"

He could see through the light from the street that her eyes were still closed. He elbowed her lightly again. "Are you Buddhist?"

"Huh? Phila, please, it's late." She turned towards the wall.

"Actually it's early. Tell me – are you Buddhist?"

"Phila, I have class tomorrow. What's this all about?" She turned back again, opening her eyes, allowing them to adjust as she looked for Phila's face. Confused, she asked again, "What's this all about?"

"Please answer the question."

"No. You know I'm Christian, at least nominally. What's this all about?" she asked, rubbing her eyes.

"I dreamt of Buddha, and am not sure what he wants, if he even wants anything."

She raised her head, considered his statement for a while, then answered in a throaty, sleepy voice. "Perhaps you're looking for a religion without God. Isn't that what Buddhism is?" She punched her pillow before resting her head back on it.

"I never thought of it that way."

Could it be, having grown under the shadow of the church, thought Phila, I now am longing for the comforts of religion without the constraints of having to pledge my allegiance to a deity? The only thing to really attract Phila in the Christian religion was the commendable life of Christ. As for the other mumbo-jumbo, beyond the records of how Christ wanted us to behave, as written by his disciples and interpreted by the church, Phila had reservations, sometimes even irritations. But he didn't think the whole thing was as shabby as the likes of Voltaire or Dawkins made it to be. He was just as much not interested in their egos and satanic pride as the mumbo-jumbo they claimed to dispel. I'll not serve! Most learned people were anti-authority, he knew that, which was why non-belief was more attractive to them. What's wrong with authority if it is not authoritarian? He often asked himself that question. But now, thanks to Nandi, he was discovering that he also had nostalgia for sanctity.

Nandi had fallen asleep again, which irritated Phila. He elbowed her again, this time more sternly than before, but she turned with a groan and went back to sleep. Questions went through his insomniac mind as he lay supine in bed watching the dull winter-dawn light announce itself through the window. Why would I want a religion without God? What would be the point of that? To appease my vanity? The ceiling was turning from grey to white as he went on with his thoughts for over an hour and a half until he was distracted by Nandi climbing on top of him. Is Christianity morally too demanding, he asked himself, fiddling with Nandi's breast. The touch of her aureoles quickly aroused him as usual. They made love. He felt needed and lost his thoughts. Nandi came with exquisite grace and a hint of derision in her face before dropping to the side, heaving. She always looked extremely vulnerable after lovemaking, which made her more beautiful in Phila's eyes.

"That's what I call a morning glory!" she softly exclaimed.

Phila's hyperactive mind couldn't rest. It travelled to a documentary he'd watched once, about the matrifocal culture of the Mosuo people. Apparently, high in the Himalayas in a remote corner of China an agrarian group of people still lived, who had survived for almost two millennia. What fascinated the documentary makers about this culture was the practice of what was termed 'walking marriage'. In walking marriages a woman does not take a husband. Once she turns thirteen she is given her own bedroom, a 'flower chamber' in literal translation, the translator emphasised. She could invite any man into her flower chamber to spend a night with her, so long as he left before dawn. In practice, strangely enough, perhaps even disappointingly to the modern (read Western) world, this usually didn't result in wild promiscuity. It was more like serial monogamy. The woman, even when she fell pregnant, did not expect or require support from the man. Everything was kept strictly private and separate from the daily workings of the family, of whom she was a part, and to the support of which she made her contribution. Family responsibilities, values and bonds were derived from the family she was born into; male members were expected to behave not only as male figures of the community, but fathers to her children.

With the radical decline in matrimony, and increase in single mothers in black families, Phila thought his people were closer to Mosuo culture than Western, which judged his culture harshly in things like polygamy.

"Nandi."

"Mhmm." She was drifting back to sleep again, sex, as always, being her *berceuse*.

"I think I'm losing my mind."

No answer. Then, "Can't you lose it in the morning, when we are all awake?" When he did not answer Nandi raised her head.

"What can be done?"

"I wish I knew. I wish I knew."

Phila lay with his hands behind his head on the pillow, thinking about Maqoma. "After my father's funeral," he said, "I want to visit some places around King William's Town and East London. Perhaps I see you after?"

"I shall be here."

The declaration felt more like an accusation than assurance to Phila. Shafts of daylight stabbed Phila's eyes from between the curtains. Nandi got up to go to the bathroom. Feeling in between worlds and modes of consciousness, Phila got out of bed and followed her. For whatever reason, seeing Nandi brushing her teeth at the sink with her underwear hanging on the bathroom rail heightened Phila's concerns into a panic.

Homewards, towards *Selbstfindung*, still *sich verfahren*.

He went to the lounge and turned on the TV while Nandi stepped into the shower cubicle. Afterwards, when she passed through the lounge to go and get dressed, wrapped in a white cotton towel, she asked what he was watching.

"Some professor of psychology at the Hebrew University of Jerusalem is convinced that Moses was on psychedelic drugs when he thought he was talking to God on Mount Sinai through the burning bush. I find that interesting."

"I never heard that before," Nandi said, going to her bedroom.

Phila went and stood in the doorway. "He says that's the reason Moses saw stuff other people around him didn't see."

"Because Moses was on drugs? I guess it's plausible – if there's any proof."

"The professor thought it was a psychotropic plant. Similar results can be obtained from a concoction made from the bark of the acacia tree, he said. Apparently that concoction is constantly mentioned in the Bible."

"You're too absorbed in yourself, if you want my honest opinion."

"There's hardly anything religious about it, if you mean to insinuate."

Phila felt hurt as he stripped to wash. When he emerged from the bathroom without drying himself, water dripping all over the floor, he caught the slight look of irritation on Nandi's face, but she held her mouth.

"No insinuations, Phila," she said. "I'm just exploring your state of mind. You said it is not altered? Is it more like possession, trance?"

"No!"

Nandi paused in putting on her pantyhose. "Do you know about analeptic memory?" she asked.

"Not much, just description."

"I've not studied it in depth either, but I know a little about it. Jung was interested in what he called 'the collective unconscious'."

"Yes." Phila indicated for her to go on.

"Well, I read about a case in Scotland. This guy, his name was James Fraser, was a cartwright or some such. Anyway, it was just after the Second World War. Fraser had a recurring dream, which he told in convincing detail. In the dream he was a witness to this battle, I even remember its

strange name, the Battle of Blàr na Léine. The manner with which he gave
details convinced historians that he had been there, actually seen the fray.
The problem was that this battle, which had been between the Frasers
and some other clan, in which nearly all the Frasers were killed, occurred
in 1544, centuries before James had been alive. His description of things
like the clansmen's dress, equipment, and methods of fighting could be
verified only through specialised sources – sources that could not have
been available to him at the time."

"Umh!"

"Whatever you choose to call it, flood of ancestral memory, or
analeptic memory, the thing seems to happen. Scientists say sometimes the
exteroceptive stimulations, absorption of external stimuli, in other people,
fail to perform or become too active."

"Why?"

"No one is certain. But the absorption is a necessary process for
maintaining normal waking consciousness. The altered state of mind is
caused by levels above or below this level. You say you get visits from the
historical figures you're reading about?"

"Something like that."

"Then this is my take on it. For some reason I think your concentration
and absorption when you're reading about these people causes these
fluctuations in your stimuli, causing these altered states of consciousness.
And that's when you get these 'visits'. Do you take any hallucinogenic? I
mean, anything – say, Ecstasy?"

"I've never taken drugs. You know I am just an alcoholic."

"I still feel we need to talk further, professionally."

"You keep missing the point. I'm not treating this as a sickness. It's
something that has always happened in Xhosa history, especially during
times of extreme pressure. It is what produced the Nxeles, Ntsikanas,
Mqantsis, Mlanjenis and Nongqawuses of this world."

"If you say so."

"There you go with your know-it-all condescending occidental attitude.
What if this is a normal thing in our tradition, how we deal with the
pressure, by dipping into the parallel world of the River People, *iminyanya*?
Is this not the essence of *ukuthwasa*? Have any of you psychologists
bothered to study this thing closer? Funny thing is that you yourself once
told me that Winston Churchill experienced a similar thing during the
Second World War when England was under German bombardment. He
called it his 'Black Dog'. Of course everyone respected it and thought him

unique because he was Churchill. Had he been African, black even, he would have been called voodoo crazy and superstitious, right?"

Nandi regarded Phila steadily. She put a hand on his arm. "Go home, Phila," she said. "Go and bury your father."

The River Tent is Broken

"THAT'S STRONG ENOUGH TO float an egg."

Siya handed Phila a cup of black coffee and sat down opposite him at the kitchen table. He took a swipe of it. "Aah! Heaven." The strength of the brew agreed with him. Since he'd arrived at the family house in Queenstown, they had been talking about everything except the death of their father. This made him feel implicated, but in what he had no idea. Something in his father's body had burst. All he could think about was that the shit had hit the innards. Phila felt crude in thinking about it along those lines, but he was never of the euphemistic lot. He didn't care because he felt whatever burst in his father was bobbing towards his own innards anyway. But that is not the kind of conversation you have with your sibling on the morning you are planning to see your dead parent at the mortuary.

"I was wonderfully amazed to see the apricot tree is still there!"

"Yep. And it still yields fruit in due season."

Siya was usually taciturn so Phila tried not to read anything from her brief sentences. There were hanging issues neither of them was in a mood for at that moment. Besides, neither knew where to start, or what the point would be of plucking hanging issues instead of letting the fruit fall down to be manure, or poison. The Polish philosopher Leszek Kołakowski talked about the 'law of the infinite', saying that an infinite number of explanations can be found for any given event. Some clever professor whose lecture Phila had attended in Berlin connected this with what psychologists christened 'hindsight bias': the tendency to regard actual outcomes as more probable than alternatives. The whole thing hadn't really made sense when Phila read it, but now he was either more gullible because he wanted to avoid thinking about his dead father, or else the bulb was getting some electricity. His hindsight bias was always in suspecting he could have done something to change the course of things had it not been for his proclivity to leave well alone. Could he have been more attentive to the needs of his girlfriend? Could he have suspended his moral judgement to save his firm, for 'the greater good of all'? Could he have made time to visit his father and talk things out? Could he have, could he have…? What could he have?

Primo Levi survived the brutal torture of the Nazis in Auschwitz, and had spent most of the rest of his life writing against revenge and refusing to be a victim. Then he'd jumped off the third storey of a building to kill himself when he was sixty-seven years old – oddly enough, the same age as Phila's father. Put your hindsight theory to that and shove it, he thought. We are a mystery mostly to ourselves. What we accept with our heads makes for our necessary fall when the heart has rejected.

Everything is falling, and I'm included in it, he thought as he looked at his sister's beautiful face. Made him admit that his father gave them good genes.

Just so we're clear about things: no medically trained person dies of a perforated ulcer by accidental neglect. Even the ways by which we fall come from our agency, conscious or otherwise, was Phila's last thought.

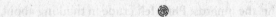

The following day they travelled to their father's rural home, seventy kilometres east of their hometown. The burden of the hours came with Phila. It had been close to three decades since he had seen the place. He trained his eye on the passing villages, the sparse, abstract shoreline of brown and turquoise hutments against the lion's mane coloured grass. The mountains, bleak and untamed, still possessed a haunted look. Progress and consumerism had caught up with the area since the change of government from the apartheid regime. Bridges had been built over rivers; electricity installed for those who could afford it; purified water coming out of installed communal taps, free of charge. Things were changing for the better, he thought, but what, he couldn't help wondering, would Dr Samuel Johnson have had to say about it – Johnson had been of the opinion that change of governments makes no difference to the happiness of ordinary people.

The earth still heaved towards the craggy cliffs, building up to green mountains where the river snaked in a labyrinth to create the valleys where, for six generations now, his forefathers had lived and planted their fields. From there the road can take you no farther, what with the prince of the mountains, Lukhanji, standing in your way and casting its shadow over everything. The mountain sent water down the sedimentary donga, creating streams that acted as bloodline arteries for the valleys. This was where his father had hidden his defeated life, here among scrawny-looking sheep and an austere cluster of rondavel huts. This lonesome hill, with its echoes of the muffled screams of the dying river.

Traditionally, it was Phila's home also.

It was evening when they arrived, the day before their father's funeral, and the activity was already widespread. Bundles and bundles of wood lay around. A bull was being slaughtered at the kraal, because his father was a first-born, which traditionally mandates a bull falls with him. Pots of samp, cabbage and potatoes were boiling at the hearth. And the last containers *zamarhewu* were being brewed and distilled. Everyone had something to do but Phila. When he wanted to lend a hand he was directed away to something else, mostly some less arduous task. He became used to the dismissive gesture. "This is not for delicate hands, *yezifundiswa*."

Being classed with the namby-pamby educated class irritated him. But he was clumsy in basic things like logging, keeping a straight line behind a cattle-drawn plough, or milking cows. He walked from kraal to shed, hearth to kitchen, pen to graveyard, looking for something to be useful at. No one required his help. His only usefulness was in driving a car or tractor to fetch the elderly. Whenever he met up with his elders Phila had a strange inclination to act more sombre than he actually felt in order to look for their commiseration. He felt he had to demonstrate to them the fact that he loved his father. Internally this made him feel like an impostor. Of course he felt loss for his father, vague as it might have been. He suspected it to be more about sentimentality, his tendency to idealise loss or absence. Absence does not get more permanent than death.

He walked past the graveyard, thinking how the Jewish culture was better in these situations. Everyone was allocated their own role to play. As children they would be obligated to visit the graves of their parents; to frequently recite prescribed memorial prayers at the graveside. Phila felt this prescribed mode of mourning ritualised loss better, giving it direction, perhaps even purpose.

He went on a gadabout riverward, to ponder things out. Standing on the river bank, in stilled attention, listening to the sounds of his childhood, remembering how he and his cousin used to trap crabs here when he was about seven, open their 'purses' to look for the coins they were told they contained. A line from TS Eliot's *The Fire Sermon* trespassed to his mind:

The river's tent is broken: the last fingers of leaf

Clutch and sink into the bank. The wind
Crosses the brown land, unheard. The nymphs are departed.

And there came his cousin, driving a cart pulled by two oxen, wearing gumboots, chaps on top of his dirty jeans and a tattered checked shirt, and with a gleeman song on his mouth. A suede hat sat precariously on his head. They greeted. Talked about days gone by. But the natural innocence of youth had been lost even between them, leaving behind awkward silences. His cousin was the one who knew all the cattle by name and colour, not just number like the rest of them. He was the one who knew what to do when the rains didn't come to avoid the crops failing or the stock dying. He was the one who knew what his father thought in his last days as the ulcer bore into his innards. Phila knew in his heart of hearts that his cousin should be the one to inherit all that was left behind by his father. After all, according to the messiah, the meek inherit the earth.

"You remember, *mzala*, how we used to fish the rivers?" his cousin asked as he sat down, lighting his dagga pipe.

"I was just thinking about that. We used reed poles to tie the fishing lines. And no reel. I remember how once the pull slashed your palm ..."

"Indeed!" His cousin extended his hand for Phila to examine. The scar was still there, smaller than Phila was imagining it in his head, but nasty all the same.

"What is happening to the river? Why is it dwindling, drying up?"

"They dammed it for water for the town folks," his cousin answered without much concern. Phila, on the other hand, felt anger. They talked about when the dam was built by the apartheid regime with no consideration given to village people. "The fish of our youth died with the river," his cousin said. As he got up to continue on his way with the cart, Phila wondered if this was one of the reasons black people were angry, burning and damaging things – because they were looking for their youth.

The day coiled like a spring in his mind. His father had told him the drive to swim upstream, for the spawning run, was always strongest when the fish sensed the dying light. After circling in the river bed, to avoid obstacles and rapids, they suddenly bunch up when the light goes down. His father, an amateur fisherman, had said all fishermen when they go to the river are in pursuit of their moment of art. It is an ancient tryst between them and the fish, when both are aiming to give a head-start to their spoor at the chow line, upstream. Explaining the difference between catadromous and anadromous fish, he had told Phila how the river left its identity on the scale map of the fish. That ichthyologists are able to study the conditions of the river from the scales of the fish who are born of it.

When they went hunting, and had to wait out the rain in the caves sometimes, his father explained the difference between stalagmites and stalactites to Phila, who busied himself with dreaming of ways to get out of the cave.

Then came the storm, the divorce, placing fate in the driving seat. But because Phila was born of the river that snaked the craggy mountains he couldn't get rid of the river murmur on his skin, not even by the roaming of his roving mind. Stuck in that cave he traced his steps riverwards, heavy with speech, like shoal seeking to spawn upstream. But the river had dried out; only the willow branches waved. What now, Phila wondered, the stabbing shafts of the dying light on his mind. He plucked a stem of dry grass to chew and then laughed at himself: this was his father's habit. We're our father's sons, he thought.

At last, his father found his art moment, in death. Because you can't love anything without loss, and no one is ever entirely in charge of their own consciouness and genetic moves.

Tears tiptoed down Phila's cheeks. He cupped his hands to cover his eyes, squinting to watch his cousin drive the spanned oxen up the hill, continuing with his gleeman's song walking in lunging steps. Phila entertained the idea of hanging around a little, while he was still stranded, to clarify issues in his head, plant cabbages like the proverbial Hadrian, become one with his people, *a hewer of wood and drawer of water.* He imagined himself doing something constructive in the village, like building a school or a clinic, to etch the memory of his father on the rock. But when the money issue came into the picture he felt discouraged. Untangling himself from such thoughts, he took a better look at the view that had harnessed his father's life. Again, he tried to see the nobility of living with a spirit of poverty hovering on one's shoulders. It's pride, damn stubborn pride masquerading as humility, he thought, no longer thinking about his father. He surveyed the wide domain where speeding winds crossed the lea. There's a snake in the grass, he thought to himself. The truth is grounded in stronger pain, in groping the wound until the poison is drained out of it. Pain and consciousness cannot be separated, as the stoics saw it a long time ago. Phila was now also convinced.

The sun, low and big, sank with ill-placed drama behind the mountain brow. A trail of ashen clouds, like blooded fleece, bleated the pain of Ramah, Rachel weeping for her children. Sheep stood stupefied in the fields where women were threshing.

Phila didn't really want to live chained by modern standards, but he did not need to look deeply within himself to realise he was too accustomed to modern comforts to ever give them up for frugal living and stoic values he hardly understood. From that realisation the spirit of his dissatisfaction rose. He ceased interrogating himself further and walked back, closely tied to the apron of his grief. No thinking, no thinking! We're in mourning. Minute by minute the darkness settled on the hills whose shadows chained Phila's cumulative memory. He understood now that grief was a last gift of love we unconditionally give our loved ones.

During the funeral Phila stood close to his paternal grandfather, so close he could see himself in his eighty-nine-year-old rheumy eyes. The bonding warmth between them no wreaths could define. When he noticed all the male members of his family had shaved their heads, Phila felt shame that he had not done so. Why had they not asked him to? They treated him differently. This had the effect of isolating him. His failure to shave might have been misinterpreted by the others as belittling his father's death and lack of respect, but they were always cutting him some slack, viewing him as an anomaly.

It was an extremely cold day. Phila had never seen the mountain slopes in the area that white with snow. It felt like he was listening to the funeral proceedings in German.

Eulogies came thick and wide. Phila always felt this to be the worst part of African funerals: lengthy, irrelevant, turgid, sanitised hagiographic versions of the deceased. The situation was rescued by his father's neighbour, a frail old man with a falcon-like face. With tingling sincerity in his voice, his undeceiving eyes spoke of old traditional wisdom and blunt dignity. His speech had the quality of biblical economy. Phila immediately adored the old man for trivialising the false sacramental gravity of other speakers; for being blithely indifferent to death. He could feel his own parasitic *Augenblicksbeobachtungen* awakening to translate the old man's speech, spoken in Xhosa, in his mind. He jotted down now and then on the serviettes parts he did not want to forget from the speech; while translating it in Thucydidean mode inside his head. When he finally had it jotted down he was frustrated by how he had lost its natural bluff humour and living energy. Only those who still live with a carry-over detail of oral culture can manage such things, he thought, in excusing himself. The only thing he got right, he felt, was its pristine intensity:

"Today my soul is filled with heartbroken revolt against my own life. I do not know why we should be spared when our children are felled. To bury your child, as Mzoli [Phila's father] was to me, is a harsh reality and cruel fate. [Stopped for a while to catch his composure.]

"Mzoli, you 'feign-hell'. [Laughter lashed through the crowd. 'Feign-hell' was Phila's father's leitmotif whenever something went wrong. Hitherforth it became the harlequinade on the day of his interment. The old man stammered on with a slight lisp before continuing.]

"I don't know who you think will turn my fields, sow my seeds and pluck my tares when you decide to join those fainéant you call your ancestors. All right then, *Ndlovu*, have it your way. One thing I know: the maggots will be at you tonight. We're coming too, so don't get too comfortable, occupying spaces of elders. It makes no difference that you go there first; we're still your elders.

"Your departure shook our hearts but does not agonise us. Nobody *osisimaphakade* in this world. It did not happen to you what does not happen to others. You suffered the fate of all mortals. There's no resisting death. It levels and calls all bluffs. I'm old as the hills; my hair is white like ewes on the fields, but yesterday I dug your grave with a spade on my own hands, against the protest of my family and friends who feared for my health. What do I need my health for if the likes of you are dead? Nothing made me more happy and proud as digging your grave. We're even then, *Ndlovu*. Don't you be asking for any favours when I get there where you sleep with those striplings you call ancestors.

"Your wordy and obsequious friends from town here say you were going to be a preacher. That's bunkum. *Iyilo* like you. Still, you were a mast in our village. We're the people who'll feel the loss of your departure most. [He trained his eyes on the audience.]

"Allow me, people of my hearth, to lick my wounds in quiet. Nobody should drink this common crock more than a mouthful. It's on its dregs already. Load every memory of him, wreaths if you wish; but now let us bury Mzoli and be done with it.

"We're getting fewer by the day. Damn it! This land shall not see the likes of us again. May God give us the light of His wand in this

death journey." [He sat, deliberately slow.]
Phila really admired such hermetic eloquence.

The following day, he and his sister drove back to town. Phila had a headache. It was quiet in the car except for the fan blowing hot air and comforting odours. Soft showers, with occasional snow, fell with the memory of the departed. Cars, sliding, dancing and getting stuck in the snow, blocked their way now and then. Phila tried to strike up a conversation with Siya, the only non-talkative person he knew to be worse than him.

"The mountains and rivers have an ancient quiet stir that haunts those burdened with history or something."

"Mhmm" was the only answer he got. He subsequently drifted to sleep as his sister drove.

'I had a father, too, a chief, for that matter,' said Maqoma from the back seat.

'Before you start your monologue, please know that I'm very tired, and not in the mood for talking. Please! I've just buried my father. So if you don't mind ...'

'I'm sorry. That was a little insensitive of me.' He kept quiet for a while. Then, with whimsical stubbornness, he added, 'I noticed you didn't shed a tear for your father.'

'And what is that supposed to mean?' asked Phila in anger.

'That you were not affected by his death in your depths?'

'Give me a break.'

'Your hero, Boethius, says the Roman emperor Nero refused to shed a tear for his beloved mother when she died.'

'That's because that mad fucker had her killed by drowning.'

'*Stabbed the belly which brought forth such a monster.* We still hear her voice here screaming that she's caught up in that permanent moment. My point though is that others have done worse than not crying for their parents. You've nothing to be ashamed of. I forced myself to break the calabash when my father, Ngqika, died, but it was not something coming from my heart. We had grown distant during his last years.'

'Tears are not the only signs of grief.'

'I know. You summoned me by other means, like desire to understand.'

'You are my understanding? So far you have not been much help in that regard; if anything, you're confounding my confusion.'

'The year is not over yet.'

'How I wish it were. The sooner we part ways, the better.'

'You think?'

'Okay, my understanding, tell me this. What happens to my father now?'

'I'm not supposed to tell.'

'Some understanding, you are.' Phila resigned himself.

'I'm here to make you understand things connected to this life alone, not those that go beyond.'

'You impose yourself on my life, telling me you're my understanding, only you can't make me understand things I really want to know. Meantime I'm supposed to listen to you rant about your past?'

'I was told to narrate my life experience to you, that's all. I think it's supposed to help you make better choices.'

'Well, there hasn't been much information so far, except for your long monologues. Excuse me, I'd really like to rest, the past week has been hectic for me.'

When they arrived in town, the only place Phila felt he was good for was a shebeen. The loud music screeched on his nerves, drowning his thoughts for a while, but he danced to it. After the fourth beer his head started feeling light, but lacked the rush vitality alcohol usually gave him. If anything it reinforced the dull sense of things. He took a seat in the lounge, not in a mood to socialise with people around, who kept giving him probing glances. Empty beer bottles thickened before him. He felt the main theme of his life was obscured in the details of his father's but didn't know how to retrieve them. He was dismayed by his suffocating grief.

It was after two in the morning when Phila walked home. Lying on his back on his bed he gazed up at the ceiling in meditative integrity of darkness, considering the light and a glint of anger he didn't quite understand. After a while Maqoma's voice reached him through the dark.

'In any case, Gcaleka and Rharhabe were twin brothers of the last king, Phalo, of the united Xhosa nation; Rharhabe being ...'

Phila tried to close his eyes and ears, but to his dismay discovered he could still clearly hear and see Maqoma.

'When *iMbokotho* was broken, the sons of Phalo fought from their mother's womb. We saw bulls of the same byre gore each other, opening wide the gates for the enemies to flood in. When he got older Rharhabe crossed tributaries, like Izeli River, near the drift, where he killed *inyathi*. To show he harboured no ill intent to his brother he sent its breast and leg

45

to the great place as a tribute. His brother Gcaleka accepted the gesture, although they had recently been in conflict. The gesture meant Rharhabe was subjecting himself to the paramountcy of Gcaleka. Thereafter, Rharhabe called that river Nyathi River.'

'So that is why it is called Buffalo River?' Phila couldn't contain his interest.

'The area was still too close to Gcaleka so Rharhabe continued roving.'

'You know they've named that whole region Buffalo City now?' Phila was finding renewed interest in the talk.

'Yes, I noticed. Nyathi would have been better, but Buffalo will do. Rharhabe settled for a while at Amabele, near where the white people established their town.'

'Stutterheim?'

There was silence and heavy breathing. 'Are you still with me?' Maqoma enquired.

'Yes! But my head is starting to rill.'

'Do you know Qumrha?'

'Why would I not know Qumrha?'

'I couldn't find it on your map when I looked for it.'

'That's because it is called Komga now.'

'Why is that?' Maqoma looked puzzled.

'Because white people couldn't click, what else? The same has happened with Ingqurha, it is now called Coega.'

'You don't say. Their takeover of this country is complete.' Maqoma's skin wrinkled like leather when he was shocked or laughing.

'Guess who we've to thank for that?'

'Are you implying that we sold the country to white people?'

'I'm not implying your lot handed it over in a hot plate. While you were busy fighting each other, they stole the land from under your noses.'

'You don't know what we did to resist and keep the Xhosa nation united. You must not talk about things you've little understanding of.'

'As luck will have it, I have you to be my understanding, which just makes things worse.'

'Is Qumrha still a sacred place of the Gcalekas?' Maqoma asked.

'How should I know? I'm not Xhosa. I'm Mfengu.'

'Oh yes,' Maqoma smiled tauntingly. 'One of the sell-outs.'

'I'm a sell-out? Then why did you choose me?'

'I didn't choose you. You chose me. Mfengus were good-for-nothing sell-outs who facilitated the draining of this land to white people.'

'I'm sure they've other views.'

'Rharhabe held *iziVivane* sacred where travellers passed. Travellers looked to them for protection and direction.'

'I hope they were paid in kind.'

'They tied long grass near ravines to express wishes and prayers, food and shelter, supplications and all. The visitor on Rharhabe land was required to throw a stone *kwiSivivane* for luck too. *IziVivane* were regarded as the holy ritual of peregrinations, which amaRharhabes were known to be. These places grew to be formidable stone hills all over Rharhabe land.'

'Hellenic people had their temples, Romans their shrines, and you guys had *iziVivane*. To each their own. I really am in need of sleep now, if you don't mind.' Phila was tossing and turning in bed.

'I cannot make you do something you don't want. You're not sleeping not because of me, but because of your own thoughts.'

'Isn't that the whole point, though? You're in my thoughts.'

'Not without your invitation. Only you can banish me.'

'And what's that supposed to mean?'

'I come to your thoughts only per your invitation.'

'I invite you out of my head then – now!'

'You must not only say it, but believe it. It is about belief. That is why I'm here. I was summoned by your belief.'

'Do I look like I believe in *iziVivane*?'

'You cannot build without a good foundation. I'm here to lay it.'

'Could you lay it somewhere else tonight, please? It's four in the morning, for Christ's sake.'

'Christ? Our nation died because of Christ's sake. The missionaries ...'

'Here we go again.'

'Rharhabe had reverence for ancestors ...'

Phila closed his eyes again, but continued to toss and turn. Maqoma's voice was still present like a clacking cymbal. He tried drowning the voice by yodelling: 'Halaa-lo-halaaaa! Loooo!' but it didn't work. The only thing he succeeded in doing was wake his sister, who came into his room.

"Are you all right?" she asked.

"I'm fine. Just a bad dream. Go back to sleep."

As soon as she was gone Maqoma continued.

'He slaughtered a cow every opportunity he got. They say he derived his strength from his strict observance of ancestral worship. The dead live! You see? They've certain powers over their descendants. They communicate with the living through mediums like dreams and diviners, who must in turn minister to their needs.'

'Are you my ancestor?'

'That's not important.'

'It is to me. Are you?'

'Ancestors look out for the good of their people. I look out for the good of you.'

'So that makes you my ancestor. Now why not do something useful, like let me win a lottery, for instance? Believe me, that would be good for me.'

'Let's get back to Rharhabe.'

'I'm tired of hearing about Rharhabe. The dude was your hero, I get it, now can we move on?'

'Rharhabe moved to and fro across the land he had recently acquired, encountering numerous nations, like the Quena and Otentottu people. He met their chieftains, Queen Hoho. He wanted to marry her, no doubt for her beautiful apricot skin, but she'd have none of it. Rharhabe forced her into seceding her land in exchange for tobacco, dagga and dogs.'

'Yes, you guys stole their land, we know. We touched on that, remember?'

'Rharhabe went on to cross Nxarhuni to Gqunube before sleeping along the sea, eKhwikhwini, where they were met by engrossing mist and swarming locusts.'

'Those rivers are now called Nahoon and Gunubie. And your Khwikhwini is Quigney now.'

'They moved eastward to cross iNxuba, because the waters of that river get impregnated with salt during summer, making the grass sour and poisonous to cattle.'

'Fish River.'

'Went past Tyelerha, as far as iNqweba.'

'Sundays. I don't know the other river you're talking about.'

'They found salt lakes eNgqurha; swam on the green waters of Qagqiwa before finding themselves up on a gumtree because of snake infestation.'

'Qagqiwa they call Zwartkops now.'

'He could not stand the snakes towards Tsitsikamma so he turned towards the mountains of Vuba.'

'Zuurberg mountains.'

'In these peregrinations Rharhabe incorporated fugitives, malcontents and small tribes into his own tribe; bribed others by kind and kin; blackmailed others with protection; persuaded others by force and rancour into joining him.'

'Kei and Keiskamma is what they call the Nciba and Qoboqobo rivers today.'

'Rharhabe's authority was bestowed by the natural esteem his people had for him, and his generosity, which he was always prepared to support with force when necessary. Even his brother Gcaleka learnt to moderate his authority over his brother Rharhabe. When Gcaleka died early, Rharhabe took advantage of the situation by attacking his son, Khawuta, when he refused to subject himself to his authority. The Xhosa nation at large would not allow that, so they came to Khawuta's assistance. Rharhabe was defeated and driven off to the west, and as fate would have it set his progeny, us, on the scene to encounter the white people out of the sea. It was in the north that he encountered the fluid and restless Thembus who sealed his fate. In one of the skirmishes with those non-reliant Thembus, he and his son Mlawu died. Thus his life ended in defeat, after such a glorious, promising start.'

'The Thembus are now something of heroes because of their son, Mandela, who became the first black democratic president of this land. I would watch my words, if I were you. Rharhabe seems more like a glorified rover to me.'

'I thought, as a Mfengu, a wanderer, you'd readily associate with his spirit and plight.'

'Well, not really. By the way, the historian Tacitus sheds a doubt on the story of Nero being responsible for his mother's death. Of course that has not stopped drama-inducing writers, like Montaigne, adding the juicy bits about Agrippina screaming as she drowned. Do you think Nxele screamed as he went under? I mean, we have to admit, Nxele does seem like the hollering type. He wouldn't have missed an opportunity to create such noise, even if for the sake of drama.'

'In my life experience, drowning people, besides manually thrashing against the water, do so quietly. But it wouldn't surprise me to learn that Nxele didn't go quietly; after all, he was a noisy fellow ...'

Maqoma faded as Phila bumped out.

The Apricot Tree

PHILA WOKE JUST BEFORE MIDDAY. The house had taken on a strange impoverished look of neglect; with an uncanny peace, it felt also like a bowdlerised version of his home. He tried in vain to locate the energy they grew up with: the silent kindness of his father's face; the frenzied frustration of their mother, who must have had premonitions of running out of time. By the time he went overseas to study his mom was five years underground, disappointed at the matrimonial betrayal of her husband, which had hastened her cancerous departure. During her last days, Phila associated her room with sulfuric anger, the torment of the ammonia smell of her chamber pot. His father's descent into a defeated life fast-tracked after that. He felt trapped in a life he'd never really wished for. Cherishing *vita umbratilis*, a life in the shade, he dreamt of an idyllic pastoral life whose possibility had been overtaken by the times.

Phila opened the window, stood, with autumn in his heart, in the gardens of his life's spring. The smells and the colours were still the same, even the manner in which the wind shaved the swaying apricot tree. The carcass body parts from his father's blue Jeep van still lay there. He recalled the day they came to drop them. It was almost the carbon copy of this day except the parents were now gone. Phila had stood at his bedroom window, spying on the combat battle between his parents about where to put the parts. Something about his parents' lives seemed to be descending into disorder at that time, and for a boy with Phila's observational powers it felt like watching a tragic accident in slow motion. His father was being unreasonable, wanting to cut down the apricot tree, instead of the wire fence on the other side, to create space for the parts. His mom would have none of it. The eleven-year-old Phila, who had learnt to stay out of such things, eventually took a pair of pliers from the kitchen drawer and went outside. He began cutting the wire fence, creating space for the delivery van to reverse and unload the things where his mother wanted them to be, which was exactly where they still were today.

Phila had invested many an afternoon with his mother on that garden. When his father came around, their eyes met. Nothing was said. Phila refused to be browbeaten this time. Those two seconds defined their relationship henceforth. Embarrassed, his father turned back and went inside the house. He had discovered his own stubbornness in his son's eyes and felt found out. Found out because he had not been in the house the whole week. Found out because he had no integrity to demand authority. Found out because he understood that his son had decided to step up into the berth he had left vacant by deserting them. Found out because he had been unreasonable and childish, made himself too ridiculous to recover his dignity. Thus had he speeded up the moment of power exchange between a boy and his father. Growing up shocks us, Phila reflected, because it always carries a price of humiliation, whether of ourselves or those we respect most.

Phila turned back with a smile. The swaying of the apricot tree seemed much more vigorous in the memory album of his mind. Now he could see that it was just a tree, getting hollowed from within by the ant nest inside its stem. He almost finger-whistled for his dog, Baby.

"Good morning," he greeted Siya as he sat at the dining table. She had prepared a breakfast Phila had no appetite for. The eggs looked lumpy. He apologised for waking up late. He felt nauseous, miserable as snow and somehow impatient with himself. His headache, dormant under the alcohol rush, was pulsating again. It was not just a mere babalaza from the previous night. More like a crashing of unacknowledged childhood fantasies, the realisation that it was too late for the future.

"No need to be embarrassed. I woke around ten myself. Yesterday was a long day," said his sister, uncharacteristically making an effort to remove all irritation from her voice regarding his drinking. They ate in relative silence. Phila felt lonely, not for himself, but for his sister who had chosen to stay. Her face had grown thin and strained, prematurely aged even. When he could not stomach it anymore he stood up. He was going back to PE via East London, he told her, to run what he called "a personal errand". In actual fact he wanted to trace the migration of amaRharhabe that Maqoma had described. Phila could see his sister was relieved at this announcement – not for any sinister reason; she had become accustomed to being alone. It was not a matter of not liking each other; they respected each other. Phila was proud of her as a human rights lawyer.

He followed her career, mostly through the media. It gave him hope. Both their characters were leopard-like, solitary. They didn't do well as a pride. There was also the issue of their father's death, which both had nothing to say about at that moment. They were also avoiding situations where they would be compelled to comment on it, or worse, examine it.

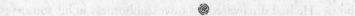

The moment he drove away from Queenstown and took the road towards the even smaller town of Cathcart, Phila could feel Maqoma's presence, but he was baffled by his uncharacteristic silence. Initially he thought he might be angry because almost everything around here was named after people who had been his arch enemies, like the town, named after Sir George Cathcart. In 1852, in the middle of the 1851-1853 Frontier War, after Maqoma had humiliated the British in Waterkloof, Governor Harry Smith was recalled and replaced as Governor by Cathcart, with orders to finish the war. In a way that was the last real war Maqoma fought against the British, in proper command, before handing the reins to his younger brother, Sandile. Maqoma was fifty-five years then, beginning his life-long battle with rheumatism. He also nearly died from dysentery during this war, the most cruel and the biggest the Xhosas and the British fought.

When he saw the Hogsback signs, and looked upwards to notice the start of the Nkonkobe mountains Phila realised that Maqoma was having bad memories, especially of the day he was nearly caught as he lay in a cave there, suffering from dysentery. Defiant as always, his wife Katye, who was taken prisoner with other women and children, when asked by the Governor if the leopardskin blanket was Maqoma's, replied, "Did you find him in it?"

They were driving on the flanks of the escarpment of the Nkonkobe mountains, which held so much meaning for Maqoma. From the west, the mountains extend to join up with the Amathole mountains, where the majority of the Frontier Wars were fought. These mountains elevated the settings for the wars and enhanced the armature of Maqoma's character as the most brilliant general of the Xhosa warriors. He used them for what came to be known as the bush wars against the colonial encroachment on their land by the British. Nowhere else had geography determined history to an extent as large as this, Phila thought. The bottom slopes of the mountains were forested with yellowwood, stinkwood and assegai trees. The plantations of pine and other timbers came later, and were cultivated for commercial use. The farmers, originally Germans, still planted Xhosa staples here: maize, sorghum, pumpkins and wheat. They began sowing when the snow-capped mountains started to thaw, sending torrential white waters leaping from the cliffs. During that season the sawmills had to operate on skeleton staff, because their Xhosa lumberjack employees went back to their villages to plant fields. This, to a smaller degree, was still the pattern today. The Xhosas lost their self-sustenance as a result of losing most of their arable land to the British colonial government, which was handed over to white farmers in 1853 by Cathcart. In almost all the Frontier Wars the British fought with the Xhosas, it was land that was the central issue.

Maqoma held his tongue all the time they went through the land that was so dear to him.

When he reached Stutterheim Phila followed the exit sign that directed him to the site of Sandile's grave, which he reached after passing a series of lakes and dams and driving through plantations of trees. The grave was tucked in between the graves of two British soldiers, to guard 'his rebellious spirit' from ever rebelling against the British crown again. Knowing the psychological weight the Xhosas assigned to the graves of their kings, the British had devised this ruse to keep the living Xhosas in check.

Sandile was Maqoma's younger half-brother. Until Sandile was old enough to assume the throne Maqoma had acted as regent. Growing weakly, under the shadow of Maqoma, the young king had had to work hard to prove himself as capable as his older half-brother. Unlike Maqoma, he was not a natural leader and he nearly bungled the well-orchestrated Eighth Frontier War where the Xhosas gained significant victories against the British.

This was not the first time Phila had been to visit Sandile's grave. He had been taken there as a child when on a fishing trip to Xholora, but the information hadn't really registered on him then. Now he sat there recalling one of his happiest family days, when his father woke him early to get his clothes on, without washing, let alone brushing his teeth. He was about eleven or twelve years old. It was in the early eighties and getting stopped by the police when you drove during the hours that needed your headlights to be on was a frequent occurrence. Headlights attracted white police cars of the Special Branch – they all drove Valiants – to chase you and pull you over. So the moment they pulled out of town on the N6 to East London they were flagged down by the police. Instantly the blinding torches were on their faces, shining at them through the windows on all sides of his father's Ford Custom. When one of the cops realised who his father was he stepped up.

"Damn, chief!" – people called his dad chief then, especially the white ones he played tennis with; the whole town, including white people, tested their salt as tennis players on Phila's father, something that made him famous – "Where you going at this ungodly hour?"

"Thought I'd give my son a taste of real fly-fishing in Xholora. He's quite keen to learn how to properly cast the line. So we thought we would give the fish a head-start, especially the dippers who drop their guard before dawn."

"Well, good luck to you both," said the policeman, who was on Phila's side of the car. "Hope you bring a catch to gut this evening. I'll radio you a pass to our guys ahead so they don't give you any more trouble. Hope we can catch up on the best of three next Saturday." He moved the torchlight off Phila's face and brushed his hair with his hand to indicate all was well. "Oh! You've got a cheeky one here," he laughed.

"Oh, he's just angry I woke him up early on a Sunday morning. Take no notice. Ready for the game whenever you are," his father said as they pulled off. Phila thought he was going to get a scolding from his dad for the frown against the cop, but he never even mentioned it.

After they got to Stutterheim they changed into their fishing gear. His father led him to the waters for his maiden deep-water fly-fishing lesson. His father was a trout fisherman. This Phila understood in retrospect each time he recalled his hallmarks when wielding a double hander. But that day his father still had more knowledge than Phila on fly casting, so he began with a lesson before showing how it was done. Phila had got stuck on the rookie jump-steeple-circle spey, something he still blamed on his father's trout fishing hallmarks, and had now resigned himself to as his factory fly-fishing fault. He usually ran too high to keep a fly where he aimed it to be; as such his tended to be whipped away in seconds by dippers. Or worse, he caught leaves with every third cast or so. That day this was very discouraging for Phila, especially when he fished next to his father who seemed to draw a yellow fin with every fifth cast. Phila's thirst for knowledge was what kept him going. And his father, on these trips, became forthcoming about issues, life plans and all. For instance he'd learnt on one of these trips that his dad had a dream of going salmon fishing in the Scottish Highlands one day, even of owning a cabin there, if it were possible, because, "A man's thoughts come easier with such clear mountain air." Phila used to think it was because his parents had grown up under the shadow of the Scottish missionary influence that his father chose Scotland, not Norway or Canada, for his salmon fishing dream. But now he knew better. The geography of an area is crucial in building the spirt of a person, a tribe, or a nation. The similarities between the Scots and amaXhosa – their obsessive grip on rustic culture, despite the pressures of civilisation – were not accidental but bred, by evolving for centuries on similar mountainous landscapes.

Phila never loved his father more than when he was a casting silhouette against a gurgling river, even as he later learnt to understand that a river ran through their characters in other things. And, to date, few things excited him as much as the break of what his father called 'river silence' with the thrashing of a trophy fish.

Phila drove another hundred kilometres or so to arrive in East London as the shadows were lengthening. The pin-prick of the lighthouse, at the Windmill, where he sat eating fried fish and chips, was barely visible through the low-hanging sky. The grey light intensified the cold wind from the harbour. The area, of course, stirred old memories – some of them kind, some not so pleasant.

When he felt the echo of depression he decided to go to the B&B he was booked into, hoping for a good night's sleep.

He woke at the first streak of dawn. Memory scars itched. He made himself coffee, which he drank on the balcony. The peace of the morning was distracting. The golden sun on the sea had the effect of amplifying things in his head. His first assignment of the day was hiking the Amathole mountains, where the gourd of *iMbokotho* broke. He felt the excitement grow with every sip of his coffee. I'm walking in the full daylight of our history, he thought to himself.

He went inside after finishing his coffee. An airline magazine on the coffee table, with a photo of the late Nigerian poet Ken Saro-Wiwa on the cover, caught his attention. He turned to the article but found it to be bland and poorly researched. He remembered when he had heard the news of the poet's death. It was the first time he and Arunny had sex. He was still in Berlin then, working late with Arunny, who was originally from Cambodia. She had felt like smoking dagga, so she'd asked Phila if he had any. When he said no she was disappointed. To redeem himself, as a darkie, Phila remembered reading from the papers that Görli, the

Görlitzer Park in Kreuzberg, was the best place to score. He informed Aru. They got their coats and left. The next thing he knew they were standing at Görlitzer Bahnhof U-Bahn station waiting for a train to her apartment, where they went to have stoned sex. After they laughed off the micro-aggressiveness of Berlin against people of colour – it had taken them an uncharacteristically long time to get their stash at Görli because people kept approaching them, assuming Phila was the drug dealer, or at least Aru's pimp. "Wie girl?" became their private joke and mating call for the duration of their two-and-a-half-year affair. He'd been smoking out on the balcony that evening when Aru called him inside. She was excitedly pointing at the TV where a visibly angry Mandela was spewing lava against the Nigerian junta who had just executed some political activists, including Saro-Wiwa. The price of serving the truth, Phila had thought to himself. He had always known about the natural contention between news and poetry. To him the duty of poetry was to historicise the news; to refine and define human experience, unlocking the mysteries of the world through a private view. When the poet has done this successfully, that is, mined the aesthetic rigour of history, then it is transformed into culture. But that poets in his era still paid with their lives for doing this came as a shudder-inducing surprise.

Aru was of the New Khmer Architecture school of thought, and had an appreciation of Vann Molyvann. A Bachelardian himself, Phila and Aru had in common their outlook towards organic architecture and the need for a structure to be a poetic emblem of its environment, as opposed to those who thought architecture should stand out of causality. Although they had known each other for at least nine months, that night was the first time they had really talked. They settled quickly with each other like bugs on a rug, perhaps even loved each other a lot. But, despite what the romantics tell you, there are things even love cannot conquer. The irony was that the poetry Aru loved so much was, when he distilled things to their essence, what tore them apart. Phila was unable to break the bond of solidarity between imagination and memory, something otherwise known as nostalgia. It might have been easy for Aru to up and go to Switzerland so that she could learn at the feet of her master where the rulers of Phnom Penh had exiled him. The deeper urge for Phila was homebound. At least she still signed her emails to him: 'Your Morning Star'.

Helen was almost as devastated as Phila was when Aru left Deutschland. They were already behaving like in-laws and were extremely fond of each other. Helen was Phila's second mother, the one responsible for his scholarship application to Germany. Phila had first met her when he was nine or ten years old, the day his father took him to the dentist to take out a rotten tooth. They were still a family then but the storms were already gathering, something even his ten-year-old self could not ignore: the constant disappearances of his dad, especially when he was doing night duty; the subsequent shouting from his mom. His father had taken him to an Indian, maybe a Chinese dentist – Phila hadn't possessed enough sophistication to distinguish between races or ethnic groups then; but remembering the pockmarked face and bulbous nose, he would now bet on Indian. Also, each time the dentist bent to look in his mouth a wave of curry reached his olfactory receptors – two words he learnt from his medical nurse dad that day when he'd tried to explain the sensation. The dentist was the type who kept lollipops for children; firm with instruction and certain in diagnosis. One thing Phila remembered about him was how he did not talk down to him in the manner of many adults.

"I have this needle, which I am going to prick your gums with. It will hurt a little. But that will help you not feel the pain when I take your tooth out. If you don't move much, I am gonna give you a lollipop." The instructions were direct and clear. Phila did not make a single move. He had this strange practice of dissociating himself from pain, a trick he first learnt when he kicked his toenail out on a rock when he was playing soccer. Because his mom had told him not to go out he had had to keep mum about the pain. Only the trail of blood on the kitchen floor told him out. His mom cleaned and bandaged the wound with a promise that it would heal soon enough.

Another time Phila broke his arm at school while playing rugby, but he didn't know it was broken until the doctor confirmed it. In the morning, when he could not lift his spoon to eat his porridge his mom knew something was amiss. The pain that had kept him awake almost all night had already disappeared by then, but his parents insisted on taking him to the doctor anyway. Phila came back the proud owner of a cast, making him the envy of his coevals at school.

By the time he visited the dentist he had already mastered the art of dissociating himself from pain. The dentist and his dad must have been friends, because they had chatted a lot about different things, mostly tennis. People said things about his father like: "Had it not been for apartheid, your dad would have gone professional." They meant it as a compliment, but Phila, who was not too shabby at tennis himself, always felt it as judgement of his abilities, meaning that, even though in his era they had more opportunities, it was Phila who was falling short. Phila's dad found his voice among strangers, which seemed strange to those who knew him to be taciturn within the family. It was a strange thing to observe a different side of his dad when they were out. At home he seemed to assume that the family could read his mind, barking angrily when they got things wrong.

Phila's English then was still faltering, but he got the gist of his father and the dentist's conversation about "a puppy for my boy". That part he definitely got because he had been dying to have a hunting dog like everybody else his age in the village. Being his father's son, taciturnity and all, Phila didn't mention anything to his father about the dog, waiting for him to introduce the topic or produce the surprise. He got concerned as the day matured, with his father not mentioning anything while running errands for the general dealership he owned in the village. They went last to the wholesaler, Metro, for shop supplies. Coming out of the wholesaler's his father said they needed to go somewhere to collect his present – "because you were a good boy at the dentist". When they climbed the bridge over the railway line, Phila knew they were going where white people lived and instinctively also knew it would not be a pleasant experience if the police found them there.

He was not exactly sure about the details of why they were not supposed to be there, just that it was the apartheid thing everyone talked about all the time. When they stopped at one of the houses with whitewashed walls, picket fence, manicured lawn and military-haircut-style hedge, his father told him to remain in the car while he went inside. Phila knew they were on a surreptitious and risky mission, so he started spying for signs of danger, staying alert. All approaching cars were a source of anxiety, especially police vans. But the only sense of danger, as Phila waited for his father in the car, came with the refuse truck. He was confused as to what to make of it. In the township where he stayed there was no collection of refuse and such – hence rubbish was strewn everywhere or else burnt. Blacks then didn't have much refuse to dispose of anyway because they lived poor, from hand to mouth. The truck interrupted Phila's admiration of the white people's streets, how open and clean they were; neat and orderly compared to those of blacks, who lived on crowded dirty streets, with sewerage permanently leaking from public toilets. White people's houses had clean white walls, well-groomed lawns and manicured gardens. Black people's houses were mostly just mud dongas. Later on when he read Orwell in *Down and Out in Paris and London*, what he described as 'leprous houses, lurching towards one another in queer attitudes, as though they had all been frozen in the act of collapse', Phila felt Orwell was defining their township. Strange to Phila also was the fact that there was no one walking drunk on the streets, or women shouting or laughing at each other walking with buckets of water and bundles of laundry on their heads, ambling towards the communal public lavatory, the only place that had running water. These things he associated with the superiority of white people, without understanding why.

Just when he was starting to panic about the truck coming closer to the house his father came out laughing, followed by a white woman. The white woman came to greet Phila in the car, continuing the strange thing of talking to him like an adult, spoiling it only by pulling his cheeks after handing him a puppy.

"Happy, are we now? We have a new puppy! You must take care of it. Feed and clean up after it," the woman declared. She had ginger hair and pale legs. Her eyes, the colour of a tumultuous sea, were trained on Phila, who acted bluff for fear of embarrassing himself in front of a white, though he was dying to scream with joy. His dad looked as though he had been playing tennis, sweaty as a racehorse.

The first thing that struck Phila about the puppy was its humbug round eyes. She, the puppy, looked at him more with confusion than curiosity. As they drove off Phila was in a fierce burst of happiness.

"Isn't Helen nice?" His father, too, was now on this thing of treating him like an adult, asking for his opinions and all. Phila nodded his head while concentrating on the puppy, which was trying to chew his finger with its tiny teeth.

It took Phila more than thirty years to piece the puzzle together. All those times when she made him juice during tennis matches at the psychiatric hospital they all worked at, the scales did not fall. Or when they met her in town, or how, when Phila was wearing the Christmas navy suit his dad had 'bought' him, she handed him a ten rand note after talking at length with his father. Or when he went looking for his father at the hospital kitchen she came out of the room adjusting her skirts, and his father came out tucking his shirt into his trousers, both of them out of breath. Nothing about these encounters seemed odd to Phila's mind at the time. People were always out of breath after playing tennis. Helen was just a kind white woman, with a strange accent, who used to be married to an Indian dentist his dad played tennis with. Only after Helen collected him at Frankfurt airport, twenty years later, did Phila finally connect the dots.

On their drive home to the township Phila fought the butterflies in his stomach each time the car looped the bridge. His father, now and then, looked with pride at Phila and the puppy, a match made in heaven, if ever there was any.

After a while he said, in a stern voice, "Know that this dog is your responsibility. You must look after her, make sure she eats and she will be your friend for life."

Phila ran his hands over the puppy's soft black fur, studying its face. The puppy was eager as mustard for play, whining a bit, and gently forcing its nose into his fingers when he stopped his playful hand gestures. His father said they must name it Baby – he was always naming things endearing to him Baby. So Baby it was.

They drove a short distance before his father stopped at the fish shop, as was the norm when they went home after a town visit. Phila was left in the car with the puppy, its heart pumping against his ribs like a caged bird. He dared not disturb its sleep by changing positions though he felt a cramp developing in his left thigh.

Coming back, his father embarked upon a lecture about German Shepherds. "... one of the most intelligent dogs on earth. They are very loving and highly protective of their owners ..."

And so it proved to be later. Phila's solar plexus contracted as they reached the apex of the climb of the motorway bridge under which the trains passed whistling to Johannesburg.

When they arrived home the puppy became apprehensive about the strange surroundings. Phila became the object of its trust, being the only thing vaguely familiar to it now amid the cackle of chickens, the mooing of cows, the cavorting of calves, the snorting of pigs and barking of alien dogs. She sniffed the warmth of his arm and buried her head under it. With that Phila's purpose in life was defined. When Phila was at school, his mother said, the dog spent the whole day in a bad mood, snarling and yelping at those she did not know, with inconsolable whimpers and whines.

But Baby was rubbish at hunting when she got older. True, she made up for it twice over with her sunny personality, more human than dog. The hunter instinct was completely dormant in her. Once while hunting they fell on a warren. Phila rubbed Baby's nose in the rabbit urine and pellets, then signalled her to go hunt. Promisingly, she did. When the rabbit jumped Baby was so startled she turned around and ran towards Phila. That sealed her hunting fate. Nobody was interested in teaching her the skill after that. It puzzled him, though, because she was an extremely intelligent dog, even if a lazy runner. Whenever Phila pointed her towards the hopping and scampering rabbits, or impala, intending for her to follow, she would look at him quizzically: are you crazy? Or she would just turn her back on the prey and begin a wolf howl. In the eyes of the community she was a failure, a glorified pet. And she was a rubbish guard dog too, only interested in sharing Phila's bed. She had about her a human poise and dignity; she refused to slap and snap at food with other dogs, so you had to give her an individual dish.

To protect her Phila stopped going to *amalima* – hunting parties. They took to going on solitary mountain climbing expeditions together instead, which Baby relished, because it meant Phila's attention was on her. She was good in the quick identification of snakes – just about the only thing she was good at with all that intelligence. Phila loved her to distraction anyway.

Kuyaliwa Ekhaya

A SHARP SQUALL SUDDENLY SPURTED heavy, violent rain, accompanied by thunder, when Phila reached the foot of the Amathole mountains where his hike was to begin. He waited it out inside the car, lit a cigarette, and watched shafts of sunlight struggling to break through grey clouds. There was a fierce intenseness in the air.

'The problem was the internecine struggles between our different tribes.'

Maqoma was back, sitting in the passenger seat and smoking a pipe that smelled like burning grass.

'Most interesting to me,' he continued, 'were the happenings of fate, the fact that the Mfengus, from the east, and the whites, from the west, arrived at just about the same time in our area. Your ancient Roman friend saw fate as an unchanging plan in the mind of God, who was immutable, and governed everything. Who can argue with that? The Mfengus would have remained our vassals in perpetuity without the arrival of white people who armed them to fight. Perhaps in the end the British, with their never-ending supply of redcoats, would have eventually prevailed over us, but it would have taken much longer without the helping hand of the Mfengus and the KhoiKhoi people, and they would have suffered very long and deeply for it. The question I discovered late, after my body had been the property of maggots, is why fate, after building us, would want to break us up into pieces.'

'Are you trying to say it was the plan of God that the Xhosas lost their land to the Mfengus and the whites?' Phila asked.

'I'm saying the plan of God, as Ntsikana saw it, and I discovered late, was that nations must mix. That they clash in doing so is in the nature of things, because of human intransigence.'

'So it is the inspired ecleticism you like in Boethius? I was wondering.'

'Ntsikana taught me that, but we shall talk about it later. I wanted to wait until I was here before telling you about our war with amaNdlambe. My father, Ngqika, was by then isolated from other chiefs, because he was deemed to be too close to white people, a sell-out, so to say.'

'Ndlambe was your father's, Ngqika's, uncle? Who became a regent when he was still too young to reign?

'Indeed. But by then we were virtually in a perpetual war with him, and with those who broke from our tribe to follow him when he refused to hand over the reins. He had been looking for an excuse to engage us in war; raided the kraals of our minor chiefs and of the white farmers who were our allies. Then, on the brink of crisis, Ngqika was asked by the colonial authority to assist the commandos that had come to recover the white people's cattle. Ngqika attempted to negotiate the handover of the cattle with Ndlambe. Ndlambe refused and was joined by many others from the imiDange tribe. Nxele, the war prophet whom everyone was by then calling Makhanda, because he practised witch-doctoring, was the one inciting people, knowing very well it would eventually provoke war with the white colonial government. Seeing the source of trouble, Ngqika demanded from Ndlambe that he hand Nxele over to him. Ndlambe refused, citing that he recognised only Hintsa, across Inciba, as a king; in similar manner Rharhabe, before, had recognised only the paramountcy of Gcaleka. He was basically claiming the kingship of amaRharhabe. Ngqika was furious at such insolence. He could be heard around our hearth murmuring, "I'll show that dog Ndlambe that I too am a king."

'All this, of course, was just part of heightened tensions of both Ngqika and Ndlambe wanting to reunite amaRharhabe under one house. Ndlambe continued attacking and confiscating cattle from our sub-chiefs until, compelled by the whites also, we had no choice but to take his actions as a declaration of war. The only way to unite amaRharhabe, we thought, and save our nation from the wrath of white colonial rule, would be first to finish off Ndlambe as the main chief of amaRharhabe. Needless to say, Ndlambe, under the tutelage of Nxele, had similar thoughts about Ngqika. We all wanted to unite amaRharhabe, but who was Ndlambe to think he could be the paramount chief of amaRharhabe, when my father was a legitimate heir? They used the excuse that my father was conniving with white people to trickle the land away from the house of Phalo. What was my father to do when they isolated and united against him?'

The rain, though still drizzling, was showing signs of slowing down. Phila opened the car door to get away from Maqoma's suffocating pipe smoke. He looked across to the mountain cap that was bandaged in white mist. Hannibal crossing the Alps in his campaign against Ancient Rome was the only other time he could think of when the cartography of mountains had played as crucial a role as did these formations in the Eastern Cape and Lesotho. The escarpments of the Amathole mountains travelled to join up, in a disjointed way, with the Nkonkobe (Winterberg) spurs to the east, moving to the ridge of the Thyumie valley where amNgika were densely populated, prompting the Scottish missionaries to build a station there, where the first Xhosa converts to Christianity, like the Sogas, resided. The mountains became craggy before they towered into the greenery of the Waterkloof in a series of flat tables as they moved west. By different graduation the Nkonkobe ran to jam up with what began the Ukhahlamba (Drakensberg), though still just a tangle of mountain ranges. Then they formed a solid wall that belted the Eastern Cape from Lesotho, from KwaZulu-Natal, before guttering towards Somerset East and Graaff-Reinet to the east, in rock-falling fastnesses, and, to the west, in solidifying granite, serenading the south-west coast until they hugged the sea to form a solid scrim curtain for the mother city – Cape Town – whose eyes were to the occident and back to the African continent.

For the Frontier Wars, the major action was on the fastnesses of the Nkonkobe and Amathole mountains, the latter named so by the Xhosa because they resembled cavorting calves.

Noticing he had gotten wet, Phila got back in the car to join Maqoma, who appeared to be in deep thought still.

'Don't get me wrong. There was, of course, an element of opportunism in Ngqika's allying himself with the whites. He had first turned for help to the turbulent and disunited Thembus out of frustration. It was the main reason why he married the daughter of their chieftain, Suthu. But the Thembus were too feeble and weak to be relied on. It was a foolish thing to rely on those mercenaries anyway, who'd sell even their own mothers for a sack of corn. Then, out of desperation, Ngqika appealed to the colonial powers, telling them other Xhosa chiefs were uniting against him since he wanted to help white people recover their cattle so we might all live in peace. But no material help was really forthcoming from the colonial forces. We had to brave the war on our own.

'I had just come out of circumcision school then. AmaJingqi, the newly formed warrior tribe, was under my command. It was our tribe's pride and hope, with agile young men of my age. Everyone in our tribe looked upon amaJingqi to deliver not only the tribe but amaRharhabe into a strong nation.

'We had internal problems too, like the group who followed the new religion under the leadership of Ntsikana. These people preached pacifism around our tribe. That was fine under normal times, but when the evil times were upon us they became a nuisance.

'Nxele and Ntsikana held the major spiritual forces of our times. When Ndlambe fell under Nxele's influence Ntsikana came to our tribe to influence Ngqika against the spirit of war Nxele was preaching. Myself, I didn't fully understand Ntsikana. I suspected he knew more than he was telling us about his prophecies. I kept wondering what his real intentions were. Was he commissioned by Ndlambe to make us effeminate? I didn't want to upset my father with my suspicions. But I grew more suspicious by the day that Ntsikana had come to our tribe on some clandestine mission.'

Phila was beginning to take serious interest in what Maqoma was telling him. He knew Ntsikana and Nxele as folklore figures of their history; and there was a proverb about the coming of Nxele, the origins of which were vague. Ntsikana, of course, was known as the prophet who predicted the arrival of white people with money and the Bible, but beyond that Phila knew very little, not even the fact that Ntsikana and Nxele were contemporaries. He treated that history the same as he did biblical stories: not really sure if they happened but, for cautionary purposes, went along with them. His eyes started opening when he began reading the history of the world, and discovered how the Hebrews interpreted historical events as the actions of God, something he still found most fascinating about the Old Testament. It now felt to him as though Maqoma was reading the South African Testament to him. He listened further.

'I thought Ntsikana was just under the spell of the white people's God. To have a good understanding of my thinking you must also recall that amaCirha, Ntsikana's clan, were the oldest Xhosa royal family. Their lineage went as far as the era when Tshawe, who was the grandfather to Gcaleka and Rharhabe, overthrew Cirha to usurp the Xhosa throne. So there were bound to be some suspicions against Ntsikana on our part; thinking his flaring popularity had something to do with the resurgence of amaCirha to reclaim their crown.

'Ntsikana had come to our tribe because he thought we wanted to avoid war with white people – Ngqika was then seen to be in collaboration with white people. Ntsikana was my first misjudgement as an incumbent prince. In one of our war councils he approached my father, begging, "Chief, please do not fight with your brothers, because if you do you'll fall. *Siyimbumba yamanyama!*"

'When he did that I was certain my suspicions were confirmed against him. I wrote his name on my knee as the first person I'd acquaint with the coldness of my spear when I returned victorious from the battle with the Ndlambes. Fortunately, or rather unfortunately, our pro-war faction had the support of most councillors. Never have I appreciated Manxoyi's hard-headedness, which irritated me under normal circumstances, as I did that day. He was the one who crushed Ntsikana.

'Just when we were about to leave, Ntsikana pulled a stunt that sent shivers down my spine. He let fall a gourd that smashed on the ground before us. Pointing to its shards he shouted: "That signifies our nation if we go to war with each other! This thing that has entered me" – he was always going on about the thing that had entered him, which they called The Word – "is telling me. My last word is that your strength can only be found in unity. But if you go to war now, you will forfeit your land. You shall be slaves of other nations. Your land will be a constant curse to you." But Manxoyi put everyone back on track again within no time.

'The following week we held a ceremony of the Strengthening of Warriors, presided over by our trusted *amatola*. AmaJingqi were officially given feathers of Indwe as members of the first warrior circle *yamafa-na-nkosi*, the happy-die-with-the-king. We ate raw beef, mixed with bitter herbs, and other witch-doctor medicines to ensure victory at war. After that we left in full battle regalia. I, wearing a chief's leopard band around my head, with a plume from the feathers of a partridge to signify my regiment, led the regiments; a plume of the blue crane, as our highest regiment of Indwe, I wore on the other side to distinguish my highest warrior status. Ah! I can remember that day. My shoulders were bare save for the python skin bands on my upper arms that had been sewn by my twin sister, Nongwane. The snake, especially the mamba and python, was our escutcheon. A necklace of hyena's teeth hung around my muscle-corded neck. The loin-skin, crude and rough from buffalo hide, fitted snugly to facilitate ease of movement. And around my calves I wore leggings of buffalo tail. My assegai, shielded by an elephant's tail skin, completed my war regalia.

'As we left, several *imbongi* incited us to war with chants. The only blemish to the party was Ntsikana, who persistently shouted like a prophet of doom: "Terrible things are coming to the land of Phalo! You're flirting with destruction, my people! You're flirting with doom! There cometh a cloud from the sea that will flood and clog your springs of sustenance ... Beware if the enemy seeks to draw you in! Do not follow them, because you are being led into a dangerous trap. Male issue of my nation! I saw your heads devoured by ants in the wilderness."

'His words haunted me like a perpetual nightmare the rest of my life.

'The day we left for the battlefield was sinister in colour, like bird's entrails. Womenfolk sent us out with a haunting *Ntlaba Mkhosi*, a war song that showered us with tears.' Maqoma began singing:

Hoyo ho!! Kuyaliwa ekhaya (2)
Yoma ho!! Kuyaliwa ekhaya
Nase Mthontsi!! Kuyaliwa ma
EHohita!! Komkhulu ekhaya mna
Kuyaliwa ekhaya mna (2)
Hema yo!! Yemolo yo ho ho!
Heya ho!! Kuthiwa ekhaya mna (2)
Xel' eKhobonqa kwaLunqongo
Kuyaliwa ekhaya mna (2)
KwelaseQombolo kuCentane
EQwaninga kuGatyana
Xela kuyaliwa ekhaya mna (2)
Yoma yo!! Hoyoyo mama
Umlo usifikele thina!!

There's friction at home (2)
My mother ho!! They're fighting at home
Even at Mthontsi!! There's friction ma
At Hohita!! The royal house of my home
They're fighting at home O! me (2)
Wait yo!! Greetings yo ho ho!
Here ho!! They say at my home O! me (2)
Tell at Khobonqa, the home of Lunqongo
There's friction at home (2)
In the land of Qombolo at Centane
At Qwaninga, the home in Gatyana
Tell they're fighting at home (2)
My mother yo!! Hoyoyo mama
Doom has visited us!

'I wish I could summon my coevals to relive the emotive force of that song. It has a funereal pathos about it, and a plaintive falling cadence.

Remind me to teach you how to sing it.'

Maqoma opened the car door. Silent and animated, Phila followed him. A rainbow arch was forming in the sky. Of his own accord, Phila bent to pick up Maqoma's stick, which he had seen drop while the old man was getting out of the car. It was only when he failed to make physical contact with the stick that he remembered and began following in Maqoma's virtual footsteps. The grass and stones, wet and slippery, made things difficult for him as they climbed the mountain. As soon as Phila caught up Maqoma continued his narrative in a plaintive voice.

'When I cast my mind back, my heart wrings in hearing that song still.'

'We still sing it,' Phila told him, 'in jubilation though, when we have traditional celebrations. It is usually in mock battles people enact when they have had one too many.'

'You mean mock stick fights?' Maqoma cheered up a little.

'Indeed.'

'Are you any good in a stick fight?'

'No! I'm rubbish at it. I was always getting bullied about it in school.'

'We must remedy that.' They fell silent for a moment before Maqoma continued.

'We marched out, trance-like, with a marked sense of order and calmness. We didn't like to mask our fear with undue jolliness. It was saddest because we were going to fight our own brethren. We knew death awaited us on the other end in their hands, our own brothers, whose only quarrel with us was that they chose to follow Ndlambe. We mastered our fears for what had to be done since it was our long-awaited chance to prove the valour of our unit, amaJingqi. That day was grave and unswerving. The thing with our nation, for instance, unlike the Zulus who've always been a little belligerent, is that we first do everything, and almost anything, to avoid fighting. But once we decide on it we commit. We prefer non-reckless bravery. We admire valour more when it is tempered with moderation.

'We marched until we reached Ntaba kaNdoda – out there.' Maqoma pointed to the mountain across from them.

'Your grave is there, isn't it?' Phila asked hesitantly.

'So I believe. But how that came to pass I will tell you in due time. As I was saying –'

'I read somewhere that it is rather neglected. Perhaps I must apply to the municipality to fix it? Then we can remedy that.' Phila felt embarrassed for the whole nation.

'We bivouacked for the night at Ntaba kaNdoda. It is impossible to describe the feeling that comes with sunset when a man is on the peak of a high mountain a day before what might be his last.'

They were now halfway to the summit. Phila stopped to survey the distance they'd covered, and to give himself a breather because he was feeling slightly dizzy. On the flanks of the khaki-coloured hills Xhosa villages clung like spit on a wall. The mountain chain was heavily forested where it was not covered by copses and scrub. Some hills stood in dull relief against the clearing sky.

Sunsets, in this land of longing, bring a crescendo of pain, reminding one of the inevitability of tears in mortal things, Phila thought to himself.

'The sun was quick in taking the moon out of its pocket that evening. The moon took her time bringing her flock of stars out to pasture. When they came out the dark night became ghostly. Dawn, with its pink fingers over the mountains, came as it must the following morning. I had had a restless night. It was my custom to meet dawn at the top of the mountain. I went to a high hill to watch the sunrise in its rosy splendour, listening to the counsel of the sounds of daybreak. All I could think was, if this should be the day I join my ancestors, I hope at least there is a sun as beautiful as this where they are.

'Where I am now, there is a man who was a king in a white man's world. He says he also liked climbing mountains to watch the sunrise. His name is Hadrian, an emperor of Rome in his time. His favourite mountain was Mount Etna. We get along fine with our ritual of meeting at dawn. In the days of my living it earned me the pet name of Jong'Umsobomvu – the one who watches the sun's lustre. My mind works better in the early hours. That is why I made it a point, especially when I had important things to consider, of rising early and sitting upon the highest point, to contemplate things. High mountain scene to sprawling land below has always been dear to my heart. I had hoped when death came for me it would find me on the mountaintop somewhere at dawn. Well, things turned out differently, very differently, for me.

'We marched early towards the open Debe Flats. When we stopped on the last hillcrest to descend in single file, yonder, we could see their warriors waiting for us on the declivities on the plains of Amalinde. Mdushane, Ndlambe's son, led their army. It is going to be a battle of princes, after all, I thought to myself. I was glad because I knew vast, plain fields would play to our advantage. We were more disciplined, younger, agile, more organised and passionate.

'Round about the time you rest your first plough-share, in the late morning, I led my men in a mighty charge. Hastily the enemy came to meet us. Our raised weapons clashed. If you've ever heard metal ring against stone you know the sound of battle. That sound echoes in the ear of your soul, eternally. I sometimes hear people, who have probably never been to war, speak of war as if it were a noble thing. War may be necessary, but there's nothing noble about it. It is a foul, stinking zone of blood and ordure that lingers in your nostrils for days. If by some kind of scatological perversion you enjoy shit running down men's legs whose faces are twisted beyond recognition with fear, perhaps war will be noble to you. The majority of us see no grandeur in that waste of life. If you have ever seen the face of a young person, full of uncomprehending bewilderment, dying, you would despise war forever. I've never met a man who does not believe in God on the battlefield. The battlefield is the platform of naked needs; in such, God is never far away.

'We forced them to hesitate and retreat. We advanced, forgetting all about Ntsikana's warning. Those days were the days Shaka was routing other tribes with a battle strategy called a 'bull's horn'. Ndlambe had a lot of Mfengus on his side who had learnt this strategy from Shaka *impis*. The first time Ndlambe tried it was on us that day. Late did we learn they were not retreating but withdrawing the centre of their battle line in order to entice us into going deeper. It worked. With us deep in the centre of the phalanx of their broken bull's horn circle they gave a signal for some of their warriors who were hiding on the bulge of the hills to close in. These were mostly the Gcalekas, led by Hintsa himself. As soon as I saw them I knew we were done for. My only wish was for my men not to panic. The enemy had also chosen the battlefield well to suit their strategy. The plains were guarded by small hills from both sides where the Gcalekas hid.

'As they closed in on us, like vultures on a carcass, our flanks panicked and dispersed. From there the battle became a massacre. Those of us who were caught in the centre fought with unabashed candour, checking them for the greater part of the day. I believe that morale and perseverance are the ultimate determining factors in war. We had more of these but, unfortunately, they had numbers. The blood of our men blotched the plains.'

Maqoma slowly raised his hand to point at the sacred grounds of Ntaba kaNdoda when they reached the summit.

'All we could do was attempt to open their circle and break the trap in desperate assault to free ourselves. I received terrible assegai wounds on my thigh and my neck. I owe my life to the valour of our Indwes. Matshaya, especially, didn't give up on me, even though things looked forlorn. Wishing to spare some of them, I commanded they run and save their lives. But they chose to stay and fight until they opened a path with their assegais. Eventually, they managed to penetrate like a wedge through hostile lines and carried me to the mountain safety of Ntaba kaNdoda. I lay there for a long time, begrimed with dust and surreal from the impact. Around sunset most of our warriors had managed to break through the wall of the enemy and, sensibly, they ran for their lives. The enemy pursued them all the way to our villages. Some of the enemy force remained behind, feasting on our dying, impaling the wounded and burning our dead; gambolling around and congratulating themselves. A holocaust smoke rose to the bare heights of the lonely sky as I watched from the mountain safety. I could not believe I had given command, my first one, for so much death sprawl.

'I have never been the one to be broken by power of leadership, but that day? My coevals, ones I had grown up with, the only people I knew and trusted, were lying dead, burning in sacrifice for the never-satiated god of war. We left Ntlukwana there, the valorous father of Neku. We left Nteyi, the indefatigible father of Tyhala. We left Tolwana at the tender age of having seen only four *zilimela*. We left even that benign fool Zakude, hard-headed as ever; he had charged like a bull to the centre when he saw I was injured. We left the whole generation of amaJingqi in those fields of death.

'Once you see so many people you know die on the same day, you lose something of yourself, something deep and unidentifiable. Their screams and whimpers visit your sleep, their stirring faces of reproachful innocence. I lost my youthful innocence that day.

'As I struggled with death on my chest, Ntsikana's words came back to haunt me. I needed someone to blame my anger on, but none was reprehensible but me. I tried to marshal some arguments to excuse my inexperience, but anger and grief came to possess me. I became hateful in my own heart, and swore to avenge my men, even if it took my whole life to do it. I didn't know whether to kill or respect Ntsikana after realising he must have learnt of the ruse through the wind, and had come to warn us. As time went on the things he foretold came true. But that too was to cost me dearly later on in my life. So, in a way, Ntsikana double-cursed me. But now it's too late, the deed has been done. The fault was not yours, son of Gaba, but our itching ears.

'As I lay, my face to the grass, Matshaya, my whilom friend and adjutant, softly said, "Strength against strength, we could have taken them. They won the day by cunning." I knew what he said was true, but truth offered me no consolation at that moment. Battles are remembered by who wins, not by who was most virtuous.

'Disaster followed hard on disaster as the enemy turned its bloodbath orgy to our villages. It seemed as though destruction, not conquest, was their purpose. They visited our villages with a satanic blast, mowing down everything they came in contact with, leaving behind only death and desolation. The dirge voices strained from our women who carried blood-stained hands on their heads crying, "Destruction, destruction all over! We're trapped in our own ruin!" The battlefield and our villages reeked of a slaughterhouse. Vapours of putrefying flesh invited wild animals from their forest lairs. Scenes of hyenas thrusting their sharp teeth on the insensible bodies of our men were common. Dogs tore the rotting flesh of their masters in an attempt to fight their hunger. The skies were dark with vultures feasting on dead bodies. Desperate women lay strewn all over the place. Nothing like that had ever happened before in our nation. In our custom women and children were sacred. Not that day. That's why I say their intention was annihilation, not conquest. Every nearby tree bore marks from the blood-stained claws of the birds of prey painting the trees a russet colour.

'More than three hundred men of my first command fell that day. The enemy seized more than six thousand cattle from our kraals. My father, Ngqika, had to flee beyond Tyumi and Ngcwenxa to Khobonqa for safety. And from there he remembered the words of Governor Somerset. "If you keep me, I'll also keep you." He appealed to the colonial powers for help.

'As for me, that is the time I really learnt how to hate. To think I had only seen twenty-two winters. The destiny of a male child in our nation was that of an ass, carcass for crows and vultures. His entire life, birds of prey hovered above his head. Where he lay, be it on the mountain slopes or plains, he was bound to be carrion.

'I led what was left of my Indwes back to the bogs and bushes of the Mthontsi forests at the Nkonkobe fastness there, where we could lick our wounds and recuperate in peace. That was when I first discovered the fort-like protection of the mountainous cliffs and caves of Waterkloof, which would serve me well later on for the bush wars against the British.

'Our enemies congratulated themselves, thinking they had dashed the last hopes of amaNgqika. Then they made the daring mistake of going to the heart of the beast, eRhini. We, amaNgqika, were the only Xhosa tribe that didn't join the all-out Xhosa battle against the colonial government. But more of that later.

'They say a man's worth is revealed during the time of his greatest need. I tried to discover myself during those months when the certainties of youth deserted me one by one. I saw myself victim of my own braggadocio. My men deserted in droves, some to the white man's religion, some to join the winning side, Ndlambe. Some stayed only to calculate which way to jump. Others stayed out of unflinching loyalty. My confidence in myself was shaken. Inwardly I couldn't command the thoughts I was forced to live by. As I stood on my humiliation I was filled with shuddering loathing for myself. Only those who had remained gave me any semblance of strength by their confidence and their expectations of my leadership.

'Rumour ran on winged feet, reporting that I was dead. This came as a relief to my enemies, who laughed my memory to scorn. But, within no time, I pulled myself together. White people helped us recover some of our cattle, most of which – and more – they confiscated for themselves. In my heart of hearts I knew we would eventually pay for their assistance with a pound of our own flesh. When you bring home a nest full of maggots you must expect a visit from the lizard. That race of thieves had seen how vulnerable and dependent on them we were. I knew it wouldn't be long before they exploited that vulnerability.

'Later, during my incarceration, I spent a long time thinking about my life. Even then it looked as though my life had amounted to nothing but a path of blood, knitted from a black fleece of destiny. Fate was unkind to me, unkind to the life of wrath and pride it allotted me.

'Once a man gets done with the vicious stream of vindictiveness and accusations he lands naked before wisdom. In his heart he cries: *It is all vanity!* Then, if he is humble enough, from there wisdom comes to take abode in his heart. Once you live long enough with wisdom you learn not to appreciate even the hollowness of victory, and the uselessness of revenge. There's nothing to take pride in in this life except counsel with wisdom. But we must first despair in order to gain wisdom. Only Qamata fills the gap of what we've lost. If it was Qamata's will that our nation should drudge for other nations, then there was nothing any one of us could have done. Our fate was too strong for us. Death is the end of weight, and the soaring of the spirit, that is why it comes as a relief to a wise man. Be not anxious about anything, not even of death as relief. Let death's shade close upon you if it must, but let your heart yearn for nothing except goodness. Do not allow yourself to be caught up in pride, that satanic weakness. Perhaps you'll reach old age, the age of your greatest needs. I pray that, unlike me, it does not find you in fields that are encircled by howling waters.

'I refused to ford where Nxele dared. I refused to swim where my sister dared, in the arms of white men and their hypocritical religion.

Yet wisdom found me all the same. I, Maqoma, am my own self; son of Ngqika, who comes from the noble Xhosa lineage. Even when my star was paling I dared to say my end would be my own. It was written in the stone of my destiny, so I could not escape my fate. My life ached like an unhealed wound during the last days of my life. White people delivered my death, but even in the end my spirit was never broken. When I took my last blanket, I cursed the devil in white people's ways and went to my permanent sleep with the wind at my back.'

Vagabonds

DUSK AND DAWN, PHILA'S FAVOURITE TIMES of the day, are when creation eloquently comes to the defence of the transcendent spirit, according to his grandma. When the nature of things assumes fervid calmness with voluptuous plenitude. "I grow young at dusk," his grandma used to say. Obviously, Maqoma, also, grew young at dawn, hence his cognomen, Jong'Umsobomvu.

Phila went down memory lane with dancing motes of dust, where Maqoma manifested to him.

'By now we had no choice but to consolidate our ties with the colonial government, because we were weak and dependent on their protection. But then came a man by the name of Graham, a demon if ever there was one to our people. He claimed he was sent by the white Governor, another devilish man, by the name of Cradock. They were the two people who made it clear to us that our land no longer belonged to us. They were not satisfied with sweeping off the Ndlambes, who in turn became a boil on Chungwa, eCawe. I might claim that we bore the brunt of white man's greed in our land, but no one bore this more than Chungwa, who had to deal with them coming from the Gamtoos side, from the Zuurveld, across Fish River and from the Vuba mountains. Right to his grave Chungwa was caught in the vice of war from every direction. Hence, to this day, amaXhosa call a person with whom everyone picks a fight *uchungiwe*, from Chungwa's name. He hid himself in the whistling caves *zase Bunyameni nase Cawe*, from where amaNdlambe and the whites chased him out to establish the present towns of Alexandria and Port Alfred. That time Graham was busy sweeping the Zuurveld region clean of all amaXhosa.

'The thing that concerned me most with the coming of the white people was not the violence of war, conceived by their greed. It was the new stirrings of religious excitement that brought with it the destruction of our traditional ways, and the dissent from custom. I mean, we were used to the spiritual gale that came with the outpouring of fear and emotional fever during times of war or drought. But the Christian thing was different; its hold was a vice-like grip on the captured person. It made people disinterested in everything but their risen Christ. We will talk about that when we discuss Ntsikana further, who was the first black Christian proselyte in our villages. For now, suffice to say Ntsikana founded the first Christian movement in our villages. Though propulsive, it still retained some semblance of our indigenous ways, although eventually these were weeded out as regressive superstition by the repulsive Wesleyan missionaries who came after the Scottish Presbyterians.

'Ntsikana possessed a spiritual drive before the arrival of greater missionaries. Like the rest of us, he met and liked people such as uNyengane, known as Van der Kemp in white man's language, and Khula, Coenraad de Buys. Both men were benign white people who understood our ways, for our mutual gain, who settled first with us way before the other pestilence followed. When the spirit of the eternal ruler, the one he called Qamata kaTayi, entered Ntsikana, it released in him an insurmountable drive for the mystic. As my father's councillor, he was indomitable. He gave voice and authority to lower caste people to speak against chiefs and kings. As such he became suspect in my eyes. I didn't so much mind their preaching values of sobriety and moving away from witchcraft because of repentance – that was the claim to their salvation. Their spirit made them thrifty and hard-working, something I very much approved of. But when it taught them to forget their hierarchical positioning in life – with the talk about self-advancement, and the disrespect and abandonment of our customs, our moral cement – I developed a problem against them. It made them impertinent and disrespectful of their caste superiors and elders. Masses gathered in valleys and dongas, listening to Ntsikana preach, and were carried away in passionate conversions that inspired communal fervour no chief could tolerate. But things got worse when Ngqika, my father, got caught up in it also. Like my grandfather Rharhabe, who opposed his sickly brother Gcaleka when he became *isangoma,* I knew something needed to be done.

'Rharhabe was my life's role model. By the time I came the field of glory had been harvested by him.'

Maqoma went on in praise-singing mode about Rharhabe:

The mast of Nomagwayi!
The great perturbator of the nations!
The sharpness of the piercing stick!
The usurper of Amathole Mountains!
From the KhoiKhoi chieftess Hoho!
To build a nation.

After collecting himself, he continued: 'Rharhabe perambulated the land of Phalo, up to Umzimkulu River, which checked Shaka's pride, over to the house of Sivanxa. Even went as far as the back of the land framed by Ukhahlamba, and followed the fence of the sea. He found that land pinned to the thrall of oppression, so he went back homewards.

'In his era the settlement of the royal house of Xhosa was at the foot of the mountain of Mkentane, the place called Mbinza in the lower parts of the Gcuwa River. Through the sagacity of old Majeke he nearly gained the chiefdom of Xhosa, though he was only the right-hand son of Phalo. Phalo's elder son, heir of amaXhosa paramount, was Gcaleka. From Gcaleka came Khawuta, who bore Hintsa, the father of Sarhili, Kreli *lenkazimlo*. That became the royal house of Xhosa. Phalo was the last chief of a united Xhosa nation, a son of Tshiwo, of Ngconde, of Togu, of Skhomo, of Ngcwangu, of Tshawe, of Nkosiyamntu, of Malangana, whose father was Xhosa.'

Phila, who had by now resigned himself to the fate of having Maqoma around and, despite himself, had been drawn into the history, wasn't altogether prepared to tolerate all of the old man's narrative style. 'Could you at least spare me the biblical narrative version?' he asked.

Maqoma gave him an amused look. 'Rharhabe's conspicuous energy and valour made him outshine his brother Gcaleka in the eyes of the Xhosa people. Gcaleka, a pensive man of sickly health, was exposed to illusions of fancy. He allowed himself to fall into the hands of *amagqirha* and *zanuse*. He frequented esoteric rituals on the banks of Gxingxolo, near Qumrha. *Izanuse* hid him there for three moons, the usual period for *ukuthwasa*, claiming to be "consulting the shades, the underworld". They lied to the people by saying he disappeared into the river to learn ancient ways from the ancestral River People. A beast had to be slaughtered to enable him to emerge. When he emerged he was known to be a diviner, having completed the initiation *yokuthwasa*. Such things wearied Rharhabe into disrespecting his elder brother.'

'Can't say I blame him,' said Phila. 'But wait up, wait up. Would you say then that what is happening to me, I mean, having you around although you are long dead, is part *yokuthwasa* in me? Does this mean I must go seek my answers from amaGqirha? I am sure you eavesdropped on my conversation with Nandi that night I spent with her in iRhini. What would be your take on it? '

'My only take is that I am here, and that has nothing to do with those liars and their witch-doctoring. Suit yourself if you want to waste your money on them, but don't drag me into it, or make me the excuse for it.'

'Then tell me this,' Phila said, aware that his frustration was visible. 'How am I supposed to deal with you, I mean your manifestation? They are a strain on my body, I feel it. I have headaches.'

'You're supposed to listen to what I tell you and learn what you must from it. It will soon be over, and you'll be back to your normal life soon enough. Meantime you'll be provided with all the strength you require.'

There was silence. Whether the sudden tears Phila felt on his face were tears of frustration or benediction, whether they were because of his father or because of himself, or because of Maqoma's intrusions, he didn't know. All he knew was that after a while Maqoma continued talking, softly at first, then in his strong, persistent voice. Perhaps he would reach screaming point – Phila did not know, how could he? – but he had no option but to be true to his stoic spirit. The hiccup of this quiet flow of tears was all he allowed himself. Then, after blowing his nose and even as the salt still stung his eyes, he felt lighter.

'As I was saying. Bad health dogged Gcaleka. Nothing – from herbs to letting blood through cupping with a cow's horn, to administration of purgatives so he might vomit the poison, which amaGqirha prescribed as the cures – worked, and he blamed his weak health on sorcery. This made him resort to witch-hunting. *Amaxukuza*, and their specious influence to expose the culprits, made Gcaleka acquiescent to smelling-out ceremonies where witches were identified and killed. He engaged in the wanton and superstitious killing of people, mostly people close to him, whom he accused of witchcraft because *amaxukuza* had told him his death was in his hearth pot. By doing this he hoped his health would improve but it didn't. The witch-hunts drained his prestige among the people. When you're a chief –'

'I'm not a chief,' interjected Phila, attempting to re-enter the conversation and feeling simultaneously surprised by the sense of empathy he was developing towards the old man.

'I know. Priest or president, same thing, different jargon.' Maqoma showed no signs of irritation. 'My advice might enable you to judge presidents and priests better,' he continued. 'There's an advantage in respecting the beneficial magic that accompanies the business of living in one's culture, but things can go too far, whereupon a chief has to stamp his foot. As a chief you must be tolerant of your people's eccentricities when they don't threaten the existence of the tribe. The most important thing for a chief is to respect his duties towards the ancestors and shun witchcraft. Witchcraft is the quickest way of destroying a tribe.'

'You mean to tell me you believe that hocus-pocus actually exists?'

'"Believe" is not the right word. I tolerated it for the sake of good governance. Once a chief gets involved in witchcraft, the tribe is sure to wither away. Rharhabe condescended towards Gcaleka's theatre of superstition disguised as mysticism.'

'There's plenty of that going around even now in the name of tradition, or religion.'

'When Gcaleka lost the respect of his people he gradually withdrew himself from their eyes and tribal activities. Rharhabe lost patience with him for being too associated with diviners. When he found no way of celebrating his valour without degrading the reputation of his effeminate brother, Rharhabe decided to leave his homeland. "Where will it stop, if even chiefs shall be susceptible to witchcraft?" Rharhabe asked, beginning to assume the tone of condescension and command against his brother.'

'So, basically, this is the reason why today we have two houses of amaXhosa, divided by Rharhabe crossing Inciba to move away from his brother Gcaleka's authority.'

'Now you are getting it. I'm glad to see you have been paying attention.'

Algoa Bay

DOG TIRED AFTER HIS HIKE IN THE Amathole mountains, Phila went back to his accommodation in East London and slept, for once undisturbed right through the night. The next day he paid his bill and got in his car. He decided to take the coastal route back to Port Elizabeth, wanting to pass Port Alfred and Alexandria, but also to avoid passing, and having to stop over, in Grahamstown. He was in no mood to be psycho-examined by Nandi. Besides, he was eager to get to PE, to pack his stuff and be done with the place.

Port Alfred was a town of felicitous waterspots for the affluent. It had the quiet grandeur of many small seaport towns: a clutter of masts and mizzens, bobbing yachts in the harbour, the sky the deep fiery blue you found almost everywhere in the Cape. The Dutch architecture of whitewashed walls predominated in the small town, which once was a major estuary for the Cape Colony, used for merchandise and materials destined for the then east capital town, Grahamstown, about sixty kilometres inland.

Back in PE Phila started tidying up his affairs in preparation to leave the city. Misfortune, collaborating with fate, had encouraged him into the decision. He regarded this week as his last opportunity to visit places he'd always wanted to visit in the vicinity. One of these was the township of Bethelsdorp on the outskirts of the city. It had started as a KhoiKhoi mission station, founded by Reverend Read and Van der Kemp, or Nyengane, according to the Xhosas. Nyengane had quoted from the Bible in naming the place: *Then Jacob said unto his household ... let us arise and go to Bethel.* Hence Bethelsdorp.

On the day of the visit, two days after his return, Phila carried with him an old book by the Scottish missionary John Campbell, published in 1815, called *Travels in South Africa, undertaken at the request of the Missionary*

Society. Part of the book concerned Campbell's visit to Bethelsdorp in 1813.

Phila arrived almost simultaneously with a tourist mini-bus. He could hear the voice of the guide above the shuffling. "Bethelsdorp has a historic association with English settlers of the early nineteenth century. It was here that the London Missionary Society established its first mission for the KhoiKhoi, in 1803. Since then a horde of famous, and infamous, settlers and missionaries have been associated with and have written about the place. From Van der Kemp, Henry Lichtenstein, Thomas Pringle, to poets like Thomas Baines. As you can see, ladies and gentlemen, nothing much of its earlier boom remains here now. The missionary site comprises only those tiny stone and corrugated-iron cottages."

Phila gently moved away from the guide's range, allowing the voice to begin to fade. "Unfortunately, soon they, too, will be gone ..."

Places like Bethelsdorp, he thought, should be visited by those people who have the ability to see beauty in barren places, or those with a pressing nostalgia or need to understand the colonial and missionary mischief. For the rest it was probably just a place of desolation where people now termed coloureds had gathered to escape the violence of colonialism. Now its surrounding township was the most violent and murderous in the province. Interesting heritage for Bethel Town, a Holy Place or a House of God.

What was left of the mission station looked stranded and baffled. Aloes, with their inordinate capacity for surviving the harshest conditions, thrived, beaten only by the choreography of the stratospheric winds of the Windy City. Phila lacked energy and interest to register anything else. Most of the KhoiKhoi who stayed in the area were Stuurman people, from the Gamtoos River area. They had flown from the white man's violence after killing the Boer commander Adriaan van Jaarsveld in revenge for an incident in which he threw a bag of tobacco for them and then mowed their warriors down while they were busy collecting it. That started what he would call a fourth war encounter with the white people, which was joined by imiDange, themselves angered by the loss of their land around Algoa Bay.

Nyengane acquired Dyani, uTshatshu, to be his companion because, being *umNtide*, who mostly took wives from the KhoiKhoi people, and were close to the missionaries, he could speak three languages: Dutch, Xhosa and English.

Phila looked at the hustle and bustle of township life around him and felt undifferentiated murkiness, something similar to the eerie feeling one gets from places of grief. Fleecy clouds tried to usher tranquillity but it was in vain. He decided to leave Bethelsdorp's fatalistic resilience and stoicism to the aloes. As he drove off, he saw a sign that pointed to Redhouse. It provoked his interest.

To his pleasant surprise, he discovered Redhouse to be a quiet sanctuary of old houses with trellised verandas and trees twisted by salt-prevailing winds, treasured by those who like quiet village life while not being very far from the convenience of city amenities. The area was under the shade of those leggy, ubiquitous invaders from Australia, eucalyptus trees. When he reached it Phila investigated the ruins of a fort and some deserted colonial-looking houses, with deep circular cellars that, it was evident, homeless bush dwellers used as toilets. Jeremiah's prophecy came to mind: *I shall make Jerusalem a heap of ruins, a haunt of jackal; and I will lay waste the towns of Judah so no one can live there.*

That aside, the place gave him the impression of contained energy, serenely quiet, with the exception of rich folks from the affluent suburb of Blue Bay down the estuary speeding up and down the river on speedboats. Phila sat near the river bank and watched a kingfisher dive into the water and come up sporting a small fish in its beak. The tranquillity settled him into gentle sleep.

Soaked in cold terror from hearing voices he felt his mind going *in die Irre,* astray, into the mystifying process of imagination valorising him again. I am becoming exotic to myself was the last thought he remembered.

'I don't feel too good. It's getting late. I need to be going,' Phila cut Maqoma before he could speak.

'Going where?' Maqoma asked as though surprised that Phila would have somewhere to go.

'Not that it's any of your business, but I don't live on river banks.'

'You could have fooled me.' Maqoma hesitated after that failed attempt at irony.

'I'd understand if you chose not to come along, if you've places to go. In fact I'd be glad. I'm kind of tired of hanging around dead people.'

'Do I look dead to you?'

'You got me there. Whatever you are, frankly, I'm really not in the mood to discuss different states of being today; my head is spinning.'

'Your head is always spinning.'

'The world makes me dizzy ...'

'Your breath smells of ice.'

'How do you know how my breath smells? You know what? Never

mind. I don't want to know.'

'It's these books you always have your nose in. No wonder you end in no man's land.'

'Says the man who meets me dead. Is that the name of the state we meet in?'

'I'm not supposed to talk about that. I'm not allowed to take you out of time. I can only take you into history, past and present.'

'But not future?'

'No. That you must figure out on your own, otherwise it would be cheating.'

'*Mfxim!* Why did I know you were going to say something like that? I'll see you when you please.'

Phila left Maqoma morose, sitting under the gumtree. The road, initially poor gravel, quickly became tarred, at which point Phila discovered he had a flat. Cursing, he brought the car to an abrupt stop before going to the boot to take out the spare, spanner and jack.

He discovered Maqoma there before him.

'Well?' questioned Phila. 'Are you just gonna stand there without helping?' The air clicked with the noise of crickets. Phila had a headache.

'No, thanks. I'll sit this one out,' Maqoma said. 'Besides, I thought you didn't want me around.' He made to sit on the grass.

'Since when do you let a small thing like not being wanted stop you?' Phila held his head for a while to off-shoot the dizziness before getting to jacking the car. 'At the river bank just now, when you said my breath smelled of ice. You did that deliberately, didn't you? You knew it would remind me of Keats's poem?'

'Something about you reminds me of Keats.' Maqoma gave a fizzing laugh before continuing in mock poetic tone.

'*You're a dreaming thing, a fever of yourself.*'

'Quoting poets is a long way from being a warrior, isn't it? It must be nice being dead. I doubt if Keats would be impressed with that stunt.'

'The *one whose name was writ on water*.' Maqoma teased Phila. Then, after a pause, he said: 'Knowledge is communal where I come from.'

'So is river water, but it does not mean you should drink from a man's well without asking his permission after he has collected the water on his own.'

'The two of you have a lot in common.'

'You've met Keats?' Phila couldn't resist the question.

'Dead people meet each other, especially those in the same sphere.'

'You mean you are in the same state of being with poets? How interesting.'

'The same state of being. We are! We're just in a different state to yours. You're plunged in the dying moment, and we are on the rising one.'

'So poets and warriors occupy the same plane?'

'Why not? Instead of words warriors are poets of physical deeds.'

'Help me change the tyre, or give me some space.'

'I don't know how to do that sort of thing.'

'It's not really rocket science.'

'No, thanks. As I said, I'll sit this one out.'

'Thank you very much. You are quite a useful ghost.'

'Sarcasm is the last resort of cowards.'

'Kindly stop misquoting people.'

By the time Phila finished changing the tyre he was almost blind with fatigue.

Lights. Blinding lights in his eyes. And pain. Phila tried to sit up but someone was saying something, pushing him firmly back down. He realised with alarm that he was in a hospital, lying on a hospital bed, and that a doctor was doing something on his nose.

Phila had a faint glimpse of Maqoma at the window, where the sky was beginning to be streaked with early morning light. When the doctor was finished bandaging his nose, Phila was wheeled into a recovery room, where he found Maqoma fiddling with gadgets. He summoned enough strength to ask him what had happened, but Maqoma only exacerbated his confusion by talking in allegories.

'Hyenas got to you,' Maqoma said nonchalantly.

'Hyenas? In the middle of a town's roads?'

'Ja, three of them. They attacked you with knives. The first one stabbed you in the shoulder. Then others came in on the party. You would not have survived if I had not been there.'

'Oh, ja? And what did you do, instil the fear of the Lord in them while they were stabbing me before becoming their understanding?'

'Something like that. The important thing is that you're alive, thanks to me. Some taxi people came to your rescue, and your car was not taken. I think that is what they were after.'

'I don't really feel grateful. I would have preferred to lose the car and keep my nose.' Phila felt murky and aggrieved as he watched morning light seep through the window. He knew it was bound to happen sooner or later, with his solitary investigation of secluded places. He felt irrelevant, insignificant, as he watched people through the window hurry past to their respective places of care.

Seeing Baudelaire's 'forest of symbols' in everything, Phila thought about the neutered life of hospitals. The doctor had told him he was going under the knife again in thirty minutes, to adjust his nose, which was still a little skew apparently. Phila took his word for it because he couldn't see his nose under the bandages. A nurse gave him an injection, which did nothing for his tenuous grasp on reality. A teabag rotating in the cup someone was stirring was the last thing he saw as he began to fall asleep. Through all of this he continued to hear Maqoma's voice. He was beginning to accept that Maqoma was welded to his imagination closer than Deianeira's tunic on Hercules.

He woke up in a different bed, next to an Afrikaner guy with slicked-back hair, who wasted no time telling Phila he was "an eternal bachelor" and promising to take him for a spin in his Dodge "when things go on the normal side". Apparently, he had come for "an eye tuck", the Botox injection, in order to create the false appearance of youth. Phila listened to the man talk up a storm, mostly reading aloud from *Esquire* magazine: "… *casu frazigu* cheese … which is supposed to be packed with so many live maggots … called *kopi luwak,* the Indonesian words for coffee and civet, to get a delicacy with a mark-up so steep it would make a drug dealer weep." And, "They say the devotees fork out as much as $600 for a pound. Read it here, bru."

Phila looked at him with a wearied eye, his companion's voice coming at him as if from an underground cellar. Fortunately, he soon found himself succumbing to sleep again.

Eight hours later, feeling nauseous and still with a dull headache, Phila managed to climb off the bed and go and look out of the window. He realised that the roaring hub of a taxi rank outside was responsible for much of the noise that filtered through. Evening fell with its usual mood of impatience. The moribund hustling of costermongers created a stir and fidget that refused to be drowned by the noise of the traffic. The cicada rhythm sent telegrams, summoning the night. Phila marvelled at the mixture of commercial, industrial and residential cosmopolitanism of Korsten, which was where he recognised he was. The sophisticated gimmick in the next bed had been discharged, but he had left a note for Phila on the plastic bag containing his magazines, telling him he was giving them to him. Phila was touched by the gesture – they'd clearly meant a lot to the fellow – but sadly they held no value for Phila and he left them where they were.

❈

Maqoma appeared after a four-day hiatus, just when Phila was starting to think he might be cured of him.

'I was begining to think we had parted ways. What is it? You don't like hospitals?' asked Phila in mock seriousness.

Maqoma ignored Phila's question. 'I used to come here, eBheyini, to consort with the devil,' he said.

'What do you mean to consort with the devil?' asked Phila, not caring to press the hospital issue.

'It's no secret that in my time I was partial to the princess's tears. We used to come to this seat of the devil whenever we wanted to see who the white man was bringing from the seas, and drown ourselves with the fiery waters.' He looked at Phila's face, as if trying to study his reaction, before continuing. 'I tried to lead my men by example. But there were times of crushing despair that revealed how trapped in clay my feet were. In those times I drank myself to oblivion. Drinking carried me to a happier past and soaked my spirit with consoling falseness. I tell you, there's nothing that deranges like the daughter of Ludiza wearing a white head-dress of silk; the seething cold drink; quencher with a sting ...'

'Okay, I get your point.'

'I see you yourself are partial to it. Anyway. Coming here put quite a strain on my body. The presence of white people in our land added to the natural dangers of travelling. We not only had to contend with wild animals and treacherous weather when we travelled, but now with white people too. It meant one had to take extra care before starting a journey; fortify oneself with charms and herbs such as *inyongwane*. Do you still use it?'

'I don't know. You might find some people in the rural areas are still using it, but none I know of. It has a scientific name now, *Dicoma anomala*.'

'In any case, we also had to carry extra bundles of spears and sticks. As a chief, wanted by colonial forces, I had to travel incognito most of the time, with a minimum of compatriots and less provision of live cattle and dried maize kernels so as not to attract attention.'

'Too many forested mountains?'

'It was a never-ending journey, not to be undertaken by the weak.

There were mountains, crowding shrubs, gurgling river after murmuring river and rolling, ribbed sand dunes. On foot, with no wagons, was not a child's game. It might look easy now with your new wagons that need no horses to pull them but back then it was rough going. The road sometimes brought us precariously close to white farms where we stole our cattle back for provisions when we ran out of meat and when game was scarce. My favourite venison is wild boar. Have you ever had the smoked meat of a wild boar? You'll never want anything else. Ratels, porcupines, antelope and buffalo were still common in our land then, before the white men hunted them to oblivion. Slaughtering anything in the wild meant inviting lions and the cunning of howling hyena. Hyena, unlike lions, do not care even if you sleep next to a burning fire. They'll steal a full-grown man and eat him alive if he is not careful.'

'I get the picture.' Phila could see Maqoma was in a reminiscing, rambling frame of mind.

'As if that was not enough. We had to pass dense woods of miombo trees, yellowwoods, dense with erythrina – which we loved for the bee hives. Wonderful thing to hear the voice of a honey-bird leading you to the hive. We were fearful around the spekboom, the favourite of elephants, the most dangerous animal in the wild if you come too close to its young. We chopped sneeze-wood, because it is stronger – we also made solid rafters for our houses with it – to put its trunk across raging rivers. In open plains we had to rely on the long *qungu* to hide our movements.'

'It is called *tambookie* grass now. I guess after the Thembus?'

'*Mfxim*! In any case, we hid in the grass from the curious wagons of white people. Without warrior strength and tenacity we would not have survived. There was still sap in these old bones then.'

'Who were the dudes you went with?'

'What are dudes?'

'Guys you hung with.'

'Nobody got hung on our journeys.'

'I mean, who were the friends you went with?'

'Oh, I see. Well, I remember Thongwane, a man of incorruptible ways and clarity of mind. Once he was nearly killed by a wounded buffalo. He made the cardinal error of hunting with only one spear because he trusted his steady hand too much. We saw the buffalo herd in the morning and decided to screen it, going before them to hide in a valley we were certain they'd pass. Thongwane decided to make things more interesting by hiding in a low hog-back hill very close to where they were grazing. He was the first to release his assegai. Unfortunately, we were too far away to assist him. His first throw was not fatal, and the beast charged towards him, kicking divots and felling trees. Luckily we had men who were not only nimble but quick with assegai hands, warriors who could throw the quiver of an assegai at full speed. The beast stood no chance, but it was strong; at some stage, although it was trailing three assegais, it managed to lacerate Thongwane's leg before fatally falling down. It fell right at his feet, upon which Thongwane took out his panga, slit its throat and wrenched out its liver so as to eat it still hot.'

'He must have been shit scared!'

'I put that question to Thongwane later on, when we were flaying the skin and cutting gigots into thin strips to roast over the fire. "I'm afraid to feel my pants for fear I shall discover my disgrace, my chief," he answered as he emerged from dressing his wound to join us at the fire. The humour was ripe around the fire concerning that topic.

'"Nothing wrong with fear, Thongwane," said I. "The poison is giving in to it. We're all ageing with the moon." Then I took the chance to gently reproach him and re-inculcate our motto. "In our youth your careless mistake would have earned you an immediate dismissal from the Jingqi clan. But that wound looks galling; you'd better find yourself some medicinal roots. Do you still dispute Diba's belief that the hornbill we saw was a sign of bad luck? Ask Diba to brush your wounds with the feathers of the blue-flowered plumbago to reduce the pain."

'We ate our food next to a detumescent river whose banks exuded dank, sickly rottenness all through the night as we slept under the black sky, harassed by windblast and driving rain, and serenaded by hyenas, who stole our provisions after they had surprised us to flight with their sniffing curiosity and barking threats. Sometimes we were stunted by the boldness of lions, waking to find them standing right in our midst despite our smouldering fires.

'I remember that particular night as if it was yesterday. The moon peeled out a slash on the broken, ashy clouds, drenching the fields with tinted silver. Thongwane's groans kept us up all night. We lost him, not from those wounds, but in the Battle of Amalinde, near the hills of Ngwarhu.

'*Awu madoda*! When they fail to come back they're lost. Call the memories of those who die with the chief. Things that despatch the arrow with dust or dripping blood. *Unozulu*! The sharp end of the stick. Disperse earth, you conceal!'

Maqoma fell silent after that, looking tired from the weight of ages.

Phila woke up feeling tired. Not only had Maqoma sapped his physical energy, but his muscles felt dull from the surgery. The medication still in his system also made him lethargic. Silence dripped from the eaves to the ceiling of his heart. A nurse came in and put his medicine next to his untouched supper tray, giving him an uncomprehending look before proceeding to check his drip.

'You're a suspect in their eyes,' Maqoma said when she had left the room.

'What else is new?'

'You're a strange young man.'

'Stranger than a ghost from the nineteenth century?'

'I guess every lot has its crumpled rose leaf.' Maqoma moved across to the window. 'This place, Korsten, is just as busy as it always was,' he said. 'A place of commerce, where selling and buying was the order of the day. The chief occupation of people here was to chase after wealth and women. It seems nothing has changed.'

'There are wealthier places of commerce now, called malls, some even just up the hill there, where a "cleaner" kind of trading takes place. But when you take away the pretensions it's all the same thing really, so I get your point.'

'One was always able to find all kinds of interchange in the markets here: bakers with blacksmiths, with bricklayers and carpenters, with dressmakers. There was always a lot going on in the town. Military levees, balls, supper parties and horse-racing, everything sparkling with gaiety. Our people, those who were not in *tronks*, were employed in everything, from being gardeners to grooms, to errand-boys and even cooks.'

'As I said, nothing much has changed. It was never meant to change anyway, it just grew bigger in scale.'

'At night, however, this place was another story. Corrugated sheds used as trollop houses, where men who wanted to drown their sorrows were greeted by minxes in fripperies offering sexual ministrations. In those houses bearded men tippled, gambled and fought, and settled their disputes over wenches with fisticuffs, sometimes even with knives and guns.'

'We still have houses for that sort of rainbow decadence,' said Phila. 'You still can buy yourself fleeting moments of sensual pleasure on every street corner also.'

'I took fascinated delight when I went to a tavern earlier, while you were snoring. The noise, dirt, grease, mess, slop, drunken confusion and disorder – it is all the same. Only the smells from drinks are different. It fascinates me. In your taverns things are a little hidden from the eye, but it is still easy to be punched, jammed and elbowed, I noticed. I was accustomed to rough food and plain living but these places took that to another level. Men playing cards, drinking all the time, not going to till their fields. Having had a feel of the myriad fleas and bloodthirsty bed-bugs in their rooms, I was not surprised they were not keen to go to sleep. Sleeping in the wild is precarious, with scorpions active, and lizards and snakes rustling close by, but the vampire fleas in those damn taverns made it hell to sleep. Damn places – you picked up all sorts of diseases.'

Phila chuckled. 'We call them different names – backpackers, hostels, even still taverns – these days, but in essence they're the same thing. Probably the hygiene has improved in most though.' He arched an eyebrow. 'Looks like you sowed your oats in your time?'

'Oh ja! I scattered my salt, with indecent women, jugglers' boxes, sodden skirts, tavern taproom, painted and decorated to excess. At times of non-activity lust took an upper hand in my life. Initially I was disgusted, and concentrated only on quenching my thirst. But after a few cups with these ladies I conceived an ungovernable passion for them.'

'I've never had the ability to take comfort in the oblivion of a stranger's body, especially the one who has no power to choose her circumstances.'

'Well, I wasn't exactly philosophising. I was just having a good time. I met a KhoiKhoi woman of loose morals here. Later on I was amazed by the ease with which she penetrated my emotions, so I married her.'

'Didn't you feel diminished, though, when you paid for her bed?'

'No! Okay, sometimes, wavering between gratitude and disgust perhaps. Remember, I've never made myself hostage to Christian morals with hypocrisy turning up on every bush, falsely following the dictates of its book with the red mouth.'

'I don't think it's a Christian thing. It's just natural for love to be exclusive. We call it human.'

'Well, I've seen your human thing; it doesn't look very different from the Christian one from where I'm standing ...'

'Perhaps you're right. It's Christianity without God. We killed God in our hearts because we could no longer stand His demands. We want to make our own laws, live according to our desires, without God poking an eye in everything we do. We could no longer stomach all that Victorian rubbish they tortured you by.'

'And whites tolerate that?'

'Actually the idea of killing God in our hearts is theirs also. If you care to know, it is black people now who are more religious, reminding everyone about God; to an extent that some of our black priests travel over oceans to re-evangelise countries of white people there.'

'Have they managed to steal any of the white people's land while giving them religion?'

'White people are too clever to fall for the trick they duped us with.'

'I'll be damned! I thought white people said there was no meaning in life without God?'

'Perhaps there isn't. But we are too busy entertaining ourselves to bother with those things now.'

'The last time I came here was not of my own will. My brothers had begun a war against the colonial government I had no appetite for. I told Calderwood, the British official responsible for our area, I was not part of the war. To be sure I was telling the truth they asked me to move away from our land and be accommodated here at British government expense. They found a house for me and my wives to stay, right here in Korsten. That was when I really grew to know the taverns of this place, and the lifestyle that came with it. I spent most of my time with my KhoiKhoi woman, so as to get news of the war quickly. Her bed was my solace, even though I could never get used to the smell of another's man's energy on her.'

'How did you two come to an understanding?'

'She told me if I turned my back on my chieftainship, to make a house with her, she'd make herself into a respectable woman. She wanted me to turn my back on all that had defined my life, for a cosy little room with her somewhere in an anonymous corner here. Though tempted, I knew what she was asking was beyond me. This was how she put it in trying to dissuade me: "I shall not forever be satisfied with being caressed by blood-stained hands, Maqoma. I do not understand your insane stubbornness. You shall never prevail over white people. It is not wise to be courageous against fate. I don't value your glory if it must be purchased by your death. Nothing good will ever come out of this obsession of yours."'

'And what happened to the two of you?'

'The tenderness on her face at first caught me by surprise. But I regained my mind and hated her for the truth she exposed in my life. She had no proper understanding of what she was asking. How could I allow the blood of all those men who had died under my leadership to have been spilt in vain? To avoid resenting her I tried to make her change the topic, and quietly I sang our tribal song in my heart: *Sponono ndiyeke ndi sebenzele isizwe*. When the Smith incident happened she understood the impossibility of what she was asking. There was my virility also, I suppose. But something told me she'd passed that stage of being impressed by a little tingle in her body. In my alcoholic hazes, to my eternal shame, I promised her more than I could give her. It is not hard to promise people who're useful to you. In my own heart I always knew I'd never acquiesce to the obliteration, or allow my people to be subsumed by the expansions of a mad empire, so long as I lived. So her plans had no room in my life.'

'Tell me about the Smith incident. Are you referring to Harry Smith, who was once a Governor of the Cape Colony?'

'I shall tell you in due time. But yes, it is Harry I am talking about, very pompous and full of himself. He eventually made himself into my arch enemy among the British officials. He challenged me in such a way that I could not back down with my honour intact after he, literally, placed the heel of his boot on my protracted neck. We had had our scuffles when he was a mere commander of their soldiers during the previous wars, before he left for another land, called India, in what we thought was disgrace. I even managed to bury the hatchet of his killing and decapitating Hintsa, our paramount, something for which we (wrongly, as it happened) believed the British had demoted Smith. But no, when the British changed their queen the new king favoured Smith. He made him into a chief of the whole colony, what they called a governor. He came back triumphant and more boastful. Mine was the first name on his knee, because it had been losing against me that had caused his demotion and departure to India. The humiliation he meted on me, in front of my wives, children and the rest of the people, demanded I act on my honour or fall on my blade. I chose the former. You'll be surprised how many wars of the nations could have been avoided if only the rulers had better personalities. Smith had a low-born, vulgar personality that could have done better with good breeding.'

'Waterkloof was inspired by this incident?'

'Indeed! I was also making inroads with the KhoiKhoi and Mfengus, people without whom I knew we could never defeat the British, or so long as they fought with them. They called that war the first clash of the races in our land. The truth of the matter is that it wasn't. Yes, we managed to convince some of the KhoiKhoi, led by Matroos, and later on Botha, to join our cause in a rebellion (it became known as the Kat River Rebellion), but the majority still fought with the British. That became poignantly clear to me at Waterkloof when we stood killing each other, I mean black people – Khoi, Mfengu and Xhosas – while the white people would sometimes not even bother to move away from their fires, instead standing aside to cheer their vassals on as they attacked.'

'At least you won that war?'

'At what price though? At what terrible price?'

The Gadfly

AFTER HIS RELEASE FROM HOSPITAL, Phila went back to Redhouse. It felt confrontational, somehow suicidal. Danger fertilised his imagination.

Maqoma came with a tremor, disturbing the birds.

'I see you're learning tricks of ostentation,' Phila said drily.

'I thought it might impress you. I love river banks. It is where I got bitten by the gadfly. Did I ever tell you about Katye?'

'I'm sure you are going to tell me again. I've never understood this Xhosa saying of calling falling in love being bitten by the gadfly.'

'If you'd ever been in love, you'd understand the itch and the nuisance. I've noticed that you hardly see any dragonflies beside the rivers these days.'

'I know!' Phila enthusiastically answered because this was something that had been a worrying notice to him also. 'When I was growing up rivers were full of dragonflies. Now you're lucky if you see the damselfly. I think it's because the rivers are polluted and dying.'

'Strange. In any case. I met Katye when my face was starting to line. Hers was fresh, hardly touched by time. She was slim as an arrow. When I first saw her a tingling feeling set fire to my nerves.'

'Aha!' Phila snorted a laugh.

'You should have seen her inviting nakedness lying supine under the drooping willow; listening to the gentle wind shake the trees. Her shrunken nipples, raisin-like and sharp as moles, sent me to ecstasy.'

'I thought Xhosa elders didn't talk to the young people about these things?'

'Tired from working in the fields the whole morning, we went to the riverside around noon to recover our strength. The dragonflies were tunnelling rhododendrons and hovering above the fluffy sponges of algae that carpeted the river surface. The weaverbirds, hanging on the fronds, cooed the drowning drone of the river. The summer air was fragrant with the scent of cerise and bellflowers.'

'Things women make us feel.'

'The girls had been swimming in the meandering Ngcwenxa, the river that traversed our village, shaded most of the time by rushes and grassy banks. It must have been in the middle of spring because we were on our second phase of cutting open the fields with ox-drawn ploughs to prevent the hardening of the ground during the summer dryness. We usually repeated the process again after the first rains, before planting. This was necessary since we used plough-shares that were not fitted with shoulders like the ones white people introduced. As soon as the soil was ready it received seed. The casting was done by hand in those days, and seeds subsequently covered by sods drawn by wooden hand-rakes. Sometimes we attached a tailboard on the ox-pulled plough to draw the seeds, but this required a craftsman's skill.'

'I buy my food at the supermarket.'

'That there is where part of your problems lie. Late summer the ground between the rows of sprouting corn was hoed and weeded by the women.'

'Poor things. It could not have been an easy thing to be a woman during your era.'

'What do you mean? They had everything easy. For one thing women were not expected to be carrion for vultures when wars came, and wars were numerous. In any case, harvest followed in autumn. The ears were cut off near the top of the stalk by means of a hand-sickle. We had no threshing sledges or rotary-sickles and such things that came with white people. Some cornfields were left to dry on stalk, to be harvested dry and stored in granaries. During winter those were what were pummelled for samp and beans. The best village sight is to watch your children bring lowing cattle from the mountains; to watch the cavorting of calves when they hear the bellowing of heifers. That, my son, is life. It's testimony that you're alive. The smell of corn, sorghum, barley, pumpkins and lucerne – to supplement the feed of our cattle – in our granaries. We didn't plant much else. We grazed our cattle on stubbles of harvested fields during winter, and rough herbage that grew spontaneously in fallows. But continuous cropping with the same crops and the absence of a balanced rotational system gradually caused a loss of productivity. We solved that by often changing grazing and ploughing land – something that became impossible with the arrival of the white people with their greed of land occupation. With white people's arrival, meadows for pasturing became very scarce. We planted fertilising crops, like beans, to restore the productivity of the soil. You knew when the caterpillar treads were back, then that land was ready to yield a bumper harvest again.'

'Looks like you guys were quite accomplished crop planters. Why, then, did you never opt for commercial farming?' This was something that had always baffled Phila.

'Commercial farming is something we learnt when we adopted the greed of white people's ways. Before that in our villages excess harvest was meant for the poor and widows. You could use your cattle wealth to barter, but it was anathema to barter with the earth's yield, something for which the ancestors would bring you misfortune.'

'Let's get back to your gadfly,' Phila said. 'I prefer that topic to this lesson on ancient agriculture.'

'The day I first laid my eyes on Katye we had risen early as usual to plough the fields. It was a steely-blue morning. I was not feeling too good, having indulged on *umgqombothi* the previous day, because Aunt Hobe's son was going to the mountain. This was a son of her shame that cursed her against a married life.'

'Cursed?'

'In our era we were not as free-going as you. Nobody wanted to marry a woman who had already had a child. She and my father brought shame to our tribe because of their excessive libido. Not that I was immune to it myself, but I had ways of concealing my shame. We thought Hobe's son would come out fair skinned, because she had a tendency to frequent our white visitors' beds. I remember the shame her advances brought to Nyengane. Khula by then had married Keke, my grandma. Keke – let us say she had appetites. It was she who was the source of high heat in our blood, if you know what I mean. But I digress. Our wooden plough broke towards midday. The sun was too hot so I decided to hide under the willow shade while the oxen drank water and others fixed the plough. That was when I saw Katye. I watched her for a long time with innocent desire.'

'Come on! You lusted after her – you admitted it earlier on.'

'The moment she stood and went to wash her long legs in the river I knew I had to make her mine or lose my mind. There and then I understood Ngqika's madness over Thuthula.'

'Who was Thuthula?'

'I'll tell you some other time, but she was the girl who wrecked our nation.'

'Oh, I read about her. She was something like Helen of Troy, hee? Don't you find it interesting that your father and your uncle fought over her, almost destroyed amaRharhabe in the process, and yet the way you say it, *she*'s the one who destroyed the nation? And you know for a fact that in your era a girl hardly had any say about who she got married to, especially if, as in this case, it was a chief or a prince who was courting her. The whole thing was decided among men – her father and other male relatives.'

'I never really looked at it that way,' said Maqoma, frowning.

Then he attempted to make light of the situation. 'When a man is stricken by such beauty he can never be right in his mind, unless he implicates himself with it.'

But Phila was beginning to find his voice against Maqoma. 'Yet if she herself is stricken also, and yields to a wrong man who leaves after deflowering her, or worse still, she gets pregnant, then her life is ruined. All of a sudden she's cursed?'

'Well ... the times are different now.' That seemed to settle it for Maqoma, who quickly recovered his jovial mood. 'I was enchanted by Katye's coyness. I said: "This is she who must rule my mind."'

'Every decent man must have a woman to lord it over him,' sighed Phila.

'She was startled by my appearing out of nowhere; she nearly jumped out of her skin. The girls must have thought they were alone. "Who are you, dirty voyeur?" she asked with an irritated look. "Oh no, I'm no voyeur," I corrected her. "I'm the chief around these lands." Then I mumbled something like, "Yet what does that avail me if I fail to move your heart?"'

'Not really the stuff that would make her want to meet you by the river, was it?'

'You're telling me! She gave a sarcastic answer. "Oh well, if that's so, I'm chieftess around these lands. Shall we go to our royal abode, your highness?" But in fact I missed the sarcasm, and took her for earnest.'

'Oh, Maqoma!' Phila covered his eyes with the hand.

'I foolishly asked if I should send my people to introduce me to her home. She became more defiant. "Get away from me, you dirty voyeur. If I catch you doing this again, I shall report you to the elders." That was when I understood she still did not believe me. I looked around for something with which to convince her, but my entire royal regalia had been left in the fields, under the apricot tree. I tried harder to convince her, to no avail. Luckily, I had a leopard tooth around my neck and she recognised it. Only chiefs were allowed to wear leopardskins and jewellery in our tribe then. Her tone immediately changed, and she carried herself in a far more respectful manner, which disappointed me a little. I liked her initial boldness more. The burden of chieftainship is that people can never be themselves around you. You never really know what they feel. "You're cruel, my chief, in your fondness," she said, only now in a shy voice. "How can you take notice of a low-born like me? There can never be anything between us. Our tribal decorum would have none of that." A seductive tease accompanied her voice and feigned smile.' Maqoma paused and his face grew sad. 'To think I might not live to see that smile again,' he said. 'Cruel is the fate of mortal man.

'On our wedding day Katye spread a paillasse bed on the floor for me to share. I spread the skirt of my kaross over her and knew her. We took undemanding pleasure of each other. Her delighting my senses made no demands on me, which was why she was my favourite wife.'

'And how did Katye feel about you marrying other women? You only mention her in regard to yourself and not as her own individual.'

'I was already married when I met her, married to two wives, and I took more after her.'

'More like four more. That's a strange way of demonstrating your fidelity to your true love.'

'You wouldn't understand it. It was something that was demanded by our times.'

'And pretty convenient for your chivalry also, I suppose.'

'Katye wanted nothing from me but love, not even to shine in my presence. She was kind, forgiving and dependable; things that make a person beautiful in my eyes.'

'And to her you were ...?'

'For me habit usually dulls appetite in sexual matters, but not when it came to Katye. Our lovemaking ...'

'Perhaps I'll see her side of the story one day.'

'When we were in the fields I couldn't wait to see her appear, against the beauty of our land, bringing me food and refreshments.'

'Please, man, let's not go to agriculture again. Life is too short.'

'Often, in order to stay longer with me in the fields, she'd prepare the food the day before and leave with us in the morning. She'd busy herself hoeing and digging holes until noon. Then I'd put it to her. "Katye, you're a princess now; it is unbecoming for you to be hoeing fields and digging furrows." To which, suppressing a smile, she would retort: "Maqoma, you are a prince; it is unbecoming for you to be tilling and planting fields. And grown men are forbidden to touch a broom ... so what were you doing this morning in the courts of our house?" With that we'd both laugh a laugh of love. Then she'd come closer to me under the apricot tree and softly ask, "Do you love me, Maqoma? I mean, do you really love me? Would you carve my name on the tree?" She made her lips into a flower blossom. And I would answer: "Pull me by the ears and give me a handle kiss." That kiss pressed to the depths of my soul.

'Then she'd update me about what was happening around the house; how my other wives were cruel to her because she was my favourite. They disliked her more because she was KhoiKhoi. She would tell me ancient stories of their praying mantis gods her people told around the fire. She was the best company to travel long roads with; her resourcefulness for water and root bulb foods was amazing. And then she'd sing and laugh in a hypnotic voice, accusing herself of having no counsellor. She lit my fire. That woman lit the fire of love in me. When they allowed me to bring one wife with me during my first incarceration on the island I chose her.'

'I'm glad you at least had a taste of that.'

'"If you loved me, Maqoma, you'd take me far away from here, to where only you and I exist under Qamata's sky. And I'd bear you warriors to defend your old age." That was something she liked to say after our lovemaking. All my women had this desire of taking me away from the violence of my life. The only blemish in our love was her mother, who opposed our marriage from the start – with uncanny precision of maternal instinct, I must admit.'

'Aren't all mothers-in-law like that?'

'She refused us her blessing, saying to Katye, "I do not understand why you want to entangle your life with a doomed man. What's your obsession with this Maqoma? He carries trouble." In retrospect, I respect her insight, even if I still don't agree with it. She must have seen how my future would be; that my life would be buried in atrocities. Luckily, the more she objected the stronger Katye's love grew for me. "My love for him overflows to the rest of my life. I would die for him." That was what she said. And she did.

'Awu! *Isithandwa sam.* Every day I thought about her, my love, and my heart throbbed. They'll be blowing shrill blasts when we meet again. They'll be carrying sounds through the veld, rushing out and furiously blasting and drumming when I fall into her arms. Then my eyes will only be for her, my eternal desire.'

'Come on, man, let's not be too sentimental now. Besides, aren't you both dead? Haven't you again met somehow?'

'Not yet. I must still finish with you. Perhaps now you'll understand why I need to get done with this assignment, so I may move along.'

'Hey, don't let me keep you from your true love, man. You can leave me. I'll be fine.'

'The ultimate powers that bring me here do not think so. I must linger a little while to finish my assignment.'

'What is it you are supposed to do with me, really? You still haven't given me a satisfactory answer.'

'Tell you my life story so as to dissuade you from …' Maqoma fell silent.

'More like *One Hundred and One Stories* then,' Phila sighed, 'only here the night lasts a year?'

'Something like that.'

'What happened to Katye?'

'What else? She ended up with the white man's iron in her bowels.'

Maqoma kept quiet for an uncomfortably long time.

'Okay, we don't have to talk about that,' said Phila, although he wanted to hear more.

'They lied, those cowards. They said they could not distinguish in the bush between warriors and women. Meantime shooting women and children was their sport and policy whenever the scales of war tilted against them. They said they wanted to kill the brood of vipers that replenished our guerrilla warriors. They said, "Kaffirs breed like rats; we must cut the numbers of their brood."

'When my Katye was cut off from this life, so young as to have given me only one son, a crown was taken from my head. I lost my reason to live. She left me lost in the prison halls of fate. The son we bore together was doomed also to die of the white man's iron.'

'Hey, look, man, I'm sorry about your wife and all. Don't cry, okay.'

'That's all right. It was a long time ago, although the wound still festers. After that the rumour was that I too had been killed during that raid. In fact it was my comrade, T'Zebe, whom I had assigned to protect my family with his life, who was killed. But the rumour served my guerrilla purposes well. I raved and raged like a wounded buffalo, killing every breathing white thing in my path. That's how they got to name me the "cacodemon". It was then that I realised clearly that we would have to fight the land issue with white people to the grave. I lost all hope for peaceful resolutions with the death of my Katye. I also lost my will to live. I became careless with my life, which other people interpreted as bravery.'

Maqoma then disappeared from Phila's eyes and ears.

Feeling a little guilty, Phila went the next day to the library to do some research – and to return library books he'd taken out – to find out if there was any mention of Katye among the British official records of the time, or from the many journals written by officials, soldiers and missionaries. He found what he was looking for in the writings of Colonel Lennox Stretch, by far the most amiable British official of the era towards the Xhosas. He wrote that Maqoma's wife fell when the colonial parties were combing the lower parts of the Amathole mountains looking for Xhosa warrior fighters. Apparently their patrols were cornered near Burnshill with no proper covering, so they decided to shoot indiscriminately at every moving thing. Describing what he saw when he came to the spot after the shooting, Stretch wrote:

> *I was completely horrified to behold a most interesting female Caffre, one of Maqoma's wives, mortally wounded and one of the attendants slightly wounded. The expression of fear and pain exhibited in the countenance of the former was so truly distressing that I felt ashamed of being in the command. The [cannon] ball had passed through the fleshy part of the stomach and broken the thighbone. When I arrived at the spot I found a female occupied in stopping the blood and soothing the cries of the infant that would soon be motherless. It was too much for me, and as I could render no assistance I hurried from the melancholy scene lamenting I was ever employed on such a duty.*

Phila bought a take-out coffee from a kiosk around the corner from the library. He drank it, too quickly, sitting on a public bench in the City Square, admiring one last time the clean Edwardian architectural lines of the municipal building, the flying Georgian buttress roof of the Main City Library he often frequented. The coffee scalded his lips and he cursed as he spilt some of the liquid on his sleeve. There was a biting wind this afternoon, so cold that it stung his eyes.

Wagons and Moods

THE USUAL WHIFF OF STALE AIR FROM THE South African Breweries factory was strongest on Thursday evenings and Friday mornings in kwaMagxaki, the place on the hill Phila still called home, even as he was planning to leave it behind. This was a Friday morning. The warm porridge air suffused the house when he opened the window. Beyond the factory buildings the metro train raced the river line towards Despatch and Uitenhage.

After taking a shower he walked to the bus stop, taking the same route he had walked almost every weekday for close to a decade: past the community centre, past the yard with the well-fed Rhodesian ridgeback that always came crashing the fence to bark at him. Today was no different. The dog's owner, a retired coloured man, who spent his mornings polishing his Hyundai sedan ("because my wife gets cranky in the morning"), came strolling to the fence to chat to Phila, gently airing the dust cloth as he came. It always made Phila panic that he was going to miss the bus. Meanwhile the dog kept up its barking frenzy, prompting the owner to shout "Voetsek!" so that they might hear themselves talk. Then came the subsequent jog to the bus stop when Phila heard its rumbling approach, and the worry when he sat down in his seat and realised he had never introduced himself to the man he chatted to almost every weekday morning and now it was probably too late. And the realisation that he procrastinated too much frustrated him further.

Phila sat quietly on the bus, listening to the passengers talking around him. Their concerns seemed mostly to be about a soccer match between the giant clubs Kaizer Chiefs and Orlando Pirates. He fought the urge to stand up and survey the faces he knew he'd probably never see again. His sentimentality took him by surprise. From his window seat he watched in motion the difficult black lives doing hand-washing, in amazing high spirits, outside the corrugated-iron structures that were their homes. At some stage, almost giving in, he half stood by impulsion of *Sturm und Drang*, storm and urge, to say something. He wanted, somehow, to indicate that he was part of the toiling masses, perhaps even starve the chameleon inside tugging to break loose from them. Noticing the probing glance from the mama seated across from him, he sat down, in shame and silence. He thought of something Maqoma had said regarding the need to leave the places we love in order to train the torch of love on them.

Upon reaching the city he didn't feel like going anywhere else except the beach, and was tired of the bus so he walked the three kilometres or so across Humewood to Summerstrand, which helped clear his head. At King's Beach he strolled past the screaming seagulls, those primary guardians of the sea. The carnival atmosphere was absent since it was before noon in the middle of the week. It pained him to see the gulls hustle dust-bins, like scavengers, competing with homeless people for thrown-away food. The pavement smelled of pigeon feed.

Feeling physical exhaustion from the walk, he found a bench to sit on. In no time he was joined by an old white man with a turkey neck and ashen varicose legs.

"May I, mate?" He pointed to the seat.

"By all means," Phila replied politely.

"Lovely day!" the old man said.

Phila sensed a suppressed Cockney accent.

"Indeed!" he politely replied.

"Any particular plans for it?"

"Not really. Just sitting here, cultivating wakefulness."

"Ah! Clever bloke, are ye?"

Phila just smiled.

"That's a nasty scar ye have right there, mate. What happened?" The guy craned his head to investigate Phila's sutured nose.

"Aah … it's a long story."

"I can see you have a story," the man said, giving Phila another appraising look, which made Phila shift along the bench a little.

"You can, can you?" What was it with old men who thought they could just intrude on his privacy?

"Yes, I can," the man said. "I have what you might call a gift."

"A gift?" Phila gave him a suspicious glance.

"I can read a person's aura. May I …?"

Phila tried to suppress a flash of alarm but then he thought, why not? He sat very still while the old man ran his hands over his face, gently closing his eyes with his fingers as he went.

"You've a green aura. With blotches of black, I'm afraid. That's high mystical energy. And a tinge of sadness."

"You know this just by feeling my face?" Phila opened his eyes and gave him a sceptical look.

"I can read palms too."

"Good thing I've been watching the flights of birds to discover the divine purpose. Perhaps I can offer you my interpretation of the nimbus around your own head?" Phila was not really in a mood for games but decided to bottle the egress and play along.

"Aye! A man of letters too? Ye speak with a force of intelligence. We're all immemorially known, mate."

"Something you read on a Hari Krishna flyer?"

"Jung, actually. Weber, too, was of the opinion that dissipation is just a loss of horizon. The devil seeks to frighten us with the accumulation of ills. Now ye've woken up the priest in me!"

"A man of the cloth who believes in superstition? Interesting."

"Retired Anglican clergy. And mysticism is not superstition. It's closer to astral physics than ye realise." He halted to take a breath before continuing. "Averse to complex narrative, eh?" He had an unattractive droop to his left eye when he asked a question.

"Suffering from dialectical dizziness actually, or in your language, mysticism in dreams."

"I knew you looked like an interesting bloke."

"Well, I'm growing tired of dreams. Maybe I'm losing interest in the habit of living with the absence of God. Or maybe I'm suspicious of the sterilisation of history. Take your choice."

"Loss of belief? Pessimism of despair?"

"Are you sure you want to engage with me on such topics?"

"Well. Job tried his luck with God."

"And look where that got him. Any case, I don't dispute God's existence. I just doubt His absolute justice. Mine is the God of Job indeed. As Job knew but tried his luck anyway, I don't have the strength to wrestle with God, because I know He'll overpower me. So, like Simone Weil, whom you should know, being clergy and all, I just wait on. What complicates things is that I admire His silence, unlike Job, who was livened by it, because I cannot believe or trust in a God I can comprehend."

"I know what ye mean. And His priests ... well, we've been rubbish at explaining His intentions."

"That's because you wrongly assumed that He wanted them explained."

After some time of sitting in contemplative silence together, the priest suggested a drink at his flat, which he claimed was nearby. "Then we can properly interrogate this absence of God against the music of Wagner."

Phila was almost enticed until he recalled that Wagner's music stupefied him, and he politely declined. Staring stolidly at the sea, he thought about Nietzsche's fool drinking up the ocean.

An ice-cream man jingled his bell as he rode past them on his bike. The priest made another offer. "Let me buy you an ice-cream at least?" he smiled, standing up, and deliberately touching Phila's thigh.

Phila declined again – something about Greeks bearing gifts teased at his mind – but his protest fell on deaf ears. After dickering with the ice-cream man the priest came back with two Magnum ice-creams. He handed Phila the death-by-chocolate one, which happened to be his favourite. Before Phila could protest further, he extended another invitation, this time to an Anglican music service that evening. "You might even enjoy it," he said. "Our church is beyond the PnP building. Ask for Roger. I am the choir master also." Phila promised to consider it, but more out of politeness than real intention.

Something about the insouciance of nature had always bothered him. He thought about how the dunes, rocks and hills had looked down at their ancestors, who met here on the beach in tones of military aggressiveness, violently killing one another as a precursor to the Frontier Wars. Even then nature could not be bothered, as it was not bothered now when they met in friendly banter. Nature plays its part, he mused, by providing the stage, whatever the outcome.

Two historical odysseys – the great Bantu terrestrial one and the European maritime one – resulting in a rendezvous of epic proportions at the foot of the African continent, the protracted bloody struggle of the nineteenth century known as the Frontier Wars, also produced the enlargement of human conscience that made it possible for Phila and this priest to sit on a bench at the beach, beneath the scintillating African sun, discussing the moral ambiguities of Weber, Wagner and Nietzsche, and the absent existence of God.

Political or social conscience came at the price of tragedy. Of a Mandela spending twenty-seven years imprisoned on the quarries of Robben Island. And a Biko dying a gruesome death in a lonely prison cell at the hands of cowards who would not even own up to their nefarious deeds.

Phila, looking at the ocean as the mirror eye of the distant past, wished he could lift the mist of myth, to excavate traditional oral narratives that were buried by colonialism, so that he could properly make out what was present in the authentic landscape of history.

"I usually know that I am taking too much of my congregation's time once they become quiet. It's a sign of suffering." The retired priest looked Phila in the eye as he said this.

"I think we are way past that," said Phila. "I was just thinking how our ancestors had probably fought each other on this beach."

"Ye mean when the 1820 settlers came ..."

"Even earlier than that." Phila gestured towards the ocean. "Many ships – *Hercules* way back in 1786 was one – were wrecked around here."

The priest looked interested so Phila continued. "Chief Tshatshu was living in this area at the start of the nineteenth century. In fact he was probably the first black to have had a good command of the English language. He acted as an interpreter for your first missionary, Van der Kemp, whom the Xhosas nicknamed Nyengane, because of his stone stubborness."

"Nyengane means stubborn?"

"Something like that. *Nyengane* is hard molten rock found around the river or sea. It gets its hardness from the rapid cooling of lava where it comes across the water. Because it made excellent rock tools but was difficult to break or mould, amaXhosa called it *inyengane*. Van der Kemp was the first to try to convert amaNgqika who, though amused by the story of the devil and all, were confused with the explanation of God involving the whole of humanity in His quarrels with 'His boy'. They were annoyed with missionaries like Van der Kemp for trying to take advantage of their kindness – they regarded Nyengane as a poor wanderer, a 'bushman of the sea' – and trying to make them his converts. That was how they viewed the whole matter of Christian conversion. I guess nothing much has changed. We can make an example of what happened between us just now. You offered me your kindness, which I refused because I felt no need for it. You proceeded to buy me the ice-cream anyway, even though I had declined it. What does this tell me? That you either do not value my opinion; or you condescend in your kindness, because you think I do not know what is good for me. In similar vein to Van der Kemp, who became angry with the Xhosas for rejecting his gospel. You put me in a situation where I must violate my own wishes in order to be polite to you; or be rude to you to maintain my own independence. What you are really after is that the basis of our interaction must be your *gestalt*, so we may proceed in triumph of your hegemony. That, in general, has been the problem between our nations: only your views matter and no one else's." Phila spoke decisively, with emphasis but without anger.

"Ye misunderstood me, old chap," the retired priest told him. "It's not like that at all. I am not like that. Van der Kemp was not like that. Van der Kemp was a man of profound faith who felt in himself the missionary spirit of St Paul –"

"That's my point," said Phila. "He was filled by the anxiety of salvation for others to the point of neglecting others' points of view. Also, he forgot to live by the principles he wished others to adopt. That is usually how it goes with you guys, and your missionary lot. Van der Kemp preached against youthful brides, but could not contain the burning of his own loins for a seventeen-year-old Madagascan slave girl he kept as a concubine before marrying in his old age. He was already sixty when he absconded with her to Mauritius."

"Aye. And that sin tortured his soul as a thorn in his flesh."

"Don't misunderstand me. Nyengane and the Reads were good people, probably the only real Christians among that missionary lot, hence amaXhosa also loved them. Myself I'm rediscovering our shared history. The other gang that came later, Wesleyans and Anglicans, were an imperialist bunch, who came with the white man's burden of Christendom rather than Christianity. That is why the likes of Maqoma despised them with a vengeance while, at the same time, they liked Nyengane and the Reads. The colonial government of the time loathed Nyengane, and the Reads also, and no wonder. You cannot doubt the wisdom of the Xhosas in regarding missionaries as the precursors of British colonial and mercantile aggression, what today is called war capitalism in learned centres."

The priest was looking somewhat bewildered – doubtless he was more at home with Western philosophers and ice-cream – but Phila took no notice.

"Be that as it may," he went on, "when he could not make any converts among the Xhosas, whom he found too argumentative, Nyengane came here and found fertile ground among the destitute KhoiKhoi people, and Tshatshu's people, whose chief had recently been murdered by Cuyler's tragic trickery across the Gamtoos River. Naturally, your government, founded on crime, rewarded handsomely such murderous acts. Cuyler was appointed a landdrost of Uitenhage, whose jurisdiction covered this area."

"I –"

"This scar you asked about?" Phila touched his nose, which was still tender. "I got this scar after a recent visit to Bethelsdorp, just a few kilometres north-west of where we are sitting. Did you know it was the first Christian mission station in this area? It was founded by Nyengane, founded to protect the KhoiKhoi against colonial violence. It still stands today, with a flavour of its inherited violence. As I indicated, Nyengane and the Reads were good people. But this does not mean they escaped the trappings of your condescending culture."

"I have been to that mission station," said the priest. "I know the one you mean." He seemed uncertain about where the conversation was going. "We cannot fault its foundations because of what the area turned into."

"I didn't say I was. I am saying also to you that, where the natives of the land were left alone, in the rural areas, for instance, they developed organically into peaceful societies, if poor ones. But where they were aggressively touched by Western civilisation and its religion they developed into violent societies. Why?"

The priest shook his head.

"In any case, these were not really my thoughts when you found me; I shared them with you only because you asked," said Phila. He got up and threw his ice-cream paper into a bin, causing a flurry of seagull wings. "I was actually thinking about a young man who walked these streets once, climbed these hills, with great sadness in his heart. His name was Tiyo Soga, and he lived a very short and tortured life." Phila pointed out towards to the bay, where sunshine sparkled on the surface. "Having just got off the wharf, towing his white Scottish bride, he was welcomed by racial scorn and hatred. He was torn apart and cut to the core by the pain of seeing his proud nation, the Xhosas, falling into slavery. He composed one of the greatest Xhosa songs from the effect, *Lizalis' indinga lakho Thixo Nkosi* ... The Xhosas had just committed national suicide, urged by the superstition of Nongqawuse, by killing their cattle, their major sustenance. The superstitious call fell on fertile ground because the Xhosa cattle were dying in numbers already. The white people had brought with them the rinderpest, a disease that cut to the core of the Xhosa's self-sustenance by killing the cattle their lives depended on. This confused them and made them extremely vulnerable. In a way it made them the nation of servants to white industry you see today. All I am saying is that the whole thing has too much coincidence about it not to see the intelligent design behind it. Now, whether we call that fate, or the God of Job, thus of the Hebrews, is immaterial to me. I just find it impossible to ignore."

The priest frowned. "The first error of the young, mate," he said, "is being angry about history. Ye cannot change history, no matter how hard ye try."

"But you can recover what you lost from it. History is the father of the present and the grandparent of the future."

"History is like the created; it cannot be changed."

"But the present and the future it gave birth to can be changed by learning lessons from it."

"I don't see what's to be gained by being imprisoned by it."

"So you'd prefer us to erase the past realities of expropriation, slavery and colonialism from history to maintain the sham of civilisation?"

"We can talk about this until the cows come home, mate," the priest said, getting to his feet and stretching. "The most important thing is what we do with where we are now." He held out his hand for Phila to shake. "Cheers! Lovely meeting you, mate. Employ less anger, and you'll see a little more clearly."

There are no footpaths in the water, thought Phila.

He sat for a while, turning over in his mind the historical events that gave birth to his cultural identity. He tried to think about the history taught in South African schools, all about the British, the Boers and Shaka Zulu; for whatever reason, Shaka was the black monarch included in their textbook. He now regarded it as little more than demonology, and a cult of villainy heaped against black people.

Stale heat hung, solid as a wall. He lit a cigarette. He wiped his perspiring forehead with his T-shirt, drawing suspicious looks from a huddle of housewives walking past.

He walked back to the city, aiming at passing the harbour, where he hoped to have a glass of beer.

To Phila the harbour of Port Elizabeth was little more than a depot for car manufacturers to load assembled cars and ship them off to different regions of the southern hemisphere. Most of the space was taken by them, the fishermen and the yachts of the rich, in that order. It had no spirit beyond the industrial. In fact, almost everything about the city gave Phila the impression that it was attempting to provide a pedigree for a more consistent form of cultural conservatism that combined economic levelling with traditional and local ways of life.

As he entered the harbour, he spotted the station tower clock, which was right only two times a day. He remembered that there was a heated, ongoing debate about tearing it down to erect a statue of Mandela. As was

always the case with these things in his country, the division on the debate
were drawn along racial lines. The progeny of white settlers felt the clock
was their heritage, and the black native felt no nostalgic association with
it; if anything, it formed part of their jarring history. Then there were those
people such as Phila who didn't really give a toss, but just objected to the
settler mentality the new government was adopting, of building statues on
land stolen from natives, like the Statue of Liberty in New York. It also
seemed extravagant and unnecessary to Phila for a nation that had not
even been able to solve its basic needs, like feeding, housing and clothing
itself. But then again he was not a politician.

Phila sat down at one of the harbour bar's wooden tables and took
in the view: a forest of cranes rising into the air; the vast spread of the
sea, smooth as a mirror, and something that never failed to impress
him. Container ships lay at anchor in the harbour, cranes labouring the
intermodal activity above them. Above, Prospect Hill – insouciant nature
– distilled the essence of the activity ready to outlast all intent and time.
He ordered calamari and chips for his lunch from an Indian waitress with
an unassuming natural beauty. And added a draught of Windhoek lager.

Phila could not get away from the Mandela statue thing. He began
speculating where specifically it would be erected. He identified a spot
he thought would be visible from afar against the bustling activity of the
cranes. He thought about the words engraved at the base of the Statue of
Liberty on the Island of Manhattan: *Give us your tired hands, your foreign
song* ... and all that jazz the majority of Americans no longer believed
because of their growing fear of black immigrants – the irony of a nation
founded by immigrants being afraid was not lost on anyone. He wondered
what they would write on Mandela's, something tired like *Long walk to
freedom,* he presumed. What would be the best epithet to fit the area and
its history? His thoughts were interrupted by the waitress bringing his
food. She put it on the table and asked Phila if he was from around there.
He never knew how to answer that question so he just smiled to imply
either yes, or I don't really wanna talk about it now. The waitress seemed
to take the benign side of the assumption and smiled back before turning
to another customer.

'The wind from the coast was troublesome to us,' said Maqoma
introducing himself with a bang.

Perhaps it was the rustle of alcohol in Phila's brain that had summoned
the old man; or maybe he'd been sitting there all along. The words, however,
resonated immediately. That was it! That would be a great epithet to put

on Mandela's statue: *The wind from the coast was troublesome to us!* He smiled to himself in satisfaction.

'The wind brought the landing of British settlers and redcoats.' Maqoma looked panicky and darty-eyed.

'Good afternoon to you, my warden. How has it been in your wanderings around the earth, bottling winds and kicking storms?' Phila attempted sarcasm, to which, of course, Maqoma had been impervious from the beginning.

'We don't have much time left. I cannot fail.'

'Always, I, I, I,' Phila feigned irritation.

Maqoma looked at him as if to investigate his state of mind, licked his lips and continued with his talk.

'The wharves, alive with clutter, foghorns and calliopes, have always made me nervous.' He spoke in uncharacteristic tip-toeing tentativeness, looking around all the time as if fearful that someone would see him. Something strange was beginning to happen to Phila. He was now also feeling Maqoma's moods directly in himself.

'People we had given up for dead were here. As serfs, wagon drivers, tailors, cobblers, smiths, woodcutters, wheelwrights, herders, farm overseers, foresters, gardeners and so on. I had always thought people who reported these things to me were just scallywags and falsifiers who wanted to ingratiate themselves with the chief. But then I could see with my own eyes that everything they said was true. Kaffirs clothed themselves in white people's dress; their women stood on smooth boulders on river banks, knee-deep in water, senselessly beating linen against the rocks. I was told it was a way of cleaning it.

'It's amazing how industrious the white man can be – erecting stone walls and dikes to arrest the pride of the ocean. All along the seashore the white tents of rude settlement sprang up, close together on the shifting dunes. I could not believe what I was seeing: white people everywhere, frolicking in picnic parties of pleasure, playing skiffle music, giving themselves to drunkenness and brutal passions. Up the hill, more tents, but those were better ordered, neater and pitched reasonable distances apart.'

The echolalic noise of rap music drifted down from Prospect Hill, a sign that the denizens were now black middle class.

'Unlike the merry lot above, down below others sat on boxes and bundles, under the wagons, with tents pitched alongside, scaring away hungry wild dogs and jackals. Wagons were a strange phenomenon to us then. Even those that later became common, the ones covered with great tarpaulins and drawn by sixteen or eighteen full-grown oxen.

'Those wagons were wooden bodies of twelve to fourteen feet in length then, and about five feet in width, in white man's measurements. Their belly-plank, which was stoutly put together, rested on the under-structure of two strong axles carried by four stout wheels fixed together on the long wagon, and drawn by means of a pole – the *disselboom* – to which was attached the *trekgoed*, or drawing gear. The sides of the wagon were made up of strong boughs of wood reaching a height of eighteen to twenty-four inches. These were bent around and attached to each upper edge of the sides, forming a structure that was covered with painted canvas, with long flaps covering the front and rear. *Trektouwen* – *riems* tied up together to make strong ropes – were used to fasten yokes. There were no buck wagons then, just rudimentary stuff; no chains to gear, and axles were made of wood. The ropes, strong as they were, were apt to break, especially in wet weather. It was not an unusual sight to see a wagon capsized, its *disselboom* broken.'

'You seem to know an awful lot of detail about these wagons for someone who just called them a "strange phenomenon",' Phila remarked, downing the remains of his draught beer.

'We had to know the wagons well for when we staged ambushes,' explained Maqoma. 'We had to know exactly where to find what in a hurry. A thirsty person went under the wagon for the *water-vaatjie*, which was almost always slung there. If you wanted things like firearms, powder-horns and bullet-pouches, you went for the *jager-zakken* on the sides of the wagon. On the front was the *voorkis* and at the back the *agterkis*, which was where all sorts of requisites for the journey as well as daily provisions like sugar, tea, coffee and rusks were stored. The *agterkis* was where a hungry raider went first.'

As the beer kept coming Phila's mind wandered away from Maqoma's monologue in a duality of his own thoughts that were still obsessively caught up with coming up with an epithet for the proposed Mandela statue.

Deny the past and soon despair of the future.

'As we sat watching from the bushes on the hilltop of eBheyini we observed their busy morning, heard the cacophony: wagon drivers, mainly Quena, chasing and driving untamed oxen, wild as buck; many knockdowns and kicks, and running after oxen that pulled away before inspanning could properly commence; hollering from their white masters; wailing babies fallen off the wagons; white women scolding their Quena servants whose job it was to bear them aloft on chairs. When the wagons started moving the oxen became wild, galloping, pitching with their sharp horns and tossing their heads. Those leading them, running like mad, leaving the drivers, passengers and cargo dependent on chance. You could see the backs of the oxen were sore from excessive whipping.'

Obsess with the past and soon get lost in its labyrinth.

'The most drama and noise came when everybody went hollering in pursuit of oxen that had run into the bush. Puppies, not to be outdone, whined for their bitch mothers while horses joined the fray with incessant neighing. When the span of oxen was eventually reduced to working order, there were satisfied exclamations and cries: "*Gee! Wow! Trek! Loop! Trek!*" The crack of whips cutting mercilessly into the oxen's backs could be heard all the way to Stony Valley. Then the undulating silence of the bush took over. The poor beasts shied, shoved their heads between their legs and tugged on.'

Whatever happens to the past will happen to it posthumously.

'Meanwhile, there was much activity down below. Men in what I later learnt were tailcoats and knee-breeches sat on veld stools bartering their merchandise, which they spread out on planks and mats to beguile the public under every shade. Rich Mfengus, proud as peacocks, with heads ornamented with jackal tails, ostrich plumes and girded in kilts of monkey tails were the wheelwrights, busy making yokes and skeys. Some were brick-makers and builders. It was a boisterous and distressing state of affairs.'

'Not too different from now, I guess,' Phila said as he finished his food.

Despair patrols a grieving heart.

'I recognised many of those men down there on the white people's wharves, busy like ants, loading and offloading different materials onto their boats: kegs of powder, tin boxes, ropes and anchors from the ship whose sails hung loose in the rusting hulks. A thought of recruiting them into contributing their steals (for they were already stealing for personal profit) to our cause against the white man entered my mind as I observed from where I sat. And, as it happened, most of them were enthusiastic about the prospect; and in due time, when I sent messengers to collect gunpowder, they didn't fail me.'

'Tomorrow I shall leave this village city,' said Phila. 'I'm grateful to it for many things, but it is too mono-dimensional for me. I am rotting at my moorings here, and circling the drains as I drown.'

'Geography in itself isn't the change of anything,' said Maqoma, who, unexpectedly, seemed for once to be listening to what Phila was saying.

'But it's a start.'

113

Phila woke with the birds the following day. He wanted to visit a few last historical sites before he left. He started at Sacramento, where some Portuguese in the mid-seventeenth century, travelling on Spanish warships, ran into some serious rock trouble that wrecked their ship.

The Old Seaview Road in Port Elizabeth was an enchanting one that smelled of the sea. He parked among the boulders, carved over centuries out of the rock-face by pounding waves. Morning mist fell softly, like the memory of a departed one. The wind whistled cold notes to brush away the dust of past years. The rising sun robed everything in golden fire. After a while, something about the sea's ancient effort, ebbing and flowing, drawing breath, now in rage, now in serene overlays, wearied Phila, so he left, ditching his plans to visit other areas.

The day was getting warm by the time Phila got going and had filled up his tank and bought a bottle of water.

The freeway out of Port Elizabeth bisects Bluewater Bay, a secluded residential area of psychedelic colours before it climbs over the Swartkops estuary and skirts the fynbos-clad hills that conceal the black township of Motherwell and the pounding sea that floods the freeway when Poseidon boosts the rim of the ocean. It proceeds through the salt hills of Ingqurha towards the giant sand dunes and bushy hillsides around the Sundays River. You lose the sight of the city as you climb the hills.

To wait out the plugged wires of the blinding morning sun Phila stopped at Sundays River, which the Xhosas call iNqweba, and admired the dunes. For a while he lay on the car bonnet, resting his back against the windshield, reading. A car, driven by a white lady somewhere in her late forties, took the parking bay next to him. Probably deciding that no one who reads books could be physically dangerous, she opened the door of her car, coming closer to investigate what Phila was reading. She was the sandals-and-socks type, with a long swishing skirt, most probably a lecturer in the humanities department of the local university.

"What are you reading there?" she asked, with what Phila took to be genuine interest. He closed the book in silence and handed it to her.

"Campbell? Interesting," she said. "Do you understand it?"

Phila, trying not to be rude, ignored her.

"If you want a better feel of how the white settlers suffered to build this place, try Pringle too," she suggested, undeterred. "He was one of

114

the 1820 settlers. Then at least you'll see we didn't just come as parasites. Perhaps that will stop all this talk of land, this land that you people think is a solution to everything."

Nothing put Phila out of mood like the term 'you people' in white South African parlance. He refused to spoil his morning mood, so he reclaimed his book, excused himself and drove off.

With the sun almost high above him now, he started feeling sentimental as the city sank in his rear-view mirror. At the immediate summit of the hill he noticed, late, a black lady, with a child hemmed on her skirts and another on her back, hitchhiking on the side of the road. He decided to stop. Having already passed her, he had to reverse while she collected her plastic bags and sauntered to the car.

"*Siya eRhini, bhuti,*" she said, more in question than declaration.

"Hop in."

"*Heyi usincedile, besesinexhala lokuba late,*" she said as she settled what looked to be a three-year-old boy with drooping eyes, before taking the one on her back down and sitting him on her lap on the back seat. It took her some time to get settled in the car. Phila, who had never found out the origins and meaning of the Xhosa word for Grahamstown, eRhini, decided to try his luck with her.

"*Lithetha ntoni sisi eligama lithi Rhini, kudala ndifuna ukulazi?*"

"*Yhuu! Hayi, bhuti, undibuza ukwenda kukamama kengoku. Ndiza yazelaphi mna lonto?*" She laughed in amused embarrassment because, as she said, it had never occurred to her to ask the meaning of the word, hence her proverbial answer that Phila was asking her mother's wedding day. Phila always marvelled at the Xhosa practice of speaking in proverbs when under some form of pressure. Hence the British officials, most of whom had no knowledge of Xhosa to speak of, and even those who had a rudimentary one, didn't have enough to understand the deeper meaning of proverbs. So they just treated the phrases as childish gibberish. Asking someone about their mother's wedding day was concomitant to mystery or futility since they would, traditionally, not have been born then.

In need of what Kant called the "quickening art", Phila took the opportunity to put on some music. As they drove off he realised he had another hitchhiker.

'At times when our wars with white people were stagnant,' Maqoma said from beside him in the passenger seat, 'I liked to visit their homesteads, especially the missionaries and *amajonis*. It's amazing what you can learn from a man who is in his cups. The white man's alcohol makes a person foolish; and it's highly addictive.'

'As such you did not heed your own caution?'

'I've always been of the belief that he who commands his mind commands the day; but even myself, I'd constantly lapse into my curmudgeonly ways after a nip or two, and thus reveal my revengeful resentments. When the white man's spirits get into your head it confuses you. Perhaps it's because our ancestors don't agree, and that's what makes the head spin.

'I remember one day attending one of the social missionary gatherings at the Kat River Settlement, or so I gave as the official reason for my being there. I can't recall. In truth I just wanted to see the land that I held dear above all in this country, the Ngcwenxa area. It was during our banishment, when they had exiled us, giving our land to the KhoiKhoi. We were under strict orders never to travel beyond our allotted lands without permission from the magistrates of our regions. The missionary in my area was a certain blasé gentleman by the name of Kayser. He was so stolid not even other missionaries liked him. He spoke funnier than the rest, with an explosive fricative and robust manner. Others even excluded him from their gatherings.'

"*Uyathetha, bhuti*?" The lady from the back seat got concerned when she noticed Phila seemingly talking to himself.

"*Ndiyazithethela nje.*" Humming to the song, he replied.

'I was made bold by my needs. The missionaries at the Kat River Settlement let me dine with them now and then, which in turn satisfied my tippling needs and quenched my reserves. Once, a sergeant by the name of Sant, if I remember well – he was from the group of Cape Mounted Rifles, my permanent enemies – unceremoniously interrupted one of these dinner arrangements with my white German friend. The young man, bleary-eyed from drink and slurring his words, made a scuffle with me. He demanded I make myself scarce from the vicinity of the colony, post haste. Because I had, on me, no magistrate's permission to be on what he called colonial land.

'"Just as soon as I finish the tea these wonderful people have placed before me, young man," I replied, remaining seated.

'"Damn you, if you don't move from that table, Macoma!" he said, pointing a loaded musket at me and pronouncing my name in that English way. I could see that he was furious and nervous, so I didn't want to give him an excuse to do something foolish. I stood to leave as he had ordered. He came closer, touching me with a flask of brandy, demanding to know if I wanted to sample his stuff as he had heard that I was partial to it. What the origin of his grudge against me was I honestly had no idea, but then again there must have been a lot of white people then who wanted a piece of me because of our success in resisting them in the previous war. I appealed to my missionary friends not to afford Sergeant Sant opportunity for staging a quarrel with me, which, I was sure, would no doubt compel him to shoot me. To tell you the truth, I was scared as a rabbit. There were many dangers I was willing to face, but a bullet in my back was not one of them. So my missionary friends accompanied me to the border of our lands and there we cordially parted, to the chagrin of Sergeant Sant, who was certainly spoiling for a fight. Many people claimed I was hot tempered. Maybe so. But I knew how to control my temper. And knew also how to bide my time. As for the white man's spirits, the muse of fire – yes I was partial to those, but spirits never made me do something I didn't want to do, or caused me to lose control. If anything, it cemented my resolve by putting iron in my will.'

"*Ungasimisela wethu, bhuti, apho ngasegaraji. Nazi ilekese zakho, bhuti, usincede kakhulu.*"

"*Hayi, sisi, uthengele untemekana izinto ezimandi ngayo. Nihlala kweyiphi ilokishi? Ndinga nibeka kuyo.*"

"*O! Ungaba undicedile nabantwana, nalemithwalo. Sihlala eFingo wethu, bhuti. UThixo akusikelel!*"

Phila declined the fare the woman offered, a legacy of his father who always refused to charge people he helped. He also offered to drive her and her children to the township of Fingo where they stayed.

Driving back to town Phila could hear the wheel of history turn in creaks like a chariot of dusk. He had resisted the urge to ask if the woman, like him, was Mfengu. He knew that the original people who stayed in Fingo were the descendants of amaMfengu who'd fought on the side of the British during the Frontier Wars, hence the proximity of that township to the main town of Grahamstown; while the township of Tantyi, the traditional Xhosa area, was on the periphery.

Makhanda

AFTER DROPPING OFF HIS HITCHHIKERS, Phila went into the town centre for a drink, settling for the first bar he could find after parking in Market Street. He remembered seeing it when Nandi and he had bought groceries at Shoprite. The bar was squeezed between a rough stone building that hosted a bookshop on one side and the supermarket on the other. The bookshop was mostly where he waited for Nandi, browsing the shelves of books he had no wish to buy, mostly about and by dead white men he had read about ad nauseam.

Phila was relieved to escape the stiff breeze of the streets as he entered the bar. He had never been inside before. The place had the forlorn atmosphere of an American Midwest movie, and the smell of decay. Most of the patrons were ageing white men with weather-beaten faces, drinking Castle Lager draughts and betting on racehorses. They lifted their heads at the sound of the door chimes. Their gazes lingered in the realisation of Phila's race. They looked like they were decaying in sync with the town and their bar. The bar synopsised their lives. Most, Phila suspected, felt degraded by the nature of things, like having to be governed by kaffirs and told how to run their farms; resented being made to share their watering hole with them; hid their disgust by ordering more brandies and Coke, washing them down with Castle Lager. And most, later on, would take out their anger on their *vroue en swart plaaswerkers*.

Everything here belongs to the past, Phila thought, as he walked over to a table. In fact, the whole town matched his oneiric mood of detachment. He was pleased, after sitting down, to discover a racially mixed group that looked like students from the university seated at the back tables, where there were no betting machines but TV screens that showed local and foreign soccer matches. This lot carried a carousing atmosphere. They were loudly discussing something that involved Fanon and Biko because those names kept popping up. Phila called for a draught of Windhoek Lager, when the barman gave him attention. The barman looked to be a hard-core exercise and weight-lifting fanatic. His biceps and tattooed shoulders did not erase his effeminate face. He had a sense of contentment with his place in the world that Phila envied. He wondered what the barman thought of him; the restless kind with hyphenated identity, dust and anxiety on their faces.

"Anything else?" the body nazi asked politely, wiping the table with a wet cloth.

"No, I'm good." Phila dropped back in exhaustion on the chair. He drank the beer without relish, gaining awareness of his thirst as he slaked it. He lit a cigarette, took a long drag and shot a column of smoke to the ceiling. The body nazi immediately pointed to the no smoking sign behind, and directed him to the smoking area, which was where the students were sitting. After an hour or so, into the dregs of his second draught, Phila found himself thinking about Nandi, knowing very well it would be impossible for him to drive, as he was getting drunk already. The thoughts took him back to the days of their youth, of intense hope, fear, ambition, anxiety and, lately, dread. He was surprised by the depth of fondness he felt for her. He thought about the requirements that would keep him in the City of Saints, as they called Grahamstown. He would need to adopt new hobbies to amuse himself, pretend that its farm spirit atmosphere didn't bother him and, after fifty, start chasing after student skirts to prove his failing vitality was still in *élan*, and with that earn Nandi's resentment. Unless she herself would be keeping a student Ben 10 to plumb her pipes. He didn't feel much attraction to that life.

He ordered another drink to break his chain of thought. Everyone became increasingly expansive with the passing time. Phila, hyper-analytical as always, lent his ear to the students' discussion. The white one was overcompensating by his knowledge of Biko's *I Write What I Like*, although he seemed to have memorised rather than internalised it. His speeches were peppered with unacknowledged Biko quotes. The girl among them, mostly quiet and slightly embarrassed when the white dude spoke – denoting to Phila that he must be her boyfriend – was more intelligent. She kept driving the discussion to what she called the 'existential paradox' in Fanon's work. It pleased Phila that she was also quoting Kierkegaard, who identified the paradox of achievement requiring failure, and flight from anguish involving a deeper anguish. Phila shared the girl's suspicion of Senghorian Négritude, which conveniently wanted blackness to be subsumed into the light of white civilisation to prove its worth. In fact, the thing Phila respected from men like Césaire, Fanon, Du Bois, Biko etc, was the manner in which they disguised their hope with anger. But Phila had realised a long time ago that he did not share their hope, that his world outlook was too bleak. His only salvation was the fact that he not only accepted God's silence but understood it also. And so his faith in humanity was based on God, not humans who squashed his flickering flame. Even if, with Job, now and then he wondered when God was going to return his camels and daughters, he accepted as necessary for a creature like him the inability to comprehend divine reasoning with equanimity if not humility. His eagerness was more for the fireside chat in God's house than this perishing house-of-clay feet.

The short student who liked using convoluted terms walked to the counter to order another round. On his way back to their table he invited Phila to join in a toast – although he didn't say to what. Out of curiosity Phila joined them.

"Nostrovia!" The students cheered before drinking their vodkas. Of course he had to introduce himself, buy most of the rounds later on, and engage in pseudo-philosophical discussions that exhausted him. When the girl asked what he thought about the existential crisis he admitted that the fact that we are alive at all was a crisis when not looked at from a religious point of view, which saw life as gift. Tactically extricating himself from the discussion, he added, "But I've not yet thought things beyond that, if I ever will."

"Rightly so, my man!" the overcompensating student loudly declared, giving Phila a high-five, which seemed to seal his acceptance into the gang. "Anything else is a distraction from the rich who want to keep us docile." This was followed by a roar of laughter. They were all intent on polishing off the bottle of whisky Phila had bought, and looked set to continue into the early morning hours.

At some later stage the overcompensating white boyfriend directed another question to Phila, who was by then quite tipsy. "Would it not be far easier to just cash in the ticket, if all the fuss is only about that?" Phila had not really caught what the 'about that' part was about but decided to play along anyway.

"Ah! The operative word being easy. Far too easy. Some of us have a bigger problem than that. We're interested in this world even when we can't stand it – *especially* when we can't stand it."

There was momentary silence while the students tried to make sense of what he'd said, followed by a chorus of laughter, indicating that they had either missed his point or understood it far too well.

Feeling privileged and ill at ease, Phila left them. It was after two in the morning. His favourite overcompensating dude lay on the lap of his girlfriend with the wind knocked out of him.

When he got to his car he softly hummed his favourite poem from Aeschylus' *Agamemnon* while fiddling to open the car door:

> *Were my destiny not prepared by gods from getting more than its share, my heart, outstripping my tongue, would be expressing these things. But as it is, it mutters in pain in the dark, not expecting ever to accomplish anything in time, though my mind is on fire...*

'Mortal that you are, do not try to be wiser than gods.'

It could only be Maqoma.

Phila adjusted the position of his car seat to recline. Smoking a pipe, Maqoma regarded the drunk Phila with amused indulgence. Phila looked around furtively before answering, fearing that some of the students might have followed him. He didn't want to lower their regard of him.

'Since you come from the gods, or with the gods, or whatever you come with, why don't you enlighten me?'

'I listened to you debate with those students. I think you are still to realise that on this side of life the best you can hope for is perspective. The sum of truth is beyond human capability, especially those still caught up in time.'

'What are you doing here then?'

'Helping your perspective; clearing the fog so you may see well. Gather to yourself the flowering fruits while time permits. There comes a time, so to say, when you can only be what you've become without possibility of change or self-invention.' Maqoma said this with startling intensity.

'Feels like I'm Nietzsche's fool, trying to drink the sea.'

'Give to the language of your soul the virtue of fidelity, and keep your thoughts ahead of your tongue. Put kindness in your heart and honesty in your ways. The rest shall be added unto you according to need. And always be true to what you've heard and seen here. Always be true.'

Phila felt something solemn and wise was happening to him, but he did not know how to interpret nor profit from it. 'I see you're in a philosophic mood today. I know what I don't know, and the silence of God, though I accept it, terrifies me sometimes; that's when I don't ...' He could not think of a single thing to say.

'Find a way to live comfortably with your cloud of unknowing, but not complacently. In a way, we are in closer position than you think. Imagine you had drowned in the river and came out on the other side only to realise you have lost all your senses but can discern, more sharply and more urgently, everything in one permanent moment. That is what being dead feels like.'

'Whoah, whoah! Were you not the one who told me to be wary of drowning people, because they take down with them whatever they can hold onto? You even made an example about Nxele who drowned with our nation. Are you saying something different now? Please be consistent.'

'The worst of it is not being able to feel time. Nothing is more isolating than that for a fledgeling soul, fresh into the dead moment that is its rising into eternity,' Maqoma solemnly answered.

'You mean to tell me there's no companionship where you are?'

'I mean you arrive blind there too, and you must slowly acquire ways to recognise things by immersing yourself in their essence. We live as souls, with personalities we acquired here because we're not corporeal. But you don't need to know all of this because it doesn't concern you for now.'

Maqoma kept silent for a while, allowing for the revelation to sink in, before continuing on another topic. 'I never liked this place. In our era it was the seat of colonial oppression. I always enter it with trepidation.'

'Nothing much to it now, except a Supreme Court and the university,' said Phila. 'But you're right on another level. There's always that restless austerity I don't like about this town, as if someone is planning something against you – your doom. In any case, I don't like strange cities. The noises they make I cannot comprehend; I don't know their meaning.'

Maqoma's vitreous eyes were trained on the street lights. 'Our doom was contrived from this place,' he said.

'I'm planning to see my friend Nandi here, the psychologist. Your doom might be at hand again.'

'Not really. I told you I will never make you do anything you don't want to do. I don't have those powers.'

'And I suppose that makes you an innocent party in all this.'

The ensuing silence was interrupted by a bergie knocking on Phila's car window with an extended hand. Phila rolled the window down while trying to fish for coins in his ashtray. He handed them to the man, who left without thanking him. Phila kept the window unrolled, to let in some air, reminding himself of the crucial need not to let his left hand know what his right was doing.

'I'm getting on a couch anyway.'

Maqoma gave Phila a mischievous smile. 'If you ask me, you just want to see her, and perhaps see if you can get into her pants again.'

'And I'm supposed to give to a dog that bites me?' Phila rolled the window up.

'Let's talk about something else then. In our era, anyone who fancied some popularity called himself a prophet. The diviner business boomed.'

'As it does today also,' Phila interjected. 'Our people tend to go white, mystical and religious when under tremendous national strain.'

'Indeed! Very perceptive of you to notice. Along with mystical longings went shouting and jabbering in the streets, the declaring of visions and all manner of things.'

'Nothing much has changed, believe me. They just call themselves born again now, and rant in the name of Christ instead of Dal'ubomi – which, I guess, is the same person.'

'Those who had run their lives foul went to the wild for a few days, ate wild spinach, honey and locusts; came back calling themselves prophets –'

'– or men of God, in this era,' Phila interjected again. 'They feed people snakes, make them eat grass and drink petrol and chemical detergents, in the stupid hope of cleansing themselves internally.'

'Then we were all supposed to drop everything and listen to what they were telling us. I became impatient with most of them. Makhanda, alias Nxele, and Ntsikana were no exceptions.'

'Tell me more about Makhanda – I mean, since we're in his territory. This municipality has been renamed after him now. I hear he got his madness from a white man, a priest or something?'

'That's the thing about madness people do not notice; it is contagious. I was wondering why his name is written on everything I come across around here. Have they named anything after me?'

'A tourist route around Stutterheim, I am told, but nothing much else. Sorry, man. Public opinion is very fickle. You must not read too much into that. King David didn't have a single book named after him in the Bible, yet his name appears almost in all that came after him.'

'Not even at the Ngcwenxa territory and Ngqegqe?'

'I don't think so. I might be wrong.'

'Yet they honour commoners like Makhanda with a whole district?'

'Well, we have this democracy thing now, which means princes and kings have no real hold over us, just a ceremonial one. If the majority of people think Makhanda contributed more than you for our freedom, then his name gets to be on top of yours.'

Maqoma made a noise of disgust. 'Contributed more than me for the freedom of our people? Makhanda? He killed thousands of our people with lies and stubbornness! Makhanda was the son of a commoner who worked for a white farmer. That's where he picked up the white man's tongue and religion. He learnt a lot by observing, whetting his curiosity on the ways of the white man here eRhini.' He paused. 'Are you sure they have not named anything after me? Surely I did more to keep our nation off the shackles of the white man's ways than Makhanda? In any case, why should care, as if I need my vanity to be bolstered by mortals?'

'I'll ask around. But why do you care? I thought you were not vain?'

'This is different. Nxele's strength was always in persuasive lies. Like all liars, he sought to mystify his origins. And he had strong powers of speech, providing creative answers, not necessarily proper solutions, to the things that dumbfounded the nation. I'm afraid you lot have fallen for his tricks too. He always was able to endear himself in the eyes of the people, being a learned man in the white man's ways. When he gained a substantial following he started seeing things in his own light. The missionaries who had initially showered him with praise could not stomach it when Nxele saw himself as the brother of their Christ too, demanding equal status with them. They wanted him to know his place. When it became clear that they'd never admit him as their equal Nxele, correctly, receded from them and established his own following.'

'That, in our eyes, makes him the founder of the Pan Africanist Movement. Do tell – have you met Steve Biko down – or up – there, if I may digress? I myself am of more Black Consciousness persuasion, a movement founded by Soga but developed by Biko in our land.'

'What does it make me, who devoted his entire life to preserving the independence of our people? Anyway, I am neither down nor up there. I am just in the ether.'

'Whatever. Did you meet Bantu?'

'Yes. Quite a feisty, headstrong young man.'

'Perhaps you could bring him with you sometime? I would like to chat with him.'

'I'm assigned to you, not Biko.'

'Touchy!'

'As I was saying. Nxele started with the white man's religion, which he picked on a Dutch farm his mother worked on. But when white missionaries refused to accept him as their equal he began the process of *ukuthwasa,* with the usual hysterical symptoms that gained him a following as a flamboyant clairvoyant: nervous paroxysms, dreams, visions and so forth. When these became too frequent he went to live in the woods and fields, refusing to eat any prepared food. He was of the view that prepared food was contaminated by the sins of those who prepared it. When he had been with the missionaries he preached against polygamy, witchcraft, adultery, incest, warfare and so on. But on his own he started saying different things, peppered with mystical ravings. The people took him as being possessed. They seized him and gagged him, put a rope around his neck to hang and burn him as a witch. That was when a diviner called Qalanga saw signs of *ukuthwasa* in his madness and rescued him. With that he turned a madman into a diviner and, eventually, a prophet of doom.'

'I'm kind of tired of this *ukuthwasa* thing in your stories. Didn't you people have anything more interesting?'

'I'm trying to make you understand what's been happening to you also.'

'What do you mean?'

'The spirit of the ancestors sometimes chooses to come into the individual they feel would be the best instrument to transmit the message they want to convey.'

'Don't freak me out, man.'

'There's nothing nefarious about it; the interpretation is still yours. They just concentrate on the visions provided by incidence and opportunity. Remember when you dreamt about being assailed by a swarm of bees?'

'Yes. Wait. How do you know that? And one of them stung me?'

'That was me. In fact three of us were allowed to sting you: myself, Soga and Mqhayi. They will take over after I am done. This is the infusion into essence I was telling you about, my soul into the bee essence. Where we are now we're being taught to infuse ourselves into the divine essence, more like seeing through the godhead.'

'And with me? Us?'

'You and the bee are a slightly different thing, not as comprehensive as assuming divine essence, just your physical nature. Your body, of course, takes strain from running both our minds, hence the headaches you keep experiencing. But they'll go away as soon as we're done. Meantime, let's continue with Nxele – he's part of your syllabus for now. Nxele came back from the school of witch-doctoring speaking of Mdalidiphu, god the creator of the deep, whose son is Tayi. He said his god was angry with white people for killing his son Tayi.'

'That must have excited your lot?'

'It gained him a substantial following. In fact, there are many similarities between Nxele's and Ntsikana's messages. The differences are mostly in the details and their respective attitudes towards white people. Our people figured any god who was angry with the white man must be a good one and their friend in turn. This god, according to Nxele, was going to plead the case of the Xhosas against the white people, and those who die believing they would be resurrected.

'Ndlambe, in whose chieftainship Nxele resided, could not ignore Nxele's popularity. He decided to utilise it for his own ends. He stirred Nxele's teachings towards a more militant tone against the colonists, largely because they were allies of his arch enemy nephew, Ngqika, my father. Mdalidiphu was now not only in opposition to the white man's religion, but actively going to throw white people back in the sea for murdering Tayi.'

'I see now why they say Nxele was the founder of the Pan Africanist Movement.'

'White people's guns would fire water, Nxele said, if a united Xhosa nation believed in Mdalidiphu and went to war against them. He went around the land proclaiming these prophecies and inciting people. I remember hearing him once, shouting and spinning like a dying fly. I took him for a madman, of course.

> *There they come!*
> *They've crossed the Qagqiwa!*
> *They've crossed the Nqweba,*
> *Only one river more,*
> *The Nxuba*
> *Then they'll be on our land.*
> *What'll become of you then?*

'He was preaching to the converted. And his madness became contagious because it was narrating what was happening as the white colonial government kept confiscating land from us through the leading hand of Graham. The Ndlambe had just been expelled from their land across iNxuba. Thus Nxele managed to raise himself to the eminence of a great chief without being born into aristocracy. When Ngqika, whose light was waning then, realised there was no escaping the power of Nxele, he tried to bribe him into the ruling class by offering to take his sister's hand. Nxele refused the offer with contempt. There's no worse humiliation for a

chief than to be refused marriage by a commoner. It is a clear indication of
a fallen power. Just about the only people who still invested the authority
of chieftaincy on Ngqika at that time were the colonial government. He
had lost popularity with most Xhosas because he had shown his weakness
by ruling through fear rather than consensus, something amaXhosa, with
their deep streak of democracy, do not tolerate.

'Nxele moved further away from Christianity. He rejected the white
man's clothes, went back to his ochre, as the saying goes. He married
two young KhoiKhoi women as a sign of his rejection of the white man's
teaching against polygamy; started demanding cattle *zokuruma,* like all
diviners. He summoned people to come and witness the resurrection of the
dead beneath a boulder at the Gompo River, at the foot of the Amathole.
There he ordered them to enter the water and wash. The people entered
the waters in tumult, as though they were charging at an enemy, bellowing
war cries and throwing water on their breasts and shoulders. Nxele tried
to dissuade them from this but they did not refrain. When the promised
resurrection of the dead was not forthcoming Nxele informed them that
it was because of their obduracy, their refusal to stop shouting war cries.
This, Nxele told them, scared the dead people back to their graves.'

'Oh dear! Were people really that gullible?'

'Nxele had a mystical hold on them. Since they saw fit to follow their
own headstrong will, and did not listen to what he told them, said Nxele,
they had only themselves to blame. He dismissed them. Told them to go
back to their homes to repent. The people saw the error of their ways and
went back to their huts, repentant. Thus did Nxele's reputation remain
intact. How he was not killed in the riot of that day says a lot about his
persuasive skills.'

'It is always easy, in retrospect, to see the ingenious manner by which
the likes of Nxele lied and fill the gaps of cosmological beliefs,' Phila tried
to contribute, but Maqoma cut him off.

'The problem was we had no successful belief for dealing with
the question of what happens after death. So when white people came
telling us about resurrection, they gave substance to our vague longings,
and explained a lot of things to many. All of a sudden, because of this
resurrection thing, life did not appear absurd. We always suspected we
would meet our loved ones again some day, almost in the same manner
we believed our ancestors to be alive somewhere. The white people came
with a concrete teaching about it, written in their magic book with the red
mouth. Hearing such things from the mouth of one of our own, Nxele, gave

people assurance of things to come. Nxele, unlike Ntsikana, was cunning enough to conform his prophecies and teachings to the expectations of the people. That is why he was more successful in the short run.

'Ntsikana, on the other hand, spoke from a non-compromising inner conviction of the truth. He gave an unadulterated version of his visions and dreams – hence he was a failure in the short run. People everywhere are never partial to the truth before it overcomes all their lies. They drink it only like medicine, as a last option. Ntsikana came to our tribe objecting to Nxele's prophecies, though not completely to Tayi, whose father, according to him, was Dal'ubomi, whom the Xhosas knew as Qamata. This was how Ntsikana phrased his teachings:

Things are bad at Gaga. Nxele has told people lies. Dal'ubomi
is coming to fence this land against lies. The true God is
Mhlabazihlangana [Nations-mix] and is Ndikhoyo-Naphakade [I
Forever Am]. His son has lightning supernatural eyes, and is Sifuba-
Sibanzi [Broad-Chested Tayi] with love for all nations he wants to
unite by and in love.
Sele! Sele!
Ahom, ahom, ahom!
He came to me at the Lake of Arms [Breakfast Vlei].
Nation of Phalo!
Respond! Respond!
You're being called by Heaven.
Hom! Homna! Hom, Hom!
The sound says as He comes.
Proclaim this at Gqorha!
Proclaim it at Mankazana.
He is the shield of truth!
He is the maker of stars and Pleiades.
He amalgamates flocks rejecting each other.
His name is Dal'ubomi.
The creator of all life!

'At some stage all these prophecies got so confusing that nobody cared a fart about the name of the true god if only he promised to chase white people away from our land, and bring an end to droughts and new diseases brought by white people, like rinderpest. That's how Nxele and his faction got to be so popular; a wretched thing that was to finally bring our nation to its knees.

'I often asked myself, when I was incarcerated at the leper colony, if the lure of the River People became too compelling for Nxele when he was on the island. Or the remembrance of things he left behind, at home; the familiar mountains, rivers and valleys of our land. Did this lead to his daring the salt waters that swallowed him? How I envied him when the longing for my hearth and kin overtook me in that dungeon. When I imagined the sights and smells of our aloe-scented plains. If you must take me home one last time my gratitude shall be eternal.'

'Can't you do that on your own?'

'I know the dead are not your responsibility, but I can see things bound by time only through your eyes. At least Nxele died like a man. After his popularity and moral fall at Gompo I worried about the reproaches his soul must have been making against the water dungeon of Robben Island.'

'I've been meaning to ask you about your death. There's something not right, almost a mystery about it in the government chronicles of Robben Island.'

'It was a long time ago; left well alone. Let sleeping dogs lie. No, my death was not from natural causes; it was more on the lines of your friend Steve Biko.' Maqoma looked more sad than angry.

'I thought as much.'

'I was the nemesis of white people in the colony. Many of them held a grudge or two against me. When I was incarcerated, at the white government's mercy, many came to pay me back that grudge.'

'The white government, naturally, encouraged that sort of thing.'

'They did nothing to stop it. Once, at the leper colony,' he lowered his voice, 'when the tired face of the moon sailed the sky, its luminous shafts washing the night with a silvery shine, I saw things on the sea. Nxele came riding the back of a sea beast, leaping from one rock to another. In the water it swam at an amazing speed, but once it got to land it stood up and walked on its legs. The legs had seven-inch toes. When I approached Nxele, wishing to learn where he came from since everyone was expecting his imminent return back home, wanting to know how come his horse swam with such alacrity on water, he took fright and ran to the sea with the animal hot on his heels. I tried to chase after them but my joints were stiff with rheumatism. I stood no chance against the agility of that duo.'

'So you people really expected Nxele to come back after the British incarcerated him on Robben Island?'

'He was the hope of a defeated people, their last hope. It was by then becoming clear that white people had been taking the land, and with it were fast enslaving us. Nxele promised to come back with the River People to fight our cause and chase the whites back to the sea.'

'What did the Russians have to do with these River People of yours?'

'In retrospect, I now understand that the Russians and Chinese were also starting a war with the British then. The whole thing got jumbled up in our people's telling, from ship news they received now and then. The people were still nursing a vague hope that either the Russians or the Chinese would rescue them from the oppressive British hold.'

'Amazing how nothing ever really changes.'

'So Nongqawuse, when she talked about the coming of the River People, was giving colour to our people's vague longings and mutterings. Hence her so-called prophecies were received by ready ears. They were meant to raise revolt against the British and they appealed to people's credulity and superstitions.'

'With that, the final doom of the nation came?'

'Indeed. But I am now putting the cart before the horses. Many things happened before we got to that point, things it is my duty to tell you about.

'The day Nxele visited me I walked back to my cell-house when I could not catch up with him. But things took a turn. When I turned I saw Nxele approaching me again, more hesitant this time. His mild face was suffused with sadness and distorted by what I could only read as grief. The strange animal again flanked him. When I tried to address him the animal raised its hackles, denoting its displeasure at my attempt. Try as I might I couldn't find my voice. Nxele spoke to me in a falsetto voice, his skin appearing as if he was under histaminic attack. It looked like a white person's skin gets when they're distressed. "You're wrestling with fate, Maqoma," he began. I'll never forget those words so long as I live.'

'You mean so long as you're dead.' Phila attempted a chuckle, trying to banish the rising fear within him. Maqoma didn't appear to notice his ironic wit.

'I wasn't sure what Nxele meant. I remained confused. Then he spoke again, this time more decisively, his whole body rearranging itself, growing fur, or something of animal integument, as if afflicted by lycanthropy. "What you see happening to this animal and me," he told me, "is an allegory of your life. You shall live like a wolf, swimming in the dark forest in order to forge war on your enemies. Your agility to move around the forest shall be like you saw this animal swim in the sea. Like it, you shall be able to walk on land also, inspiring great fear in your enemies and brethren." His voice sounded ancient, like one tired with the burden of world age. It seemed as if he himself was slightly astonished by his prophetic knowledge. He continued: "We're only men, Maqoma. The indomitable wheels of fate grind us into powder, or raise us to great heights, with or without our volition."

'He talked to me of many things, like what he called the indomitable strength of the British Empire, "always aiming to emulate the Roman vice". He narrated how the city of Rome became the proud mistress of the universe by organising a band of ruffians to effect the plunder and rapine of its neighbours. How the city was made rich by oppressing millions of people around the world. "What at first it obtained by violence and plunder assumed the softer name of revenue when they instituted themselves as an empire. The power originally usurped by the fathers was inherited by the sons, who tortured it into their inheritance by legal invention. What they could not achieve by fraud and murder, like their parents, they devised legality to make it law and called it enterprise. To steal land was not enough. They needed to write it on paper so that it gained legality of rule of law by ruse of governance invented to serve their rapacity. They keep systems of oppression by the intrigue of their courts of law and then call it government. Then establish heads in their leading bands of robbers, calling them kings and emperors, presidents and prime ministers. They parcel out pieces of land around the world, dividing it into dominions that serve the coffers of their empire. And, as is always the case in these things, they begin to quarrel with each other, thus sowing the seeds of the downfall of all of us."

'Some of what he told me I later I learnt here from my friend Titus Petronius, who used to be the son of wealthy Romans and courtier to Emperor Nero in his living years. Titus and I are assigned to the same level of the living dead in the house of ancestors. At present he's somewhere in the United States on a similar assignment to mine. Petronius and I have a lot in common, although we lived centuries apart. He spent most of his earthly days carousing through the back alleys of Rome, dallying with prostitutes and loose aristocratic ladies; making himself a nuisance in marketplaces, drinking places, temples, crowded tenements and aristocrats' villas. I relate to that. But Petronius had enough sense to see through Roman pretensions of greed. His famous line you might know: *The Fates are bent on war, the search for wealth continues ...*'

'Nothing has changed much,' Phila tried to assure Maqoma, suddenly aware of how many times he had said this, 'except, perhaps, the pretenders to the empire have acquired more subtlety, calling their quest "wars of freedom". The quest for greed and power still goes on. Modern Rome drains the world for insatiable profit of commerce, pursuing peace by perpetual wars of greed.'

'Empiric strength is the cause for wanting to be in wars of possession. Nxele said to me, "As for you, you say in your heart they'll never take your land while you are still alive. Well, Hector alone killed Patroclus, yet to avenge him Achilles became a veritable killing machine, until the river Xanthus choked with the bodies of the Trojan dead. Where does it end, Maqoma?" I felt like Damien, torn to pieces by the horses of my passions.'

'I see Petronius has been teaching you a lot of classical literature.'

'A penetrating silence fell between Nxele and me. His rheumy eyes fastened on me a while, inviting my own nakedness towards my heart, before his image extinguished itself from my eyes. That was just before I was freed by the colonial government from my first incarceration at the leper colony. It took some time for me to understand the full meaning of the dream. I learnt later that it is misfortune that teaches us to be true to ourselves, not dreams.'

'Am I dreaming?' Phila, who by then had goosebumps, asked, expecting Maqoma to ignore him as usual. 'Or am I in the arms of misfortune?'

'Only you know the answer to that,' Maqoma replied.

The Coming of Nxele

PHILA WOKE AT 5AM. HE HAD FALLEN asleep in the car, which was still parked on the street. He opened the door to be greeted by the pink fingers of dawn caressing the hills, building confidence into the day. His head felt clubbed and his neck strained. He cupped his hands to strike a match and light a cigarette.

'Your smoking sticks are strange; don't they burn your mouth?'

'No, they just give us cancer.'

'And that's a good thing?'

'I still want to know more about Nxele. I fell asleep yesterday, well, this morning.' Phila looked around to see if there was a shop open for coffee but could not see one. Good coffee was extremely difficult to find in small towns anyway, he consoled himself.

'I'll tell you more some other time. Now you need to take me somewhere.'

'Where are we off to?' Phila was sure his mouth smelled like a sewer. 'I need to brush my teeth.'

'I need to check things from that hill.' Maqoma pointed beyond the Settlers Monument. 'It was after the Battle of Amalinde I came here, still sickly but relying on the effects of the sleep-inducing *Cuika* water to cope with my nights and days. The humiliation of defeat at Amalinde was still fresh on my mind. If it is true about the child being the father of the man,' he said as he waited for Phila to fire up the engine, 'then the children we were in that battle killed the men we might have been. Had I only taken heed of Ntsikana's admonishments, our enemies would not have prevailed over us.'

Phila drove to the foot of Monument Hill, where he parked the car. They began the climb on foot. The steep rise was tortuous.

'You keep saying the glamour of our nation dimmed with the renunciation of Ntsikana's vision. Explain, please?' Phila asked, more

133

resigned to his fate than excited by the prospects. He was also trying to take his mind off his suffering body. The playful respect of a grandfather and grandson was now getting established between them.

'Oh, how I wish we had listened to the son of Gaba.'

'People never listen to prophets; not ones from their hometowns anyway. We're blind when our temperaments rush us to our fates.'

'I used to think that if there be blame in the whole matter, it lay with my father, Ngqika. He should have known better than to let young hot bloods lead so important a war. Now, having had time to think and confront myself, exposed to my own weaknesses, I know better. It requires much courage and relentless light to expose one's psyche to truth. Our fates are not in the stars, but in the gauges of our bile.'

'Tell me about it.' Phila's mouth tasted of bile, and his head hammered. 'I am often amazed how the turn of a historical event, wars, could have been averted had the main actors had better characters.'

'Sadly, that extends to Harry Smith and I, but let me not put my wagon before the oxen. Desire for vengeance made me bold. My hatred for Ndlambe made me bold. My needs made me bold. I was sometimes led astray by the seductions of victory, intoxicated by the strength of youth. After the Battle of Amalinde, Ngqika's star, never resplendent, went on the wane. He started giving himself up to white man's liquor.' Maqoma's face took on a forlorn look of wistful remembrance. 'Ndlambe's mistake lay in being taken too much by Nxele. He decided to embark on a premature stance, going for the eye of the octopus – the frontier capital here, eRhini.'

'I read that it was organised suicide.'

'That it was. Don't get me wrong, such an attack had to be done, in the long run, no question about it. Perhaps even his timing was great, because amaXhosa were still intoxicated by the unity gained in Ngqika's defeat. And the colonial government was still a weak rumour of a few white settlers, more stranded than established in the beginning. He could have nipped the white expansion in the bud had fate not been armed against him. But his preparations were dismal. AmaXhosa still did not possess the proper ammunition to go for an all-stakes war with the colony. I kept telling my people: we must first learn enough about the white man's ways, unite completely among ourselves, before going on an all-out war with them.

'Nxele was at the height of his influence, spoiling for glory. His word was basically law among amaNdlambe. I was sickly, but curious to see for myself the all-out war led by Nxele, who had never even been to battle, let alone led a war. It could only be because of old age for a fine war strategist like Ndlambe to allow his armies to fall under the command of a war novice like Nxele. Perhaps Ndlambe trusted Nxele's sagacity too much, and his son's military strategy.

'Their first error was choosing broad daylight to attack the fortified buildings of white settlement. I watched from this hill.' They had finally reached the top with Phila sweating profusely and dizzy with tiredness from the climb. 'There was still a litter of boulders here then, which elegantly broke the sky. I see them no more now.'

'They carved away a portion of the hill to make way for the tarred road,' said Phila. The traffic to PE, or Peddie in the other direction, sounded like the movements of the seas from up there.

'As you can see, the place is a naturally raised coliseum.'

'That's why white people chose to build the Settlers Monument nearby.'

'I had often heard Nxele preach from the adjacent hill. It was known as his pulpit during our era. White people subsequently called it Makana's Kop. The two hills dwarfed the eminence of the town – still just a huddle of houses then. Around the town there were rolling woods towards the banks of the Fish River, making for an easy disappearance under need. From there I watched the tragic spectacle of Nxele's war. Opposite, that way towards Gwanga, are those numerous other hills and ravines where Nxele and his warriors hid. Further behind, in the thick Fish River woods, the attacking warriors had left their women and children, with the promise that by evening they would all be occupying the town. Mats, pots and cooking utensils were brought along by those Xhosa who had been driven away from the area by the operations of Colonel Graham. Meanwhile, the warriors went on an errand of death.

'I watched the to and fro movements of Mdushane's horse early in the morning across the river. Mdushane, my arch rival at Amalinde, acted as the captain of the day, waiting for a command from his supreme commander, Nxele. Behind the brow of the hill stood a myriad of ant-like warriors, mostly on foot, carrying assegais and cowhide shields. The only hope they had against the white man's guns rested with Nxele's prophecies of turning white people's bullets into water.

'There are always those last-minute doubts when you're about to engage in battle, when you begin to ask yourself real questions. What is the value of that for which I'm about to shed the blood of these young people? What certainty of honour even in victory justifies spilling so much blood? I didn't envy Nxele at that particular moment. Those questions must have been even more intense for him whose supreme hope rested on the prophecy he knew to be a lie. Not that I blame him. When you're going to war you use everything at your disposal to build the courage of your men, because, in the end, wars are won mostly on that.

'I sat wondering what might have been on Nxele's mind that very moment. Was he thinking perhaps it was not too late to call off the bluff? I don't think Nxele was insensitive to other people's sufferings, but he was more consumed with seeking glory for himself.'

'Like all brave people – Caesar, Napoleon, Shaka, Hitler – he was a sociopath. You great men of war are great by the expense of young men's blood.' Phila's growing anger caught even himself by surprise, but Maqoma did not rise.

'Early in the morning, on the side of the British army, I saw the garrison commander, Colonel Willshire, go out to inspect the detachment of the Cape Mounted Corps. He must have learnt of the pending attack of kaffir warriors through the green flies; probably from that treacherous elephant hunter Boezak. All of a sudden white people began assembling their troops on the adjacent slopes. I took fright for Nxele's sake, because the attack was to happen at noon according to Nxele's plan. We learnt later that it was the Khoi, Ngcuka – whom the white people called Nootka – who was once my father's interpreter, who had informed Willshire that he saw kaffir warriors hiding towards Kaffir Drift. While the British platoon went to patrol the area of Kaffir Drift, Nxele was to attack the town.

'The colonel almost fell for Nxele's trap all right. He sent some of his troops to patrol the direction up to Kaffir Drift. And those patrolling troops didn't return until the battle was almost over. But he himself, escorted by about twelve soldiers, galloped in the other direction towards where Nxele's warriors were hiding, to satisfy himself, perhaps, that there was no danger there. Whether he was tipped off or not is now a moot point. Nxele panicked when he saw them coming. When the colonel and his escorts crossed the dongas to round the gorges where a few of them were hiding Nxele ordered an attack. I'm certain the Xhosa warriors who were at the bottom of deep gorges further on were not in immediate view of the colonel and his troops, otherwise the white people would not have been so stupid as to expose themselves like that so close. But as I said, Nxele panicked. That is the usual tell-tale sign of a novice on the battleground.

'Nxele's warriors, who were hiding in the ravines, waiting for noon to attack, climbed out at his command. The moment they realised the danger they were in, the colonel and his men made an urgent about turn, pursued by the frontal point of Nxele's warriors. The chase would have been comical if it were not so tragic – the bullet-speed fury of the colonel and his men, chased by a few mounted Xhosas who were followed by the hordes of foot warriors. The warriors caught up with and killed a few of the foot soldiers, but the colonel and the rest of the mounted soldiers got away. The colonel later boasted, when he presented me with a dock-tailed roan as a sign of goodwill between us during one of our armistices, that the swiftness of his steed, Blucher, saved his life that day. "If you take care of your horse, groom it well, it'll be a loyal friend and take care of you."

'When the colonel and his men came galloping they raised the attention of their army. The carnage was about to begin. White troops, assisted by white farmers, shopkeepers and so on, assembled at the town's municipal building, which was built like a fort. Meanwhile, Nxele's warriors hared downhill. With their artillery, the whites formed laagers and waited. The street above the watercourse, next to the site now occupied by that stone church, was the major battleground. I narrowed my eyes and saw on the plains, through the haze of dust, that Nxele was whipping his followers into a frenzy with an animated speech, getting ready to cross the river to the town centre. Apparently, he even promised the aid of the spirits to assist the cause. "The spirits will countervail the boastful prowess of the white man's fire, turning their bullets into water!" they say he kept shouting in frenzy above the din. We heard the first British artillery thundering on the descending hordes. Battery fire raked Nxele's warriors. Shells flew with a roar. The destructive musketry didn't need to aim much to find targets. There were just too many warriors for any fire from white men to miss.

'Nxele had drawn his army into three columns. One column went for the municipal building on the west side. The main one went for the barracks, the first point of British defence in the middle, made up of mostly KhoiKhoi and amaMfengu. The Xhosas looked like a cloud of whirring hornets coming down, despite being raked by fire. On the first attack, across the river, they met up with Mfengus, whose location was between them and town. They passed through with relative ease when the Mfengus turned back to the safety of the municipal building, joining the laager of white people who were garrisoned there with armed troops.

'With no cover of darkness or forest, from there the warriors were sitting ducks as they charged. I couldn't help shouting to them from up on my hill, as though they could hear me: "Break up! Break up, you fools! Break up into little knots so the cannon shrapnel shells do not harvest you!" As if they had heard me, two columns went for the square, which was where the concentration of British fire was, and the other column

137

continued towards the barracks. Furthermore they broke into little knots of about fifty men as they charged. I was smiling and about to doff my hat at Nxele's sagacity when I discovered none of them had throwing spears. They had broken all their spears in anticipation of a close combat. How was he hoping to get a close combat against the British in broad daylight and under open field attack? The fool! How did he hope to get close to the enemy without the diversion of throwing spears? That was Nxele's second fatal error. While still thinking about that, I noticed that they had again organised themselves into continuous clusters in the firing line of the soldiers. Thus the real reign of terror began. I threw my hands on my head and turned away, but anxiety drew my eyes back into the massacre.

'All the soldiers needed to do was fire in the right direction and their shots found targets. Nxele and Mdushane were busy cheering the warriors into the muzzles of the soldiers' guns. When it was clear the warriors were falling in droves, unable to engage the enemy in close combat, butterflies fluttered in my stomach. My nerves tautened into little bundles. I would have given anything not to witness the slaughter, yet at the same time there was nothing I would not have given to witness it. It was only a matter of time before the Xhosas realised what was happening and turned back helter-skelter.

'The colonial force rallied behind their stone buildings, raining murderous fire over the warriors. Dust mixed with lilac smoke blinded me from seeing the gruesome action in detail. After the concentrated attack from the warriors I could see the firing from British soldiers slackening, which lit the fire of my hope. They must have been exhausted. They can't keep up their fire for long, I thought. The warriors are just too many, outnumbering the soldiers by more than a hundred to one. Then I noticed something that alarmed me more than anything else. The hired mercenaries of Boezak's elephant hunters were rushing along the river bank. Late did I notice what they were up to. Their marksmen were targeting and eliminating the chiefs one by one. Boezak was familiar with our ways. He knew that most of our people would lose courage once the chiefs fell. That made for the turning point of the battle. Most of the warriors lost courage. Believing they could not sustain the attack, when they saw their leaders fall wild panic set in. The majority retreated in disarray and confusion. A cheer went up from the soldiers and although the white people's garrison was by then already feeble, they fired with renewed alacrity. All the warriors needed to do was hold their attack. As they had been taken by surprise, the white people were bound to run out of ammunition. The warriors didn't think about taking advantage, however. In fact, I'm certain, had Nxele not promised them the assistance of the spirits they would not have been brave enough to stand on their own and fight it out. The warriors took the fall of their chiefs as a sign of dissatisfaction from the spirits and ancestors. It was this realisation that sowed confusion among them. They realised no spirits were coming to their assistance to turn the white man's bullets into water. All that was left was for individuals to save their own dear lives.

'The moment the warriors started retreating they fell like flies. More perished in that retreat than in the advance. Many leapt, wounded, trying to save themselves, into the Kowie ditch, where they were easily shot by the soldiers from the barracks. In vain did some try to conceal themselves by thick grass or weeds; the soldiers burnt the marshes and fired at anything that came out of it. As a result most of their bodies lay lifeless in the Kowie ditch. That was how the river got its name, Egazini, the place of blood. Many warriors died there that day. Ndlambe lost three of his sons.

'I surveyed the scene of slaughter a little before we left. Bodies with distorted faces lay hopelessly dead. The eyes of those who were still alive were drunk with pain. Crows and vultures were already wheeling in the red evening sky. To this day, the pines and firs in the area bow mournfully, remembering, perhaps, the bones that enrich that soil.'

Phila went down the slope with a heavy heart. The calm of the day had graduated into an inferno. Maqoma's voice was relentless.

'I felt terrible relief as the battle came to a close. I'm not sure I would have been able to stomach more. The carnage was too much and painfully one-sided. When the mournful hues of the evening shadows came upon the wounded, my men and I headed home. I was still struggling with weakness from my wounds. My legs wilting and drooping like stalks of crushed corn, they trembled as I mounted my horse. A stagnant scent of marsh dampness made my stomach heave. The scrunching sounds of horses' hooves crushing pine-cones made me sick. When the evening shadows deepened we camped on a coppice near a river bank somewhere – I can't remember which river. The iron planted by war took root in my heart that night. The chill of death was in the air. We took out corncobs from our leather carrier bags to cook and eat. I tried chewing and swallowing but it was difficult. Somebody passed me a peeled prickly-pear; the seeds were too hard for my weak jaws.

'Silence howled as we lay defeated against hope of ever prevailing against white men. At the break of dawn we prepared to leave. "We might find ourselves in awkward situations, my chief," said one of my escorts, meaning we might come across colonial patrols, or be surprised by feeding elephants that abounded the area. "We'll ride it anyway," I said, feeling agitated. We went through very steep and rocky cliffs into the thick of bushes. In the morning, the thunder of the white man's cannons resumed; we heard their stuttering shatter the anxious silence now and then through the trees. Branches lay crashed to the ground. They chased amaNdlambe all over the place; some more to protect their cattle. Luckily, none of them spotted us. We emerged from the woods with death laid on our shoulders like a sand-bag.

'One of my escorts sang softly against the bluish grey of the sky. His voice sounded comforting against the crumbling background of cannon fire. No matter what, we always have songs to comfort us, I thought to myself. The calm of the sky felt like an insult to our mood. The horses pricked their ears now and then as the thunder of gunfire reached us. Turning back I could see smoke hovering in the sky from a long way off and I knew in my discouraged heart that another black man had just fallen. Each cannon pound pulled in strained a muscle in my heart.

'The newly minted sun raised lazy swirls of mist over the hills. The wind travelled aimlessly across the scree. Clouds began to mass in the distance, shading the sky into a tender smoky lilac beyond the tops of the mountains. We proceeded cautiously, dashing for the protection of the woods whenever we heard the creak of wagon wheels or the rattle of stirrups. There's a run downhill before you reach upper Nxuba when you cross towards Double Drift. There we met up with elephants drinking water. We filled our calabashes before fording the river, knee-deep, towards a very steep hill. My horse slid on an elephant carcass and nearly dropped me. Only the tusks had been gouged out by the hunters; they had left the carcass to rot. The mischief of white people followed us everywhere.

'The river disappeared around a sand bend and parted ways with us. We proceeded by way of hills, rugged and bold. Baboons looked down at us from hanging cliffs, howling and barking in derisive banter: "Baagoom! Baa! Baargoom! Boorg! Baa!" Whenever they got too close for our comfort we cracked the whip to scare them off. Curious hyenas came to investigate, laughed and lost interest when they discovered we were not stranded.

'One of my escorts managed to shoot a porcupine, which made for a great roast in the evening. We bivouacked at the foot of a cliff with a challenge of hyraxes rolling rocks down at us in their migrations. We fed our horses oats, stolen from white farmers, and ate bitter lemongrass, which grew wild on the river banks. The proliferation of orchards of oranges, lemons, figs and other strange fruits amazed me as we passed towards the eMthontsi forests. White people were working the land. Ostriches roamed the plains with steady strides. When we reached the place where Fort Willshire was eventually built to threaten our villages, I was dog tired. A ramshackle of colonial buildings was already starting to go up there. We avoided attention. In time, it became a scene of enterprise, women with bundles on their heads and babies on their backs, head turbans and skin mantles trimmed with buttons and beads, assembled under the trees that surrounded the fort. Bartering was taking place in a cacophony of loud strange languages, giving the impression of a flock of vultures over the dead carcass of an elephant. I became weary of the nature of things.

'By the time I reached my house I was gnawed by black potencies and ineffable weariness. I could see the concern and questions in the eyes of my followers. What now? I had no answers. My mind lost its clarity. I admitted none of my wives into my hut that night. There was a feverish cloud of mental stress in my mind. I took the tin of fat with a piece of rag for a wick to light as a lamp. It had been a gift from the Governor to replace the thin smoky strips of wood we lit for light. A moth buzzed around the flame with nauseating insistence. Pallid ash gleamed from the hearth fire. Disturbing thoughts crawled through my mind like snakes. I can never completely delineate the depth of bitterness I felt that day.

'The Battle of Nxele convinced me once and for all that it was futile, suicidal, to engage white people on open plains. We had to come up with some better tactics if we wanted to engage them successfully. It became clear in my mind that in warfare with white people you have to hit and run on forested battlefields. Ambush was the best tactic against their murdering fire. The best time for attack would be when it rained, because their muskets did not work properly then, and their wagons were not as swift. Or at night, when they could not see you from a distance. White soldiers were useless in the forests, especially without the KhoiKhoi and the Mfengus as guides. These thoughts went through my mind as I lay on my mat that evening.

'After the colonial government vanquished amaNdlambe and amaGcaleka, white people followed after their remnants like a disease. Instead of falling on his assegai like a coward, Nxele did the manly thing. He first held a ceremony at Gompo to invoke the rising assistance of the shadows, the ancestor spirits he claimed would help our nation. People gathered there overnight with lit fires and slaughtered beasts. Again the ancestors failed to show up.

'Still defiant of the white man's rule, Nxele surrendered himself, with his two wives, to save the nation, since white people were not going to be satisfied until they captured him. He handed himself to the white authorities, not crestfallen, but boasting that he would be back with the River People to deliver our people from serfdom. The white government took him to the colony of lepers; banished him to be damned by howling winds.

'People believed Nxele would come back soon, would come back victorious. The news spread through our villages like wildfire. His personal belongings were preserved in expectation of his return. Mqantsi, the rainmaker, kept Nxele's fire burning. When the rains were late in coming he blamed it on missionaries and urged people to drive them away. He held rainmaking ceremonies at different river spots, discouraging people from going to the missions at the threat of lightning. But nothing much came out of his ceremonies. The drought continued.

'Then people went to the missionaries, who were rich in harvest because they employed irrigation schemes to water their fields. The nation had to wait for Mlanjeni to gain another witch-doctor close to the powers Nxele wielded during that difficult period. Even he, Mlanjeni, gained authority and power from the support of Nxele's son Mjuza, who kept the faith that revived the 1850 war, which became known as Mlanjeni's War.'

Phila, plagued by thoughts of Nxele and unsettled by Maqoma's words, absent-mindedly walked through the black township of Fingo.

Like all other South African townships, it was a ramshackle conglomoration of tin houses and spaza shops, with occasional government buildings – schools, clinics, a post office, a police station – and a proliferation of *shis'inyama* shebeen spots, all swept by dusty poverty and buoyant misery. He felt *sich verfahren* again, losing his way, looking for a foot to stand on, driven by *Unruhe*. The more he walked the louder the clanking of his father's armour sounded. He didn't even know what he was looking for, or if the township, with its soft violence of poverty, was even aware of its tragic history.

Ntsikana

THE WALK AROUND FINGO MADE PHILA awake to the scratchings of his dust, his complicity in the nature of things. He found himself longing to hear Nandi's voice.

"Hey!" Nandi answered her phone.

"Hello! I'm in town. I thought I would give you a ring." Phila was slightly hesitant.

"I figured. You never do unless."

"You make me feel bad."

"Oh, it's not an accusation. I'd be worried something was wrong. It's your nature. It is what it is."

"Listen, I was wondering if you wanted to go out for dinner or something tonight? You could show me around?"

"That would be lovely, if you don't mind company. A few of my friends already made plans to go out. In fact I think you would love to meet them. We're celebrating a production of a play one of them wrote."

"Cool. I'll be at your place in twenty minutes or so. Would love to have a shower first."

"Perfect!"

The apartment building Nandi lived in was a sort of old Chelsea style, the houses interconnecting, distinguishable by the interchange of wooden French shutters painted different colours – green, blue, purple and white. Each apartment had a small garden with a lawn in front. Nandi had planted flowers along the paved path to the door. The walls were weather hardened by ingrained sandblast – British style: something done to prevent dampness from penetrating internal walls during the epoch when cavity walls were not yet invented. The house had a pleasing Victorian feel about it.

Nandi gave him a brush kiss after she had opened the door for him. She was dressed in blue and white traditional Xhosa *umbhaco*. When she noticed the surprise on Phila's face she explained.

"We're going to an Ethiopian restaurant so I decided on traditional wear." She frowned, feigning seriousness.

"I don't have anything traditional to wear," Phila protested.

"Yes, you do. I bought you a shirt when I collected my dress from the seamstress." She led him to the bedroom, took out the shirt from the wardrobe. "You see, you're not the only one psychic here."

Phila smiled at her, then took off his clothes and jumped in the shower.

A low moon serviced the night, drawing the evening away from dusk into deeper night as they walked to the restaurant. The air was typical for middle of winter in the Cape, clear with a polished steel kind of coldness. The white dots of *umbhaco* on Nandi's face glowed against the moonlight. She looked happy and this made Phila feel happy; somehow he managed to escape the feeling of constriction inside. He restrained the urge to talk about the wounds of the past as they passed the stone cathedral in the city square. The healthy openness of the streets was a shock to his mind after his afternoon of wandering the streets of Fingo, with the impression it gave of a slum, of many people living in a small, congested space.

The resturant had the simplicity of a student canteen, with gingham checkered tablecloths and citronella oil table lamps to repel mosquitoes. They were seated at a table in the garden section, under a tent canopy, with gas heaters on every corner. It was Grahamstown Festival time and the place was buzzing with visitors. Phila was pleased to discover they were the first of their group to arrive; he preferred receiving than being received. He ordered a double whisky and asked for a glass of water when the waiter came – a jovial young person they later discovered was a music student at the university. Nandi ordered a glass of sauvignon blanc.

"Why would they have tables, not cushions in an Ethiopian restaurant?" Phila wondered aloud.

"Can you imagine white people eating on their sides?"

"Why not? Romans used to."

First to arrive was Rebecca, or Becca as everyone called her. Phila didn't catch how Nandi knew her but apparently she was in the legal department. Nandi introduced him as a childhood friend.

"Who's crashing the party. Sorry about that." Phila stood up, extending his hand to greet Rebecca. He also took the opportunity to order another double when the waiter came with dumpling bread, asking Rebecca what she would like.

"I'll have a single of what he's having."

"You sure?" Phila said. "It's Singleton, rather peaty. Perhaps you want something Irish?" Even as he said it Phila felt it was rather presumptuous of him.

"I prefer Scotch actually," answered Rebecca, who didn't seem to mind his forwardness.

Luckily the last of their crew arrived at that moment. Phila had a bad habit of not catching a guy's name while never forgetting his face, and never remembering a woman's face from a first encounter but never forgetting her name. So when the bespectacled philologist professor, who had written the play that was being staged the following day at the opening of the festival, kept chatting to him he felt embarrassed for not retaining his name after they'd been introduced. The boyfriend had Nordic features and a brogue, which most probably meant he was Scottish. He was more circumspect than his partner. After everyone had ordered the professor came back to Phila.

"Nandi tells us you're an architect? What would you say is your specialisation?" He made it sound confrontational rather than a friendly way to pass time. Phila decided to indulge him.

"Only TV show architects can afford to be specialists, or at least only the well-to-do ones. The rest of us take whatever jobs we can find."

"But what was your thesis on at school?" He was probably Phila's age, or younger, so Phila was taken aback by the insolence in his voice until he connected the dots. He was probably a friend of Nandi's married lover.

"Frank Gehry," answered Phila, making an effort to be polite but not go so far as to elaborate.

"Oh yes? Why Gehry?"

It was Nandi who started shifting restlessly in her seat. Phila smiled, took a swipe of his drink, and asked if anybody minded if he had a cigarette. The professor minded so he put his pack back in his pocket.

"Well, it was more like Gehry chose me than the other way round. Frank, like me, grew up with the legacy of fishing from his dad. It made him interested in curvilinear forms. Hence you see most of his buildings are that way, like a fish in motion."

"And they have scales for walls," Nandi added playfully.

"Yes. He's probably the leader of the movement of putting art and playfulness back into architecture. This does not entail building structures only, but public spaces, interior designs, furniture and so forth. I am interested in that sort of thing. And he can hold his own as the poet not just of structures, but words and concepts also. He does not seem to distinguish between poetry, philosophy and the theology of the environment ..."

"Theology of the environment?"

"I'm not drunk enough to discuss that. Suffice to say that some of us believe there's a theology to the environment, which we violate at our peril."

They changed the topic to the reason for the gathering – the play the professor had written, and which he described as a hybrid of Western sensibility and Xhosa history and culture. It sounded interesting, if vague conceptually, so Phila decided to reserve his opinion until he'd seen it. Rebecca excused herself for a smoke break – "Since we're not allowed to smoke at the table." Phila liked her a lot but decided not to follow, for the sake of Nandi, if not the professor. When Rebecca came back the table conversation had bisected. There was Rebecca and the blonde partner talking about drama and acting – he was a postgrad drama student – and Nandi with the professor deep in analysis about the points in the play the professor thought would resonate with the white audience and those with the black. Phila stood to go to the toilet, passed the bar for another double shot and went outside onto the pavement for a smoke. He came back when he saw their waiter carry the *gebeta* to their table. When he was seated Nandi broke a piece of *injera*, scooped up the paprika goat stew, and smiled at him. "*Gursha!*"

Phila gobbled it down. The wild earthiness of the taste was amazing.

The professor got bored, confirming Phila's suspicions. "Why don't the two of you get a room?" he suggested.

Phila was amused. As if to make amends, the professor tried to turn the conversation back to Phila's profession. "When you look at the spatial videography here do you see any difference to the apartheid years?" he asked, while Rebecca seemed to be continuing a different line of conversation, which had probably been interrupted by the arrival of food and which Phila had been half listening to.

"Well, the majority of the students are black, for one. And we have black judges at the High –"

"If you have ten students, eight black and two white, then the university admits only five, and chooses the two white students and another three from the eight black students. Would you call that a majority and fair?" Nandi interjected.

"If they were all chosen through merit. Meritocracy is what we strive for in a democratic system."

"Not justice?" asked a visibly angry Nandi

"Meritocracy is a major part of justice."

Phila read between the lines these were probably common arguments among this crew and so he decided to stay out of it. It went on for a while until they finished eating. He went outside for another smoke break, returning just as the waiter was serving the pot of Ethiopian coffee he'd asked for. The professor asked if he could try it and he lifted the *jebena* before Phila, who had been going to suggest putting a strainer on the spout to reduce the ashyness for a beginner, could stop him.

"It's salty!" protested the professor.

"Yes, they pinch it with salt to release the flavours."

"Not my cup of tea – or coffee," the professor grumbled, and they all laughed as he wiped his tongue in exaggeration. "What about you, old chap?" he said, moving his attention once more to Phila. "Do you also think desegregation has achieved nothing?"

"I wouldn't go as far as that. But there's no arguing with the point that the apartheid spatial geography has hardly changed."

"But surely you can see that the suburbs are filling up with the black middle class?" he asked.

Phila looked at him, thinking the question was in jest, only to discover the professor was being earnest. "I think what black people resent in this Mandela's rainbow reconciliation thing is that it came at the greater price of justice, thus only ending up being a catharsis for white people and nothing much else. If you ask me, the people who got the rawest end of the stick are the black middle class. Because they joined institutions that were designed for white people, bringing with them ninety per cent of being black problems, while in reality being barred from eighty per cent of white privilege. They have to straddle the divide, making themselves a nuisance to both sides."

"But surely we can't blame the institutions for that, or call it racism?" The professor wasn't giving up on his course of thinking.

"Oh, I agree. I don't think it's racism, not the overt kind anyway. It is just that the whites have not adjusted to the situation of living with blacks on equal terms, without having authority or hegemony over them. The black people sense this, and resent it. I think that's where we are in our generation, just over a dozen years into democracy. Of course, the truth of the matter is that the refusal of most institutions to transform means, despite the freedom rhetoric and all, the white male in particular still has authority and hegemony over most. Most white people sense this also, and according to their individual characters, it either embarrasses them or emboldens them."

"Let's just say I am not conversant with your thinking somehow. It is getting late. We need to get going. Big day tomorrow."

The professor called for the bill but the women indicated to the waiter that the night was on them, to help him celebrate. He thanked them, then took the hand of his lover and they left.

The air was nippy by the time they left the resturant, the stars more resplendent in the black sky, and the crickets chirping and the moon shepherding them as Phila and Nandi walked back to the flat.

Suddenly there was the clip-clop sound of horseshoes on a road and then a horse pulling a carriage passed them at a saunter.

Phila, who was rather drunk by now, pulled Nandi to a halt by the arm. "Please tell me you saw that," he said.

"Of course I saw it."

"A horse and carriage?"

"It's a circular service offered to night-time lovers. The ride starts at the university lawns and goes to the city square. A round trip will cost you R150."

"So ... do you want to ...?"

"Really? I never took you for the type!"

"No! I don't care about the rubbish ride. I just thought it was one of ... you know ... my visions."

They both laughed.

"And I was thinking they're even getting funnier because I could have sworn the horse was wearing diapers."

They both burst out laughing again, Phila laughing so hard that he couldn't continue walking. He stopped and sat down to catch his breath, while Nandi, tears of laughter rolling down her cheeks, sank down next to him.

"They wear the diapers because the municipality fines them for the droppings if they don't clean up after the horse," she explained, still chortling, which made Phila start laughing all over again. After a while he caught Nandi's face fixed on his in silence. He became quiet. They kissed. And kissed again.

"It's been a while since I've seen your laughing face," said Nandi as they stood to resume their walk.

"It's been a while since I've heard something to laugh about."

Just as they were crossing the last street Phila mock marched the goose step, reciting a Rilke poem:

Berge ruhn, von Sternen überprächtigt;

aber auch in ihnen flimmert Zeit.
Ach, in meinem wilden Herzen nächtigt
obdachlos die Unvergänglichkeit.

Nandi stopped, bending down and laughing with her hands on her mouth. "Do that again," she begged.

"You look so sexy when you do that."

Phila crossed the street back to Nandi, again reciting the poem, but this time in English:

Mountains rest beneath a splendour of stars;
but even in them time flickers.
Ah, unsheltered in my wild,
darkling heart lies immortality.

"No, no! I want it in German," Nandi said. "With the accent. I like it more when I don't understand what you're saying."

Phila bent down to kiss her more. They crossed the street hand in hand.

Nandi opened the door after a jingle of keys. She went to the kitchen, while Phila went to the living room to connect his iPod to the music system. He felt like the blues. Nandi came back with two glasses of whisky – one neat and another with an ice block and soda water. She handed the neat one to Phila as the song began.

"Oh no! Not sad music. I thought we were playing happy tonight."

"Sad? Blues, sad? Where do you get such a notion? Blues is what Albert Murray calls the 'music for good times earned in adversity'. It is the tool of the muse that feeds the subconscious. The blues, man."

Phila took Nandi by the waist to slowly dance to the shrill old voice that was recorded on American plantations.

O Lawd, de cotton am so grassy, de work am so hard, and de sun am so hot dat I b'lieve dis darky am called to preach!

As they moved they found themselves humming along to the banjo rhythm.

"The blues, man, is the sigh of God in human spirit," Phila softly murmured on Nandi's neck. "It is the testimony of the indomitable human spirit under a black skin. The blues, man. How can you call the blues sad?" They were still dancing slow, and Phila was almost whispering in Nandi's ear. "The blues is not a cry of those too dumb to avoid strife, as the slave masters thought in the plantations. The blues is the response of human spirit to the fallen nature of man; a burning smoke of the transcendental spirit to its maker. Not a cry of the one who has lost control. The blues is the power of control by the one who has lost hope in human affairs but keeps discipline to the promised hope of the divine. The blues finds all tools, including music and language, inadequate; the spirit strips bare to become the blues. The blues is the condition of hope for the hopeless and the price the spirit pays to rise to higher consciousness. The blues – shit, man! The blues ..."

The song ended and they sat on the sofa. Nandi lay down with her head on Phila's lap, who was seeing diamonds against the lights.

@

"What is the name of his play again?" Phila asked as they left the flat to go to the theatre.

"*Thuthula wamaRharhabe.*"

"Interesting." Phila's emotional nausea, mixed with the babalaza from the evening before, quickened with the busy festival streets.

"We can watch something else if you like?"

"*Thuthula* is fine." Phila cut her short, like a blade that went through his own heart too.

They walked on in silence, Phila too fast and Nandi deliberately strolling.

"Are you coming?" Phila turned round, frowning.

"Are we in a hurry?" Nandi, dawdling, gave him an amused smile. His moods always amused instead of irritated her.

Phila knew he was being silly and unreasonable but could not help himself. He continued at his moody pace.

The town was a warren of marketplaces and bars. The closer they got to the taxi rank, the more crowded the streets became. Phila, irritated with everything now, turned to look for Nandi. He could not see her. It was only then that it occurred to him that he didn't actually know the way to the theatre. He asked the first person he thought would know and was informed that he had passed it about four blocks back. It irritated him further to find Nandi waiting for him at the entrance with a sarcastic smile on her face. They went and sat in the cafeteria without really talking to each other. Phila ordered an Americano, and Nandi a skinny latté. He regretted not having enough foresight to bring a book or something to while away the twenty minutes before the show. He had lost interest a while ago in the vacuous gossip of newspapers. Another complication developed after he finished his coffee. There was no way he was going to ask Nandi where the toilets were and conflate her already ballooned ego. He stood to walk left, hoping to meet someone he could ask for toilet directions.

"The toilets are that way," said Nandi, pointing in the opposite direction he was heading.

He wanted to deflate her by telling her he wasn't looking for the toilet but he knew it was pointless. She knew him well enough to know that coffee always went straight through him.

"We might as well go in," she said with irritating smugness when he got back. He plotted her downfall in his mind as they walked into the swallowing dark of the theatre.

Half an hour into the show Phila heard a familiar voice.

'This is not what happened,' Maqoma whispered. 'They're making Ndlambe seem innocent in the whole thing.'

'You and your beef with Ndlambe,' Phila whispered back. He felt Nandi turn to look at him.

'Ndlambe was a cunning man. He had no designs for giving up power when Ngqika came of age.

'He assured his rule by a prodigality of generous gestures.'

'Could we talk about it later on?' Phila replied in a quiet voice, feeling uneasy, although by now he should have known better.

'Ndlambe made himself colourful in the eyes of the people, bribing them by relaxing things like cattle fines and so forth. He wanted to live in their mouths even after death. These people are showing none of that.'

'From what I heard,' Phila whispered fiercely, 'Ndlambe was a good chief. Which is more than can be said for your father, Ngqika, especially when he was young. Ndlambe fortified his chieftainship by driving the menacing chiefdoms west of the Fish River, like the Gqunukhwebe.'

'Why did people want him out then?' Maqoma hissed.

'Because they were superstitious and thought it bad luck not to be led by a blood chief.'

'Ndlambe was a divisive menace.'

'And besides, he was like a father to Ngqika, raised him. And Ngqika betrayed him by sleeping with one of his wives – Thuthula.'

'Fathers do not try to steal crowns away from their children, or get infatuated with their girlfriends. Thuthula was Ngqika's girlfriend first. They were sweethearts growing up.

'Ndlambe got infatuated with her and put her into his seraglio, tried to legitimise it by calling her his wife to spite Ngqika.'

'Too many versions about this story of Thuthula for my liking.'

'Oh, but she was a beauty, with a calm face no man ever grew tired of. Ndlambe seduced her. That sowed the seed of our tribal destruction. When Ngqika reclaimed his woman other chiefs saw it as immoral, saying it was like taking his mother to bed. That was how Ndlambe manufactured support for himself. War broke out. Ndlambe was defeated and taken prisoner by Ngqika. When he was a prisoner his followers smuggled messages of rebellion, telling Ndlambe to, "Always keep your leopardskin and goats in sight," because they would be rescuing him soon. In due time they stole him in a daring act that led to daylight combat against the few guards assigned to hold him. Ndlambe and his followers fled across iNxuba.'

'And thus amaNdlambe, your perpetual nemesis, were formed.'

'A little more complicated than that, but yes. And about two winters before our last war with amaNdlambe, a cloud of locusts covered our land like a blanket of doom, making the skies quake with their sinister whirring wings. Those nefarious insects devoured the whole year's harvest in a matter of days. The diviners, ever ready to allocate evil to nature's idiosyncrasies, saw in them an omen of terrible things to come. They attributed this to the incestuous relationship Ngqika had entered into with Thuthula. They said by becoming bewitched with Thuthula he had allowed a curse upon the tribe. "Calamities we know," they said. "This is not a calamity but a curse." To exacerbate the situation Ngqika's youthful lack of prudence made him sack most of the councillors who were critical of him. He abolished Mxhamli from office and created what today we call *ixhiba*, a corporate body of councillors. Mostly these were made up of his lackeys. He laid grievous yoke upon the people, introducing things like seignorial taxes on domestic stock, wanting to acquire the inheritance of all commoners who died without heirs in their direct line, and so forth. As a result more disgruntled people crossed iNxuba to follow Ndlambe.'

'Verily!' Phila attempted sarcasm by mocking Maqoma's pattern of speech. 'There're only a handful of stories, and even those are just variations on legends and folklore.'

The lights came on. It was interval. Maqoma was nowhere to be seen.

Nandi and Phila filed outside with the rest of the patrons. They sat at the bar, where three of Nandi's colleagues joined them, the bespectacled professor and his partner from the previous evening and a skinny looking redhead, as the waitress delivered their drinks. Phila was slightly disappointed Rebecca hadn't made it. Because she was born in Maine, in the US, they had started talking about shad fishing towards the end of dinner and he'd have liked to continue that conversation.

"So how is the play so far?" the professor was eager to know, although as it turned out the man seemed far more interested in telling them his opinion of the public reception than hearing theirs. When he finally stopped talking, Phila tried to think of something interesting to say about the play but couldn't really come up with anything substantial. Quoting Maqoma he said: "There are some historical inaccuracies, but the humour makes up for them."

"It's a play, not a documentary," the professor said, rather rudely, with a grin. Then he went on, without irony, to teach Phila about what he called the "inner life of Xhosa culture". Phila remembered the dude had been introduced as a philologist. He had unified theories that were supposed to explain everything. He decided, for Nandi's sake, to be polite.

"I hear what you say," he said, "but the major error is not in humanising history, but in misrepresenting known facts."

Phila glanced over at the Xhosa royal house representatives who had been invited to the opening, and who were at a table close to theirs. They were deep in discussion and he wondered what they were saying.

"You people need to learn to differentiate between drama and history," the professor persisted. He had a voice like a bassoon.

Phila, as usual, switched off after the "you people" thing and took advantage of the lull created by the returning waitress to change the topic. "I'll have another double," he said, gulping down the remains of his first.

The professor raised his bushy eyebrows. "We're certainly fond of our Russian Mule, aren't we?" he said.

"Leave him be, he's better company when he's had a few," Nandi said.

The situation felt irredeemable now in Phila's mind, and as such the professor's sarcasm didn't affect him. But knowing that Nandi was addressing him through the professor – this offended him.

"I'd like a glass of white wine, please," Nandi ordered without looking at the waitress, but keeping a steady eye on Phila.

"You seem fidgety, Phila," said the professor, tightening the screw.

"I've a lot on my mind," answered Phila, feeling Nandi's eyes on him.

"Nandi tells me you've some problems – somatic delusions, I think?"

Phila wasn't fooled by the mock pretence of care in the man's voice. He shot a look at Nandi, more in disappointment than anger. There and then, something broke between them. Nandi was looking down, in shame and mounting anger against her colleague. Phila knew better than to take the bait, so he kept quiet as he sipped his drink, and the group changed the subject. At Nandi's insistence, they began instead to scrutinise the play. It baffled Phila to learn that, "The script was written in the shade of Plato's moving image of eternity ..." and that it spoke of "death as the Freudian aim of life and desire to return to the safety of the mother's womb ..."

After a while of this, he felt an attack of Kafkaesque anxiety, looking now and then for an appropriate moment to say something so as not to be regarded as boring. He wanted to be neutral without being hostile. The problem, he thought to himself, was that you had to be rudely assertive to speak in such groups.

Nandi looked at him. "You're awfully quiet, Phila?"

"I'm keeping watch over the dead."

There was uneasy laughter around the table.

To cope, Phila assigned a theme song to the babblings as he drifted into his own dark corner – Duke Ellington's *Mood Indigo*. Henceforth he wore an idiotic smile, occasionally nodding, pretending to be impressed with their talk.

In no time Maqoma came to fill in the gaps. Phila was surprised at how relieved he was to hear Maqoma's voice. It also concerned him that perhaps he was not just becoming anti-social but was crossing the divide, becoming more at home with the dead than the living.

'That was just about the time Ntsikana came to our tribe. Ntsikana had been born of our tribe before his father, Gaba, left with the faction that followed Ndlambe. He got into trouble for disputing Nxele's prophecies among amaNdlambe.

'Ntsikana openly disputed prophecies that ran with the bent of Nxele on authority "of the thing that had possessed me, stirring against things Nxele is saying". The thing was telling Ntsikana that the "Cape Corps would destroy Xhosa warriors with gunfire if they went to war with white people." Ntsikana painted such a gruesome picture of death that most people were relieved just to get rid of him, as though he was the carrier of the deaths he was prophesying. This hoisted Nxele's petard among amaNdlambe. Ntsikana came to us in disgrace when Nxele's followers made it extremely difficult for him to stay.'

'Your times were quite confusing.'

'Yes! It is told that one day Ntsikana woke up early, as was his custom, to watch the sunrise. He saw the rays of the sun leaning strangely against the entrance of his hut. When he came close they came to rest on him. "Do you see what I'm seeing?" Ntsikana asked his servant boy, who was separating calves from heifers in front of his house. The confused boy replied in the negative. Three times Ntsikana asked the boy and three times he got the same answer. The rays left Ntsikana, proceeding to the cattle enclosure, where they came to rest on his favourite ox, where they stayed for about as long as they'd stayed on him. Ntsikana sat next to his kraal for a long time contemplating these happenings.

'At the hour when the sun reaches its highest peak, Ntsikana went inside his hut to prepare for a tribal dance taking place in the village that afternoon. When he left for the dance he was still feeling a little queasy.

At the tribal dance, an uncanny spirit carried him into a mild trance. The moment he recovered he stopped and sat down, feeling queasier. He recovered when the spirit momentarily left him. Having caught his breath and feeling better, he stood up to dance again. The same thing happened. Three times this happened, until he gave up and called his entourage to accompany him home. When they were about to cross the river he had an irresistible impulse to cleanse himself. Stooping over the waters, he washed the ochre off his face, threw his beautiful leopardskin kaross away and demanded they give him something less pretentious. People were astonished. They asked: "What has fallen over Norhongo, the heifer that stints its milk?"

'Ntsikana answered them by saying, "There's an insistent voice within me that says, 'Let there be prayer! Let everything bow its knees to Dal'ubomi.'

'When they reached the house Ntsikana told them again about, "The thing that has entered me, commanding me and all of you to pray ceaselessly. It tells me we must convert from our sinful ways and not listen to that liar, Nxele, who is misguiding people." His thought developed away from Nxele's and moved closer to Christianity, which caused him a lot of troubles in Ndlambe's land as Nxele then was at the peak of his power.'

'And you guys, amaNgqika, distrusted Ntsikana also, thinking he must be Ndlambe's spy when he came to you.'

'Exactly! He spread the prophecy thing too thickly for my liking, screaming all the time that, "The people are being lied to by Nxele at Ndlambe's place." I thought it was one of Ndlambe's ploys.'

'But Ngqika trusted him?'

'Well, my father's credulity took Ntsikana to heart from the start. By taking Ntsikana under his protection he also brought us more to the centre of the controversy.'

'And then Ntsikana went around converting people to Christianity?'

'Which made me hate him more.

'His first converts were the councillors of our courts, men like Noyi and Soga, the grandfather of your friend Zisani.'

'Zisani? You mean Tiyo?'

'His name is Zisani. It was his mother, who fell under Ntsikana's influence, who named him Tiyo – after Nyengane.'

'Oh … Van der Kemp's name was Theodore … hence Tiyo? In the manner the Xhosas like to Xhosa-ise English words?'

'Exactly. Soga's father, Jotello, was my coeval. When my father married Ntsikana to Soga's sister Nomkhini, I knew we were done for. Soga was one of my father's trusted courtiers, who had secretly been given the task of investigating Ntsikana's sayings. I was impressed by my father's sagacity in this matter until I discovered that Soga was already a convert of Ntsikana's. Where's the sense in sending the convert to investigate the converter? The whole thing was rigged.

'As I expected, Soga came back on fire with Ntsikana's religion, and wasted no time proselytising too. My father, wavering, spineless character that he was by then, became one of the initial converts. I almost despaired for our tribe. They handed Ntsikana a dwelling place near Soga's, between the villages of Thwathwa and Mankazana, which was subsequently called a sacred place. From there Ntsikana took hold of Ngqika's palace, from the royal palace at Tyumi and Gwali to beyond Nciba. We were everywhere plagued with kaffir pseudo-Christians, people turning to the "Word". When Soga came to report to my father he said: "The Word has given birth out of our rocks. KwaGqoboka rocks are flowing water, the desert has given birth to rivers in the wilderness." I could have easily killed him but for my father's credulity. The Ngqikas were possessed.'

'You must admit, though, that Ntsikana's teaching had a moral effect on the land.'

'Granted. Men whose lives had been base and dissolute changed their habits and punctiliously practised the duties of the tribe. Everyone talked about belonging to Ntsikana's denomination. They spoke in mystical fashion about the thing that had entered them, preaching the message that people should pray so that sins might be forgiven, while pointing to "the great … who art in heaven". People spent their days praying on mountaintops with Ntsikana. He composed songs, one of which they called *Thou Art Thou*. Let me remember how it went:

Thou art Thou.
The stronghold of Truth.

Thou art Thou.
The thicket of Truth.
Thou art Thou.
Who dwellest in the highest ...
Who created birds and certain kinds of animals.

'And they would name birds like doves and eagles; land animals like gazelles and lions; sea creatures like fishes and dolphins. Then the song went: *You who's not like Satan, who in trying to create birds came out with bats and owls ...* And so forth and so forth. It was madness. As people sang they tilted their heads and their eyes rolled back to give an impression of what they called a holy trance. The whole thing spread like fire fanned by a strong wind on dry grass. Conversion was the *dernier cri*. My concern was that it created a loophole for white preachers to infiltrate our villages, and commoners to disregard their chiefs. I was ready to follow the example of my mentor, Rharhabe, by letting amaNgqika go to the dogs; leave with my own followers, amaJingqi, to start afresh somewhere far away. The only problem was that there was nowhere for me to go. What land other tribes did not occupy was taken by the insatiable demand of white people.'

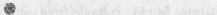

Phila's head was pounding. The din at their table, where everyone seemed to be talking at once and at cross-purposes, made him tired and the place was hot and crowded. He decided to get away from them and attempt a conversation with the entourage of the Xhosa royalty in the far corner. He went across and introduced himself as a journalist who was interested in doing an in-depth interview about the opinions of the chiefs regarding the play. They pointed him to a young man with fair skin and leopardskin band on his head. When the king stood to greet Phila his bodyguard-cum-praise-singer rose first in praise.

"*Ah Nkosiyamntu!*"

The king wore an expensive suit, along Gucci lines. He set Phila at ease, appearing relieved to be rescued from whatever it was his group was discussing. The two of them were of the same age and similar views. They actually hit it off very quickly, mostly talking about the pleasures of travel across the European continent. The king was an economist who had studied in Oxford. He told Phila he was in love with a Scottish girl whom he could not marry because of his royal duties. Phila chose not to probe.

He was fascinated by the king's knowledge of Xhosa history and promised to visit him for a more in-depth conversation.

Just then the bell, ending the interval, was rung. They exchanged contact details and Phila went to rejoin his own entourage after expressing gratitude to the royal group for allowing him to intrude.

He was hardly back in his seat in the auditorium when Maqoma, seemingly pressed to end his own narrative, was at it again.

'Meantime Ntsikana founded his own clan, amaCirha, which was growing at an alarming rate. His wife's people, amaJwarha, were also foremost in the conversion and became the new royals of amaNgqika. Almost all of them belonged to Ntsikana's new movement. I've often thought about what it was that made people so receptive to Ntsikana's message. In those days people were desperate because it was clear the chiefs had no answer to white people's encroachment. White people had come with strange diseases we had no cure for. Drought was also prevalent. All these things made people gullible to the supernatural. But more than this, Ntsikana's strength lay in his flashes of divine milieu, unfurling the immensity of things to come. He had, for instance, foretold the coming of two nations in our midst: one from the west and another from the east. He foretold that the English, "Would be white as the sun, with golden flowing hair like cobwebs from maize ears. And they will bring with them a button with no hole." The button – which was money, of course – was a conflict bringer, said Ntsikana. "Our nation must be careful not to adopt its habits." He said the white people would also bring a book "with a red mouth" containing "the word". By this, as we came to know, he meant the Word of God. "We must listen to the word. Accept the word," said Ntsikana. "Your land will be filled with wagons, wire-fenced kraals and mimosa-thorn paddocks. The sites of your villages will be grazing sites for flocks of sheep. Don't fight with the Word. Nxele is a liar. He is misleading people." So went Ntsikana's prophecies and all of them came true. "Even when you've faltered, Sifuba-Sibanzi will bring you back from the mountains where your skulls shall crush against rocks and be eaten by ants." We did not have long before that prophecy was to come true – at the Battle of Amalinde, which I already narrated to you.'

Nandi passed a packet of wine gums to Phila. He took two and returned the packet. Instead of taking it she held onto Phila's hand. Phila tried to break out of his mind world but Maqoma held just as tightly.

'On the day of Ntsikana's death his ox came home early from the grazing fields and bellowed melancholically around the house. People tried to chase it away, saying it was a bad omen, but Ntsikana remonstrated with them. He said if it had vocal cords it would sing a dirge for him. "It is doing all this to pave my departure. You must not eat that bull when it dies." With that he entered the world of his ancestors after a long sickness.

'*Awu! Madoda!* The grass rustles when a tall tree falls! The tree falls on it and it rustles!

'Before Ntsikana died he employed people to build him a coffin from uMhlungu wood. He often visited the site of its construction to measure if he fitted in it. People found this behaviour strange but tolerated it because it was Ntsikana. Subsequently, everyone wanted to be buried in coffins. On his deathbed Ntsikana called his bosom friend Soga, the son of Jotela, and admonished him to educate his sons Kobe and Dukwana. He pleaded with him to leave with both their families for the missionary area near UmGwali where uNyengane had been given permission by Ngqika to start a school. The younger boy was called umSimelelo, the one before that Mfundo (educated in knowledge). They all went for white man's education with the Sogas. I also sent my children to learn the white man's ways in Cape Town, even as I desperately fought them against taking our land.

'Having looked deep, in an affectionate manner, on both his wives (the white people gave up trying to convince him to give up one of his wives), he said, "When I uprooted these ladies from their father's kraal I swore an oath that I'd love, protect and nurture them. My blood and theirs now is the same. I do not intend to go back on my word. If this is an error, I'm prepared to answer for it before uQamata.

'Ntsikana closed his eyes. With that umCirha of Qangqolo, uNyembezana, the son of Gaba, kicked the bucket. *Awu*! The frost lay over the pelt of Gaba's bull, *mfondini*! The messenger of the leeward side of truth, whom even the whites could not confuse. He refused to renounce his second wife, Nontsonta, umQocokazi. As a result even today her resting place is on the side of Nyembezana. The greatest prophet the Xhosa nation has ever had.

'I can still see the son of Gaba in one of his mystical dances – singing, rejoicing, leaping into the air, crying out. "Ki-ki! Ki-ki!" Ah! Such times will never come to this land again. Give me a piece from the bark of *umthi wamaphupha*, the tree of dreams, and let me sleep with my ancestors. I'm tired. Yet I must go on. I see the heavy thunderstorm approach from the land of Kreli. The land will soon resound with thunder. Look at the Quena, doing the dance of thunder, invoking the brave-sounding Nquru on whom he must whisper all his guilt. They confess! They confess according to their culture, each time before a thunderstorm as the clouds darken. Me, I say, to everything a unity of line! The Quena don't want to carry their guilt to the next world; or be deleted because of it, should thunder extinguish their lives in this one. We come! We come! *Mz'ontsundu,* we've come!

'What rock my youth was shattered against. Lie there, my troubled thoughts, lie there. Gold, you cannot corrupt. On that we are at least all agreed. Let us continue and be ever so vigilant not to disturb Nquru, the son of the thunderbolt. *Nde'gram*! I disappear!'

❀

"You seemed preoccupied during the second half of the play. Did you not like it?" asked Nandi on their way back to her flat.

"T'was all right."

They walked in silence with the pale outline of a moon peeking through racing clouds.

"Do you know anything about the prophet of amaXhosa, uNtsikana?" asked Phila, to break the tension.

"I read about him once; he sounded like an enigma to me."

"I think he was an enigma to his contemporaries too; always telling people about the thing that whispered in his ear, to which he must always be true. At least he didn't mislead the nation like Nxele did."

"But Nxele got the better of him in the end, isn't that so?"

"Depends on how you look at it. Strange things were said of Ntsikana after his death, like that he fornicated with his ox," Phila attempted jest.

"Surely that can't be true?"

"Of course it wasn't true! Just jealous people who wanted to tarnish his image. I mean, he was extremely fond of the bull. It also behaved intelligently – it was like a pet – as animals that are exceedingly loved tend to do. His sin was taking white men's religion seriously without necessarily adopting white habits and culture. It made him distrusted by both the black natives and white settlers. Ntsikana was conservative but progressive, where Nxele, aka Makhanda, was opportunistic and regressive. Nxele usurped the notion of Pan Africanism when it suited his purpose. The Xhosa progressives, led by the likes of Soga, took to ploughing and hoeing gardens, which in their culture then was the women's job. So they were seen as effeminate. Of course white people took advantage of this. The white missionaries were forever flocking in Tyumi, around Soga, trying to convince him of this and that, and helping him in his fields. They wanted to prove that Western ways were far superior to our ways so that he might be the example for others who wanted to follow him. They eventually established a mission there. Things were still friendly between them, hence Chalmer, who manned the mission station, then sent his son with Soga's to Scotland for education."

"The fact is that Xhosa communal ethos was hostile to innovation," Nandi said, looking Phila in the eye.

"Xhosa chiefs didn't see things quite that way. They were irked at people like Soga. All that selling of produce was too much for them. Ntsikana preached against our nation adopting the practice of monetary exchange, but it didn't even take a decade after he was dead before his protégés adopted the practice, selling things with money at the market and all."

As Phila and Nandi entered the flat, evening was falling like a shroud. They went and sat on the balcony.

"Dawn and dusk remind me of my father," said Nandi. "I used to wake each time he went to work at about six in the morning." She rested her head on Phila's stomach, making it impossible for him to talk back except with an occasional grunt. "My father would ruffle my hair as he walked out, saying, 'Be kind, princess.' I'd watch him climb on his bicycle with the right side of his trouser leg tucked into his sock. I liked to watch him ride the bike against the mist until he was swallowed by the streets. It felt as though he was going to slay some dragon each morning."

"Hmm. He worked at a dairy?"

"Ja – you remember?" Nandi twisted her head and looked up at him.

"Why wouldn't I?"

"Yes," she said, settling back down. "He would come back late in the evening with buttermilk. I hated it. It smelled like fart, but it was our staple diet. My mother would cook *umphokoqo* to mix it with. It got to a stage when I couldn't stand anything associated with dairy. I didn't even like ice-cream, which he bought us every Saturday when we met him at his work place."

"That must have been hard, especially as he must have thought he was giving you a treat."

"It was a little. But I liked the fish and chips he bought for us to eat on the bus back. I didn't want vinegar on mine, the smell reminded me of buttermilk. To this day I can't stand vinegar." Nandi wrinkled her nose at the memory, then went on: "As you know, my mother was not that educated; worse still, she was a miser. Whatever money I gave her she saved, afraid bad days would catch her unprepared. I mean, we were indigent, but she made things worse by always worrying about tomorrow. She was plug-and-play, though, when it came to taking care of the house, although I suppose there wasn't much to take care of. Old rusted metal kitchen unit, a crumbling wooden table, a kist on its third generation in the bedroom, and a chipped fake imbuia wardrobe; sagging flea-ridden sofas, a pinewood wall unit with a display of three generations' photos."

"I remember there was a framed photograph of your grandma in your dining area," said Phila. "I always thought she looked so regal in her red Methodist Women's Guild uniform."

"It was rumoured once that a mine in Carletonville, where her husband worked, was collapsing and she prayed so hard it stopped."

"Whhomm!"

"There wasn't always enough food to go around in our house of three children. Sometimes my father didn't go to work for weeks. But thanks to my generous neighbour I at least always had something to eat." Nandi twisted her head again to look up at him. "How did you know I needed that food?"

"I didn't. I was just happy you relieved me of what I didn't want when I offered you. I was not fond of food then, and my mother force-fed me."

"I admired your mother. She always looked so clean and smelled very nice. To this day I remember the perfume she used because it was on the dressing table the day you popped my cherry." They both laughed. "It was called Opium. I tried it on my wrist and was never able to forget that smell. She was the only black professional woman I knew, your mom. Because of her I wanted to be a nurse. And of course I was in love with you."

"It wasn't just a crush?"

"It was more than that, and I have your bloody sheets to prove it. How did you wash them? I often wondered."

"You left me with a serious problem. I put Jik, Handy Andy, Omo, nothing worked. The bloodstain refused to come out. I think my mother just assumed I had been hurt." Another mutual laugh.

"I liked that you let us play with your toys, stuff, records and all. It was at your house I first watched TV, which you surprised me by not caring to watch yourself. I had never met a person who was that fond of reading before, to the extent of disregarding TV."

"I still don't watch."

"It felt unfair that you had a TV when you didn't care about it, while we who wanted one didn't. I liked the silence that fell on your room when you lay in bed reading. The smell of fabric softener in your bed. You smelling of Blue Stratos. I don't think I could have coped without you when my father died. You became my refuge. Of course, you probably just wanted a shag."

"That I did."

"There's a lot you did. I remember how devastated I felt when you left for Europe. I even read racial connotations into it, as if they were always robbing us of things we love."

There was silence for some time before Phila continued. "I do not know how to mourn. I just get angry about everything."

"There's no formula. You just need to stay true to your feelings."

"Often I have difficulty identifying my feelings."

"You don't need to identify them, just live them."

"Live is a loaded word. Most of the time I feel nothing where I am supposed to feel something, and everything where I'm supposed to feel nothing, and it all confuses me."

"Take the advice of the philosopher who responded prophylactically to Heidegger's vision of man as living 'towards death' by advising against thinking too much about it. That is where your first problem lies. *Carpe diem* is best honoured by caressing the quotidian details and appreciating the ordinary. Feeling nothing is also something. I think you were thrown in alienating situations too soon, too young. It made you rely only on yourself. And now you don't know how to create space for others in your your life."

"Something compares to nothing to me."

"Feel that and let me know."

"I'll write you from there, when I'm ready to share with you the gift of my nothingness."

Whichever Way the Wind Blows

PHILA LEFT GRAHAMSTOWN EARLY THE following morning, driving into the blinding sun. Somewhere between Ngqushwa and Qonce the mountains slipped into grand focus, making things grow nearer to his telaesthetic sight. The genius of his nation fell heavily, bending him like the Nilotic reed. The unclaimed burnt marshlands of history lay before the eye of his mind. He pulled over and stopped the car. *Ubuthongo bentlombe kaNtsikana* took over. The sedimentary smell of life lulled him. The last sounds he heard were the pit-pattering of birds.

The voice was insistent. 'You must speak! You must speak!' The thing that entered him told him: 'You must speak before darkness overtakes your mind.'

Phila felt his body go taut as a rope, then begin twitching in uncontrollable spasms. He felt himself having a fit, his head hitting repeatedly against the headrest. 'The gadfly! The gadfly!' something said in the depths of the boiling tumult of his mind. 'Ola hu! Ola hu! Oh!' the thing screamed. Then a deep peace descended over him, tranquillity such as he had never felt before. Across the fence a tractor tilled the soil, leaving ochre scars where its blades cut.

'Now that we are about to enter the seasons of my life I think it proper I give a formal introduction of my life,' Maqoma said solemnly. 'I was born a twin to a girl who could not fail filling our father's kraal with her *lobola*. Her name was Nongwane. Our umbilical cord is buried at Egxukwane, near what in white man's language is called Middledrift, just beyond this mountain. Our lambskin swaddle clothes were skinned from the kraal whose sheep drank the waters of the Qoboqobo River – we'll pass the river soon. In our era those waters made an oxbow before entering Debe Nek. They passed through a succession of valleys before joining Tyumi River. In those cool valleys Nongwane and I were born of Nothonto's pangs,

164

the daughter of Nxiya, a maiden of the Ngqosini clan, of Sotho and Khoi ancestry. The banks of the Tyumi River, where if you're sick they give you a concoction of aloe's honeydew and burn *umhlonyane* in your nostrils – an unsavoury thing of tremendous medicinal value – were our playing ground. I learnt to carve oxen using clay dug in those banks.' Maqoma pointed in front of them, wavering to indicate further down.

'For us, in the Xhosa royal families, it was easier to be closer to your mother's children than your paternal siblings, who were more or less your rivals rather than brethren. But Xhonxo, who was rather namby-pamby, was my favourite brother, though we didn't share the same mother. The three of us grew up close. We played pebble games together, fished for crabs in sloots; made whips for sham fights from rushes we picked in the open watercourses where we also learnt to swim. We killed birds with sticks and stones, roasting them over wood fires before devouring them, bones and all.

'Xhonxo and I were fond of taunting our sister Nongwane for her burgeoning over-zealousness with her newly found faith, which later was propagated by the cryptic Ntsikana. She grew such a long beak because of that religion that she was wont to preach whenever she opened her mouth. It was almost necessary to trim her wings now and then. Her religion made her smug and priggish. Bhulineli, whom the English called John Brownlee, took over where Ntsikana left as her chief priest when Ngqika gave him permission to open a school eMgwali. Nongwane attended that school and learnt white man's ways. I, meantime, couldn't be bothered with such effeminate things. I had wars to fight and my father's cattle to tend. Besides, I didn't like what I saw in my sister. You couldn't even joke with her about anything anymore without her taking umbrage, or becoming sanctimonious. Her world became grey. In no time she shunned our rituals and celebrations, saying they were barbaric and encouraged immodesty. I tell you, it reached a point where being around her became a strain. I didn't know what to talk to her about. Very soon I understood why the whites had to crucify their prophet. If this Christ was half the nuisance Nongwane became the cross was his come-uppance. It is difficult to coexist with such self-righteous bores.

'Nongwane and her cabal raised a lot of noise and fuss about prophetic visions that made them drunk with religious fever, jabbering nonsense with their heads tilted to one side. Most of us were interested in the new teaching at first without really letting the whole thing go beyond the surface and circumstances of our lives. The fables of the new religion were intriguing but over time they grew tepid and lost their novelty. What irked me more than anything else was their followers' inability to handle criticism. They preferred to wrap things in enigmas instead of discussing issues straight up. Whenever I said this my sister accused me of incomprehension, saying I had been blinded by heathenism. She felt I was deafened by the shallow wishful thinking that prefers lazy familiar traditional ways for no reason except that they're old. Whenever we laughed at her, out loud, she'd burst into frustrated tears and then our father would reprimand us, warning us not to be rude by making fun of other people's beliefs.

'We named the converts and all those who were ever ready to believe in the spick and span *amagqoboka* – turncoats – who caught every passing wind because they lacked anchor. Since then those who trust too easily in the novel before understanding the old were called *amagqoboka*, because they've turned their hollowness inside out. Unlike my sister, I couldn't afford to be indifferent to the verdict of our society. I was being groomed to be a chief. "A man's foes shall be they of his household," she would quote from their book with a red mouth to me whenever we heard arguments like that. But I could see she was grieved by what she called "the obtuseness of your heart". It tore me apart too to see her religion dividing us. I still maintain, faced with all the malice of the devil they painted so gruesomely, and the restraints God supposedly imposes on us, as they preached, I'd choose my forefathers' ways. I wouldn't want to spend eternity with a God who's so shallow as to be stiffened to hostility by mere creatures.

'In those days it became notorious for people to carry their life disappointments into some form of a religious calling, wanting to implicate the nation in their personal ambitions, like Nxele who made himself into a war doctor and the national Makhanda. Mlanjeni, with blanched body, pale and gaunt as a reed and weak as a sloth – because he spent his waking hours submerged, up to his neck, in rivers – came a decade after Nxele. These false prophets confused our chiefs with their belligerent prophecies about the people of the river, who were supposedly well disposed to us, and those of the foam, coming from the sea, who, though ill disposed to us, were also coming to rescue the Xhosas from colonial power.

'Before the tumult that came with white people settling in our land, Nongwane and I, during our teens, were sent to live with my uncle in the vicinity of the Mtontsi forest. On the given day we set out at dog's distending hour, when you can just about discern the cow's shining horns. Still we didn't beat my father's *imbongi* and the sending-off party. Immediately we started the journey his praises accompanied us, half-singing, half-reciting against the background of crowing cocks, barking dogs and bellowing cows:

Sasombuluka isikhotsholo sehlathi laseMthontsi,
Yasombuluka inkuzi abayikhuz' ukuhlaba ingekahlabi,
Hazi bothinina mhla yahlaba.
Sasombulaka isilo samaRharhabe kwakhal' izakhwasha
Hizan' nibone ubuhle bomfanaqwa buk' Nothontho
Qabintulo, qabintulo, nderham!

There distends the flying cobra of Mthontsi forest,
The bull they wonder about its gouge before it gores,
I wonder what'll they say the day it impales.
There distends the ogre of Rharhabe disturbing guinea-fowls,
Come and see the beauty of Nothonto's mirror image,
Rock lizard, rock lizard, I disappear!

'Thus went our send-off party. We travelled until about noon when the sun became unbearable. Then, at the wadi of Ncerhana, just before the confluent waters, we sat under a willow tree. When the afternoon wore away the heat of the forenoon we continued and reached the kraal at ghost hours the following day.

'Many places I've seen, but there are none as dear to my heart as the alluvial soil of Ngcwenxa. This is the area the white people called the Kat River valley. This was the place for which my friendship with Stockenström was broken, because he betrayed me and confiscated the land, through the colonial government, as an experimental settlement for the Khoi and amaMfengu.

'The area is fenced by Nkonkobe mountains. It has the spurs of Waterkloof and the ridge of Tyumi on the west. I am sure you'll also rarely in your life see land of such beauty, with its high green and rugged rolling hills whose sediment makes the valleys down below so fertile. My character was formed there under the sharp eye of my maternal uncle Kota. At the foot of the Nkonkobe mountains was where I learnt how to cut the furrow straight when turning the soil. That was where Nongwane brought me food from the pestle and the millstone of Nothontho. We would have starved beside those willows had Nothontho not been industrious with her grinding stones, kibbling the golden harvest. What would have happened to us if the leaning wind hadn't given her a hand in winnowing the chaff? Who would have fed the pigs with cobs if Nongwane hadn't hurried from collecting wood in the thickets of Mthontsi, where treetops tamed the fury of sunrays and the dimness checked the pride of the British during our bush wars? Where trees were reflected in the soft dimming glow of Ngcwenxa's still pools.

'*Awu madoda!* I saw a gleeman accompany my mother's child with flirtatious songs as she went to fetch water at the river. Nongwane scorned him with pretended bashfulness and lips twitching with a controlled smile when she saw me. "Have you brought me some cow dung to smear your rondavel, Maqoma?" my sister asked, glad to change focus from her embarrassment of me seeing her with a boy. "Your room is disgusting." And, labouring her point: "I've been telling you to stop smoking *umgqutsapere* with your friends." But she was flattered. I could see my mother's child was flattered by his attention. Her smile was from one cheek to another, her dimples like stars in donga-coloured skies. Then we would go home. I would help her carry the bunch of wood she'd collected from the bush, while balancing a crock of water on her head. Then I'd sit at the hearth, watching my mother's child snap beans, wring chickens' heads and pluck their feathers. I would watch her as exhaustion from working in the fields settled on my shoulders and eyes, as she shucked corn and dug eyes out of the potatoes in preparation for the evening meal. That was the time when we would pass a silent word of gratitude to women like Nongwane who provided for us men.

'And it was there that I also met my first love. Be done, work! Be done, chores! I have a tryst over the hill. *Isiponono sami sindilindele.* My inamorata is waiting for me. "Don't hold me too close, Maqoma. You're a warrior, you'll soon leave me with a sore heart. It is not wise to give one's heart to a wandering warrior. People are talking," said *isiponono sami* as we rolled, frolicking in the grass like calves. Oh, she was a buxom, stout and rumbustious thing – I made her my first wife. We talked of fickle things under the mimosa tree until the sun said, "Buy me if you can and I'll stay. If you can't, why are you still here? Do you not know that my setting wakes *ucelizapholo*, Venus, the shepherd and lovers' star? Who'll milk the cows if you linger here whispering sweet nothings? And you, young lady? Are the pots standing in your hearth?"

'That was perhaps the quietest and most fulfilling period of my life. Little did I know it would be those well-watered foothills of the Kat River valley that would provide those thieves with an incentive to banish me and rob my people.

'We lived eMthontsi for four years. Then word came from Tyumi, summoning me for the school of circumcision. I went to the school of circumcision *eBlayi*, fitting of a chief's son. I had companions and coevals to accompany me. That sealed our fate as blood brothers for life. They would, for instance, never marry without notifying me, likewise myself. When we grew up they became my first councillors. We established a tribe together called amaJingqi. Matshaya, one of them, became *isandla sam sokunene*, the hand of my chiefdom, my main assistant, and the others were the core of my council.

'We remained in the *boma* as initiates from seedtime until harvest, coming out of the school during the calving of the herds and lambing of the flocks, so as to be fed *umthubi*, the richest, first yellow milk. During the day we went in search of firewood, and hunted with dogs, sticks and long spears for our meat, as far as the Nkonkobe mountains. We would pilfer chickens and any other food we wanted from village homesteads – everyone understood and were lenient, by custom, to the needs of the initiates. No one minded, since everybody, except the white farmers, knew it was what *abakhwetha* did. In the evenings, or at dawn, we sang initiation songs, most of which were our traditional anthems. We sang them whenever we wanted to invoke unity, like when going to war. We were tested on our knowledge of initiation language, age-old Xhosa wisdom, and beaten by sticks when our knowledge or memory failed us. *Amakhankata* dressed our wounds pretty roughly to test our endurance and strength, and often it happened that:

> The goat that had not bleated
> When its throat was cut
> Cried out when it was skinned.

'We ate poor unsavoury, unsalted food. Water was mixed with ashes in the first weeks. If one is to become a man he must learn to overcome hardship, humiliation and disgust, we were told. It was a hard six months away from the village.'

'A whole six months?' Phila asked. 'We go for a month these days, sometimes less if one has to go to school.'

'And go back to the village with a fresh wound? No wonder you people have become so weak in bed, and can't handle more than one wife.

'Making premature contact with village people, especially women, weakens your virility.'

'How exactly?'

'Witchcraft. What else?'

'*Mfxim*!' answered Phila in amusement.

'It also affects your healing powers. After those six months we washed off our white ochre. We burnt the grass of our *bomas*, and emerged for the great ceremony that marked our acceptance as adult males and warriors. Never had I seen my mother so proud, ululating, singing, dancing and prancing like a young buck. Then the festivities began. We were given our *imisoko*. My father, Ngqika, gave me, together with *ilifa lam*, as part of my inheritance, a white bull with dotted spots I coveted very much. The bull was magnificent, streaked and spotted black. Its pedigree went to the ancient of times in our tribe, and had a bizarre effect in the village. People called it *Isitshingitshingi Jingqi* because it swept through during our oxen race tournaments, and was lethal when fighting with other bulls. My father seldom made me as happy as he did that day. Other minor chiefs of the land and the surrounding areas came to pay their homage, giving me gifts; as Ngqika's first born they gave me *amawu*, choice gifts. Even Hintsa sent a delegation, something that pleased me much, as it meant he recognised me as the possible heir of our chieftainship. Ngqika, in view of everyone, placed a necklace of red beads around my neck to signify my stature as his potent heir.'

'They turned into a system of patronage?' Phila taunted the chief. 'Seriously, though – you named your tribe after a bull?'

'Or the bull was named after the tribe. I can't remember which came first now. As amaJingqi then we were in a league of our own; full warriors who spent almost all our time in stringent exercises and gruesome hunting expeditions. We started as a warrior camp of amaNgqika before eventually developing into a fully fledged tribe. We were young, sharp, charged and fed the usual honed speeches about our land that was seeping out like a ripped maize sack under our noses. Ngqika did not beat about the bush as he told us what had been happening in the land while we had been gone.

'"You push your livestock in the morning to graze on the mountains. When you come back there is a white flag in the field where they lay the previous day, and a white man wielding a white paper, telling you that it entitles him to build a farm there. That means you can no longer graze or hunt in that area. He insults you, calling you lazy for not tilling the land that is empty and yearning for crops. The following day it's the same story in another area. They need huge acreages to farm. All you're good for, you're told, is to be a good, biddable, hard-working kaffir who knows his place. To work for your white master and learn the ways of civilisation.

Fields we used for grazing were now filled with waving corn – barley and wheat everywhere. Where were our cattle supposed to feed, was the question we asked, after we've fed ourselves with white man's bread?"

'Later that day I noticed that the colour of my father's face had changed. Sorrow and sad anxiety from the confusion of his mind was written all over it. He looked sickly, nervous. The light had gone from his eyes. After he had satiated himself on the "tears of the queen", he took me aside to explain what was troubling him. His middle-age paunch trembled as he said, "The children of pride are upon us, my child. They have no honour. Their spirit is animated by greed. They speak peaceable and believable words with deceitful hearts. I've seen the sign of things to come. Our future is strewn with blood. They are going to subdue Phalo's land, take its spoils to their occidental hives, and make all of us their vassals and tributaries." I was alarmed by the manner in which he talked, but I answered calmly, trying to downplay his fear. "You speak like a demented man, father. You need to get some sleep. Everybody knows white people are your friends."

'"Friends? Friends? I'm scared shitful of them. Sleep? What sleep? I've not had decent sleep since the day I saw the first white man, and how much death their magic pipes can sow with just one roar. Did you see what they did to Ndlambe's men with *mbayi-mbayis*? Sleep went from my eyes since the first day I laid them on those cannons and heard with my own ears the rumble and tumble of death they cause. My heart has been cast on the sea of anxiety. The hope of holding onto our land has fallen away from my heart. They say they bring us news from heaven, yet they fortify the devil in our midst."

'A sepulchral silence fell between us. Fear hung heavy as frost in my father's eyes. I pleaded with him. "Father, please try and get some sleep, we'll talk again in the morning." That was all I could say before clothing my disappointment in dignified silence. Too late I understood that my father's weaknesses came from too much insight playing havoc with his courage. His was a sad story of a purebred racehorse put to work hauling water. In the end, it didn't matter what we did. The stars were against us and the tent of the River People was broken.'

Phila woke with the sinking sun and expanding shadows. A river ran between the newly tilled fields and the scowling mountains. He started the car and drove off. As he crossed the Buffalo River to enter eQonce he recalled this was where Rharhabe had killed *inyathi* and sent the upper arm to appease the wrath of his elder brother Gcaleka. Several people were hitchhiking there, with mini-bus taxis stopping at intervals.

Taking a deep breath, Phila entered eQonce, where he had booked a room in an old colonial hotel. The town, known to the British colonists as King William's Town after their then newly crowned monarch, was once the colonial capital of the so-called Adelaide Province. It amused Phila no less that its regality had returned, because it had, again, under the current dispensation been made the provincial capital of the Eastern Cape. Harry Smith, who basically founded the town as military headquarters, tied its establishment to the geography of the area for military defence. He designed the town's main streets to radiate like the spokes of a wagon wheel towards the system of forts he had founded on the feet of the mountains they called Amatola and Winterberg, while amaXhosa referred to them as Amathole and Nkonkobe, respectively.

In the past the town used to be a fearsome symbol of colonial power and febrile activity, where amaXhosa got what was then referred to as 'kaffir truck' – useless low-quality goods and rejects from recently industrialised cities in England such as Manchester. Nothing much of Smith's ingenuity and reign of terror was to be discerned today, Phila observed, as he negotiated the heavy town traffic, which suspended all known rules of the road, among the boisterous bustle and hustle of commercial activity. But equally useless low-quality goods for amaXhosa were still for sale everywhere, only now they came from China and were referred to as *amaFongKong*. The collective decay of many colonial Eastern Cape towns had caught up with it. Its rusting buildings had the icing-sugary glitz of screaming facades of McDonald's and KFC. And like the others – PE, Grahamstown – it was rich in symbols of colonial rule on every corner.

The hotel had something of restrained Edwardian buoyancy to it, and also something of the confused ornamental diversity found in the decadence of the late Victorian age. After checking in, Phila climbed the baronial staircase in urgent anticipation of a bed. Upon entering the room he dropped his bag on the floor, kicked the door closed with the heel of his shoe, and threw himself face down on the bed. He slept *obentlombe* to wake up only the following day around nine. Already the intensity of the heat was oppressive. One of the reasons he had come to the town was to attend the initiation of a distant cousin of his into a school *yobu gqirha*, to be a witch-doctor. And then there was the awkward wedding of a friend and former girlfriend. They had sent him the invitation out of guilt, most probably, not expecting he'd be daring enough to attend. But Phila was curious. And daring.

He took a shower and put on his Sunday best before heading for the wedding ceremony. In fact it was a dull thing. Phila stayed only for the official part and to congratulate the groom and the bride. At least he felt his coming was not a waste of time because it made him realise he no longer believed in petty wars. In Leonard Cohen's words, the enemy was sleeping, and the woman was free of his thin gypsy heart.

When he came back to the hotel in the afternoon there was nowhere else to go so he went on a fool's errand at the bar by the pool. A SYF, with bright hair extensions the colour of the Swedish flag, extreme nails and all, was pretending to be consumed by a chick-lit book while eyeing his every move. There was hardly anyone else around, with the exception of staff members. He took a dip in the pool and went to a shaded corner to read his book. Immersing himself in Kafkaesque internal displacement, bordering on insanity, did not have the effect of escaping into fiction. It made him think about the wrong turns his life had made. The thought had a flattening, desensitising effect, so he directed his mind to the SYF across the pool. He decided to take the bull by the horns. He stopped by her umbrella.

"I'm going to the bar. Would you like something?"

Silence. He peered beneath the umbrella and saw that she had dozed off. He took the opportunity to read the title of the book on her bosom: *The Bride Stripped Bare*. He felt awkard. To leave without arousing her attention now would be suspicious. The barman was already giving him suspicious looks, though pretending to be busy packing glasses. Maybe he was thinking Phila was about to steal from the sleeping woman. He felt no choice but to wake her up, so he lightly kicked her shin, hoping she would not get cross.

"What is it?" she asked softly, taking her shades off.

Phila was glad she showed no signs of irritation. "I was just going to the bar to get something to drink and thought you might like something. I didn't realise you were asleep. Pardon me." He made to turn with an apology. It worked.

She gave a faint smile. "Actually, I would like a Manhattan."

"Sure. Crushed or on the rocks?"

"Crushed. Thank you." She raised herself from the reclining pool chair. "Gee! I didn't know I was so wiped out."

Phila exchanged a couple of perfunctory remarks with the barman before paying for the drinks and hurrying back to the SYF.

"Here you go – crushed and hopefully balanced."

"Much appreciated."

She had pellucid eyes. Phila always noticed the eyes first, because he believed them to be the the seat of the personality. He lingered a while to be invited to sit, but then sat down anyway.

"So? What do people do around here when it is this hot?" he asked. The sun was still baking down, but he didn't feel presumptuous enough to invade her umbrella space.

"Stay around the pool and, like, drink piña coladas – or Manhattans, if they are lucky."

They both chuckled.

"That's the life!" said Phila. He waited a little before extending his hand to introduce himself. "My name is Phila Sobanzi."

"Matswane Motleng." She threw her hand on his.

She had soft sweaty palms.

She was not from around here, a good sign, Phila thought.

"Don't ask me much about the vibe of this place," Matswane continued. "I'm, like, 404 when it comes to it. As far as I can tell, the town is dead. I survive on Sillywood here, thanks to my square-headed spouse." She pointed to her closed iBook next to her chair. "I've, like, never watched so many movies in my life. Good thing I kept saving them on my comp."

"Good for you!" Phila's mind raced into decoding the term 404. He was sure he had heard it somewhere (just as he had recently learnt from a *Cosmo* that SYF meant single young female).

"Are you staying long in the hotel?" Matswane enquired.

The position Phila was seated in made him an uncomfortable voyeur each time Matswane opened her legs to cross them. He took uneasy pleasure in it. "Just for the weekend. I came to attend a wedding; a friend getting married to an ex."

"Wow! That must have been tough?" She sat up again, and seemed a little restless.

"Not really." He remembered that 404 was a web-error message when you ask it to search for certain information and it can't find it: "404 Not found". So it must mean clueless, thought Phila.

"How did it feel?" She focused her gimlet eyes on his face.

Phila took some time to think about his answer. "Like the hot air you get from a train you've just missed, I guess."

"Taking it like a philosopher, hey?" She twisted her face to feign pain.

"I heard somewhere it's the only profession still left struggling truthfully with its own demons."

"I prefer art, so let's not even go there."

"I also heard that art misleads with false unities."

"I'll bookmark that. I'm, like, not aiming at being a saint or something."

"That's too bad. Aims, at least, should be ideal, even if we fall short. Where are you from, if you don't mind my asking?"

"Mother City. I mean, I'm originally from Tembisa, on the East Rand, now Ekurhuleni, but I work in Cape Town; studied there too. I've been staying here for the last three months or so. I work for an actuarial firm. We were hired by the Eastern Cape government." She spoke English with a Model C accent.

"An actuary. You don't see many of those around; certainly not as beautiful."

"Really? I understand why. Like, this has been my Elvis year, but I already feel like going postal. I'm tired of Dilberting for an egomaniac old coot whose specs are, like, Pentium 1."

"Leave then. Life is too short. One minute you are in love with someone, the next you are marrying them to your friend."

"So it does still hurt!" They both laughed again. "I just might do that one of these days. I mean, I'm, like, paid ribs 'n dick compared to the old coot I slave under, yet he delegates everything to me. The chairman founder of the firm is, like, a seagull, flies in now and then from the UK to shit over everything we do and bails as soon as he comes."

"How did you get into the field?"

"I actually went into actuarial science sort of by accident; like a process of elimination, if you like. My mother wanted me to be a doctor, but I despise seeing blood, so medicine was out. I couldn't see myself under a hard hat as an engineer either, as my dad had hoped. But I happened to be good in math and fancied something on the creative side, perhaps architecture." She laughed. "But I was horrible at drawing."

"Oh, architecture's not about drawing; perhaps a little joining of dots here and there. People tend to confuse architects with draughtsmen. Architects design – they don't draw."

"Now you tell me? Are you an architect, or, like, just an alpha geek?"

"Well, it depends on what you mean. I was trained in the field of architecture, but I am kind of out of things right now."

"Out of things? Get real! What does that mean? Out of a job? I thought there was a great demand for architects and engineers in this country?"

"Maybe so, but none of it has come my way. It's mostly been taken by big foreign firms. I think I'm ready to take another dip in the pool now."

"Why? Am I blowing your buffer?" She waited for Phila to answer but Phila was already moving towards his corner. "Wait up. I'll join you."

Matswane threw her towel down and Phila noticed that her swimwear revealed more than should be legally allowed – and that blew his buffer. By the way she dived into the pool he saw she was an accomplished swimmer. Phila was not a fish but would not drown when thrown in water. He hated chlorinated water, though, because it gave him a splitting headache when it got into his ears. After three lengths he got out and went to recline in his chair again. Matswane continued swimming for some time. As she walked back to her chair Phila noticed that her nipples had shrunk under her almost-transparent-when-wet swimwear. Cool early evening air began atoning for the sweltering afternoon.

"I grew up not very far from here," Phila said. "We always knew, no matter how hot the day was, there'd be this breeze from East London in the early evening to temper the heat, bringing much needed relief."

They ordered another drink and moved their chairs together under the umbrella. They continued talking, exchanging tentative details about their respective lives, until it began to grow dark and was time to go inside.

"Would you like to join me for dinner?" Matswane asked as they gathered up their things.

"It would be my pleasure," said Phila.

"I'll meet you in the dining room. I need to take a shower first."

Phila kissed her on the cheek as they separated.

In his room Phila felt the return of *Weltschmerz*. He also felt muddle-headed, with practical considerations concerning dinner. He had a cold shower. Putting on his last clean pair of jeans and the cotton shirt he had worn with the wedding suit, his mind hinted caution about the night but his lust pushed on. He liked the way his jeans hugged him and the confidence they inspired. They were Guess; he'd got them second-hand at an Oxfam shop. He splashed cologne on his face to hike his mood before going downstairs.

A white guy, a rare species in the former homeland, with a goitre and kind manners, asked for Phila's order when he entered the dining room. He ordered goulash for his main meal and chocolate cake on some exotic sweet sauce for dessert. He spotted Matswane sitting at the far end of the room in a bare-backed white dress. She looked like something out of an affecting dream. He didn't realise he had taken as long as he had, and felt a little embarrassed that she'd got there before him.

They exchanged information about the food they'd ordered, commenting on having had to place their orders at the door. "How strange is that?" Mat – because they were now that familiar with each other – said. She had ordered the lamb tagine and artichokes thing Phila had been too suspicious of to choose. In the end her choice, though sounding too exotic, was the better meal of the evening, so they shared it and left the goulash, which looked and tasted as if it had been made of kitchen leftovers.

After dinner Mat invited Phila to her room for drinks.

On top of the TV Phila saw there was a photo of her, in slim-cut jeans and a cropped jacket, revealing a toned midriff. A clean-shaven, crew-cut guy hugged her with too much confidence to be just a friend.

"That's my soon to be ex-fiancé," Mat said unprompted when she noticed Phila's eye lingering on the photo.

"Sorry to hear. What happened?"

Matswane poured two glasses of whiskey, Jack Daniel's. Phila secretly wished, if they were going to drink that sort of thing, it could have been Jim Beam, which had a less nauseatingly perfumed taste, something he disliked about Tennessee whiskies.

"Appletiser with it?" Mat asked, raising the glass.

"No, thanks. Just ice is fine." Not one to look a gift horse in the mouth, Phila gulped his first tot.

"I usually have mine neat, and follow it with a glass of Appletiser," Mat said, settling into a chair. Then, taking up the conversation she'd left off at dinner, she talked at length about her dissatisfaction with her job, her fiancé and her parents (who were always asking her for money). She seemed to be dissatisfied about a lot of things. Phila suspected the problem might be with her.

"What can we do tonight? I was told there's a festival in town?" Phila asked after a third glass, feeling more confident.

"A *fête champêtre*. It's like a boring show-off of agricultural produce. I already checked it out."

"I would like to check it out too."

"Festivals are so passé. Seen one, seen them all."

Silence fell between them. Phila liked overbearing women; they compensated for his indecision. He went out onto the balcony.

"I've been thinking about your train thing," Matswane called out from the bathroom. Phila could not hear her well because she had just flushed the toilet so he walked back to the room. "You are right. There's always another train scheduled to leave next."

"The trick is in managing the time at the platform before the next train arrives – staving off the void," Phila added, lowering his voice on the last part so Matswane wouldn't hear.

Night was falling fast outside. The stars hung low in the sky. Phila and Matswane talked nineteen to the dozen. After the sixth drink or something, Phila came back from the bathroom to be greeted by Matswane lying semi-naked in bed, her transparent nylon panties revealing a Hitler's moustache on her Brazilian wax. She had a very, very attractive body. Still Phila was caught off guard, even though he had already suspected from their talk and oglings this was the direction things were headed.

"I'm not, like, asking us to frog relate or something," Matswane said when she noticed his hesitation.

Frog relate? Phila was lost for a while before vaguely remembering something about frogs mating for life. He ran downstairs to get a packet of condoms from the vending machine he had seen in the foyer. When he came back, pronto, Mat said, "Let's just go with the flow." And she opened the sheets for Phila to get in. A moral fissure opened in his mind but he ignored it as he quickly took off his jeans and jumped into bed.

"I'm just overwhelmed. I've had a salmon day so far, swimming upstream, and so was wondering if my nerves were playing tricks on me." His voice had difficulty coming out because they were already kissing.

They made love with surprising patience and synchronised movements, that seemed poised at the brink of ecstasy. They came at the same time in what Phila could describe as a mutinous arrest. After that they lay quietly next to each other for a while before Mat broke the silence.

"You're still present within me."

Phila took that to mean she was still orgiastic and made love to her again. What is under pressure in us, even concealed, is what comes out to explode in lovemaking, he thought.

When he saw that Matswane was sleeping, it crossed his mind that she might be narcoleptic. Her sleeping face had the troubling serenity of a Bellini Madonna, with hints of the coming crucifixion. He listened to the sounds of silence. I'm lost, he thought, as he put his ringing cell phone on silent when he noticed who the caller was – Nandi.

Later in his room he wrote an email, mostly gibberish poetic musings to suppress the guilt, to her:

Hey there,

Sorry I missed your call. I was sleeping. Now I can't sleep. I am on the balcony of the hotel watching the wind shave tree scalps. The trees wave the direction of the wind. Somehow this irritates me.

Remember the day at the beach in Port Alfred when your hair kept following the wind? The sea glimmered to the touch of the sun. The clouds whispered, "The wind is stealing the wetness away." You said the gulls were shouting, *I need you like rain,* because you read it in a book of poetry by Philip Larkin. We argued about his racism. You instructed me to separate the art from the man. I was not convinced by your argument.

You went to him, promising to come to me, but you never did. You said he awoke a longing in your body you could not explain. I was hurt. It made me resentful though I admired, envied, your happiness with him. I wanted to be the one creating that unexplainable longing in you, that happiness in your eyes.

I recognised that coming storm, from the gathering clouds. I suspected there might be trouble soon, and so there was, and you went back to him for good, or so you said.

I choose the vagabonding life because I know, no matter how I try, I can never fit into your decent life of theatres with the pleasantries of foaming lattés and the mocking condescension of sophisticated ignorance from your friends who mark me as the enemy before they even know me. I have a canker in my heart that gets restless around the ritualised anxieties of a bourgeois life.

She's almost everything I don't like in a woman, yet I am drawn to her like a moth to candlelight. I can't think of anything I want more at this stage, except being at the centre of her whirlwind.

I am afraid I've misplaced our hopes by my misadventure.

That's my nothingness tumbling down into emptiness for you. Perhaps, in another life. *No suitcase can hold a goodbye,* your poet says ...

We Must Attempt the Task of Living

PHILA HAD PLANS TO ATTEND *INTLOMBE*, the ceremony of *amagqirha* that morning. The full moon had been sighted the previous night, sparking the start of such ceremonies. Curious to see his cousin start her apprenticeship, he set out at dawn. Rumours had it that the whole thing cost her parents two goats, six bottles of gin, some mysterious accessories and the white cotton dresses of *ubugqirha*, on top of the hefty sum of two thousand rand. But the parents were not complaining, since *bengabantu abamhlophe,* thus susceptible to witch-doctoring. Unlike *abakhwetha*, who daubed white clay only for their initiate period, *amagqirha* permanently daubed it, wearing white cotton clothes with trinkets to denote that they belonged to the clairvoyant caste. More money would be required when she came out in six months' time. By then she might even be pregnant, since *abantu bomlambo* – the River People who have the gift of witch-doctoring – impregnate each other sometimes to transfer their powers. Apparently, sleeping with your principal was common among witch-doctoring initiates, even encouraged, so that one might acquire their aura. Contraception was anathema, as it blocked the natural transference through biological mystique.

Phila was strangely jealous of his cousin, but he wanted to observe the process. He was even tempted initially to join the apprenticeship too, but the problem was that he was not *umtu omhlophe*, which was the prerequisite for initiation. The temptation of faking the symptoms, *zokuthwasa*, crossed his mind: hysteria, nervous paroxysm, dreams, visions and so forth. In the end he decided against it.

After breakfast at the hotel, he went to his car ready to leave, only to discover the car had been broken into and vandalised on the street he had carelessly parked it on. The driver's side window was broken, shattered actually, and the door's keyhole vandalised. They had taken the car's stereo. As the morning was overcast, threatening rain, Phila thought it was probably not wise to drive the car without a window. He resolved to look for a place that could fit a spare window for him. This was easier said than done on a Sunday morning, as he discovered. King William's Town was a small village, something he appreciated better when he was not in need of an open spares shop, but eventually he found a place, owned by an Afrikaner in his early forties. When he arrived the guy was sitting on the veranda with someone he called Oom Piet. As luck would have it, they had the right window size for the make of his car. For a bit extra they offered to fit it for him. Phila accepted the offer, after complaining about how difficult it seemed to be to find an open spares shop in town.

"Eh, boetie," said the owner, bending over to open the car door from inside, and hitching up his pants to hide the builder's crack, "People here still go to church. You're lucky me and Oom Piet have a different arrangement with God." He gave Phila a smile. "It's difficult to get parts for these Sentras these days. You're really lucky. We got this only ... when was it, Oom Piet?"

Phila was a little apprehensive that this performance was designed to con him into paying more.

"Doensdag," replied Oom Piet in an indifferent tone, more out of duty than enthusiasm, from the veranda, smoking his pipe, eyes vacant.

"Bloody *skelms*. You say they broke into it this morning? I tell you, *broer*, everyone who has assets in this country must own a gun, not to shoot anyone, but to scare *skelms* away so they don't take advantage of you. They'll probably sell your radio for R50, just to get themselves a bottle of Klippies. Bloody *skelms*!" He straightened up to light a cigarette – a Royal – before continuing. "I told Oom Piet here ..." pointing behind him with a tubby, greasy hand, the only glabrous part of his exposed skin; his upper body was now inside the car. "I said, Oom Piet! Rather than gallivanting and getting our asses in all sorts of *gemors*, or being lied to by the dominee, why not we open the shop on Sunday? I mean, we stopped going to church a long time ago, what with all the moffie dominees, and besides, my wife prays enough for both of us. And as I said, the big guy and we have a better understanding. So instead of sitting around the yard, fattening our asses and farting from too much boerewors and pap, we could be making some money. I tell you, boetie! Best decision I ever made. Now I make money of three days on Sundays; and it's usually blokes from the township. That apartheid thing wasted our business. I'd have been a millionaire long ago if okes like Mandela had got out sooner, and everyone would have been better for it. You know *mos* how there in the township

181

they don't bother about God. Instead they get their *messies in die* jalopies and come fix them with me. I give them discounts, and the word spreads like fire, *broer*. Who can ask for a better church than that?"

The Afrikaner seemed to have lost his initial inhibitions. Bits of shattered glass came flying out of the window onto the road.

"I tried introducing some of my okes into coming in shifts on Sundays, thinking they're probably in need of the extra cash, but it was no use. Those who came were drunk most of the time; the others couldn't be bothered even to pitch up. You know *mos* how it is there. They just go to their shebeens, play loud music and run after skirts. Then on Monday they all want to go to the clinic or something. Only this year two of my guys died on me. What else? It's the thing that's out there. Now I have to give them short lessons before handing them their envelopes on Friday. I say: 'Boetie, *gaan lekker maak met jou geld*. I've no problem with you testing the oil gauge of other cars with your dipstick, if you know what I mean.'" He halted to wink at Phila. "'But there's this thing out there, so *moenie gaan* opening your zip with strange ladies.' I say, 'Chaps, last month it was Sipho; that other month it was Zakes. Who's next? If you don't stop fucking around *mos*, or *gaan met* a damn condom, jy sal be *dood, almal van julle*. Faster than any apartheid ever killed you. A person will have to gird with his own booty if he must, until this AIDS thing blows over at least.' *Wat*? None of that helped. Three of my guys are sick again. I had to let one go because he was too sick to be of any use to me. *Ja-nee, die kak* is in the fan."

He was silent, but not for long. "Well, boetie, you've got a mess here. They broke some frame pieces too when they broke the window. I'll have to take the frame out. That'll cost you extra, boetie. *Askies tog. Maar a Boer maak a plan vir jou.*"

As the man strolled off to go and get some tools from his workshop to strip the window frame, Phila started panicking about time. When he came back, having stripped a frame from another Sentra, a newly lit cigarette between his lips, he said, "Relax, boetie. If you want something done well you must be prepared to invest some time on it. Oom Piet!"

Oom Piet had disappeared from the veranda into the shop.

"Give the gentleman some keiner-kleiner to relax him!" the Afrikaner shouted.

The drink came in a jiffy. Phila swigged it back, prompting the Afrikaner to thunder into a boisterous chesty laugh. "*Ag man, jy es a skelm wena, suka!*" When he stopped laughing, he said, "There's a lot more where that came from, boet! As I told you, me and God have different arrangements. Just now I was having difficulties untying this screw. I put it to Him that it's rather rude to delay this nice chappy who obviously has somewhere else to be, so I'll appreciate any help He can give. And there, immediately the thing came out. God and I understand each other. The dominees and their arse-fucking tendencies just get in the way."

By the time Phila left the yard it was already ten to twelve and his head was hot from more than a few tots of brandy. There was no chance he was going to make the ceremony now. *Amagqirha* would have long left with their crew. Phila drove back to the hotel with his tail between his legs.

❦

"Did you have a good sleep?"

"Ja." Phila, sitting at the bar, where Matswane joined him, was non-committal.

"I thought you'd left without saying goodbye."

"How could I?" Phila said. "You're not working today?"

"I do most of it from the room, I don't really have an office here."

They were both quiet for a few minutes.

Then Matswane said, "I thought to myself, even if I was drunk, surely I couldn't have been that bad?"

"You were terrific actually."

'Thanks for saying, even if it's not necessarily true. I needed to get all that energy out of me."

"Glad I could be of some help."

"So what are you doing tonight? You're welcome to my room, if you wish; perhaps this time I might even recall what we did."

"Be kind."

"You'll join me again, won't you? Surely one *bêtise* doesn't make a complete fool?"

"What about your fiancé?"

"Let's go to lunch."

Matswane swung her behind under her tailored, hip-hugging, salt-of-the-earth jeans, showing confidence in her personality. Her boobs jutted under the loose shirt she wore, or almost wore. Phila followed her into the dining room. Mat opted for a canapé lunch, boosted by cheese morsels, and a salad with Norwegian salmon, which she made a big fuss about. A little irritated by her upper-middle-class poise, mannerisms and attributes,

Phila ordered ribs and chicken and grilled vegetables. After lunch they went and sat at the pool again, where light shimmered over the water with protesting intensity.

"Do you want to go somewhere with me?" asked Phila, standing up suddenly.

"Where?" Matswane asked, raising her head and looking at him from beneath her straw hat.

"You'll see. It's not far, but we'll need to drive."

"Okay."

The past is a constant responsibility, an operation of conscience for dealing with the present, thought Phila as he drove. We colonise our experiences and give them back as myths.

The wind blew strongly. "*Le vent se lève. Il faut tenter de vivre.*"

"What did you say?" asked Mat.

"I was just thinking about a line I like in Aeschylus's play *Agamemnon*: 'The wind is rising. We must attempt the task of living.'"

"You're strange."

"Is that why you are here?"

Scavenging dogs transported degrees of gloom and seediness to the back streets as they drove out of town. On the outskirts almost immediately the road reached into a rural atmosphere. The houses became frugal and the landscape green and lush.

Matswane sat up. "So, I never really asked your story?"

"Like what?"

"We're all hustlers *mos*. What's your hustle?"

"To be honest? To find a good way to live, without too many internal contradictions. Perhaps afford to pay for my own keep, if I'm lucky."

"What contradictions?" Mat asked.

They were passing through citrus farms that were in harvest. All along the road there were people, coloured teens mostly, selling bags of oranges with R5 prices written on brown boards. The selling price at the supermarkets for the same bags started at R15.

"Never mind," said Phila.

"You haven't told me where we're going. What are we looking for?"

"We are looking for … no, let me not spoil the surprise."

Seemingly in the middle of nowhere Phila took a gravel exit. Was isolation the sum of the rural life, he wondered, and the reason most people fled to urban areas? After a bumpy drive, which involved almost getting stuck in the small brown river they crossed, he stopped the car.

Matswane looked surprised. "I do not see anything to see here except a few old ruins," she said as she got out of the car. "Or are we here to admire the view?" She pointed down to the valley below, from where they had come, and looked at Phila enquiringly.

Phila followed her to the ruins she had indicated, some crumbling walls overgrown with moss. "Well, we're here to see the ruins mostly."

"Great! And I thought you were interesting. Now I am sure you're a lunatic about to murder and bury me on a deserted hill."

"The only way you can see anything interesting in places like these is by bringing something of yourself along. Provided –"

"– provided you're a lunatic?"

"Provided you have a little spark of their history. You can wait for me in the car, if you like."

"Actually, I think I'll do just that, mister flak catcher.

"This scene is shuck."

Phila gave her a grin of clemency as he strode off. There was an air of quiet dereliction over what remained of Fort Willshire. It was hard to believe that this had been the scene of one of the fiercest battles between the Xhosas and British forces. Now the ambience was quiet, somehow fey. Phila sat down on one of the stones with his ear on the ground.

After half an hour Matswane came looking for him.

"I almost didn't want to disturb you. Where do you go when you visit these places?" she asked as she sat next to him.

"I'm trying to ... I want to ... I don't know. I'm looking for something ... I don't know, something intimate, when I'm in these places."

"What do you mean, intimate?"

"I'm not sure."

"Maybe it does not want to be found, or understood."

"I think the contrary is true.

"It only wants to be understood on its own terms, so we have to eliminate the noise and the possibilities of misunderstanding."

"Is it love you're looking for?"

"Why is it, when there's something missing, women always assume it's love? I'm looking for everything that makes sense, a way to live. I suppose love is the ultimate sense."

"I want to look with you, but I want to know what I am looking for."

Phila frowned. "It's a hard, boring life, as I indicated earlier, and one I wouldn't wish on a dog. But something inside me compels me, deeply compels me."

185

The irony of him sounding like Maqoma was not lost on Phila.

He was also wary of making himself falsely sound like an enigma to Matswane's ears.

Together they walked around the area.

"I think I want to try," said Matswane in an uncharacteristically deflated voice. Usually she sounded forceful, her tone bristling.

Phila looked at her. "A firebrand longing for adventure, or domesticity?"

Matswane shrugged. "Either way, I can no longer go back to my life as if nothing happened."

Phila wanted to advise her against his foolish life but he felt impotent. "You have a comfortable life, Mat," he said. "What do you wanna spoil that for? Go back to your fiancé. In a few weeks you will have forgotten all about this, and everything will be fine. You don't really want to come with me. You just want to conquer what you see as a wild spirit. It's a woman's instinct to want to tame."

"Thank you, Mr Freud."

"This is not a life of trendy cafés and cocktails; or fancy boutiques, malls, and emporiums hawking cosmetics, handbags, shoes and all that."

"Tell me what happened here."

Phila became pensive and then generous.

"These crumbling walls are the remains of a fort. Fort Willshire. It was one of the first forts the colonial government built in the area. When they became fed up with colonial encroachment on their land, the Xhosas attacked it in 1850. They used to call it 'the seat of the devil' because it was where white people led black people for trade, exchange, with prices that satisfied white people only – things like stripped and dappled hides, tanned sheepskins, ivory, gum, knives, beads, cooking pots, fronded ostrich feathers, tallow, Dutch soap, timber ploughs – things like that. Beads and buttons served as currency; they were exchanged for live beasts and hides inland from the Pondo and Thembu people. Ngqika, the chief of amaXhosa in the region, was decadent by then. He frequented the fairs here because of his alcoholic degeneration. It was where he got most of his monetary income, by demanding tribute from those of his people who made exchanges with white people. He also got his brandy that way. To Xhosa aristocrats this place was loathsome, a symbol of how white people were cheating in exchanging crooked prices for commodities, and turning their people into a nation of drunkards that could be easily taken advantage of. They resented the fact that they were allowed to cross the river borders only when white people wanted to exploit them, as was the case during the fairs."

"Is that why you wanted to check out the agricultural show? You thought it'd be more than the fairs of before?"

"Not really. They were only allowed to cross the river from 10am, during the days of the fairs, and could only stay until 4pm. By the time most of them got here the agreed going prices for the day had been made without their contribution. As such there were 'morning prices' for white folks, and midday prices for kaffirs, and then evening prices for general farmers of the area. Mornings and evenings kaffirs were not allowed to be here – as such, those prices were not inflated. If you think about it, the whole thing is similar to the legacy of apartheid: the kaffirs must come to town during the day, work and spend their income, then return to the peripheries or urban and rural poverty.

"Impetuous dealers got a raw hand, while if you delayed too much you found yourself in the position of having to go back with your stock, or sell it at way lower than its real value. White preachers used the opportunity to convert 'black heathens' and the whole thing generally had an effect of anglicising Xhosa people, which was why these fairs were loathsome to chiefs. It was not a rare thing in these fairs to meet Xhosas wearing wool blankets, soldiers' coats, knee-breeches, silk stockings, hats, and carrying things like parasols and handkerchiefs. Some even had cotton rugs in their huts. Xhosas here acquired addictive tastes for sugar and brandy. From there they became dependent on white people, treating them like their *baas*. It was these fairs, together with the missionary activity, that were the main destruction of Xhosa social structure and the transformation of what had been their national torpor to the religious and market principle. Things like these undermined the authority of the chiefs – 'making men effeminate by compelling them to do women's jobs like planting gardens and hoeing', according to Maqoma, son of Ngqika."

"You sure have researched these things."

"During the 1851 war, when the Xhosas were joined by some of the rebel Kat River valley Khoi, and a few amaMfengu, the sky over white people's settlements became bright with wreaths of flames from burning farms and mission stations. Gunshots echoed occasionally along the kloofs whose skies were lit from the devastated homesteads of settlers. Sometimes I mistake certain sounds for the echoes of those days, because I can feel … I mean, Maqoma tells … I mean, I'm reading about things that happened in these places."

"And that's when you get lost in them?"

"Sometimes I hear the voices and see the faces of people who were there."

"In your dreams?"

"Something like that."

The wind was blustery and hot. Matswane held her sunhat on with her hand as it gusted around them.

"The Xhosa blocked all roads to the fort during that war, and held those inside at ransom. Each time the Brits sent an offensive against the Xhosas, assegais drank their blood. *Hi! hi! hi!* Xhosa bullets also harvested them from those hilltops over there. It was suicidal and hopeless to stand against so many Xhosas, so those inside decided to sit still in the protection of the fort, waiting for reinforcements since they were outnumbered with no way of escape. They were held hostage for about three days. Included among them was Harry Smith – then already a governor – Maqoma's rich enemy and nemesis. When you read the letters Smith wrote during those days you realise he had reached a dementia with fear. The letters were disjointed and incoherent. He even requested the colonial government to convince a Zulu army to come attack the Xhosas who had risen to annihilate the whites in the Eastern Cape. He was in the devil's grip. He knew the shoe was of Maqoma's stitching. He knew Maqoma was not gonna let him get out of the fort alive, not after the humiliation he had meted out to Maqoma a few years before in Port Elizabeth."

"What humiliation?"

"Coming back from England as the new Governor, Smith summoned the Xhosa chiefs, Maqoma among them, and asked them to kiss his ring as a symbol of serving him. He also asked them to kneel before him, whereupon he put the heel of his boot on each of their necks."

"Yark! That's sick!"

"Hence Maqoma had orchestrated things into this siege, to avenge himself on Smith. Smith survived by the skin of the teeth. He escaped in the morning on horseback disguised as one of the Khoi Cape Mounted Rifles according to official colonial books. But the Xhosas say he was disguised in women's clothes, knowing very well the custom of the Xhosas of not harming women even during times of war.

"Any who tried to come out of the fort were killed by the Xhosa, who wanted to reduce the garrison to the utmost dire straits, with no food or ammunition nor provisions to replenish them. Their intention was to finish them when they were weak, before their reinforcements arrived.

"According to the Xhosa plan, a KhoiKhoi man from Bhotomane's chiefdom, who worked at the fort, was to start a fire inside, creating a diversion. He was also supposed to canvas around the disgruntled KhoiKhoi of the Cape Mounted Rifles to fight on the Xhosa side when the time came. Maqoma, the chief who led the assaults, later cursed the thought that made him rush to trust the KhoiKhoi. On the given night the Xhosas descended from their fastness so as to be outside the fort's wall at first light. As soon as the saboteur gave the fire signal they were to attack. But the signal never came. The result? When daylight came the Xhosa were as exposed as a Bushman's back, white people waiting patiently, guns in hand, ready to fire through the holes of the fort. They had somehow learnt of the ruse – no prizes for guessing from whom. They rained hell on the Xhosas at first light before they could retreat to safety. Even to this day the white people do not know how they escaped from the mouth of that lion. They learnt to respect, fear and thus hate Maqoma that day.

"Fate blunted the edge of Xhosa opportunity. When they got back to their villages some Xhosa men were so charged they started attacking the missionaries who stayed in their villages, and killing white traders before their chiefs could restrain them. The missionaries were no longer safe in Xhosa villages, so they were given chief escorts across colonial borders. Some Xhosas who had converted to white people's ways, like the young Soga, who attended school at the missionary yard, left with the white people. The colonial government took such acts as the declaration of full war. And so another Frontier War began."

"Will you go back to her?" Matswane asked.

"What?" Phila was bewildered. "Who?"

"Your woman."

"Who said I have a woman to go back to?"

"Your likes always do."

"My what? ... You know what? Let's not talk about this anymore."

"Fine."

Silence fell between them. When Phila glanced at Matswane, he thought he saw sadness in her eyes. He was confused as to what he was supposed to say. When he finally spoke it was as though he was reading from a prepared speech.

"I am travelling into my life, in an attempt to read what is in it for me, perhaps even to learn to accept myself, vague losses and all. I do not yet have a verdict on who is my woman and who is not. It could be I shall not be able to live with what, who, I am. What then? I cannot drag others into the mess. That is why I am unable to be attentive to others at this time in my life. I've no mystery to share ..."

"I'm not looking for mysteries to solve, just situations I'm comfortable with," said Matswane, her tone slightly reprimanding. "And I'm comfortable with you."

Phila felt he was back to square one. "I don't have much foresight. I'm against happiness as the only goal of this life, so I shall not gel well with your type."

"My type? Against happiness, but for ecstasy? We'll see how that goes."

"I feel incomplete and unhappy in most situations. I'm sure you can see how that will eventually be a problem. You'll get bored with me very soon. People usually hate me, strongly, when they discover I cannot be turned into what they want me to be."

"I don't want to end up like you, but I'd like to go with you for a little while, to clarify some things in my own head also."

"Like what?"

"I don't know. The fact that I don't want to get married to Siva for one," Matswane said. "Perhaps I've grown too comfortable in my own life, allowing others to make decisions for me. Siva is more of my parents' choice for me than mine. I see how that can be a problem for me, perhaps not now but later on. I don't want misery, but I would like to see what else is out there."

Perhaps he had been wrong about this woman. "I thought you were happy with your life?" Phila said, hiding behind a smile.

"I am. Just not content.

"Mine is the kind of happiness that breeds blandness."

"Now you want to use me as your guinea pig, to see if there's any value in sadness?" Phila grinned, then admitted it out loud: "I might have been wrong about you."

"No, you were right. You saw the side I presented."

"I'm beginning to like the other side also."

"I want you to like me."

"You want what you already have. I'm scared for the time when you see the real me, that's all."

"What for? I'm the one who stands to lose here."

"And I don't?"

"Somehow I think everything is a gain to you."

"If by that you mean I am alive to life whatever it brings."

"You seek stories to remind yourself you're alive?"

"I was just reading from the hotel's bedside Bible this morning. The psalmist says those who are alive to life, their lives are like a story that's being told. Or something like that. What are we without the stories we tell each other about each other? Keats says it better: *I have an habitual feeling of my real life having passed, and that I am leading a posthumous existence.* I get stabbed by life: flowers, babies, homeless people, roads with or without cars, the marketplace, the silence of a deserted church building and so on. The very act of living, breathing, eating and walking is sacramental to me. That, to me, is being fully alive. Let us be going."

They began walking towards the car.

'Why is she coming with us?'

Maqoma. Of course.

'It's a free country.'

At that moment Phila recalled a dream he'd had the previous night about the Philistines. He had dreamt of terror-filled King Saul in Endor consulting a medium through the prophet Samuel. When he came across the psalm Phila was trying to find the passage of the dream from the Bible: *Samuel said to Saul, "Why have you disturbed me by bringing me up?" "I am in great distress," Saul said. "The Philistines are fighting against me, and God has turned away from me. He no longer answers me, either by prophets or dreams. So I've called on you to tell me what to do."* Phila wondered if he had called on Maqoma to tell him what to do.

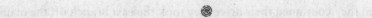

After breakfast the following morning Phila and Matswane drove to Maqoma's grave in Qoboqobo. From the Engen filling station they immediately took the right turn to climb a curving road towards Dimbaza, a black township now looking more like a ghost town. During the era of the Bantustans, when Maqoma's remains were exhumed from Robben Island to the area, it was a booming town of textile manufacturing. But they couldn't compete with cheap items from China and one after another the factories closed. Jobs faded and lean days returned. This pushed rapid urbanisation to those cities that were still able to offer jobs. Denizens from peri-urban townships and rural areas like Dimbaza formed the greater part of the informal residents who converged on big cities like Johannesburg and Cape Town.

"Are we still on the right path?" Matswane, who was at the wheel, asked a rather quiet Phila.

"Yes. Drive until you see a sign that says Qoboqobo and follow that." After a moment he corrected himself. "No, the turn will say

Keiskammahoek. They still call these places by their colonial names."

"I don't like it much when you keep quiet, babes." Mat tried to revive the conversation again after five minutes or so.

"Really, don't worry about it."

The landscape turned verdant with clumps of forest that thickened towards the foot of Amathole fastnesses amaXhosa had used as their natural forts during their wars with the colonial forces. They branched towards Keiskammahoek and drove through thickets of forest and past lakes of white waters, most of which was now privately owned by white farmers, with a dapple of Xhosa huts whose owners either worked on the white farms, or deserted them to eke out a living in the cities, living insalubriously like animals in zinc dwellings, *zamatyotyombe*. After they climbed over the Keiskamma River, Phila asked that they stop.

"Here? What happened here?"

But Phila was in no mood for talking. He trained his eyes on the hill where the Uniondale missionary school was built. It was the first post where Zisani Soga had taught when he came back from Glasgow the first time. The post was organised by his friends and benefactors, the Nivens, who manned the station. It was the first mission the Xhosas burnt down during the 1851 clash, partly in deep resentment of Zisani whom they saw as a bad influence on others for trying to convert them.

When they continued their drive they took the east branch off the main road to Boma Pass where Sandile's warriors had ambushed and killed thirteen British soldiers at the start of that war. The forest all around them was thick. Then they saw a small black and white road pointer to Maqoma's grave.

"Ah!" exclaimed Matswane.

All this time Phila had stayed silent. The burden of history weighed on him. He got out of the car and walked a couple of times around the grave. There was nothing much of ceremonial pomp to it, just a rectangle of granite stone with Jong'Umsobomvu's biographical details engraved on it. Then a few praise-song notes of his clan name. It felt wrong. The whole thing felt wrong. Matswane's presence. Maqoma's silence. His mind going blank. It all felt wrong.

He walked back to the car, climbed onto the bonnet and lit a cigarette. He lay there, supine, looking at the azure skies. The wind gathered. The forest, a few feet away, started singing. Phila listened. He didn't hear anything. He got off the bonnet and lay on his back on the grass, to get a better feel of the ground rumblings. Momentarily, Matswane joined him, lying supine too. They were quiet together for a long time.

When the forest shadows had almost reached them, Phila got up and pulled Matswane to her feet. "Come! Let us be on our way, the day is far gone," he declared.

They each put a stone on the grave before they left.

At the hotel they lay the same way on the bed, side by side. Matswane kept Phila primed with whisky. After about an hour and a half, Phila said, "I actually like that the grave has no pompous ceremony about it, even though I doubt it would stay so for long. Sooner or later a politician would come along, wanting to use Maqoma for political gain, spouting silly ideas of putting up a monument or something. I would like to think his indomitable spirit would tear down such monuments. The only thing I would change is the epithet on the grave. I would keep the biological details, of course. But instead of the clan praise thing I would let Mqhayi speak for him also."

"Who is Mqhayi?" Matswane asked.

"One of our greatest poets," Phila said. "Surely you know Mqhayi?" Matswane shook her head and Phila began to recite:

Asinithenganga ngazo izicengo;
Asinithenganga ngayo imibengo;
Bekungenganzuzo zimakhwesikhwezi,
Bekungenganzuzo ingangeenkwenkwezi.
Sikwatsho nakuni, bafel'eAfrika,
KwelaseJamani yaseMpumalanga,
NelaseJamani yaseNtshonalanga.
Bekungembek'eninayo kuKumkani,
Bekungentobeko yenu kwiBritani.

"He wrote that poem for those brave soldiers who went down with the troopship, the SS *Mendi*, in 1917."

"Oh ... I think I heard about that," said Matswane, "but you'll have to translate." She looked at him expectantly and Phila recalled that she didn't speak Xhosa. He recited the passage slowly in English, moving away from the official translation, which he'd never liked, even when they were still students and made to recite the poem. For one thing, he could never understand why they rendered Mqhayi's clear reference to Germany, in *iJamani*, to West. He now understood that translation is a third language between the two being translated; not only did it depend on the skill of the translator, but it also came riddled with the translator's own linguistic quirks. Hence, like fingerprints, no translations could be the same:

We didn't bait you by supplications;
We didn't bait you by skewers;
We didn't promise star wealth for booty;
Nor the shining spread of stars to take.
We say to you also who died in Africa,
Because of German mischief in the West.
Was it not valour for your king,
Or your dignified tribute to Britain ...

"That is powerful," Matswane said when he had finished. "I can understand how such a poet would lend words to Maqoma's grave."

"Perhaps the last part would be misplaced, since Maqoma was no friend of Britain. Come to think about it, neither were the soldiers who sank with the *Mendi*. They went there to fight for the land they had been promised if they joined the British forces."

Phila told her how in the past the government of Ciskei celebrated the day of independence at Ntaba kaNdoda. How Maqoma's bones were buried there after being exhumed from Robben Island in 1985.

"Unfortunately, death didn't find him 'on the mountaintop somewhere at dawn', as Maqoma had wished, but surrounded instead by yawning waters, incarcerated in the land of lepers."

"How did he die?" Matswane asked quietly.

"Under mysterious circumstances. Exactly how he died was never explained by the government of the time."

"He must have been quite a character for you to invest so much energy into researching his life."

"That he is ... was. I'm sure he is pleased with his bones reburied at Ntaba kaNdoda, which meant so much to him. That's where his character was formed – or so I understand from ... Anyway, it is also close to the scene of the first battle he ever led against amaNdlambe. Perhaps you've heard of the Battle of Amalinde?"

"Can't say I have," said Mat. "But I have a feeling you're going to tell me about it."

Kicking Against the Goad

'A RAINMAKING CEREMONY WAS HELD at the great house near the banks of Mgxada.'

Maqoma was in a good mood compared to the last time they'd talked. Phila felt a sharp relief in hearing the chief's voice. He had been feeling a certain mental constipation without him over the past few days.

'The ceremony was organised by Suthu, Ngqika's great wife, for the benefit of her benighted son Sandile,' continued Maqoma. 'Mqantsi, the rainmaking shaman, whose influence was at its height, officiated at the ceremony. He had a virulent hatred for the white missionaries, put the blame on them for the raging drought that was in the land then. In fact he blamed them for everything that was wrong in our land. Without rain there was no contending with white men's ways for us. Rain was a source of our self-sufficiency. The likes of Mqantsi and Mlanjeni used people's credulity for their own ends. "Since white man came in our land," was Mqantsi's leitmotif, "seasons have changed, rain has been withheld. White people raise winds, by witchcraft, that blow the rain away to the oceans." He brought cheers to the hearts of the confused nation. "Our only reprieve is in chasing them away!" More shouts of support. "They've come to our land to kill with hunger all those who do not adopt their ways."

'That was how Mqantsi invoked people's hatred against white missionaries; reinventing Nxele's rallying call. I was a little ambivalent. I liked his preaching against white people, but I wanted things to be taken at a steady pace, to prepare our warriors to fight with white men's smoking sticks of death. Mqantsi and his followers saw my caution as a sign of weakness.

'Mqantsi liked to hold his rainmaking ceremonies on Sundays so as to intimidate those who wished to attend services at the missionary bases. He made it a point to hold them close to the missionary stations so as to distract their congregations. He called for a boycott against selling farm produce, like milk, corn, eggs and meat, to the inhabitants of mission stations. If I'm not mistaken, there were about four stations in Tyumi.

'That day, as usual, the rain ceremony started with due sacredness. Mqantsi chanted the usual arcane gibberish, leading an ox (a magical rain animal) with a special leather thong across the land affected by drought. People followed him in awed anticipation and hypnotic superstition, hoping for the thong not to snap as that would have spelt unheard prayers. The thong seldom broke, Mqantsi made sure of that.

'The ceremony was half the issue. Mqantsi dragged my name through the mud as soon as the sacred ceremonies were finished. It was no secret that I didn't go for the mumbo-jumbo, whether traditional or foreign. I tolerated ceremonies for the peace of the society. I didn't mind them so long as they had some social value and – this was most crucial to me – they promoted respect for chiefs. I long learnt that orderly life among human beings depends upon the presence of some common sentiments that control their behaviour as individuals in relation to others for the benefit of all. If superstition regulates sentiments for social communal benefits, fine by me. But if it is in opposition to the people's sentiments, and to chiefdom, I oppose it, even if it is brought by an angel on a golden tablet. For me, God's voice has to take cognisance of the social order of the group; meet people where they are. I don't care about any law that does not respect the customary ways of the people it wishes to govern. By wishing to suppress, or govern by force, belief can do no good. All it will do is set a dangerous chain of reaction in motion. People will only see it as an alien agency that threatens their situation. Once you undermine people's ways, which have a very strong hold on their national conscience, friction will develop.

'So I tolerated superstitious ceremonies for the greater good of the tribe. That was why I first tried to reason with the faction that was led by Mqantsi – for the sake of our people. When they approached me for support to attack white people, I told them, "We must first wait until we establish a trusting relationship with the missionaries. From them we shall learn their tricks, perhaps even how to manufacture weapons similar to theirs for ourselves."

'"Is that the excuse you give for playing a coward now, great Maqoma?" Mqantsi challenged me, interrupting me as I was speaking. A commoner interrupting a chief while he was still talking was not heard of in our culture. It was a sign of the low opinion he held of me. It irked me, of course, but I kept quiet, giving him enough rope to hang himself. I hated the mocking irony by which he pronounced my name as "great Maqoma"!

He continued. "You know as well as I do that the presence of white missionaries has never deterred the white government from attacking and killing us for sport and for our land. What do you suppose will be different this time? Or is it as I've heard – that the fort buildings erected next to your villages have brought water in your knees?"

'It became apparent to me that the meeting had been organised to denigrate my reputation in the eyes of the people, not for rainmaking. Suthu, Ngqika's widow, had arranged it thus, so that I might lose credibility in the eyes of the people, which would be her son Sandile's gain. By appearing brave in pushing for an immediate war with the white people they thought to undermine my power and subvert my authority. Although I was fuming from Mqantsi's obstreperous solecism, I tried to minimise the damage by keeping my temper cool.

'"Yes, I'm sure you're right, Mqantsi," I said, picking my pipe with a grass stem. "But the missionary presence in our midst limits potential colonial mischief, and reduces their atrocities. When they know there are some of their own who observe and judge their destruction it tempers their cruelty. Now is not the time for us to put the flute of our anger on the lips. Let us first arm ourselves with guns. It is of little use to fight white people with assegais. Their firearms are far too advanced."

'There was open discontent in the air. It could have easily led to revolt. Most had no patience to embrace what they saw as a forlorn hope. But Mqantsi, who was obviously chosen to be at the front of confrontation against my leadership, attacked again. "Let Maqoma wag his tail between his legs and cower if he wants."

'Such audacity! I kept thinking to myself. Things had gone too far. Mqantsi was bold because he was sure of chieftain backing. I suspected my brother Thyali was in it too, wishing to capitalise his influence on the inexperienced young Sandile. Mqantsi continued, more charged. "Let the great Maqoma ingratiate his missionaries, but we, the sons of Phalo, shall not be implicated in that degenerate cowardice. We shall not sell off our forefathers' land for buttons and strange sayings, as Ngqika did. I've been suspecting that the great snake of Mthontsi has been growing weak. Now I see it with my own eyes. They've tamed the mirror of Nothontho! Maqoma was sharp as a double-edged sword in his day, but not anymore! Perhaps none braver than him shall ever come in the history of our chieftainship. But that was before the sea came to his knees."

'It is very frustrating when stupidity becomes audacious; fatal when it has the majority following of the tribe. I listened with ripe boredom and mounting anger as he continued to insult me.

'"Personally I never thought I would see the day when the scaly python of Nothontho would wallow in feminine credulity of believing what gives him joy. I say those who woke late saw nothing. They've not seen the python uncoiling itself, the star of Mthontsi appearing at dawn. The fire burning in the valleys of Ngcwenxa when the son of Nothontho lost his cool. What tragedy Ngqika committed by welcoming white people in our midst. It is he who raised those muck-eating Mfengu into pecking their necks. It is our tribe who is now living on muck. The Mfengus have outstripped us with our own cattle. Shaka was wise in eliminating the Mfengu vermin on his land. We were stupid for opening our hearts to them. Look now, our land, from Cwecweni to Ngquthu, reeks of Mfengu vermin. They flee like the sun when they move because their soles have grown callused as baobab bark.

'"Do you really think white people would live in peace with you, Maqoma, just because you want to live in peace with them? What they really want is to see the nation of Phalo annihilated and all of this land in their hands. Whatever happened to the talks you used to inflame us with that white people's idea of peace was making us their vassals? That there was an uncrossable desert between our habits and theirs?" He stopped to collect himself while making sure the cheers were heard before continuing. "So long as I'm still eating the millet of this land, white people shall feel the pinch from Phalo's vice."

'Thundering shouts of approval denoted support for Mqantsi's sentiments. I wrote him on my knee, swearing the year would not be over before he slept under the sod, wrapped in the mat of my vengeance. I knew I couldn't touch him then because his fame was high on behalf of the hopes people had in his powers to placate the wrath of the ancestors. Being a leader depends on your ability to choose your moments, to adapt your course to practical demands. You must know and be able to submit to necessity; how to build and profit by materials at hand. There's no need to go on the offensive if you know the field does not suit your tactics, and the timing is wrong. One who chooses time and place can rise superior even when the greatest odds are against him. That is the sign of true leadership.

'I knew where to tie Mqantsi and let him learn the weight of my anger. There was nothing I could do to protect my brother Thyali, however. His obduracy and myopia stood between us and drove him, stupidly, to sacrifice our people unnecessarily. I had always admired his sterling simplicity and discipline, but when he was under the influences of the warring party he lost his best qualities. Fortunately, one of my elders sensed the direction of my anger and tried to placate things by putting Mqantsi in his place. He put aside the calabash next to the crock he had just drawn from. Then, wiping his hands on the slumbering dog at his feet, he addressed Mqantsi.

'"You think you've grown so wise and popular to earn the right of lifting your lips in scowl, and laying harsh words against chiefs, Mqantsi? Since when has being a rainmaker entitled one to throw abuses at royal blood? You think you can talk the equal of chiefs just because you know how to lie to people by promising the rain you've no power of making? If you don't watch your mouth, your doom is in the offing."

'The intense reproach of the old man was agreeable to me, but things had gone too far for it to tame my anger. Others stood also to draw Mqantsi back from his insolence, to little avail. Mqantsi continued on the trail of his insults. Maidens came to sprinkle the floor with water to settle the dust. I looked into the distance with frustration. The wooded plains and slopes along the heights of Mgxada beckoned.

'Circumstances plot to the advantage of the devil's mischief when he is preparing your destruction. Two days after the ceremony the rain came down in a mad rush, destroying instead of rejuvenating the dying crops. But nobody cared. The fact was that it came, which to them meant Mqantsi stood in favour with the ancestors. From then on the grumbling wind could only fan the fire of Mqantsi's popularity. Thyali, who could never resist the temptation to win glory for his ego, which this time was fanned by Mqantsi, started rustling white farmers in flat disobedience of my orders. This gave a long-awaited excuse to the Cape Mounted Rifles, the mercenary destructive force hired by the colonial government, to come down on us like a disease. Within no time Thyali and his people were driven away from their land and forced to resettle on barren land. As I didn't think that was an opportune time to hazard a sortie, I didn't go to their assistance. My best strategy lay in remaining passive while waiting to feast on the carrion. I knew whites were dying to extend the fight to me because they recognised I still held the greater balance of power. My plan was to play fast and loose between the two belligerents. I knew Smith would not be content with only Thyali's land; his success would serve only to sharpen his greed. I sent emissaries to Hintsa, the paramount of the Gcalekas, warning him of impending white attacks on both our lands.

'In the meantime I thought it an opportune time to deal with other internal issues troubling my tribe. Matwana, a minor chief in my tribe, had been causing me some concern by pilfering followers to the Mqantsi faction. When he suddenly fell ill with a mysterious sickness that caused him constant headaches, continuous nose bleeds and strange carbuncles on his skin, I saw an opportunity to be done with him once and for all, and exterminate his infected chieftainship. I'm not proud of what I had to do to maintain power sometimes, but necessities will arise when the devil drives, and in shameful times it is normal to be ashamed. The power of a chief depends upon his ability to manipulate his people's weaknesses to his own advantage.

'With four councillors and witch-doctors we paid Matwana a visit at his base in Mkhubiso, near Burnshill Mission. The diviners I brought, encouraged by myself, suggested that death was in Matwana's own hearth. Strategic witch-hunts were made. Naturally, most of his wealthy followers took the blame for his sickness. In our tribal system when you destroy wealthy aristocratic councillors you destroy the tribe, because the power of a chief is highly dependent on the wealth of his aristocrats. We accused Matwana's wealthy aristocrats of sorcery, a sin that is punishable by death. We attached loops of *ingximba* to their doorposts, as tokens of accusation, and summoned them to the great place to answer the accusations. Many of them fled to the colony and the missionaries, which prompted the missionary Laing to request a congress with me.

'On the agreed congress day, they came with my old friend Matshaya. Did I tell you about Matshaya?

'He once saved my life, at the Battle of Amalinde.'

'I believe you did,' Phila said.

'Matshaya was living in missionary quarters then, and fully practising white man's religion. The day was oppressively hot, without a single cloud in the sky. We sat under the tree of *umsintsi* as we congressed.'

'Why did white people call the tree *kaffirboom*?'

'I don't know, perhaps because we liked to congress beneath its shade? It grew abundantly in our areas.'

'Matshaya ...?' Phila prompted.

'I was very much interested in hearing about the health of my quondam friend, who served as an interpreter between the missionaries and us,' Maqoma continued. 'He began the proceedings wearing a wary warm smile. "It's been a long time, my chief, since our eyes met. Things multiply and the grass is long."

'I always had a soft spot for him, but then was not the time for intimacies. "Is that why we don't see each other anymore, Matshaya?" I asked, rather crudely. I immediately berated myself and tried to placate him. "I know we are scarce from each other's eyes, Matshaya, but you know how it is with you there and me here. I never thought it had anything to do with the grass, or any of Qamata's designs. It only proved too dangerous for you to be Xhosa, so you found yourself other masters. I thought that was why we don't see each other anymore. Am I reading things wrongly from where I'm standing? Enlighten me."

"'I guessed you'd see it that way," he answered sheepishly.

"'The cat lies at the hearth in our villages while you drink fermented drinks with a thorn; living in the lap of luxury and trailing foreign robes. Beyond that we've been keeping well despite the pressure your colonial friends put us through. We have a hard life this side, spilt out like water since hearing the misfortunes that have befallen our tribes, but we know Qamata bends his eye on the deeds of man. Have you any news for us?"

"'I'll get straight to the point," he said, standing, casting a towering shadow with his stature and robes.

"'You never were one to beat about the bush, Matshaya," I encouraged him, lighting my pipe. "It's one of the reasons I wanted you always close to me. You are loyal, but loyalty has many faces, I guess. Your only weakness was always too much honesty, always allowing your tongue to speak before your brain. Repair yourself and let's get on with it. What do your friends want?"

"'My missionary friends feel they need to warn you that you're on a dangerous course, my chief. The green flies have reached us that you're planning an all-out attack on white colonial powers. That will be suicide. They have brought me along to assist in persuading you against such an undertaking, for old times' sake. I hope you don't mind."

'I found it funny that he should still address me as his chief while wearing immaculate clothes, and having washed the ochre off his face, carrying a book with a red mouth in his hands with clean nails. And teeth, white as kids against burnt grass. I looked a beggar compared to him. Part of me wanted him to shrink before his disgrace of choosing opulence over struggling traditional life, but he was not biting.

"'A suit and a book with a red mouth – wages of slavery are low these days, wouldn't you say, Matshaya?"'

"'If my chief sees it that way." Matshaya showed indifference.

"'You think because you walk with white men and their flowing hair your ears will reflect the sun also? Tell your white friends I want my people they harbour in their missions. Those people wish to escape their obligation in our societies. They must hand them back. Otherwise we shall have no choice but to regard the missionaries as harbouring the fugitives. How many women do you have there who've run away from *uphundlo*? How many thieves and murderers escape their due punishments to your missions into your Jesus's hands who seems ready to forgive only sins committed against kaffirs without justice, but demands the justice of white people's courts where the ill is committed against white people?" I asked cynically, still trying to bring him down from his high horse. He ignored my comments and continued with his mission, which irked me more.

'"We're not here to talk about that, my chief, perhaps later. I know whatever has reached the ears of my chief about my reasons for defecting must not have favoured my side of the story. The world gives an easier ear to slander than to truth ..."

'"Are you one with the world then, Matshaya?" I interjected. "It seems it's you who's now arguing slander." My resentment mounting, I paused, wishing to give him a chance to defend himself. But when he failed to lower his eyes in shame I saw no reason to respect someone who obviously had lost his for me, so I continued in controlled impatience. "What reached me, Matshaya, is that you've deserted the field Qamata gave you to cultivate for a less stony one. In my eyes you have no reason to be proud, not the Matshaya I know anyway."

'"In my lights," it was his turn to interject with a hard voice, seeing no point of sparing me, I suppose, "conditions that made for our traditional life no longer exist, and to resist the times is to set yourself on a collision course with the wagon of destiny. Still that's not why we're here. My friends want me to tell you that Her Majesty's government is much more powerful than the Xhosa nation incorporated, let alone the Ngqikas. If you love our people, as you purport to do, you'll realise that it is futile to resist inevitability. You'll only bring meaningless death to our people."

'I became surprised by the superior disdain his voice acquired the more we spoke.

'"They're not your people, Matshaya," I retorted indignantly. "You gave up that right when you chose to join white missions. And since when is defending our inheritance futility? So long as there's one warrior left in this land of Phalo the sons of Albion shall catch hell before they're able to confiscate it."

'Matshaya kept a momentary calm before answering. "The suppleness of your mind has always beat with intelligence, my chief. But these are dangerous times for intelligence. It would afford you a better future to assume meekness. I won't attempt to compete with your eloquence. But these are things above any one man, and these are not times for eloquence, or gallantry. We've fallen on evil times, not an epoch of heroes that was our forefathers'. Your valour is indisputable, everyone knows that, but these are other times. There is no sense in fighting an elephant with a walking stick. For the sake of the people, find other ways.

'"Instead of nursing revenge, why don't you use the white man's law against them? Take your grievances to the white man's courts to obtain justice for our people?"

'"Hahaa! You make me laugh, Matshaya. The justice of white courts is just only to white people. I've learnt that the hard way. My father's experience is warning incarnate for me. You had better come out of the sheep's close, Matshaya, and tell us what it is that your friends want before the cows come home."

'"That you stop the cruel practice of witch-hunting. That you forget about engaging colonial forces in an all-out war, as is rumoured everywhere." Matshaya found it difficult even to catch his breath as he said that.

'"Rumour is the prevailing mood of unfaithful people, Matshaya. "I thought you knew that."

'"My friends want you to trust your commands to Somandla, the Almighty. After that you shall see all things shall work out for the best."

'"Personally, I'm rather sick and tired of what white people want. It usually has no benefit for me, even when it is not downright oppressive to us. You've always had too much trust in the mysterious and vague, Matshaya. A man must tether his horse before trusting it to the care of Somandla. Lest Somandla finds blame in his careless trust. If you understood the teachings of Ntsikana, as you claimed to follow him, you would have understood that. Perhaps we'd have had better things to say to each other today. As it is now, I see no way of convincing you out of your error. I'm sure the feeling is mutual. You've been reading too many fables from the book with the red mouth. Tell your friends I've bought the path I'm on with the tragedy that is my life. It shall end when that life ebbs away." I stood to leave.

'"All I'm saying, my chief, is that in evil times it is better to listen to the wind than to brave the storm." He said those words with a resolution that reminded me of the Matshaya I knew. That Matshaya flashed before my eyes for a moment, and, for that brief moment, I was filled with tender affection for him. But the presence of white missionaries soon made itself felt and I lost the feeling.

"'And what about trafficking with the devil, Matshaya? What does your wisdom say to that?'"

"'We cannot defeat an enemy we don't know, my chief. It was you who taught me that.'"

"'I suppose asses fly also in your missions if you think you can traffic with the devil and not get singed.'"

"'We take the good with the bad, my chief.'"

"'You've always been a wise one, Matshaya. But I'm afraid we just don't see by the same eye here. Perhaps the fault was yours. Perhaps you should have left me on the battlefield to die an ignominious death. You wouldn't be faced with this problem now. But having survived that afternoon my blood will have to turn to ice before I allow white people to just waltz into our land and confiscate the inheritance of our children. That is my last word, my friend.'"

"'Remember then, my chief, what you once told me. Violence is very attractive to an imprudent man, like false gold to a fool. Whereas to a wise person it is a last resort of desperation.'"

"'Where have you been in the past few years, Matshaya? It was desperate times the moment the floating houses of white people landed on our shores. I remember many things well in my heart. The years before white people came death was just a visitor, not a master, in our villages. But times have changed. When the powers of governors grow congenitally deaf to those who don't see with the same eye they reduce them to fatal desperation. If we can't name our complaints in words, we would do so with the force of our spears, and the desperation of our vanishing days. What are we to do when wisdom is ineffective against greed, and blocked by endless profit making and the cruel vanity of white people? They've left us with only one option, to violate our own lives to pull down the pillars of their kingdom. We're trying for the impossible, you say. Well, if we'll not achieve it with our lives, we shall with our graves.

"'You're a self-regarding person, Matshaya. Your actions don't impact much on the future of the tribe. I understand why it was easy for you to yield to the temptation of ease, and I don't hold it against you. I don't think you were after profit. I know you better than that. But I'm the chief. Many people depend on what I do. I cannot be eating pie dishes of clotted cream and drinking brandy while they die of starvation because the settlers have occupied their arable land. Run away from harsh destiny all you like, if that is what is in your heart, but do not expect me to follow you to feathered pillows when we are losing the heritage of our children. I know many evils await us, but we shall stand like men and fall like warriors. Not for our sake but for the sake of our children's children; that when they look back on how the land of Phalo was sacked from us they'd at least say they had forefathers.

'"We're not fools, Matshaya. We know in our hearts our ways can no longer reign supreme in this land of Togu. We preserve, not because of fatal obduracy, but so that we may defy the cruel fate, with our deaths if need be. So that our children, and their children's children, may stand up tall until the land of Phalo is returned to its rightful owners. If defeated, we shall live in our children's hearts as ghosts or myths until the land is returned to its owners. In them we shall live until, in the chaos of history, they trace our steps and hear our voices. Then at that time, even this day shall not be insignificant, and those who shall have perished shall not have done so in vain."'

'Matshaya insisted on imploring me to change my mind with moistened eyes. "My chief, the Lord Jesus Christ is beating the wings of His angels over your head. Harden not your heart and accept His salvation for He holds all things in His hand. If only in humility you would humble yourself, He will heal our land …"

'His words filled me with anger. "I see that you've now learnt the gloomy talk and bandy arguments of priests, Matshaya. You've acquired the habit of answering simple questions with complicated, long jabbering answers. I doubt if there'll ever be any going back for you. But please, spare me the tiara pomp. I have enough problems as it is. For what it's worth, I hope all the patina of religion you've acquired does you good somewhere, and affords you some solace for deserting your people. But do not expect me to be moved by all that trumpery. You're walking over the graves of our forefathers. Were it not for the respect I used to have for you we would not even be talking still. I grew tired a long time ago of listening to the false import of Christian words. Those hypocrites who speciously take counsel with the supreme God do not hesitate to foster the devil in our midst by cruel greed. They never match their actions to their words.

'I'm weary of their vulgar talk about events they say are to overtake us after death, only because we don't lie, kill and squander in the name of their God. Christians are their own best argument against their religion. I've grown a serious aversion to them. And you – do you honestly think alleviating yourself from your responsibilities is going to afford you salvation?

'"You have your journey, I have mine, Matshaya. Mine is bound to the wheel of my people's destiny. Everyone must find his own salvation.

I'm determined to be whatever becomes of man. If that's an insult to your religion, so be it. You've always been a little rushed, careless to detail, and not very concerned with probability. Hence I was not surprised when you took on this venture. Though I must admit I thought it would have cloyed even you by now. I suppose I was wrong, or perhaps I underestimated the depths of your conversion. But please do not preach to me. I wear my memory as armour against inordinate influences. I fear Qamata, and try to honour my responsibilities towards his ordinances. That is all the religion I need in my life, and luckily I don't need to be English to accomplish that."

'By then my heart was in my mouth. As I spoke, Matshaya constantly looked at me with pleading eyes. That day we both realised the gulf between us was no longer bridgeable. I thought of the song we used to sing when we were growing up, herding cattle in the fields:

There lies too much friction between us now,
The shadowy mountains, the hissing grass,
Please, friend,
Accompany me a while in tow,
For I'm afraid of snakes
That distend in the grass.

'His missionary friends watched me with long assessing stares. As soon as I was done talking they started addressing Matshaya. Whatever they were whispering it took too long, which irritated me further. I got fed up and interrupted them. "If your friends have something to say, let them address it to me, Matshaya."

'Matshaya eased the situation by saying, "They were interested in our earlier talk so I was trying to retell what we were saying to them."

'"And what do they say about it?" I asked, not yet fully placated.

'"That you're a wise man in whom there are more things to admire than to scorn. But they feel you need some religious instruction. They say you have keen intelligence and sharp wit that can be better used for the work of our Lord Jesus Christ, instead of drowning them in liquor. But ignorance still dims your eyes and, like Saul, you're still kicking against the goad."

'"What they say does not come as a surprise to me. We're now stretching this pettiness too far, Matshaya. Tell them their Lord will have my attention if he gives us back the land Her Majesty's government has stolen from us. I thank you to be on my way."

'With that I extinguished my pipe, took my *isikhakha*, threw it on my shoulders and was on my way. Anger added speed to my stride as the rest of my men faltered behind.

'"By the way, Matshaya," I called from my horse, "tell your friends that I've nothing to do with the war plans going around. It's not a shoe of my stitching."'

Even the Cur Will Turn

PHILA SAT ON THE EDGE OF THE BED scrutinising his anxiety. Hands cupped on his chin, he wondered about the prospects of meeting Matswane's fiancé. She had told, warned, him earlier that he had got suspicious when she didn't answer his calls, and so he was flying in to East London that day and coming to King William's Town. She had felt trapped and told him everything. Now he wanted to meet Phila.

"Me?" Phila asked, a little shocked. "Why me?"

"Because I told him about us," Mat said nonchalantly, as if it was normal.

Phila wasn't really surprised; somehow, he felt, this had been her master plan all along.

The whirlwind was in the thorn trees now.

Forty minutes to seven, next to the alarm clock, his hotel bedside telephone rang. It was Matswane.

"Siva is on his way to your room and, oh! he's breathing flames!"

For a minute Phila couldn't figure out who Mat was talking about and she had already dropped the phone on the other side. He sat trying to husband thoughts to get himself out of the situation. Instinctively, though, he knew this was not going to be a situation he could bail himself out of by using Socratic dialogues.

The knock at the door was less fierce than Phila expected. He opened the door and proceeded to take a seat on the desk without even looking the man in the eye. Now that he was standing in the middle of the room, himself not exactly sure what to do next, Siva looked gigantic and smelled of too much cologne.

"I guess you're Phila," he said, looking around the room as if expecting to find another person. Phila nodded. "How long has this been going on?" The next thing, before Phila could answer, the giant was charging him like a bull. He punched Phila heavily on the jaw. For a while Phila could

208

see nothing but a flash of light. More shocking to him was the strange release from the trapped feeling the punch gave him. The punch felt like an electric shock. Like an auotopsied lab rat, he wished for more.

Although he grew up in a township, where fights were as common as the rising sun, this was only Phila's second fight ever. The first one had been in junior secondary school. He remembered how he had thrown himself at the bully that afternoon, how he had fought like a cornered cur, maniacal and unbridled, throwing everything he had. The surprise of such a violent reaction had thrown the enemy off and it was the same now. It took a while for Phila to realise he had the heel of his hand pressed against the giant's jaw.

At that moment Matswane entered the room. She looked shocked to see her fiancé lying unconscious on the floor. "Is he dead?" she asked with an accusing face. "Did you have to kill him?"

Phila went to the bathroom and came back with a jar full of cold water. He threw it in Siva's face. It did the trick. "He hit his head against the wall," he said.

Smelling the direction the wind was blowing, he proceeded to pack his bags. Matswane sat on the carpet, looking dazed, leaning against the bed. She cradled her fiancé's head in her lap, wiping his face with a wet towel.

Downstairs Phila paid his hotel bill and left town.

He drove to East London, experiencing alternating spasms of self-pity and bitterness. His mind, in irritation, wondered about amaNdlambe, whose houses dappled the hills and valleys along the road between King William's Town and East London. This was the road that had given the trapped Smith breathing room.

During the 1851 war Maqoma and Sandile, together with the Kat River valley Khoi rebels, who were led by Hermanus Matroos, had closed all roads into other colonial towns like Grahamstown and Cape Town. So the colonials had no ways of replenishing King William's Town and the surrounding forts with supplies and ammunition. But the neutrality of amaNdlambe meant this stretch of road from the port of East London to King William's Town was opened to them. As if to rub salt in the wound, Siyolo, one of the Ndlambe chiefs, decided to join the war a little too late, after the troops of KhoiKhoi mercenaries from Cape Town had passed through to King William's Town and Fort Beaufort to rescue the situation for the colonial government. Meantime, when approached to be similar mercenaries, the Zulus declined the offer, asking: why should we help the British fight amaXhosa who are deamanding their land back, when we also should be doing the same thing here?

Phila switched his thinking to the city he was going back to – anything to avoid confronting the mess he had created through Matswane – the first city he had known in his life. East London had a mixture of English smugness and German functionality about it (it and Stutterheim were founded by a group of German missionaries): old buildings and stringent quality. Everything about the place pointed towards England: Oxford Street, Trafalgar House, East London. Every time he was there Phila felt the need to deconstruct the colonial psyche.

When he arrived thirty minutes later he was welcomed by the golden lights of the industrial zone, which introduced a festival mood on the scars of the terrain. The city was truly a borderland town between isolation and nomadism, thought Phila.

After checking into his usual self-catering guest house, he went straight to his room, where he lay on his bed, prey to sapping feelings, trying to accommodate himself to his circumstances. The error had been in allowing Matswane to enter his space. It wouldn't happen again, he told himself. He decided to take a shower. With hot water falling on his neck he chose to end the struggle against the noose; with a soothing *Suzanne* from Leonard Cohen in the background he accepted the situation and his error. That which we cannot reform we need to accept, the advice of the stoic came to him. By the time he got out of the shower he almost felt his own self, passive and distant to things.

He opened the fridge, seeking something to eat. There was pastry in the freezer, ice-cream – blueberry cheesecake – and frozen chicken livers, a litre of milk that had gone off, a dish of jam and a jug of water. He opened the cupboards: uncooked rice, samp, pasta, Kellogg's and several tins, among which was a tin of beef meatballs, which he took out. Basically the groceries he had left behind when he was last there. He had told the Afrikaner woman who owned the place, Mrs Boyle, that he'd probably be back within a week, and she had been true to her promise of keeping his stuff, "If I don't become too busy." He needed to buy more groceries. He also found a packet of sour cream and chive potato chips and a packet of peanut M&Ms, both of which he took through to the lounge. Booty in hand, he turned on the TV as he sat on the couch. His cell phone kept ringing but he ignored it. After channel hopping he settled on a National Geographic documentary about meerkats. The curiosity of the buggers, their teamwork and smart ways of outmanoeuvring enemies fascinated him.

He was watching desert elephants when the door buzzer sounded. Certain it was someone buzzing in error, he ignored it. He hadn't told anyone where he was staying. After several buzzes he decided to check it out. It irritated him with pleasure to hear Matswane's voice on the intercom. He buzzed her in and unlocked the door latch, then panicked slightly when he realised she might still be with her fiancé.

"I'm glad to see you're eating healthy." Matswane tried to be flippant despite the situation, her eyes taking in the empty chip and sweet packets. After registering with some relief that she was alone, it occurred to Phila that what he was doing was not very macho – binge junk-eating away a heartache. Cracking a bottle of hard alcohol might have made a stronger, more macho statement, but he had a motto of not touching alcohol when he had emotional problems.

"I took the liberty of inviting Mr Jack to be our counsellor." Matswane raised the bottle of Jack Daniels she was holding by the neck.

"I've only water to offer," Phila said, feigning an apology and going to the kitchen to fetch glasses. He had a taste of bitterness and panic, bile and iron, in his mouth.

"Oh, I think you've plenty to offer!" The noisy programme on TV overcompensated for the silence between them. "I've just dropped Siva at the airport. Then I remembered the B&B you said you always stay at when you're here and thought it worth a try. The receptionist knows me as your wife now." Matswane laughed softly.

Phila was stunned to discover she was waiting for him to say something. He did not. He kept a tight rein on his hopes.

"I told Siva I was going with you," Matswane said.

"I suppose he was not very pleased about that," was Phila's contribution to the conversation.

"He threatened to sue me for all the costs he had already run up on our wedding preparations." They both laughed, Matswane a little harder than Phila.

"He looks like a practical man." Phila held his glass out for another stiff one.

"His reality is in numbers."

"Good for him."

After two drinks or so Matswane said what was on her mind. "It's been a long confusing day for me. The only thing I know for sure right now is that I want to be with you."

"You could have fooled me back there at the hotel," replied Phila with irony in her voice.

"What did you expect?"

The question felt like a punch in the diaphragm for Phila. "Somebody described expectations as resentments under construction," he said, feeling a giddy relief coming over him.

"Do you resent me?"

"I doubt if I can ever be able to resent you, even if I wanted to."

They kissed with more force than passion.

"I desperately need a shower," Matswane declared, pulling her body away from Phila's.

Phila pointed her to the bathroom. "There should be clean towels and all." He heard the hiss of the water and snatches of song.

A few minutes later she came out of the bathroom in his robe with life-threatening beauty. By and by, with the encouragement of Black Jack, they made love on the carpeted floor with the background of Americans killing people in some faraway desert country on the TV news. Phila, butting up against the couch, felt fallen. He needed a cigarette. He switched off the TV to replace its noise with sounds of silence and the monologue of traffic in the distance. Then he went to the balcony to light a cigarette. Behind the fiery setting sun, for a moment it seemed as if the old world was crashing down in flames. He watched the moon path grow faint on the sea. The silence of the falling evening was tangible. Halfway through the cigarette Maqoma broke in.

'Not far from here are the peaceful valleys where the Gaga unites with the Tyumi River.' Phila made a mental note of the area. 'I can't see this place without recalling the boreal wind Somerset, the first Governor of the colony we encountered. Somerset as a person was not bad and had an amiable disposition towards us. He and my father got on very well. In turn I had a good rapport with his son, Henry, who still had an easy-going personality then, before the whole thing of colonial power went to his head. He was none too intelligent but he wanted to please everyone in all things, which made him a poor leader and a liar when things went wrong. Regardless, he had an inflated sense of his capabilities, which his father encouraged by placing him in positions of power he had neither the experience nor intelligence to manage. The major problem in our relations with the Cape Colony mostly came through the blustering puppy dog Harry Smith, but Henry was to blame for that also by worshipping and flattering Smith every chance he got. You could say they tolerated each other's incompetence and unhealthy ambition. Many wars we fought with the colonial government could have been avoided if the men in power then had better characters than Smith – and D'Urban in particular, who came before him.

'When Smith made us cross the Gaga River into barren land, after all the undertakings he had given me as his friend, I knew then that the issues between us and the white people could only be resolved by war. They took my land on the Kat River banks, gave it to the KhoiKhoi, and ordered me and my people to go plough rocks and graze cattle on stones. I had done everything in my power to placate colonial powers; entertained their missionaries, returned their livestock whenever I saw them around our villages, all at great expense to my reputation among my people, who took to calling me a sheep in lion's skin. I even sent my wives, children and relatives to white schools in Cape Town, to be educated in the Western ways. But none of that was enough for them.

'Obedience, just as rebellion, is a cause for war in a white man's mind when that mind is captured by greed.

'Eventually, I saw the only way out was to fight it to the grave. Since war must be, I told myself, let it advance to the bitter end according to the nature of things. You tell me that in their books they talk about me as if I was born loving war. The truth is they made me into a demon in order to hide the facts about why we decided to go to war. I was a loyal friend to the amiable. Ask Henry Somerset, even the Rosses, who established a mission station on my land. Although I didn't care much for their religion, I used to have tea with them every Sunday. I allowed them to convert my people, teach them how to work the land. And we talked about plans of living and tilling the land together for the good of everyone involved. John and Helen Ross would vouch for that. They were the two white people who knew me best. Yes, I became a fierce enemy to those who took our land by force, combustible when attacked, intrepid when confronted by problems, preserving when tested by harsh circumstances, but above all I operated on principle and was true to my word. I believed there were rules and boundaries even under war conditions. I preserved my principles even when the white people made it clear they did not respect them, like when they killed women and children and burnt our planted fields.

'Just before the 1846 war, I stayed under the mountain of Mqwazi, what the white people called Gaika's Kop, trying not to be implicated with my brother Thyali's militant adventures. But the Cape Mounted Rifles visited us anyway, despite Henry's personal undertakings to me. I'll never forget that day, the day they came. It was like a mountain landslide, early in the morning while children were still brushing sleep from their eyes. We woke to a mad gallop of cavalry and the murderous rage of gunfire. One could hardly breathe. The air was filled with smoke. They felled unarmed people in pockets and groups, firing, stabbing and slashing with bayonets and sabres as they went. Our people didn't even get a chance to fetch their weapons. Nineteen of them were killed, defenceless, running back and forth over the courtyards like frightened impala.

'It stays in a man's mind the sight of his child being crushed and trampled by a horse; the sight of his woman running outside the hut singed and scalded like a mouse from burning sheaves.

'Imagine my surprise when I discovered the person in charge of that raid was Henry, that scaramouching and swaggering fool. Of course, he was too stupid and clumsy to pull that on his own. He did not know those mountains from his arse. He couldn't keep track of us on plains of short acacia trees even if our tracks led up to his arse and were as conspicuous as the zebra's coat. No, the mastermind of the Mounted Rifles was a man named Stubbs. The funny thing was that I had allowed Stubbs to barter in my chiefdom with copper, iron, beads, buttons and darning needles. He occasionally smuggled brandy for us. He presented himself as someone who didn't care about white colonials' rule. He told me all he wanted was a way of survival during those times of failing crops. I believed him because I saw in him the complex character of Khula. He gave me the idea that he had the same profound resentment for white authority. Like Khula, he had begun his career among us by hunting elephants and selling their ivory. He even had Khula's surprising streak of tenderness and boyish sense of fun to complement his harsh mannerism. We taught him our ways, bushcraft, tracking spoors even at night, discouraged him from plundering the gentle beast that is sacred to us.

'Stubbs told me that as a youth he had had a hard time, so he wished to form a hunting club for the unruly young men of his people, something to keep them out of trouble. It was with that group that he formed the nucleus of the redoubtable Mounted Rifles. Henry exploited them to tragic use against us, effectively so. In the end they were not just a hunting club but mercenaries devoted to the congenial occupations of arson and rape. In retrospect, I see my trust towards Stubbs was careless. Henry understood the character of men like Stubbs, knew he would be for hire when given an offer he could not refuse.'

Phila thought it best to chip in because Maqoma was now becoming emotional.

'Stockenström, in his book, says the tragic raid was not premeditated. He says the Boers of the commandos were frustrated for not catching up with the Ndlambes they were fighting, and were threatening mutiny if they were to go back without the cattle booty they had pinned their hopes on in joining the Cape Mounted Rifles.'

'That makes it right?' Maqoma asked. 'Only a fool, or someone with vested interests, pretended that the Cape Mounted Rifles were something beyond Cape Colony government-sanctioned mercenaries, a form of legalising theft and a way of elevating chicanery into a principle of governance. They were a reprisal patrol system of the so-called Spoor Law. All of them, the Boers, KhoiKhoi and government officials, were there to steal Xhosa cattle under the official collective banner because they hadn't courage for individual raids. They collected cattle they lied about having been stolen from the first kraal they came across, regardless of whom they belonged to. As a result, the likes of that whore Stubbs distinguished himself in murder and plunder during the raids.

'As if that was not enough, when I complained in anger to the government Henry told me I was the one stirring up trouble in the Kat River vicinity. He said we were too close to white farms, which might give us ideas for mischief. Meantime it was the white farmers who had expanded into our areas. We had to move further away from my homeland to settle near Mankazana, which was my brother Thyali's stronghold. Because there was a drought in our land then, the white farmers wanted my land because it was irrigated by two rivers, which meandered through the valleys. I was, at the time, busy in a skirmish with a Thembu chief whose foolishness of raiding white farms I knew would be blamed on us. I told the Rosses about it, and promised to take care of it. In the ensuing skirmish, Sigcawu, the Thembu chief, was killed by my people. More importantly, calm was restored among the farmers of the area. But those who wanted my land pressed Henry and the white government to banish me from the land.

'Thyali was a tough customer for Henry, just as manipulative and distrustful. When I quarrelled with Henry he used shrewdness to divide the amaNgqika royal house. Suthu, the great wife of my late father, Ngqika, had designs of becoming regent until their son Sandile came of age. I had by then learnt to be very tactful in dealing with Sandile. Henry, and the colonial government, sponsored Suthu to build sub-divided huts of great magnitude with ornamented interiors of double-rowed pillars of wood, plastered in strange clay that had the advantage of making her huts waterproof. Herself ever prone to decadent luxury, she appreciated these things. They also brought awe to the eyes of those with materialistic ambitions in our villages. They made it appear as though, were it not for

215

my stubbornness, and Thyali's warring spirit, this was how the Xhosas would live under the British.

'During my exile from Kat River, Thyali got the chance for his I-told-you-so. Thenceforth, Thyali and I acted in unison in opposing Suthu and the colonial government. Though a lot of bad blood existed between us and Suthu, I advised Thyali to join me in forming a triumvirate to face up to the encroaching colonialism through Henry, whose mission I now saw was to divide the strength of amaNgqika. I didn't care about Suthu but decided to fight one enemy at a time. We divided the governance of our chiefdom according to our circumscriptions. I was to be a regent for external affairs. Suthu and Thyali would share the responsibilities of internal governing. This compromise suited me well. I knew I could always back my claim as a paramount by force. Khula had taught me well in the behaviour of the Caesars. Buy time with meaningless compromises while you concentrate your energies on more pressing issues, like dealing with colonial encroachment on our land. I knew whoever controlled the warriors ruled. I had no problems with people reigning while I ruled. I made it clear in no time that it would be foolish of them, Thyali and Suthu, as virtual rulers, to command what they couldn't enforce.

'They had enough sense to understand my drift. I censored all decisions they made without consulting me first until they learnt to ask my permission about everything.

'We were told preparations were being made for us to meet the Governor, in order for us to voice our grievances. Missionaries like the Rosses told me the Governor was an amiable man, a shrewd observer of character, so we should not to be afraid to speak our minds before him. I was assured that he was a fair and moralistic man. I put all my eggs in that basket for peace, but nothing came out of those dishonest preparations. Instead we were given the usual insulting rhetoric. Men of the calibre of Colonel Stretch rescued the meeting.

'Stretch was among the few white men who were sympathetic to our cause and understood our plight. He urged us not to give up but to tell the Governor that the Mounted Rifles' raids were ravaging our villages. They told us those raids were not ordered by Her Majesty's government, and so were illegal. They told us we were to contain the spread of violence and promote peace between our people and to curtail stock theft; as an incentive, we'd be given back the cattle that had been confiscated from us by the Mounted Rifles. That was done with the loss of only two hundred head. With that I thought things would take a better turn. I came from that meeting deluding myself, thinking perhaps there was a way of living as good neighbours with white people, even though they kept driving us from whatever land they needed for their own use. I told myself this was no different to our ways. When you live next to a tribe more powerful than yours you must be prepared now and then to be shoved, pushed and bullied.

'Governor Somerset had always had a weak spot for the amaNgqika tribe. I knew I could always appeal to him. I thought him chivalrous towards his foes also. Unfortunately, the Governor was soon retired and another person, D'Urban, came instead. The new Governor had no desire to form lasting peace with us. The only native people he recognised as part of the British colony were the Mfengus, the refugees from Shaka's wars, and the KhoiKhoi. He turned a blind eye to every illegal raid white farmers made in our area. He was the one who established what they called a reprisal system by which the commandos were permitted to follow the spoor of their stolen cattle to the homesteads they were hidden on. This gave rise to rampant abuse by white people of just following any spoor and confiscating the first cattle they encountered, whatever number they happened to be. The commandos marched at night and attacked at dawn, shooting indiscriminately. Whether you were innocent or guilty of stealing cattle you were not given much opportunity to prove yourself.'

"Thinking about your history as usual?" Matswane wrapped her arms around Phila who was seated on a wire chair on the balcony and looking at the ocean in the distance.

"Something like that." Phila craned his neck to kiss her.

"Sorry I bombed out. It's been a salmon upstream day."

"Tell me about it." He grabbed the bottle to pour himself a stiffy. Darkness had settled in, ushering the twinkling stars. Phila strained to make sense of the milky cluster of stars he assumed to be the Southern Cross – he could never be sure, even when he looked through a telescope.

"So what's happening in the historical cinema up here today?" asked Matswane as she sat on the chair beside him. "What's Maqoma telling us this time?" She was joking, of course, not knowing how close to the truth she was.

The reveal of her nubile thigh from the split in the towel she had around her gave Phila a boner but he made to ignore it by lighting a cigarette.

"He's telling us about the time when one of the chiefs, Nqeno, lost his son, shot dead outside his homestead by the commandos as he came out of his hut to try and find out what was happening. This created a state of perpetual alarm and desire for war among amaXhosa. When they sent complaints to the colonial government they were either ignored or evicted from the land they occupied to make way for the Mfengus to settle there.

"Round about then, Maqoma's half brother Thyali came to see Maqoma. He was in a very alarmed state and he was also a very ill man – I suspect it was cancer he was dying from. According to Maqoma, he was looking harassed and sickly. Maqoma narrates it this way:

"'He looked at me with gleaming eyes before doffing his bright blue head-dress. He sat next to my mat, refusing to take any refreshments. After a while, he said, 'We shall never know peace in this land, whether we're willing to fight or not. Rather than living on our knees, it is better we die, with honour, on our feet like men. We're teased to war no matter what we do. They insult our chiefs, kill our princes, rape our women, starve our children and hunt us like impala everywhere we go. This is not a decent way for grown men to live.'

"Maqoma, who had come to a similar resolve, gave his brother assurance that from then onwards he was with him. 'Let's fight it to the end,' he declared in anger.

"The last straw for Maqoma came when his half-brother Xhonxo's head was grazed by a bullet from a shotgun blast. A certain white farmer, living around the region of Nqeno's people, lost three horses and a foal. The farmers concluded that Nqeno's people must have stolen them. A patrol was sent to look for the horses. When the culprit was caught the patrol took a herd of sixty cattle for compensation, on top of the three horses and the foal. This was their 'system of reprisal'. Armed warriors took on the heels of the patrol when they heard what had happened but were dissuaded from attacking by Stokwe, another of Nqeno's sons. The remnants of those warriors were not completely pacified and they followed the patrol and, just outside Fort Willshire, they attacked. The patrol reached the safety of the fort but tensions were heightened as a result of that incident.

"Such insolence and lack of regard for royalty was what enraged most of Maqoma's people. It opened up a chasm of chaos in the region. Thyali's warriors followed, surrounded and attacked all white parties after that, whether they had confiscated their cattle or not. Several fignts ensued, ending when reinforcements for the white patrol arrived from Fort Beaufort and Thyali's people fled the land. When news reached Maqoma he went

218

in jaundiced anger about his brother Xhonxo, whom he had been close to growing up. Every warrior who saw or heard about the incident went back to his hut and took out his assegai and spears, preferring to die than to live with such humiliation of their royalty shot at in broad daylight.

"'The royal blood of the son of Ngqika has been shed and can only be avenged by blood. From now on we shall meet force with force.' That was how Maqoma roused his people.

"He advised Thyali not to rush to war, however, but to give them time to organise. He was waiting for guns from some of the old Graaff-Reinet Boers whom he knew. The KhoiKhoi who were enlisted in the colonial army were agitated by the racist and unfair manner in which they were treated there; every day they approached the Xhosas, to join against the colonial government and whites in general. More and more renegades from the colony were settling on their land, advising on how to deal with the colonial government, and secretly supplying them with firearms. Many of the Xhosa warriors had not yet learnt to fire guns, so Maqoma told Thyali to delay the war a little. They also needed more time to intercept and hold up wagons for gunpowder and bullets. In the previous wars the small number of those who had guns had to resort to improvisation for bullets, using almost every metal, from zinc to pewter stripped from the farmhouses they raided; they even made wadding with Bibles.

"To buy some time to organise Maqoma sent a letter to the white commander urging him to give a satisfactory conclusion to the matter of Xhonxo's incident by returning the confiscated cattle with an apology, to help him control his people. Meantime, the Xhosas, from the mountains of Nkonkobe to the sea were aflame, seeking revenge attacks. Almost all Xhosaland stood in anger. Several of Hintsa's chiefs stood with amaNgqika also, even though Hintsa was compelled to remain neutral. His land across the Kei, Gcalekaland, became a refuge for the safekeeping of all the cattle. Even some Thembus who saw the legitimacy of the position deserted their chiefs who refused to enter the war; they went to stand with Maqoma against the colonial armies. Only Gqunukhwebe chiefs Phato, Khama and Chungwa, who feared the colony, did not join. Phato and Khama betrayed the lineage, earning Maqoma's rancour. It was very difficult for him to forgive them this betrayal, especially as they had married some of his sisters. With these exceptions, the whole Xhosa nation joined amaNgqika in what they saw as the final stand against colonial oppression that would decide things once and for all. The whole of Xhosaland was in the grip of a roaring war against the colonial forces. The white colonial government got wind of the war preparations and sent an official message to Maqoma to cease them. He sent back his answer in one line:

"Sir, when cornered, even the cur will turn."

When Phila went silent Matswane said, "Babes, I hope you don't take this the wrong way, but, had I known the sound of Maqoma's voice I would say you're starting to sound like him. It's starting to give me the creeps."

Intab'Enzima: Mount Misery

PHILA WAS STARTLED FROM SLEEP BY THE noise of the bathroom lock latching. He fought a flicker of panic before remembering Matswane. He was not used to having someone around. What made her lock the door, he wondered, as he got out of bed to open the window and let in the grainy morning light, followed by lazy warm air that carried the smell of the sea. He went to the kitchen for a cup of coffee. From there he studied the coming day while the coffee percolated. His thoughts combed through the history of the Kat River Settlement, Maqoma's land, given to the KhoiKhoi and Mfengu by the British authorities – lush valleys with gulches of black earth, and an explosion of mountain ranges with extreme inclines and terrifying declivities. Cacti and bitter aloes grew in abundance against the high rocks. Phila had always been drawn to the ragged ravines and deep gorges whenever he drove through them on his way home to Queenstown. He never suspected the terrain contained so much hidden history. The scales were falling from his eyes.

Some of that land, ever prone to participate in history, was parcelled out to black veterans of the First World War, some of whom Mqhayi had immortalised in his poem about the sinking of the ship *Mendi*. The greater part was now occupied by citrus farmers. Oranges grew magnificently in those cool valleys and were a main industry for the region.

Outside, the birds twittered. Phila sat drinking his coffee and looking into the mirror of the past. When he got up to get himself a refill he heard Matswane entering the kitchen. She was wearing a smile, blue denim cut-offs and a white T-shirt, and tying her hair in a ponytail. Her swimming eyes had a look that politely questioned the plans of the day. With a smell of Eden she kissed him on the cheek.

"I think we must visit the Kat River valley today," Phila said, pouring her coffee.

"Where's that?" Matswane asked, her somewhat peremptory tone indicating that she felt sprung upon.

Phila pulled out a chair for her, keeping one hand on her coffee mug.

"How long will it take us?" she asked. "I still need to get to King."

The thought of King spoilt the happy mood for Phila. "Aah … it's not too far from here," he said, avoiding the question. "You know where Fort Beaufort is?"

Mat shook her head.

"Well, that's where we're going. It's less than 150ks. We can proceed to King from there."

The day waved blue as they set off. In the passenger seat Phila struggled to fend off sleep. Matswane chatted to him as she drove, staying the progress of his soapbox musing. Phila sat, listening to her talk from an impotent distance, which inspired numbness in him. These days the major renown of the town Fort Beaufort was its psychiatric hospital and that one of the best agricultural schools in the country was there. Delving back into its history, Phila recalled that during the late nineteenth and early twentieth centuries it used to be vibrant with Wesleyan missionary activity; it also hosted the second biggest institute for black education after Lovedale College. This institution, Healdtown, produced the first black teachers and journalists, who became the initial catalysts for establishing the movement of black resistance later known as the African National Congress. It was there, too, that his parents had met and fallen in love. And the eventual informal amalgamation of Lovedale and Healdtown gave birth to Fort Hare College. Phila was thinking about all this when Mat broke his train of thought.

"You still haven't explained where in Fort Beaufort we're going, babes," she declared as they entered the town, which was named Bofolo according to the Xhosa, "but it looks like we're here."

They pulled into a Total service station to fill up with petrol and buy a few supplies from the shop. As they walked back to the car, Phila said, "The place we're going to is just outside town. You did bring hiking shoes, didn't you, Mat, as I asked you to?" He winked, because he had forgotten to tell her, not that it mattered anyway because she had no change of clothes in his B&B.

Matswane feigned throwing daggers at him. "I'm sure my takkies will do just fine," she said. "If the going gets too hard, I'll just wait for you in the car."

The road trembled in the heat as they drove towards Hogsback through a muted countryside. After twenty minutes or so Phila indicated that Matswane should take the next exit, which was an unmarked gravel road towards the mountain fastness and a few villages clinging onto the western hills. In the further distance still was an assemblage of wattle and daub houses with thatched roofs stuck to the mountainside like spittle on a wall. That village looked bigger but it was probably hard to get to. They drove a dusty-bumpy drive for another twenty minutes before they were literally at the foot of the mountains.

"My dear, meet the notorious Winterberg mountains, Nkonkobe to the denizens of this area," declared Phila as Matswane turned off the car's engine and allowed silence to enter the open windows.

Phila got out first, then Mat followed him. For once she seemed to have no words. They were surrounded by an explosion of mountain ranges. Phila was pointing to where the mountains started in a steep climb on the west and saying something about the Kroomie plains. From that summit were waterfalls that came down in crushing sounds, which reverberated where they stood. Phila indicated that the mountain adjacent was the beginning of Amathole, and if they were to follow that line they would reach the back of where they had been the previous day, and probably be able to overlook Maqoma's grave, or at least the brush of the forest that guarded it. And were they to climb Nkonkobe all the way up on the other side, they would be met by the small town of Cathcart, from which would be a few kilometres to his home town of Queenstown. Mat listened in fascinated silence. The realisation that they were about to jaunt up the mountain took the gleam out of her eye a little, but she was a good sport. Phila took a back carrier bag from the boot and packed the bottles of water and sandwiches they'd bought at the garage shop into it.

"And off we go to explore wounds of history," Phila joked, while Matswane was tying the laces of her takkies.

"Now, now, babes!" She clicked the car alarm and the hazards winced.

The fastness of the Nkonkobe range, of which Kroomie formed one of its biggest summits, was a natural fort for the Xhosas to hide when fighting their colonial enemies. The range went all the way to form Amathole towards East London. It had enabled Maqoma and his warriors to hide in safety, and then to stage one of the most devastating battles of the Frontier Wars, the Battle of Waterkloof. Waterkloof, shaped roughly like a horseshoe, was the highest among the broken spurs of the ranges that formed precipitous valleys and gorges.

After conquering the first hill, Phila and Matswane got into their stride.

Then began the woods, with their low light and high humidity.

"They call this Woodcutter's Path," Phila said in a low voice.

"Why are we whispering, babe?" Matswane asked. giving him a concerned look.

"Well, we're in the wild now. We wouldn't want to attract the attention of leopards or something." Phila maintained a serious visage before bursting out laughing at her expression. "I'm pulling your leg. The leopards have been pushed deep into the mountains. And they're nocturnal animals anyway."

"Shit!" Mat exclaimed. "That still doesn't make me feel any better." She panted in file after Phila. The woods were a mix of yellowwood, assegai trees and ironwood.

It was steep going and to preserve energy Phila and Matswane fell quiet as they climbed. After they had cleared the woods, where bush pheasants and whirring partridges kept scaring Mat when they burst out of the cover of the bush, the path opened into a long narrow valley before bottling into an egress. Further on the terrain became stony, before they got to a high cliff where they could see the dark mouths of many caverns. Extending between the branches of the trees dotted about were thick twists of monkey-rope. On their right the terrain was thickly wooded, clotted with underbrush and creeper vines.

They stopped for a few minutes to catch their breath and drink some water. Phila took a few steps on his own, feeling the breeze cool him through his damp shirt. When he turned round he saw Mat looking at him enquiringly. "Shall we go on?" she asked. "Before I change my mind?"

They reached the nek of the mountain where the sheer cliff drop made it impossible to proceed. Phila reckoned its high point above would be what the Xhosas called Intab'Enzima and the British named Mount Misery. If they could find a way to proceed from the other side, he said, he estimated the peak would take about forty minutes to climb. They decided to go around. Down below was a scenic cut of steep valleys, some ending in cul-de-sac dams.

"Let me guess," Matswane said as she scrambled up the rocky cliff. "There was some kind of a war here?"

"Indeed, the most decisive one."

"I thought as much." Matswane looked up the mountain, where the path before them leaped into bleak vastness. "But really? Here?"

"Imagine the British soldiers climbing here – the redcoats – encumbered with their woollen uniforms, all their weaponry and other gear, bayonets, heavy belts and all. Chasing after nimble and almost naked Xhosas, who carried with them just five assegais and a small pouch of dried food reserves; only a few of them had rifles. Stupid as he was, instead of waiting for them to run out of food, Smith ordered that they be flushed out of these woods and chased from the mountain cliffs. It was organised suicide for the Brits."

Phila, whose forehead was beaded with perspiration, noticed Matswane's hesitation and he threw her a look of kindness. "Sure you're up to this?" he asked.

Matswane dismissed his concern with a shrug of her shoulders and set off with admirable determination. Phila had to dash to catch up with her.

"Down below here, close to where the orange farms are now," he said after getting his breath back, "the British colonial government created the Kat River Settlement. It was an experiment, a conglomeration of KhoiKhoi from the Cape Colony and Mfengus as landowning blacks within British territory. They were to act as a buffer between the Xhosas and the white subjects of the British Crown. It simultaneously provided a convenient way of getting rid of squatters on white farms." He could feel his thigh muscles tensing.

"Ah! So the divide-and-rule strategy of coloureds and Africans started long ago?" Matswane commented. She stopped abruptly to avoid a terrifying declivity, at which point she gave Phila a look that intimated she was done.

"Even further back," he said, hoping to engage her interest and encourage her to keep walking. "It began in the Cape of Good Hope, then spread to Algoa Bay. What they didn't expect, though, was that Stockenström, who was basically the founder of the Kat River Settlement, had other designs. It became the first settlement where natives successfully adopted Western civilisation. On a given day it looked like a typical rural town anywhere in Britain: shopkeepers selling their wares, children going to church and to school, and so forth. The difference was that they were native children. It became the best success story for missionary activity anywhere in the world, and the Reads – remember the missionaries I told you about? – were at the centre of it. But, needless to say, the success of the settlement couldn't be taken for what it was.

The *Grahamstown Journal* used its newspaper pages to print vitriol, complaining about kaffirs gaining airs and being given ideas of revolt. The usual racist nonsense the media perpetrate.

"Maqoma's genius was in feeding the fire of the Kat River Settlement into an open rebellion, which became known in history as the Kat River Rebellion. He even married another coloured wife to cement the bonds between his tribe and the rebels. He ended up with an additional division of Kat River rebels in his warrior camps. In no time the colonial government suffered mutiny in those ranks, and for that reason decided to disband the Cape Mounted Rifles, which was mostly made up of KhoiKhoi and Mfengus. This only served to add hundreds of British-trained KhoiKhoi and Mfengus to the Xhosa ranks. They weren't much more than a collection of miscellaneous, unruly rabble who wanted to make good their escape from British law enforcement, but they were fierce and useful in war. And their intimate knowledge of the fighting ways of the British came in handy for Maqoma.

"Maqoma, always given to open-air, rabble-rousing speeches, planned his attacks: Sandile was to concentrate on the Amathole area, Matroos, the KhoiKhoi leader he had secured to his side, was to take the Fort Beaufort town area, and he placed himself here, in these mountains, in between the two for easy access when they required his assistance. They were supposed to listen to his co-ordination so that they might all concentrate the strength of their attacks in one place at a time. But Sandile and Matroos were both hotheads who wanted to steal the thunder of war glory for themselves. They had initial success, especially with bush ambushes, which was a big part of Maqoma's strategy. These fostered their daring. Matroos went for the eye of the octopus by attacking Fort Beaufort town, in broad daylight. The battle was protracted but in the end Matroos's KhoiKhoi rebels lost, and Matroos himself was shot dead in that war. The Khoi replaced him with Botha, who had a better head. Sandile, after a few successful skirmishes had whetted his appetite, made a plunder of attacking Fort Peddie, also in broad daylight. It was a replay of Nxele's war on a smaller but just as tragic scale.

"Maqoma had a hard time persuading the KhoiKhoi rebels – who had suffered heavy losses in the Fort Beaufort war – back into war, but with Botha's help he managed it. He thought this would be the last of the wars with the British, and thus wanted it to be decisive. He met up with Hans Branders, another Khoi rebel leader, and convinced him to lend his support. He desperately needed the rebel leader's skills and prowess if his guerrilla tactics were to be effective. With the ammunition from the Kat River rebels, and his knowledge of the area, Maqoma believed they had an ultimate advantage. He believed they would be invincible. This was the planning he was trying to impress on his not-so-strategic fellow Xhosa chiefs, who lacked his prudence and intelligence."

Beyond the brow the hill flattened into the green table of Kroomie.

A boy, wrapped in an ochre blanket, led a drove of mooing heifers in their direction.

"Up there would be Intab'Enzima." Phila pointed across, not sure how to circumvent the precipitous hills to get there. Matswane screwed her eyes to see where Phila's finger was pointing. "That was where the Xhosa warriors ensconced themselves during the bush war – what history would term the Waterkloof Battle. It was the only battle in which the Xhosas clearly won the day against the British."

"Surely you don't expect us to reach that height today?" Matswane asked, stopping to catch her breath. She reached out for Phila's back, took out and opened her bottle of water and took a swig from it. Above them, beyond the gorge to the summit, was a tangled maze of massifs and lengthening shadows. Phila had to agree she had a point.

Forfeiting the last climb, they inspected the mountain aeries around them before turning back.

"I think those are the Kroomie plains," Phila said, admiring the view beyond the spur that cut their path.

The sense of their flat space was overwhelming.

The teenage boy, by now very close to Phila and Matswane, looked amused in front of his drovers. He was obviously not used to human company on these heights, not the swanky type at least. He carried veldkos and flowers of thirst – aloes – in his hand. His dog, a mongrel, sniffed Phila and then, satisfied, loped off. The boy raised the hand not carrying his stick in respectful salute before booming out a greeting.

"*Siayazibulisela ebahambini. Liyarhatyela nilumke!*"

Matswane, whose Xhosa was not good, looked repeatedly to Phila to translate. "He sends us well wishing and warns us not to linger too long because darkness falls quickly on these heights."

"He said all that in two sentences?" Matswane looked sceptical.

"Well, Xhosa, especially the rural one, like all classical languages, communicates by proverbial brevity. I am translating his meaning, not interpreting his sentences. Do you know what I mean?"

"I think I do," said Matswane. "Your tone also changes quite a lot when you're translating Maqoma's transcriptions, I've noticed. Do you realise that you're doing it?"

Phila laughed. "I didn't realise. It must be because the Xhosa Maqoma speaks is tinged with ancient Xhosa; he uses language that is getting lost in the pidgin we speak now."

Phila stared at the boy sentimentally, watching his silhouette sail on into the eye of the fast-setting sun. Something about the boy pierced him with sharp longing.

Dusk started invading the plains where the sun didn't reach. Streams fell from high mountainous ledges. Long shadows spread across the yellowing fields. Phila, who knew he had an unhealthy taste for the moribund, wished they could linger but Matswane was worried, so they began their descent.

At the bottom, where they were parked, while Matswane picked bramble and briar seeds from her clothes Phila dickered for a hot meal from a man who stopped his ox-drawn cart to offer a greeting. Initially, Phila just wanted to know if the gravel road went to the town of Alice on the other side. The man said it did, prompting Phila to enquire further if the road was navigable by a sedan in the dark. The man had other ideas. Why not spend the night with his family, have a hot meal, then leave the following day, he suggested. Phila saw no harm in accepting the kindness of the stranger, but it took some time to persuade Matswane.

"The missus will be glad to have people to talk to for the night. It might relieve her moods, so you'd be doing me a great kindness. You see, she went to school, and you educated lot like to talk things over and over all the time. I am a simple man who knows only how to look after his fields and stock. This talking thing gets on my nerves most of the time. But I feel for her, having to cope with my silences. You'll also be doing me a great honour. It's been a while since we've heard news from outside this village."

It was settled. In no time they were following the ox-drawn cart driven by the middle-aged man with prune-plum skin, who had introduced himself as Zwelinzima. The span raised a puff of dust against the thinning sun. The rustic scene mesmerised Phila. The only thing missing was the pedlar's song his father loved to sing as he drove the oxen home. It took him back to thinking about the origins of his people's locomotive ways, since their descent from the Great Lakes region of the swift Neolithic transformation from hunting and gathering, to soil tilling and animal husbandry. If the Obobogo archaeology was anything to go by, his people were already farmers by the time they left Yaoundé in Cameroon.

As they reached the first homestead a young boy, about six years old, cut a caper of delight in hearing his mother give voice in loud greetings to her husband. The boy came running, throwing himself into his father's arms with the careless trust of a loved child. The woman, after giving a curious look to the visitors, continued taking washing off the fence. A girl, a little older than the boy, with a bundle of sticks on her head, nimbly climbed the fence over a stile at the back, where wind-stunted eucalyptus trees guarded the homestead in a stoop of no discernible symmetry. Two older boys crowded bleating sheep into a pen.

Zwelinzima, who had a slight stoop and a hesitant gait, introduced them to his wife in a flattered voice.

"All we wanted to know was where the road ended. Your husband kidnapped us," Phila joked as he extended his hand for a greeting. Matswane, who wasn't quite sure she had properly parked, bent down to pick more burrs from her clothes before jogging towards Zwelinzima, who waited to reassure her while Phila greeted his wife in the courtyard.

"I'm used to it," the woman smiled. "My husband has a habit of dragging strays to our house. It's a habit he acquired while he was working as a guard for a government tourism department. I keep telling him one day people will find us murdered cold here with all the unknown visitors he brings inside our walls. Even white people from lands as far as Scotland he brings here sometimes." She had a kind, welcoming smile. "Have you travelled far?"

"Not too far by road," Phila told her, "but the spirit has been sojourning. *Siya mfenguza!*" He felt comfortable with her, and was delighted for the opportunity to speak in authentic Xhosa idiom. "I see your village is amenable to accepting late-coming visitors." He squinted towards the sun whose trail of fiery streaks was still strong. He cupped his hand over his eyes to properly see the boys bolting the kraal before continuing with his clan introductions.

"*Ndizalwa ngama Ndlovu, abeDluli. Ndiyi Ndlovu edl' igoduka. Umfenguzo siyawazi.*"

"*Awulahlekanga mntase, ndizalwa ngamaNdlovu nam. Ndedele kulomzi woXaba, onoMjoli.*"

Zwelinzima joined them, introducing Matswane before his wife had finished.

"*Ngu Nosuthu lona maNdlovu. Ndiyaqonda ukuba nazene nale ndoda yase maNdlonvini. Ndimxelele ethambekeni ukuba ndathatha intombi yakwa Ndlovu, udade wayo. Yilento ndiqonde abanakude balale endleleni sikhona.*"

They went on with getting to know each other in the happy coincidence of Zwelinzima's wife sharing a clan name with Phila. The boys were asked to present themselves to the visitors after they had finished bolting the pens and kraals. Both were obsequious and respectful, extending both hands in proper Xhosa greeting. Their father continued addressing his wife.

"Times are tough, *maNdlovu*, now. You think you're accepting a visitor, instead you're inviting death to your house, but something immediately felt familiar with these two for me. I was not surprised to learn he is your clan brother." Then he turned to Matswane. "Nosuthu here claims she can hand the sickle and stay the saw. We shall see tomorrow when you hand her the blade." They all laughed heartily. The women went inside with the excuse of preparing the meal for the evening. Zwelinzima invited Phila to the fire in the court.

Phila remembered they had an unopened bottle of whisky in the car and he went to fetch it, presenting it to his host as *Ihamb' Idlani*.

"This is what we were eating on the road, *noMjoli*," he said, handing it over. Zwelinzima was extremely pleased with the gesture. They kept quiet while he unsealed the bottle. The moment the click cracked they burst into enthusiasm because it signified that the bottle was not poisoned. Dimming his eyes, Zwelinzima took a swig after pouring a tot on the ground for the ancestors. He passed the bottle to Phila, who did the same. The two men could now talk freely.

"You say you're on the sniff of our forefather Jong'Umsobomvu, *Ndlovu*?" Zwelinzima sat stock-still, chewing a grass stem in bovine studiedness, clasping his chin to signify the seriousness with which he regarded the matter.

"The chief feeds my spirit, *Mjoli*. As you know, we in the cities tend to enslave our reasoning to the desires of the flesh. At some stage this suffocates the spirit."

Zwelinzima pressed Phila to talk about the source of his disillusionment. Phila talked about loss of cultural inheritance, the hand-me-down generational trauma from events of history. When people don't know what to do with their lives, he said, they move to the cities, but sometimes this is not enough to close the void, so they try to conquer the distance by travelling to other countries. "You take yourself with wherever you go. There lies the problem."

Zwelinzima gave an occasional nod as Phila talked. Perhaps he was wondering if these were just tipsy ramblings.

They were busy interrogating this conundrum when a dog with distended teats came sniffing for something to eat. A moment later one of the boys appeared to inform their father that the bitch had whelped. Their talk was arrested by the news. Zwelinzima asked after the litter and gave orders about how its kennel should be cushioned from the cold and rain, before excusing himself to Phila so he could supervise the implementation of his instructions.

Left on his own, Phila listened to the falling darkness. He thought he could hear the echo of a vanished river carving the valleys, leaving behind the sunken beds of caked earth he'd observed earlier. He realised this meant he was seeing and hearing through Maqoma's eyes and ears.

The other boy, cocky, with obstreperous eyes, took the opportunity to get familiar with Phila. It turned out that the dust commotion earlier on the hills had been from a ferret bolting after a rabbit. The dogs and the boys, said the boy, robbed the animal of its catch and they were then cooking it. Would Phila like a taste once the stew was ready? Phila said he would, which pleased the boy. He told Phila he was very interested in city life and asked him lots of questions, saying he was planning to go work on the mines for *lobola* when his time came to take a wife. Phila knew the boy would be the bell-wether of the family. Somehow this realisation made him feel sympathy for him.

Zwelinzima came back and broke up the boy's animated talk. "*Uxolo, Mdluli. Lamakhwenkwe akufuneki uyekele kuwo qha lonke ixesha, ayonakalisa,*" he resumed, taking his seat and opening the bottle for another swig before passing it to Phila. "*Ndifuna ukuva lendawo yokuba Ijingqi liyavela lithethe nawe, Ndlovu.*"

"It's complicated, Xaba. I get *lengulo.*" Phila felt grateful he could express himself in Xhosa, because the meaning of *ingulo,* 'sickness', in Xhosa was not only a physiological phenomenon, but indicated someone who was also psychic, and as such it was regarded as an honour rather than shame. "The doctors suspect some kind of dissociative disorder. I sometimes feel a profound dissociation, emotionally and existentially, sometimes even physically. Like I will look at my own limb and not be able to associate it to myself. Try as I might, sometimes I just can't convince my mind, or feel in my senses, that my arm, or leg, is mine, because they don't feel part of my inner image. As such I am not able to move them for the duration of that phenomenon."

"*Ingxaki nikhawuleza nizikhumshe ezi zinto, Ndlovu. Ingathi intsonkothile lena yakho. Kodwa andiqali kuyive. Iqhelekile kubantu abamhlophe, ababizwa ngaba phantsi. Uthi akokuthwasa Mdluli oku kwankho? Kodwa ke mna andinalwazi lwazo ezinto. Into endinga kuxelela ngayo yimvelaphi yethu apha kule ningqi.*"

"*Ndingayivuyela noMjoli lonto. Ndifuna ukuva kakhulu ngala mfazwe ye Waterkloof.*"

"*Make siqale silinde amakhosikazi asondle mfondi.*"

Zwelinzima, who was a little tipsy, explained how he had seen and heard of Phila's sickness, and how in days gone by it was treated by consulting *igqirha*, the only person permitted to indicate if Phila was being called by the 'shadows'. They agreed to talk about the Waterkloof Battle after supper. After that he lurched to his feet and went stumbling off to check the progress of the kitchen matters. Phila sat hugging his knees, pondering the string of failures that had led him to that moment. The alcohol burning his blood brought with it the heaviness of sleep. He'd always found it difficult to understand writers like Baudelaire and Hemingway, for whom alcohol was a mnemonic device.

'Because it was a period when war succeeded war, we put sentries on every mountain corner to watch for colonial attacks.' The voice of Maqoma in his head filled the void. 'Standing on that rocky escarpment, looking down beyond the blankness, one could see everything on the wagon paths. We even built stone forts on remote hilltops. The British forces had no option but to launch their attack from there. When they came, it was first with two expeditions, under Henry and Colonel Fordyce; these were predominantly made up of Highlander and Mfengu units. They brought the first fog of war with about two thousand men. Their objective was clear to me. They wanted to break our stronghold at Intab'Enzima.'

Zwelinzima was back. "Where was I, by the way, *Ndlovu*?"

Taking advantage of his host's tipsiness, Phila decided to direct things to the head. "You were about to tell me about the Battle of Waterkloof," he said.

"Oh, I've told that story a million times in my day. It was in the spring of 1851, 7 September to be exact, Henry Somerset and Fordyce came to flush out Jong'Umsobomvu and his army here, in the mountains you see before you. The Xhosas had been there since harvest time the previous April, so they were running out of supplies, having used most of them during the winter, which was particularly cold that year." He took out his pipe, stood up to grab a burning stick from the fire, and began the process of lighting it. "The British ascended through Woodcutter's Path, the only way to take anyway if you had cavalry dragoons. That day the British forces couldn't reach the Waterkloof summit. Because they met up with Xhosas, who blocked their narrow way. Henry was panic-stricken. He convinced Fordyce that they should retreat. The Xhosas blocked all their paths except one, which, as they discovered halfway, although it had looked safer initially, had a very dangerous declivity. From deep within they discovered the path to be a dead end into an impassable cliff with white waters about thirty metres down below. They had to turn back – they were about three hundred and fifty men, half of whom were on horses. The Mfengu regiment at their rear, not sure what was happening with the dragoons in front, were too afraid to turn towards the Xhosa warriors, who were pursuing them with maddening sounds of booming gongs, bringing terrible dread. Even the trees started shaking with the reverberations.

"Then Maqoma emerged from deep in the woods, riding his grey-white horse, dressed in European clothing, giving instructions to his warriors. For a moment the British soldiers, who were fatigued from the difficult earlier climb, were mesmerised by the sight; they were not sure if they were seeing a ghost. When directed, and showing impressive co-ordination, Maqoma's warriors charged, throwing assegais that whistled and quivered as they flew. The British realised this was no apparition. The soldiers started firing their muskets, but in the confusion they killed more of their Mfengu and KhoiKhoi allies than the enemy, who were just perfectly out of musket range. The assegais, which seemed as if they were being thrown by trees, found their targets on horses and British soldiers. When the British finally gained the slope and were able to retreat onto a safer path they found their way blocked with trees, which the Xhosas had deliberately felled. They had no option but to charge and to fight the Xhosas in close combat with their awkward bayonets and swords. Most perished by being pulled into the bushes by their belts and being pushed to the edge of the precipice. Others fought on, with assegais in their backs, shoulders, legs and stomachs. By the time they managed to clear a path for retreat the British left behind about fourteen dead white soldiers, and Mfengu and Khoi. Jong'Umsobomvu also lost nine of his men.

"Not that Fordyce, new to Xhosas and young and ambitious to win Governor Smith's approval, took a lesson from it. Henry, who knew Maqoma well, was more circumspect and he begged Fordyce never to repeat such folly. His words fell on deaf ears." Zwelinzima fell silent for a moment before asking, "Do you think they're deliberately starving us, *Ndlovu*? Have we done something wrong?"

"I think they're lost in their own conversation also."

"Pass the crock, *mfondini*, let's consult the ancestors." With that they took another swig each from the bottle. "Shall we stretch our legs and clear our heads a little? It is getting too hot in here."

They walked towards the pen and kraal. Behind them was a cabbage garden Phila had not noticed before. The clouds, white as washed fleece, floated like some form of a spaceship on top of the mountains, giving the night a white tinge, as if the area was under floodlights. Zwelinzima opened the makeshift wooden pole and barbed-wire gate. Then he began weeding in between the cabbage rows. Phila had no option but to join in. It was one of the things that reminded him of his father in Zwelinzima, this inability to sit at leisure without starting some form of manual work.

"The neighbours will accuse us of witchcraft if they see us working in the garden at this hour," said Zwelinzima, at which they both chuckled.

"A month later," he went on, "the British attempted to flush Maqoma off the Waterkloof again.

"This time they met up with *iimbila zivela kusela* ..."

At that moment Zwelinzima's wife shouted that dinner was ready. Phila wanted to ask about the roots of the proverb Zwelinzima had just uttered, why meeting rock rabbits on their way from drinking water was associated with trouble, but he decided it was neither the time nor place. Instead he stopped to strike a match, light a cigarette and stave off the dizziness from not being used to manual labour. He was excited to meet someone who, like him now, looked at things through the historical lens. As he stood, inhaling deeply and watching his smoke curl into the sky, Maqoma took up the story from where Zwelinzima had left off, unable to rein in his horse.

'We prepared a welcoming assembly for them. Having cleared all our villages, sending women and children far away, some even across iNciba, only the brave and strong remained behind to plant the fields and supply us with food reserves. But I saw something never heard of before. The British resorted to dirty tricks. They were burning our fields – I mean, who does such a thing?'

'It's called "scorched earth policy",' said Phila. 'Cruelly effective.'

'Not only that, but they killed women and children when they encountered them –'

'– collateral damage,' Phila interjected, feeling sharper than he thought he ought to be with so much whisky in his head.'

"Are you coming, *Ndlovu*?" called Zwelinzima when he noticed Phila wasn't following. He was about to enter the house.

"I'll finish my smoke and be with you now-now." Phila perched on the stone kraal and trained his eyes on the mountain clouds he couldn't get enough of.

Maqoma's tone was indignant. 'Even war has rules, which the honourable never betray. Before then I had regarded the British with honour. No more after that. Where they are most dangerous is in giving a semblance of legality to their fraud. Hence you could sleep in your house and the following morning they would bring a magistrate's paper saying that the land beneath your house had been given to the British colony – against your wishes. All of a sudden you are the illegal one, invading your own land!

'Anyway, as I was saying. I instructed my men to move on cat feet. Our forces were like ghosts. We would attack and then vanish into thin air. The forests and mountains concealed us well. Our men climbed trees like monkeys, the enemy passing right under our noses without seeing us. Others of my men buried themselves for days in holes in the ground, not moving even when ants started gouging their eye sockets. When they ran their knees touched their chins – not even cheetahs could catch them. It was easy for us to go without food for days, something the colonial forces could not manage. They were at our mercy on these mountain fastnesses.

'Somerset and Fordyce undertook two-pronged sporadic assaults without any progress against us. Morale is the major part of winning a war. Your first battle is won in frustrating and discouraging the morale of your enemy. And nothing works to instil fear in a soldier like not knowing from where the enemy is coming, or when. Sowing fear and confusion is your first weapon against an enemy.

'I remember the day like it was yesterday. Fordyce's party came from the direction of the Kroomie plains. His party, made up of about one thousand men, was a mixture of KhoiKhoi, Mfengu, Highlanders, mounted burghers and artillery crewmen. Somerset's party, made up of a similar number, had a lesser mixture of men and an alarming addition of three field guns. He came from the east, where Fuller's Hoek is. I secured most of the Kat River rebels at the forest plains for surprise attacks. Another force, mostly amaNgqika, remained on the Waterkloof. This force was composed of a few of my trusted fire-armed warriors, no more than eight hundred, so as to facilitate swift attack and speedy retreat without suffering huge casualties. Other chiefs went to the Amathole region to start another war with the colonial government.

'We deliberately stayed off the seat of their government in Rhini, wishing to first finish with forts and farms before closing, in unison, the circle to Rhini. I had learnt my lesson well from Nxele.

'At Waterkloof, before you reach the summit, we had the natural fortress of the kloofs. Concealed everywhere, even on open nek areas, the colonial forces discovered too late masses of our armed men. When Somerset and Fordyce came it was in the wee hours of the morning. Fordyce's column began its arduous climb near Hermanus Hill into Woodcutter's Path.

Encumbered by their artillery and the ox-wagons of the commissariat on rugged, stony terrain, it became impossible for them to move except on foot and horseback. You should see how impassable this region becomes when it rains, especially if you want to move towards the fastness. When their train was in motion, it crawled. At the ascent points you could see the desperate whipping of their animals. At some stage they could not move any further as the road became impassable. The two parties by then were completely out of contact with each other. Fordyce had marched his men up to the root garden where the nek of the hill begins to turn. He deployed his guns halfway through the climax, passing our concealed warriors in the bush. They placed themselves halfway to the summit, having run themselves into a dead end like yourselves. Anyone who knows the area is aware that though the path is clear at the bottom it leads to an impasse. I had prepared a firing line against them from the plateau across.

'I instructed our concealed warriors not to appear until we started firing our guns from the summit, when the brigade had positioned itself as an easy target on the impasse. We rained fire on the from behind rocks, screened by rocks and bushes. From their blind rear, my concealed warriors appeared, scattering their marching lines. The colonial forces dashed on towards the cliffs, sometimes firing at each other. Half the time their troops could not perceive where our fire came from. They were as exposed as a baboon's behind. All the soldiers could see were puffs of white smoke below and above, to their left, and the only place they could run to led to murderous declivities. When we ran out of ammunition we dislodged rocks and boulders, which went tumbling down into their ranks like missiles.

'By mid-morning the enemy committed the rest of the army, led by Fordyce, in trying to root us out of the ambush points of the forested kloofs. Their artillery advanced towards the nek, veering off to the right, not seeing us to their front because they were then moving along a hollow centre of our trap. Fordyce must have guessed the danger they were being swallowed into because he started running down onto the exposed nek, waving his hat and bellowing something. None could hear him above the din of musketry and cannon shot. In the commotion he was caught by a shot from one of our KhoiKhoi marksmen who was perched in a tree. We later learnt the bullet passed through his chest. Some of his men tried to retrieve him, raising his body away from the scorching heat. We doubled the rain of fire; musketry reverberated far around the deep kloofs in double force. Never had I seen so many men dying for a lost cause.

'Eventually, they managed to carry Fordyce up the hill, where they placed him under a tree. Our men started charging in wild hurrahs along the mountain ridges and deep valleys when we noticed someone else had assumed command. We knew Fordyce must be dead, and thus the morale of their army down. I was extremely pleased with this, my first high ranking officer, although I would have preferred it be Harry, Governor of the Cape Colony at that time. But you would never find those voluble cowards in the thick of the battle; they knew how to preserve their skins.

'When they began to call the squad of Fordyce to storm back it gave me an idea. I took forty of my men, whom I knew to be agile as ermines, to belt the enemy's position. As a result, by the time the enemy tried to turn back across the open nek they were in our direct firing line again. We rained crossfire on them. Caught up in fire from all directions, even from the one they had come from, where my forty men and I were ensconced, they dispersed in disarray. Some even deliberately took their chances and tried to scale the cliffs rather than face our fire. We doubled over on the fallen ones who tried to regain their feet as they lay with mangled limbs on the blood-dyed grass, waving rifles with white handkerchiefs tied to them to signal surrender. As far as I was concerned, the rules of war no longer applied to the Brits.'

Phila entered the house at the same time as the children were joining the adults at the court where food was served. Everything was communal: four dishes – red kernel cobs, wild spinach, pumpkin stiffened with mealie-meal and boiled wild boar leg. Zwelinzima started describing to Phila how he'd caught the boar three days before when his wife asked for a moment of silence for the young girl to say grace.

"Unfortunately, it's getting harder to get boars on the hunt these days, to say nothing of impala," Zwelinzima continued after the prayer. "Most are kept on commercial farms, which in turn are only accessible to tourists because of the exorbitant prices for visiting these farms. Game farms have become the bane of our traditional living, although other people are grateful for them because, although not many, they provide jobs."

As the head of the house Zwelinzima invited the visitors to dig in first. The children were dished their portions of everything before they excused themselves and went to their hut. Phila, who sat on the ground hugging his knees, was amused to see Matswane sitting uneasily on the cow-dung-smeared floor, compared to the lady of the house who bunched her smock dress underneath her. With her black crepe *doek* she looked very dignified. They all ate in silence, Phila taking a portion of everything while

Matswane dished herself only the vegetables.

Zwelinzima took up their earlier conversation after the meal. "These things you ask after, *Ndlovu*, are a hard memory because they involve wars. And wars not only make exiles of people, they –"

"Let's take our cue, Nosuthu," said Zwelinzima's wife. "I know from experience that war talks are a polite way of chasing us out of the room. They can talk about it until the cows come home. But ask them about their own hearts, *baba yinkukhu esikwe umlomo*." She gathered the dishes together as she spoke. "What's on a man's heart, even if you can live with him for three decades, you can never know for sure. One day he just disappears, saying he wants to 'find himself'. Like our neighbour last year. Meantime women have no such privilege. They have to think about the children they brought into the world ..."

"Come, my sister, let's go do dishes," Matswane echoed. "Once you get this one of mine talking about Maqoma he goes on a spiel." She turned to Phila and said, "Try not to drink too much. Remember we've an early start tomorrow."

"We grew up to these stories of valour, *Ndlovu*." Zwelinzima relit his pipe. The smell of rum and maple tobacco filled the room in no time. "We know the grave enemies of Jong'Umsobomvu. This is the reason to this day dogs are named Somerset in our villages. That was the man Maqoma taught a lesson in these mountains. I can show you tomorrow where his unit expired trying to roar out a rescue for Fordyce's men. These things are enhanced in the telling, but the wooded invisibility of the forest made for their graves. Many of the bones of British soldiers are strewn here, hence you find their relatives still coming here to find closure. We take them around. It becomes awkward sometimes, because both our forefathers killed each other in these hills, and now we, the seeds of their loins, stand in confused grief, not sure what exactly to say to one another. All we can do is direct them to grave plates, or lead them to the cliffs where most of those soldiers hauled themselves up, taking chances with the natural order of things rather than face a stabbing assegai."

The two men talked, drinking and smoking, into the night, with an intimate frankness of people who had known each other all their lives, like brothers. When he started feeling the rustle of too much alcohol, Phila excused himself to go to bed around two in the morning. He found Matswane already asleep in the hut they had been allocated as their sleeping quarters. The door bellowed on the hinges like a house that had not been opened in a while. Inside the hut had a musty-sour smell with the permanent coolness of a thatch roof. He could not properly see Matswane but guided by her soft snoring he made his way to the bed, where he joined her without taking off his clothes. He found that he could not fall asleep, the bed was jumping with fleas also, which made him wonder if the dogs used it sometimes.

'After Fordyce fell,' Maqoma spoke, 'the war bent badly for the British and dissatisfaction spread among their soldiers. We drove them into a headlong retreat. Most fell from the edges of the precipices. Some tried to rescue others, resulting in their own deaths. I could see on the top of the hill that one of their grenadiers was deliberating coming in support of their comrades, but demurred in the end. It would have been suicide. We had pinned them in an impossible position on every side of the nek. By the time another of their column arrived to relieve them I had already ordered all my men to concentrate on Somerset's column.

'Under our fire Somerset retreated and his men abandoned their position. Late afternoon they turned back and retired to bivouac where their artillery was on the open Kroomie heights. In my estimation they had lost almost half of the men they'd climbed up with.'

'They put the number at far fewer than that in their writing, eighteen, I think,' said Phila.

'Of course they would. Where have you ever seen them write honestly about their losses?'

'Indeed. It would run counter to the narrative of a mighty British empire. Although some of their historians are beginning to be honest about these things now.'

'They tried to resume their operations the following morning, but to no avail. We watched all their movements with extreme vigilance. At night we raided their camps, took their oxen and provisions. In less than three days they were a spent force, with nothing to eat. Other regiments came to make another attempt at regaining our stronghold, surrounding the kloofs, to their detriment. This time the bulk of fighting fell on the Mfengu division. This action was short. We cut them off one by one. Torrential rain favoured our tactics, making it easier for us to roll boulders down on them. They again retreated and spent soaking nights in the Kroomie camp. We observed that most of them were rapidly losing heart. They made fires to keep themselves warm, which made them sitting ducks. Someone must have warned them because when we returned the next night for target shooting against the fires, we were met by an enveloping cocoon of darkness in their camp. We managed to slay their night patrols but were not daring enough to attack the camp. We thought it wise to fight them under our natural fortresses.

'Some of our men spent the night digging the buried bodies of our enemy, cutting their hearts out to steal their strength. I told them to leave the mutilated bodies outside the graves so as to dent the morale of the enemy. Morning brought no change to the wet weather. Even from afar we could see that the morale of the enemy had by then hit rock bottom. They gave up the struggle and made for Fort Beaufort. So ended another of their fruitless forays into Intab'Enzima.

'For his part, I heard, Somerset blamed the dead Fordyce for attacking too early, before he could be assured of support at the point of convergence. He said there were hordes of kaffirs in that mountain. I laughed later when the news reached me. For one thing, Fordyce was the braver of the two; and we certainly didn't have hordes of kaffir warriors on that mountain, as they falsely reported. As I said, at most we were just eight hundred plus. I subsequently left to organise our resistance in the fastness of the Amathole mountains. But when the Kat River rebels capitulated on their riots, the colonial forces were able to expunge our fastness at Intab'Enzima. Botha, the leader of Khoi rebels then, fled, but eventually came back to slit his own throat rather than fall prisoner to the barbarous British forces who were calling for his head. Most of us had moved on in any case. To me Intab'Enzima was about showing my strength to Smith. He never commanded anything where I was, not unless sitting on one's arse in some office is being in command of war. I later learnt that it was in their nature to lay thick colours on things when they narrate. They immediately recalled him in humiliation back to their land after that battle. I went back to the mountain fastness when I heard the new Governor was brought, George Cathcart. Not because I wanted to continue with the war – we were also a spent force and needed to plough the fields before winter came – I just wanted to get better terms of peace and my land back. It was not to be. The new Governor was not just a man of cruel manners, but treacherous also. You could not rely on anything he said. He was gone within a year, but not before doing irreparable damage to our nation. The tragic consequences were ripened by the stupidity of the likes of Mlanjeni before being crowned in tragedy by a young girl by the name of Nongqawuse. But more about that later.

'In fights with the colonial force the crucial lesson was to avoid open spaces, which favoured their firing power. It became our method of operation, whenever we attacked them, to lead our subjects to a densely forested mountain, and from there launch sporadic ambushes. We ambushed them in their churches, in their hooded wagons, in their ploughing fields; almost everywhere they were not expecting us. We learnt to move fast, in stealth, through dense forests like the black mamba. Our ears and eyes became honed, alert to the slightest foreign noise or movement in the forest. Their clothing encumbered them even when they dared to follow our paths in the forest, and their bodies did not do well when exposed for too long to the sun; and they easily smarted from the whips of thorn bushes. Their armour made them conspicuous. They glittered against early and evening sunrays, broadcasting their location to us. The inaccessible mountains provided natural protection for us from their battery. Thick tree trunks hemmed them in and prevented them from making any kind of formation or being able to plot any formal course of battle. On many occasions they ended up raking their own patrols with fire. We were everywhere yet tenuous as the morning mist, disappearing immediately when it got hot. Dense bush provided excellent cover for us, allowing us to surprise them at close range, making our assegais more effective than their guns. They deserted almost all their military posts and farms and flocked together at their capital eRhini to organise their defence.

'I noticed that whenever our fire rained, and our assegais made havoc in white army lines, most of them crawled wounded behind rock shelters and forgot their valour. They'd fall into great panic and flee in disorder, thinking of nothing except the shelter of the fort. When we pursued them, some rode their horses so hard that many of their poor beasts were killed by sheer exhaustion. Once you gave the red devils no room for tactics, and forced them to fight with sheer trial of personal strength, bravery and war skill, they broke and fled like fawns. Bravery was not their strongest virtue, that's why they hid under artillery; but they were skilled at adopting cunning tactics like – what did you call it? the scorched earth policy – burning our planted fields.

'They used Mfengu and KhoiKhoi regiments as cannon fodder, assigning the difficult task to them of acting as an advance guard to penetrate our strongholds. These regiments were supposed to make the first contact with us and lure us into open fields. This deliberately kept the white army out of the stress of the battlefield. The Mfengus were tractable because they were hungry wanderers fleeing Shaka's *Imfecane*. We taunted the whites for this cowardice, and the Mfengu and KhoiKhoi for their foolishness. When the KhoiKhoi woke to what was going on, they became intransigent against colonial orders and subsequently spent their wartime hunting game, or remaining to shoot at their own colonial allies whenever the fire heated up. The KhoiKhoi gave us signs of where the redcoats were by volley fire. We paid them in kind whenever we caught some of them by sparing their lives.

'The tragic past of the Mfengus refused them the courtesy of trusting any ally so they were tough customers, loyal only to their own survival. Hardships had taught them how to act together for their own benefit alone, and they were unwilling to completely abandon their fate to us. They kept vacillating between revolt against military exploitation by the British and assisting us – but they only ever gave us a little support. The Mfengus were a perfidious lot. They had no battle array, and seldom met any enemy in open field; all their loyalty went with the destruction of their tribehood. The only thing about them to commend is their kindness and hospitality to strangers, and fidelity to their women. Even that they learnt the hard way. Hunger and oppression has been their lot since *Mfecane* destroyed their tribe.

'Without the Mfengu and KhoiKhoi, even with no guns we could have eventually prevailed over the red devils. Their way of fighting was just not suitable for combat against us. Strong as they might be in open fire, they were almost useless in the bush, or wherever the horizon was obscure. For instance, my men and I were involved in a skirmish with one of their patrols led by Lieutenant Bailie near Ntaba kaNdoda. It was amazingly easy to lure the battalion to the Mngqesha River where I knew they'd be trapped. All I needed to do was wheel my horse around, with my men at a respectable distance. When they saw it was me they were foolishly enticed. Each and every one of them entertained the foolish honour of killing Maqoma, the great perturbator. Rising in their stirrups, they came in a mad rush with drawn swords and pointed guns. I then lowered my body to my horse's body, with my head almost touching the mane, and rode like hell towards my men. In no time I dropped from their sight as I disappeared into a ravine. They fired in all directions, not sure which way I had gone or how I had suddenly vanished. From there all we needed to do was wait on the leeward side of the krantz until their ammunition ran low while blocking their egress line. By the time they realised this they had nowhere to go except a thicket, where they were cornered like a porcupine by dogs.

'A well-trained hunting dog knows how to avoid the quills of the porcupine. They volleyed a few shots but we didn't give them much chance to reload. *Ho! Hi! Hi! Ho!* our spears went, showering a rain of assegais on those who chose to dare attack us. None of them survived in that skirmish.'

Hintsa's Head

BY THE TIME THE MORNING SUN ROUSED INTO ripe blossoming, Phila had already spent some time gardening his thoughts at his laptop. The cows, mooing their way to the fields, shepherded his thoughts when his mind drew a blank. He tamped the cigarette he was smoking and stepped outside to spy on the doings of the day.

The grass on the hills, fading into the whitish gold of a lion's mane, looked magnificent when hit by the sun as dawn slowly peeled off the coming day. The wafting morning air, swampish with the river's sour mesh, raked the rural haunted look over the dry river creeks.

"Spring is moving on stilts."

Phila had not heard Zwelinzima come up behind him and he jumped, startled. "It sure looks that way," he chuckled. "It is better for us to take off while it's still early; this sun seems to be lit by a short man."

"Yes, our tokoloshes are not lazy in this area."

The two men sat on the grass next to each other. An ancient understanding between them required no formulation of words. Fingers of mist crept up from the yellow reed bank like arrows of supplication.

"Perhaps, when you come this way again, the children will have long gone to the cities. My wife will struggle here on her own, but she is a strong woman." He kept quiet to see if Phila was with him. When Phila simply nodded he went on: "This life, our life, will close its chapter when the likes of us fold to join our ancestors. Perhaps, sometime, someone will speak of things that happened here; how we tried to push back the flood of the sea – a useless thing, now to think about it. Times move on. Those who can't move with them must remain in the graves. The best that can be done for them is to put a stone to their memory. Jong'Umsobomvu? That was a man among men! None like him shall be born of this land again." Zwelinzima's lively eyes were filled with a young boy's remorse.

Phila was mute. Something in him understood it all, though he could not explain. A dry smile was trapped on his face as he went inside to get their bags. Gently, they bade farewell to each member of the family, as though they had known each other for a lifetime instead of just one day. When he tried to speak as they drove away Phila's voice became choked with emotion. He felt, once again, the world biting into him.

"You know that he's sick? Cancer," Matswane stated, almost as soon as they were on the road.

Phila felt irritated by her need for intrusion, her lack of discretion and understanding of circumlocution in rural traditional ways, and her inability to keep quiet at this early hour. But he knew there was no point raising this with her; he knew what she would say. "I'm not like you. I don't know how to hide my vulnerabilities …"

When they got to King William's Town Phila visited the museum while Matswane tied – or rather untied – the loose ends of her contract with the provincial government. At the museum, a middle-aged guy, wearing a chiffon shirt and blue jeans, ushered him in. He seemed preoccupied as he spoke of the history of the area and the museum. Displayed in protective glass were materials that had been presented to Mandela by various world leaders. The guide explained about measuring the revolution of the country, but he talked without much enthusiasm.

In a dimmed corner hung an illuminated poster of Steve Biko lying dead on the cement prison floor. This caught Phila's attention. The face of Biko, proud and vulnerable, like a bruised and skinned plum, lacked the tranquillity of restful sacrifice. This Biko looked stubbornly independent even in death. It only occurred to him then that Biko had been born in this town. The guide, with trembling assurance that completed Phila's thoughts, framed the bleakness of Biko's last days for his information. There were many stains of exaggerated telling in his narration but Phila was too involved to speak. The part that impressed itself on Phila was what the guide said in quoting Biko: *Our culture must be defined in concrete terms.* It had always amazed him how museum and art gallery curators knew how to sieve things into their essence. You could forget for a moment that they themselves didn't really know the depths they pronounced sometimes. Still they were able to separate the chaff from the grain of history, which was a fair starting point.

Outside, the small provincial capital of the Eastern Cape had other icons of dissipation. Its people seemed glazed with strandedness. Phila lay down on the lawn of the public square, sky- and people-gazing while waiting for Matswane to collect him. Everything looked dappled, sounded graceful. Somehow he felt it right that he was there, in that town, in that park, at that moment, with those people, in this life. With Hopkins he felt deep gratitude for the dappled things and the grandeur of God that charges the world. He was beginning to suspect he might be having a mystical moment when he felt a tug on his foot. It was Matswane, rousing him. Her business done, they drove back to East London.

Phila sneaked out of the B&B very early in the morning to buy fresh bread. He drank in the fresh sea air on the promenade with the early morning joggers. As he walked he was struck by the dereliction of the dying industrial compound: rampart buildings constructed of uncut mortared stones; ghost openings where once were windows and doors; scant roof covering and timber, flaking walls, urine-drenched passages. It seemed as though the city was already skeletoning its past.

Decay was everywhere denoted by the barrack buildings rimmed by half-rotted cell doors. Iron bars, once thick as wrists and strong as mountains, bent like ghosts of failure.

This is no state of decay but of death, thought Phila to himself. Tired of visiting places of the past, forts of shame, walls of staggering imperialism beneath two centuries of delusional sinecures, he turned back. He went to the Spar for bread, eggs and such, and then, for whatever reason, perhaps to make himself less conspicuous, he also started jogging, like the rest of the people on the beachfront promenade.

When he got back to the B&B Mrs Boyle greeted him enthusiastically as he jingled the keys out of his pocket. He gave her a curt nod, hoping to get away quickly.

"Hello! We've not seen you in a while." The fug of smoke from the permanent cigarette in her mouth stifled the passage air. She was a slightly overweight middle-aged white woman with too much time on her hands. Besides a nosy personality, she was a right laugh.

"Yes – I've been out of town again." Phila tried in vain to pass her.

"You young people are always on the road. Roads today are a guillotine, you must be very careful."

"Always careful."

"Did you hear what they did to the poor woman at No 3? Three men …" She went on to narrate how three men pretending to be salesmen came to her flat and held the 'poor woman' hostage while they cleaned her place out. "Took all the furniture," said Mrs Boyle. "She was lucky they didn't hurt her. The horror of it! Times are bad …"

"Yes, they are, Mrs Boyle."

"That's why I never open my door, even if the Pope comes knocking." She took a long drag of her cigarette. "But when I saw this lovely lady in the foyer waiting for you, I knew no harm would come of it. I saw you go out earlier, probably just going to the shops, I thought, so I invited her in for tea to wait for you in my flat. Lovely girl, you must take care of her."

Phila felt a little confused.

"Come inside now. Let's not keep her waiting any longer. Mind you, it is dangerous these days to have a girl without … you know what. Come along now, she's waiting. I hope she's finished her tea. You don't know things that happen in this place; even my husband thinks it is too much. Mind you, he grew up on a farm and saw a thing or two in his day. He's not the one to worry about such things. In our era we …" She went on ahead, happy to have someone to talk to beside her husband who, between his job and watching rugby on TV, did not say much beyond calling to her to bring him a can of beer from the fridge.

"When you said you were in East London, I knew this was where you'd be staying."

Nandi spoke in her usual calm manner, as if it were preordained that they should meet here, on this day, at a beachfront guest house, Phila in his tracksuit and jogging shoes, holding a grocery bag in a trembling hand. He didn't speak, just signed a nod to Mrs Boyle, before leading Nandi to the room. He felt cold. Had it been a cold morning? He fiddled with the door until it opened. By the looks of things Matswane was still asleep. He prayed she was still asleep.

Nandi stepped inside and threw her handbag on the sofa. "So, what exactly is going on?" she demanded forcefully, uncharacteristically. "I am not putting my life on hold for you again. So you had better let me know now what is actually going on?"

"I didn't ask you to put your life on hold for me," Phila answered sheepishly, sidestepping the question. He wanted to tell Nandi to keep her voice down but knew he couldn't without giving away that he wasn't alone in this place. The door to the bedroom was ajar. If Mat was awake, no doubt she would be listening.

"Oh! But you don't have to say it. You know when you reappear I am just gonna drop everything and continue with you where we left off?

"Well, not –"

"Good morning." Matswane appeared from the bedroom, wearing Phila's T-shirt. "Am I interrupting something?"

Phila dropped back on the sofa adjacent to Nandi's.

"Is this her? This …" Nandi held back her words. Scooping up her handbag, she said: "You know what? The two of you deserve each other." Then she went for the door. Phila followed her but couldn't catch the door before she banged it. He wrenched it open but Nandi was already taking the last flight of stairs to the pavement. A flabbergasted Mrs Boyle, cigarette in mouth, and obviously trying to make sense of the sudden commotion, stood in the passage, staring. When she saw Matswane following Phila in a hurry, the penny dropped. With a surprised "Oops!" she hastily went back into her flat and shut the door.

When Phila reached the pavement Nandi's car was already rounding the corner. Slowly he went back inside. Upstairs Matswane was sitting on the sofa. He sat next to her and she leant her neck against his shoulder. "So that was your woman?" When Phila didn't reply, she said: "I think if you want to be with her you should drive back now to her." Phila remained silent. Then he got up and went onto the balcony, where he lit a cigarette.

After a while he went back inside and gathered up the grocery bag from the lounge floor. As he carried it into the kitchen he felt a lump in his throat. "I was aiming at serving you breakfast in bed," he said over his shoulder.

Matswane had followed him in. "We can prepare breakfast together," she said. "It'll be great – our first prepared meal together."

There was something about the eagerness in her voice that vaguely suggested innocence and that pleased Phila.

"Okay." He started with the scrambled eggs.

"Don't put garlic in my scrambled egg, babes. I hate that," Mat said when she noticed him making to mince the garlic.

Phila softly laughed. "We've just discovered something we disagree on. I love garlic scrambled eggs."

They ate breakfast in a mild discursive pleasantness. After washing the dishes they sat on the couch for a while, feeling no need to puncture the comfortable silence. Neither of them mentioned Nandi, and that felt okay. Mat suggested they catch a movie, but Phila said: "Tell you what, let's pack our stuff and cross the Kei to the former Transkei, and I'll show you where the Xhosa king met his ignominious death at the hands of the British. I need to go there anyway.'

"Sounds good." Matswane was getting used to him by now. "Give me a few minutes, okay, babes?"

Phila closed the door of the flat slowly and made them walk on tiptoe past Mrs Boyle's flat, but it was no use. She opened the door and said, "Off you go so soon? Take care on the road. Sorry about early on, I had not realised. And don't worry – I always keep an eye."

"Thanks, Mrs Boyle. *Ndiza kubambela ekushiyayo.*"

"*Zandi shiya zonke mntana wam, akusekho ndiyidingayo.*" She always amazed Phila with her fluent Xhosa – perks of growing up on a farm.

"And that?" Matswane could not suppress her curiosity.

"I was just thanking her with a known Xhosa proverb that says: 'I'll catch you one – a bird – that is fleeing from you,' which basically means 'I owe you one.'"

"And her answer?"

"She has subtle humour sometimes. She answered: 'They've all flown away from me, my child, and I've no interest in catching any of them' – meaning she is no longer interested in fleeing things, and would rather stick with what she knows."

Phila and Matswane giggled.

"I love Eastern Cape whites for making an effort to speak African vernaculars," said Matswane.

"An effort? She probably speaks better Xhosa than I do! Divide and rule struggled here because of our mutual dependency on farms.

"Hence most of us speak all three languages of the area: Xhosa, Afrikaans and English."

"That's great!"

"We also fought the most, fiercest and the longest."

They pulled into a service station to fill up. "Were we to ask this petrol attendant about himself, I mean his background, do you think we would learn much beyond his clan name?" Phila asked Matswane as the man walked towards the car.

"I doubt it. Perhaps it is not necessary that he does. There are other ways of knowing your identity without necessarily being in touch with your history."

"Like what?"

"Oh, I don't know. Traditional practices, perhaps? You don't have to be a historian to know and practise those; they can just be handed down to you by your parents."

"I see. Don't ask me why, but I can tell that he's umGcaleka, that is, he comes from beyond the Kei, instead of iRharhabe, who are mostly from this side of the river."

"Everything regarding you millet eaters is complicated to me. I never even knew you were sub-divided."

"All cats look alike in the dark, I guess. Mind you, I'll admit to not knowing the difference between a Pedi and a Tswana."

"Well, me too, before they speak and I am able to distinguish," Matswane said, adding, "but you can tell before they speak."

They took Oxford Street towards Old Umtata Road, then to the freeway, travelling for thirty minutes before descending the sharp Kei Cuttings. In passing the former border posts at the foot of the mountains Phila felt a sanguine frenzy. These were the roads he had had to travel with mounting dissatisfaction to his boarding school decades ago. It became clear to him now that displacement starts at home, and is a perspectival dispersion that estranges familiar landscape. He wondered if his over scrutinisation of the familiar would eventually render it *unheimlich*, uncanny, to him. It pleased him to see Mat basking in contentment as forbidding granite cliffs were replaced by hills and valleys where flocks of sheep grazed. In the distance they looked like colonies of ant hills.

Sedentary shepherds sat on the roadside in abject impotence as the road climbed towards Butterworth, with the grass getting tawny and the soil ochre. About fifteen kilometres outside the town Phila asked Matswane to stop the car. He got out, and she followed him. They sat on the bonnet looking at the vast fields and clusters of Xhosa villages.

Then Phila started heaving, as if he was about to retch. He looked at Matswane with sunken eyes.

"Are you okay?" asked Matswane, concerned.

"Yes. Maqoma is here, forcing his way."

Matswane did not understand. She had an involuntary scowl on her face. "Is he hurting you?" she asked.

"No, it's something he does when demanding my attention. He has never done this before when I was in company. I suppose he's getting used to you. He wants to show and tell me things related to his life. He says …

'We now need to go back a little to the year 1835 in the white people's calendar.'

Goosebumps stood up on Matswane's smooth arms, but she said nothing, just listened.

'We, as amaNgqika, were entering what really was our first war with the colonial government. You would remember that we had not been part of the Nxele war, and in the other wars we had been non-active allies of white people until when coming back from raiding amaNdlambe the white government attacked our people, basically declaring the first war between us. They were still in desperate need of our cattle, but they couldn't find them, or not enough to satisfy their needs. And so they crossed iNciba.

'When it proved difficult to catch our cattle, the colonial forces turned to Hintsa, the king of amaGcaleka here. It was that devil's whetstone, Smith's idea. Harry Smith was little more than a commander of their soldiers then, but somehow he convinced the then Governor of the colony, Benjamin D'Urban, to come with him. They found Hintsa already buckling under the pressure of the Mfengu revolt and Thembu skirmishes. What induced them to cross the river was to follow the vast numbers of cattle we had sent to Hintsa for safekeeping, away from their rapacity. They claimed the kine belonged to their farmers, and everyone they came across. Hintsa warned his people to take their cattle beyond the reach of white people by taking them across Mbashe River to Pondoland. Those treacherous Mfengus became bold in their daring when they saw colonial forces. They started filching the cattle of amaGcaleka they were tending. And then, in formed units of *amabutho*, totalling about seven thousand, excluding women and children, they presented themselves to the Governor, seeking the protection of the Queen of Britain as subjects. These doings put Hintsa in an awkward position. For one, amaMfengu were his subjects and servants. He was compelled to meet up with the Governor, in demand of his cattle and subjects.

'Hintsa met the Governor, with his head councillors, his son Kreli, and his brother Bhuru, on the bank of the Izolo River. He wanted to reach some understanding. D'Urban, prompted by Smith, demanded fifty thousand head of cattle from Hintsa before peace and understanding could be reached. The Governor went over the wrongs he considered Hintsa guilty of. After that, while instructed to bring half of the demands within a week as a first instalment, Hintsa was given presents to appease him: saddles, bridles, spades, blankets, duffle, brass wire and beads, and made to promise to do his best to improve the relations between his people and the colony.

'They dined, attended by bagpipes and bugles. Kreli was also offered gifts of beads, brass and duffle, and presented with a scarlet cloak ornamented with blue buttons. They drank soup, ate biscuits, potatoes and coffee with sugar like friends. Just when they were starting to be at ease, laughing and drinking – *Ha! Ha! Ha!* the fire blazed.

'The Governor tore away all pretence of friendship and demanded that Hintsa, as paramount of amaXhosa, order the surrender of amaNgqika, and compensate the settlers for their loss of cattle and horses. He was ordered to pay, on top of fifty thousand cattle, a thousand horses, one half of which were to be handed to the colonial government as soon as they could be collected, and the rest within a year. Hintsa, who all along had been shaking his head, eventually succumbed on condition that he collected the cattle himself as, "Kaffirs would not dispense with such a great number of their cattle unless the order comes from the king personally." The Governor refused. He told him to find another way to communicate the message to his people. Hintsa despatched a secret message, warning his people to drive all their cattle as far as possible from the British instead of delivering them for payment, and never to trust the white people's peace initiatives because they imprisoned a person. "White people shower with presents those they wish to imprison," he said as he was taken prisoner by Smith.

'Hintsa had entered the white man's camp under peaceful assurances that he was there to talk peace. He woke the following day to the shock of being a prisoner. He sent similar messages to me and to Thyali, urging us never to stop the war on the colonial government.

'When the party sent to collect the cattle from amaGcaleka did not return in five days, Smith – who was eager and determined to commence hostilities against amaGcaleka – urged the Governor to go back to the colony and leave him to conclude the situation with amaGcaleka. Hintsa proposed again that he be allowed to go and persuade his people to hand over the cattle. As a sign of good faith he promised to leave his brother Bhuru and his son Kreli for insurance. This arrangement was agreed on. Hintsa set off with a small patrol under the command of Smith. The company in all was made up of five hundred troops and fifteen members of the invidious Corps of Guides. Hintsa had designs of luring the party deeper into Xhosaland where he'd be in a stronger position to negotiate the release of his son by taking the white party hostage. The party marched on, covering up to fifty-two miles a day, with Hintsa always under the strict eye of Smith and KhoiKhoi bodyguards. The Southey brothers, who were the members of the Corps of Guides I loathed most, were the ones helping them track the cattle spoors. Naturally, Hintsa looked for every opportunity to escape. The Governor took Kreli and Bhuru with the main

troops and marched from Izolo to Ndabakazi, the mission station close to
the present town of Butterworth.

Matswane looked at the road sign before them; it was pointing to
Ndabakazi. Phila's eyes were closed.

'Hintsa and Smith's party camped for the night at Gwadana Hills
before marching again from the morning until evening. When there was
no sign of cattle Hintsa feigned a complaint to Smith. "You see how my
subjects treat me. They drive the cattle away from me, in spite of being
their king. I've no control over them." At about ten in the morning of
the following day Hintsa made a request. "Allow me to send Mthini, my
principal councillor, to tell my people I'm here, so that they must not drive
away their cattle." Smith agreed on condition that Mthini returned by
dusk. Hintsa was in good spirits when Mthini was allowed to set off,
which he did at high speed. "It'll not be necessary now to go as far as
Mbashe," he said. "I'm sure we'll find all the cattle at Nqabarha."

'When they reached the foot of Mbongo Hill, near Nqabarha, Smith,
who was growing suspicious because the cattle spoor seemed to be keeping
a day's march ahead of them all the time, wanted to climb the hill to
survey the area. He was not prepared to let Hintsa out of his sight so he
took him and a few of his scouts and bodyguards up the hill with him.
Hintsa, who rode a remarkable horse, led the way up the hill on foot,
to spare the animal from fatigue, while Smith rode his. At the heights
they paused to look at the hollows and knolls, valleys of dense bush and
rocky mountains all around them. At the foot of the other side of the
hill a wooded stream emerged from precipitous heights, beyond which
rose the Mbongo Mountain. Smith noticed that the cattle spoor divided
as they crossed the river. One branch took steep ascent to a hilltop that
sloped away to the right, down to a bend in the river where there were
several kraals. The other branched towards and disappeared on entering
the Mbongo Mountain. His KhoiKhoi scouts told him as much also.

'"We must follow the track to the right; the cattle that have gone to
the left up the mountain are lost to us," suggested Hintsa. The suggestion
made sense to Smith even though he was suspicious of Hintsa's motives.
Having crossed the river they proceeded slowly up the steep track. That
was the moment when Hintsa took the gap. He rode quickly towards
Smith, the only man who was in front of him, and passed him, aiming
to disappear into the small but thickly bushed terrain ahead. Smith and
the guides called out to Hintsa not to go so fast. When he ignored them
they called on him to stop or they'd be compelled to shoot. The area was

covered with thick bush, the effect being that instead of assisting the chief's escape the bush hemmed him in.

'Seeing there was no way of escaping, Hintsa smiled and turned back to Smith, who by then was galloping to intercept him with pistols drawn.

'Beyond the bushy area the bald brow of the Mbongo Mountain was visible and the terrain opened up, parallel to the wooded bed of Nqabarha River on their left. There was a village nearby at the tongue of land where the river bent a few miles further down. Smith took out his spyglass to have a better look at his troops still scrambling up the steep ascent. Hintsa, who all the time had been edging away from Smith, bolted away again, this time making a dash for the village. The guides shouted to draw Smith's attention to the escaping Hintsa, who had gained a head-start of about fifty yards before anyone noticed. Throwing his spyglass away, Smith and his party set off in hot pursuit, but only Smith's horse was up to racing with Hintsa's splendid dark bay.

'When Smith was about forty yards from Hintsa he drew his pistol and fired, but it jammed. He tried a second time and the same thing happened. Hintsa was getting away. Tossing his pistol aside, Smith spurred his horse to go faster. He caught up with Hintsa and struck him with the butt of his rifle, which flew out of his hand in the scramble. Hintsa took the bundle of assegais that were tied to the saddle of his horse, and furiously jabbed Smith with it. But Smith rode Hintsa down, desperate to prevent him from making it into the thick vegetation on the river bank, all the time trying to seize Hintsa's reins and being dissuaded by Hintsa's stabs. By then Smith was riding too close to Hintsa for the parrying jabs to have any serious effect. He grabbed Hintsa by the kaross and hurled him headlong to the ground. Hintsa was on his feet instantly. He flung an assegai, but it fell between the legs of Smith's horse.

'Smith's aide-de-camp, whose name was Balfour, along with the Southey brothers, had by then caught up with the two scuffling men. When he saw that the fallen chief was about to run for his life into the thicket, George Southey fired at him. The shot caught the chief in the left leg while he was still looking around for the best way to escape. Hintsa fell down on his hands, got up again and ran towards the river bank. Southey sprang from his horse and called upon the chief not to escape, but to no avail. Smith shouted at Southey to fire again, and he did, this time striking the chief under the ribs on his right-hand side just as he reached the river. The chief fell and rolled but, being a strong man, he was up in no time again, desperately scrambling down the steep clay bank and stumbling into the water.

'Smith, by now standing up in his stirrups, shouted that they must not let the "kaffir king" escape. As the ground was too precipitous for horsemen to follow, some of his men, among them Bisset, Driver, Balfour and Shaw, dismounted and pursued the chief on foot, firing shots at him all the time. Hintsa tried to swim across the Ngqabara River. Southey, Driver, Bisset and Balfour were the first to reach the place on the river bank where Hintsa had seemingly disappeared. When they didn't see him they knew he was still on their side of the river. Southey and Balfour entered the bush with Driver and Bisset doing the same on the other side, all working their way towards each other with Hintsa somewhere in the middle.

'Southey was the first to come upon the chief, who was not wading through the river but running along the reeds in faltering steps. As Hintsa tried to shelter under a shelf of rock Southey came up behind him. By then the chief was bleeding profusely, and he was very tired. He pleaded for his life. In cold blood Southey blew off the top of Hintsa's head. Hintsa collapsed into the water and died. He was in his fifty-sixth year.

'The ball had entered the forehead and completely smashed his skull. When Smith came up he collected the jewellery of ivory and gold Hintsa loved to adorn himself with and put it in his bag. Bisset took the chief's assegais and charm to put around his own neck. When others could no longer find any more valuables to take from the chief they cut his ears off as memorabilia. They bragged among each other when they got to their military camps. Shaw cut the skin of the king's shin. Others dug his teeth out with bayonets after they had cut off and cooked his head. To date, no one knows what happened to his skull afterwards.

'Some KhoiKhoi soldiers, disgusted by the behaviour of the white soldiers, traced where the body of the Xhosa king had been left to be eaten by hyenas. They carried it to the first Xhosa village, enacting what had happened the previous day.

'Thus did the sweet tall grass of Khala, Xhosa's royal blood, arms ringed with ivory, nails black with digging for his nation, ignobly perish for trusting the honour of the British Governor. *Awu, Mádoda!* When they fail to return they are lost.

'We were flabbergasted by such insolence. Perhaps you now understand why my resentment for Smith ran so deep. Hintsa kaKhawuta was the paramount of the Xhosas. The depth of the paramount's humiliation was too much for most of us. It fired us up to more courageous resistance. We heard the real story of Hintsa's death from Mthini and others who were the first at the scene of the tragic debacle. They rallied their followers and came to join us with intentions of avenging their chief. The day they came I said to my brother Thyali, "The Gcalekas are starting to feel the hardness of our lot and the bleakness of the situation our future is under."'

Phila opened his eyes and looked around him.

Matswane did not know what to say, her forehead was pleated in furrows with sweat pearls. The landscape was still the same but everything had utterly changed also. From being Aladdin's cave of wondrousness, now, at the storyteller's plenitude, it was a land of shame. She felt a two-thousand-foot drop to the valley of shame. By and by she said: "I'm feeling deep-seated anger."

Phila didn't say anything as they drove into Butterworth. Then, as she was parking the car outside a supermarket, he broke his silence. His face drawn and drained of energy, he said, "KwaXhosa, Hintsa's death is the wound that has not healed, probably shall never heal. His shameful death is a symbol that foretold the nation's calamity. The search for his head has become a quest for the recovery of the nation's dignity. And like the dignity, it has not yet been found."

"I remember reading something about the search in the newspaper," said Matswane, feeling as exhausted as Phila looked, knowing that words, any words, were inadequate.

"Almost in every decade, a diviner or witch-doctor rallies the Xhosas around this cause by claiming that the ancestors are not happy with the fact that Hintsa's skull has not been found. Western historians dispute this but there is a strong belief among amaXhosa that after Hintsa was beheaded, the British took his head, together with his traditional mace, to Scotland. But nobody knows for sure, or where in Scotland they might be."

Phila got out of the car for a smoke while Matswane went into the supermarket.

Everything falls according to how it bends. Everything falls according to how it bends.

Walking barefoot, Phila repeated these words, over and over. The ground felt warm and prickly.

Brother, Brother

THE TOWN OF BUTTERWORTH SWARMED WITH people going about their daily business. Some when they passed the car gave it admiring glances – Matswane's Saab had a striking out of place feel around the bakkies and Toyota Corollas – mostly Xhosa peasants with stiff crude gaits, excitedly confused by traffic in crossing the streets. Occasionally, a puffed-up municipal worker, or a clerk, or a teacher, crossed with more assurance, in ill-fitting woollen cardigan and shirt with a worn collar, and alcohol-induced bloodshot eyes. Phila found himself having to keep a permanent apologetic smile on his face in polite greetings to everyone who made eye contact with him. It wearied him but he felt compelled since he had no defined position in the structure of things in that place. He wished Matswane would hurry up.

At that moment he saw her shoving her way through the throngs at the supermarket entrance. Watching her wait for the traffic lights to change before crossing the street, he felt guilty he had not gone with her. Her face, with an expression of irritation, changed into bliss when their eyes met. There was something of Schopenhauerian *Wille zum Leben,* will-to-life, about how she carried herself.

"Oh, the floorshow of frogmarching to the till!" she exclaimed as she opened the door.

"What happened?"

"Over and done with. I got us some rosemary focaccia, it looked fresh and appetising. Some ham and cheese too." She gave Phila a kiss as she put the plastic bags on the back seat.

"Good! I'm starving. There're some picnic areas outside town. We can park and eat."

"Fine by me." She put on her seatbelt and shades and then fired up the engine.

After driving for about twelve kilometres they pulled over into a shady picnic spot to eat. There was a calm, imperturbable silence in the air, occasionally interrupted by the blast of bulleting traffic. Cows with soiled flanks grazed in quiet bovine studiousness on the fields beyond the barbed-wire fence.

"The bread is good." Phila nodded after taking a bite.

"How long until Coffee Bay?" Matswane asked, busy with her food.

"An hour or two because of the gravel road once we branch off the main."

"Super! I'm getting wiped out."

"I'll drive. There're just too many animals in the road anyway from here. It needs someone who understands the area. It takes some getting used to."

The fissured ochre land bristled with thorn bushes interspersed with yellow grass. The austerity of the place encouraged thought. Could that be why Transkei, more than any other black area in South Africa, produced so many thinkers and political activists? Phila suspected the truth lay in the fact that the Eastern Cape had borne the brunt of colonial encounter through the cursed blessing of its long littoral.

Phila took the wheel and Matswane relaxed beside him, gazing out of the window. "So this is Gcalekaland. How posh!" she declared, as they passed a sign pointing to Willowvale. Her exclamations felt out of place, thought Phila to himself. He was impressed that she was determined to 'slum it', in her garb.

He recalled how Maqoma had told him about the royal contention that followed Hintsa's untimely death at the hands of white people. How his son Kreli was still too young and depended on his councillors. The British compelled the young king to register his people for the sake of census and paying taxes. The Gcalekas hated it. This put the young king under tremendous pressure.

"So your people walked this land, climbed these mountains and fished these waters for centuries," Matswane murmured.

"Well, technically, my people did all that on the banks kuLundini loThukela, on the banks of the Tugela River and foot zoKhahlamba, the Drakensberg, present-day KZN, but I get your point," said Phila. "To my people, amaMfengu, the British were lifesavers. They had come to these lands as starving wanderers. The Xhosas called them their beasts and dogs, because they employed them to do menial jobs, like looking after their stock and tilling their land for food and shelter. Hence when the British, in the form of D'Urban, came here amaMfengu saw an opportunity to unshackle themselves by turncoating. They pinched some of the Xhosa stock they were looking after, assuming it as their portion for the years they were slaves without real compensation. Naturally the Xhosas were livid. Meantime amaMfengu became the first natives to adopt the ways of the white man."

"Treacherous bastards your people were, babes." Mat gave Phila a brush on the head while still training herself to the beauty of the Wild Coast that was beginning to appear.

"In any case, Kreli's powers were specious. Everybody knew that real power rested with Councillor Gxabagxaba in the Gcaleka chieftainship. There was too much confusion. Minor chiefs didn't want to take orders from a commoner. Others mocked the young prince's ceremony of induction by not attending. They felt he was just a pasquinade. You remember Bhuru?"

"Hintsa's brother?"

"Yes. The funny thing is that he abandoned Hintsa's son when he needed him most. When it was clear Gxaba was usurping the throne, Kreli resorted to consulting diviners and rainmakers to increase his grandeur, just as his ancestor Gcaleka had done. Kreli was forced to grow up fast. His first brilliant action was to move out of his father's shadow by establishing his own great place beyond the Mbashe River. Obviously, he also wanted to be far from the reach of the colonial government. But this brought him into contention with the Pondos of Faku. He then went back to the land his father contended with Ngubengcuka of abaThembu. They had been given the greater portion of Hintsa's land as booty by the British because they'd assisted them in the last war against the Xhosas. Kreli demanded his father's land back. The Thembus drove a hard bargain. With the assistance of Myeki's Mpondomise and their doctoring, Kreli was driven to the coast, almost destitute. And the greater area of Butterworth was given to amaMfengu, up to the present-day Peddie, by the colonial government. So Kreli, like your Maqoma, found himself without a home in the land of his ancestors. From the area of present-day Coffee Bay to Gatyana, to Cintsa, along the coast, is where the majority of the amaGcaleka were pushed in pockets of desperation. For a while, in desperation, it was where Kreli settled in to catch his breath before attempting to reclaim his land."

Feeling impressed with how much he had taken in what Maqoma taught him, Phila continued: "For a while it looked as if Kreli would amount to nothing much. Luckily for him, most Xhosa chiefs don't take kindly to seeing their king made into a plaything and a vagabond. They felt an urgent moral need to be under some form of paramount, a king of the Xhosa nation. A conglomeration of Xhosa warriors were gathered to fight under Kreli's banner to reclaim his father's land. AmaNdlambe and amaNgqika across the Kei also agreed to set aside their quarrel, a rare thing, to join the army on behalf of Kreli. They routed the Thembus and drove them towards the Orange River, where they came under the pressure of Mshoeshoe's Sothos and were obliged to press back to the fringes of amaGcaleka. Reading between the lines, Gxabha retreated to the background, handing the reins to Kreli, who re-established his great place at Hohita, where his father used to be. Hohita is here in Willowvale but we don't have time to visit it.

"Maqoma gained tremendous influence over Kreli as a result of the assistance he offered, since he was the brains behind the amalgamation. But Maqoma had bigger fish to fry. His next move was to whip Kreli into a frenzy about the treacherous way white people had murdered King Hintsa. But Kreli had other internal issues to deal with. His brother Mnyaluza was one of the group that chased the Thembus beyond Igqili. He made frequent sporadic attacks on Kreli, so that the young king never really offered Maqoma the strength he needed when fighting the colonial wars."

"What's Igqi ... Igqili, babes?"

"Igqili is the Xhosa name for Orange River."

A journey is a series of irrevocable disappearances, thought Phila, as they got closer to Coffee Bay. What if a journey was a series of re-emergings? One would have to be someone who *no longer denies*.

Phila drove carefully on the gravel road, which was belted by scarlet, winter-blossoming aloe trees. Watchful forests thickened the closer they got to the bay.

'The sources of our pain are intermingled with those of our strain.' Maqoma spoke softly. 'Thyali learnt that lesson late. He died under suspicious circumstances. In his dying, he came to visit me on a windy August day.

'I could see he was not his usual jaunty, jerky self. He looked sickly.

'"Is something the matter, *mfo*?" I asked. "You look sickly." I was a little concerned but also cautious because there was still a lot of bad blood between us.

'He rolled his eyes up in his head in a manner that denoted all was not well. "I'm nose to the grindstone, Maqoma," he answered eventually, indisposed and gloomy, which confirmed my suspicions.

'"What's the matter? Why have you come to see me in the dog days?"

'"I'll get straight to the point. The white government is changing Commissioner-General Stockenström. He shall no longer be with us. All our agents are being replaced too. Apparently this group has been too concerned with the welfare of kaffirs. No guessing the kind of men who will be replacing them. Our only choice is in refusing to accept such replacements. I think we shall soon be at war with the colony again." This was towards the 1856 war of the millennialist movement of Nongqawuse he never reached. After the 1851-1853 war, when even our success in battles, like in Waterkloof, didn't earn us back our land, I became depressed once again and reverted to drinking. "We need all of our courage; it is obvious where all this is going." Thyali looked not just like a man in disappointment, but in despair.

'"I can't even spin a word to catch a fly these days," he added, "not since I went to see Suthu. She gave me lumps of sugar. I've not been myself since." He was harassed by stomach pain. I had a suspicion in my mind.

'"Do you think she poisoned you?" I asked, genuinely shocked to believe that Sandile's mother would go that far.

'"I don't know. Would she?"

'"She'd do anything to secure the throne for her son."

'"I don't think so ..." Then Thyali changed the topic. "In any case, I knew the status quo was too good to last. The white people must be in need of more land and cattle now. Those robbers will not stop until they've taken every last arable acre from us. Their purpose has always been to drive us to arid thorn-infested land where we will dwindle from famine, and come begging to them for work and sustenance. I want you to take my people under your wing also. I'm sure very soon the colony is going to push us out of our land again. I don't have the strength for it, so everything depends on you. But you need to ease up on white man's liquor, Maqoma, because your poison is going to come through that." He looked in my eyes for a long moment. "You know what to do, Maqoma. All this will culminate in another war. Better start preparing now. I'm afraid you'll have to do this one without me. I've strange premonitions."

'After that we sat in gloomy silence. One thing I always appreciated about Thyali was the consistency of his mind. Even when most of us vacillated and didn't know what to do he was always constant. From the start he knew the only way to live in peace in our land was to meet the violence of white people head on. Whatever the situation, even in my strangled hysteria, when I was grasping at straws, throwing myself into the white man's bottle, I always knew Thyali was there to keep the fire burning in our hearth. Whatever happened to me I knew he'd think himself into calmness and continue the struggle. Now he was telling me soon he would be no more. That shocked me into sense.

'Women who had been preparing meat for us brought it, but we were both out of appetite. When they came back to claim the dishes they were surprised to find we had not touched a thing. "Anything the matter, my chiefs?" one of them asked.

'"Everything is the matter," Thyali answered as he took a long pull from his pipe. He turned to me. "I have nothing to show for my life except blood, tears and toil. I've wasted a great deal of my life enclosed like an animal in strange lands because of white people. We're like dogs going after their own tails, round and round in dizzy warring circles. Last night I dreamt I was a gnat in a blade of grass of a British soldier crushed under his boot." A look of suffering was etched in his ferret eyes. It was the first time I got such intimacy from Thyali. I had always admired him for bearing the unhappiness we were born into with courage, however savage it was sometimes. I always found myself wanting compared to him in that department. And now here he was, pouring his heart to me, and I was discovering he had the same feelings about me, the same respect. How could it have been different? We were born to the same situation not very far apart in years. If anybody, it was Thyali who understood my situation best, and I his. We were the cats of the same forest, always stressing the ugliness of life while remaining vital in our heart of hearts.

'To animate the disembodied silence between us I stood and went to the calabashes among which I kept my brandy. I poured a tot and offered one to Thyali. He refused it with indignation. He again reproached me about my drinking problem, which he blamed for my lack of attention to things that mattered.

'"Contrary to your impressions," I argued lamely, "the white man's drink expands my mind – to receive better impressions. I've seen people throw away their lives because of white man's liquor. For me it does the opposite. I find it a tolerable companion in times of crisis. On things that shattered me, Thyali – the death of Hintsa, the humiliation of our nation, the manner in which they murdered my wife in the mountains – alcohol has been my only companion, the only thing that gave me strength to cope. Have you no heart? I'm not able to face a day of my miserable life on my sober wits. It gives me the little will I have left for continuing; without it I'd be in an even worse state. It keeps my spirits up. If you cannot understand this, try to conceal your disappointment in me."

'I continued in that vein for some time, trying to make Thyali understand where I was coming from. I even became sentimental, trying to blackmail him into sympathy, but he did not budge.'

'Things we addicts say to get a fix.' Phila implicated himself in order to sympathise.

'"It's time you got your act together, Maqoma," Thyali went on. "If alcohol is the only thing that facilitates your courage to life, then you might as well be dead. There's another storm coming. I have a feeling it'll be a make or break one. If we lose we're done for, forever. So long as something remains of me I shall go down grabbing the throat of a white man. But should my ancestors call me before the war starts or is over, all will be dependent on you. You cannot expect the young chiefs, Kreli and Sandile, to be of much use. They look up to you. Show them you're worthy of their respect. Break the shackles of white men's liquor, which has such a strong hold on your life."

'He stood up, bowed his head, put his hands behind his back and walked out of the door, leaving a sense of dreariness and doom behind. His entourage and guards were waiting for him as he got on his horse. They left without once turning back to look at me. He didn't look at me again. Do you understand what that meant? My father's child didn't look back at me. That's how disappointed he was with my drinking problem. He had lost his trust in my abilities but was forced to rely on me as the only hope. And that was the last impression I had of him because he died within weeks.

'I looked around at my people. Women turned their eyes down. They were all ashamed of me. My people were ashamed that I was dependent on the bottle. I went inside, took the last two peach brandy calabashes I had and threw them with all the strength I had against the boulder at the back of my hut. As they shattered among the rocks people looked up to see what the matter was. When they realised what had happened they started smiling, clapping and eventually singing praise-songs. Women came fawning and touching me.

'"My chief, my chief! You're back from the demon of white people."

'I never felt so proud of myself as I did that day. "Gather my councillors to be here the day after tomorrow," I instructed. "We have urgent things to discuss." Then I went behind the hut to vomit the last of the white man's poison still in my system.

'Thyali died from a similar sickness as our father, although he didn't drink white man's alcohol. Everyone was of the suspicion that white people were doctoring our chiefs to death. Thyali suspected Sandile's mother, Suthu, and the lumps of sugar she gave him just before he contracted the disease. Suthu fled to the colonial authorities for safety and told them I was the one orchestrating the campaign against her. You must hand it to her, she was shrewd. She knew she was through with Thyali and now she wanted the white authorities to come after me so her son Sandile would have no contender to the throne. Thyali went to his grave wondering if Suthu had poisoned him. When he died, because his sons were still young, his chieftainship fell to Xhonxo, who was not very effective. Suthu overpowered him with the threat of a barrel of a white man's gun, and the influence of Tola. Sandile was supposed to be the supreme ruler but we all knew Suthu held the real reins. That irked me. I became, in their eyes and words, "just another drunkard chief like Ngqika". This was probably the most frustrating time in my life, Suthu conniving with white people to get rid of me.'

The Dappled Things

PHILA AND MATSWANE ARRIVED IN Coffee Bay in the soft misty rain that was common in those parts of the land.

"When it rained like this in our area we said it betakes a monkey's wedding," Phila said, putting on the windscreen wipers.

"What do you know, so did we," said Matswane, taking in the green hills that rolled into the sea. They took a few wrong turns before they were on the right road towards the beach resort they were booked into. They parked the car immediately after entering the area in front of a bungalow with a sign saying Reception.

After collecting the keys for their bungalow they drove to their unit. They carried their bags inside against the polite curiosity of a couple sitting on the veranda of the next unit with sundowners. Matswane decided to take a shower, while Phila stood at the window and looked out at the sea view. He whispered, "We've come for Light."

The river mouths are full of the Light, according to Xhosa lore.

"I am making a cocktail – would you like one?" he called out to Matswane, whom he suspected was beyond earshot, as he opened the window to let in the connotative notes of the sea.

"Make me something with mint, please," she shouted back above the sound of shower water.

Phila mixed vodka with soda water and lime cordial before realising they had no mint leaves. None the less he went outside to the veranda satisfied with his Russian Mule. He lit a cigarette and felt obliged to give another nod to the couple next door.

"Dat sunset is de schamptin out of dis werld?" the guy said, with a heavy accent Phila immediately recognised as German, possibly from Thüringen. He stood to extend his hand, introducing himself as Arno. It turned out he was actually from Herrsching, a small town outside Munich. For some

264

reason, he felt compelled to tell Phila his exact address (corner of Leitenhöhe and Adolf-Ochert-Weg), which Phila found amusing because he knew it to be a German thing. Arno, who attended the University of Stuttgart, was on an exchange programme with the University of Port Elizabeth. Phila didn't feel like lingering too long and so he chose to withhold the information that he had spent some years studying in Germany, especially since he had not even found the appropriate time to tell Matswane yet. He felt it'd be inappropriate for her to hear it in front of strangers.

"I'm more Deutsch than Schwiss, but my vader kheeps insisting dat ve are Schwiss. Last I vas in Zürich vas ven I vas twelf hears hold. My mama is German, born in Cologne."

Arno, looking self-conscious, then gave a slight giggle as he went on in stagey reluctance. "Is dis too much information?"

"*Nein, nein, ich habe gehofft, daß du mir zeigen könntest, wo die Bar oder die Küche ist. Ich hätte gerne für Bonbons gefragt.*" As usual Phila's natural sympathy took hold of him. Arno was fascinated.

"*Du kannst ein paar von unseren haben. Wir sind immer vorbereitet. Meine Freundin ist Polinisch; sie denkt an alles.*

"*Willst du mit mir zu ihr kommen?*"

He went inside to bring a sprig of mint before continuing rabid talk, telling Phila his life story in five minutes, interjecting every second line with a "*Gottverdammte*".

Late that night the couples sat around an open fire, cooking lamb potjiekos and roasting garlic bread. Martyana, Arno's girlfriend, contributed an Austrian cabbage dish, though lacking the crucial garlic ingredient. They talked late into the night about their respective lives; growing up in different provinces, countries and continents. The European couple wanted to hear more and more apartheid stories, which, in the end, slightly irked Phila because they had to keep inventing horror stories they were fresh out of. Arno said he had wanted to come to Africa ever since a tarot card reader in Berlin had told him his fate was in Africa. Phila found this quite amusing.

"What did you interpret that to mean?" he asked.

"Zat I'll know ven I get zere!" They laughed half-heartedly before the girls, in muted giggles, went inside. Arno took the opportunity to expound, still in German.

"You know what? I always wanted to sleep with a black woman. I mean not a hooker. A nice good clean black woman. It vill be different ... you know vot I mean?"

Phila felt things were fast moving from heights of politeness to buddy luridness and locker-room banter and he wasn't sure how to react. In the end he decided to be a good sport and indulge Arno, but he stuck to English. If they kept up this conversation in German, he thought, it would only prolong the luridness.

"I bet none too different from sleeping with a white woman, except for the colour of her bush?" he asked.

"I know. But ze difference in skin colour type, culture and race surely brings viz it subtlety of tensions zat are ripe for transformation into sexual energy. Do you not zhink?"

"Well, I never really gave it that much thought. But now that you mention it, I see your point."

Mercifully, the girls came back, which the men took as their signal for a change of topic. They brought with them a bottle of whiskey, dilating pupils and canned laughter. It was Matswane's turn to listen to Arno's *ben trovato*s. Rolling his eyes, Phila clicked the front door shut behind him on his way to the loo, partly to prevent mosquitoes coming in, but secretly to have a momentary respite from Arno's voice. When he came back he was offered a glass of whiskey. Arno was astonished to learn Phila drank 'zat Amerikan ding' and they all laughed, though Phila not as heartily.

The sea had risen with the wind that was gusting strongly. After they had finished eating Arno wanted to go swimming.

"I couldn't move from this stool even if I wanted to," Martyana said.

Only Matswane was game. She went inside to put on her bathing suit, and off the two of them disappeared into the darkness.

Quite how they got onto the subject of the dangers of itis, Phila couldn't recall, but soon he and Martyana were in a deep discussion. She asked what it was called in Xhosa. Phila said *ukwetyisa* and went on a drunken explanation about cud and two bovine stomachs, because in the confusing sense of Xhosa words having a minimum of two meanings and maximum of sometimes eight meanings, *ukwetyisa* meant literally chewing cud also. They went on with their malarkey, more to disguise their concern about the pair who had gone swimming in the strong sea in the dark, conjuring the notion *yoku thwetyulwa*, in Phila's mind. The Xhosas associated the high rate of death by drowning around river mouths as a call by the River People – the ancestors. Hence they also regarded river mouths as dangerous, sacred places. "Do you think we should go check on them?" he asked Martyana.

"I wouldn't worry about them. Arno, you know, is, what you say, a professional swimmer in Germany." She did an imitation of breaststroke to make her point.

Phila told her, in mock fear, that it was exactly the hour the River People called their victims into the underwater sea caves. Martyana, who had a dreamer's gaze, was fascinated by the stories of Xhosa lore Phila told, the way his grandma used to tell them as in *intsomi*.

The duo returned after an hour or so. Arno, for some reason, was naked, holding his swimming costume with the hand that was not holding Matswane's, his penis shrunk into a button. Phila was used to odd European behaviour, but he wondered what Matswane made of it.

Arno excused himself to go and sleep after an unscripted gulp of that 'American ding'. In his overbearing and blustering manner, which Phila was getting used to by now, he dismissed his girlfriend, saying she could stay up if she wished. He did everything with a predatory boldness that irritated Phila. After a while Matswane excused herself too. "It's been a long day," she said as she drained her glass. "Don't stay up too late, babes." She ruffled Phila's head as she left. "It was nice meeting you, Martyana. See you on some adventure tomorrow."

For a while things felt a little awkward between Martyana and Phila. He broke the tension by asking where in Poland she was from. "Not that I know any part in Poland," he added.

"Ummm, originally, Kołobrzeg," Martyana said. "Do you know anything about?"

"Only that it's on the extreme side of the Baltic Sea and has terrible winters, with the sun setting at midday sometimes."

"That's my home."

Her visage had a troubling humility. Phila just could not make the commonality, or connecting attraction, to the blustering character of Arno.

"So you probably don't think South African winters are anything to write home about?"

"Let's just say I've never felt a need, not once in three years, to wear a parka with a fur-trimmed hood, or put my hands in mittens," laughed Martyana. "I love South African weather." She paused to assess his reaction before continuing. "My family lives in Krakow now. I studied in Warsaw before moving to Munich. It was there I met Arno. But we begin, what you call … go out?" She looked to Phila for reassurance that she had the right words. He nodded in encouragement. "Go out, yeah … only here in Africa. Before, in Germany, we see each other, greet, but nothing much." She had a better command of English than Arno, and her accent wasn't nearly as heavy. "I go to Munich because I want to study under a very good German artist called Juerno."

Phila and Martyana talked almost until dawn. They hugged as they stood to go to bed. Then kissed. Though its meaning was vague, the kiss was accomplished without hesitation or guilty haste. Phila put it down to sheer exhaustion, being very drunk and obvious mutual affability; he really liked her quiet manner, the tranquillity it fostered with the placid sea.

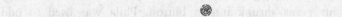

When Phila woke around noon Matswane was nowhere to be found. A note on the kitchen table said he should meet them at the river café for lunch at 12. He took a shower and had a little hair of the dog that bit him the previous night. Then he strolled over to the braai area to see if there was any of the lamb stew left in the potjie. There was plenty still. He dipped in a morsel of garlic bread without bothering to warm the pot. It tasted even better than before. Having made up his mind not to join the others for lunch at the café, he unplugged his computer, which was on the dining room table. He took the laptop outside and sat on the veranda to read up on the notes he had made from his reading and conversations with Maqoma.

"Anything could have incited war during those volatile times," he read. "It might seem ridiculous now that the *casus belli* happened to be the stealing of an axe by Tsili. Tsili was caught stealing a white farmer's axe in Fort Beaufort. He was rescued by his friends in a daring stance that involved cutting off the hand of a KhoiKhoi prisoner to whom the farmer had cuffed Tsili. The colonial government demanded that Tsili should be handed over. Sandile, as the Ngika chief then, refused. Even in the midst of grave intimidation he stood his ground. It led to another all-out war. Such are the fortunes of men under the rule of fools.

"The colonial government had not bargained on an all-out war. They were under the impression that Sandile was pusillanimous. They sought to teach him a lesson that would deal the kaffirs a quick powerful blow, to settle things once and for all. Maqoma and his brothers were in retreat. The cantankerous Thyali had just died. Sandile first engaged the British forces on the plains of Gwanga but was routed. Maqoma, who was sitting that war out, came secretly to train Sandile's warriors in guerrilla warfare tactics. The British hit them hard by burning Xhosa fields and huts, digging up and burning granaries. Both armies were disintegrating in disarray. AmaNgqika were almost prostrated on account of famine. Identifying where the problem secretly lay, the British again placed Maqoma under house arrest in Port Elizabeth under the pretence of consulting with him. Sandile's warriors were ensconced in their mountain fastness, but without victuals or provisions it was just a matter of time before they came down with their tails between their legs, or continued dying horrific deaths in the wild. Things were extremely bad. The kloofs reeked with the stench of putrefying flesh. The weather became oppressively hot, as if nature herself was colluding against them. Their sustenance came from occasional raids on white farms, relieving wagons of their loads, ransacking vulnerable posts, overpowering weak patrols, and raiding Mfengu settlements for food. They did these things with diligence and reasonable success, but it was unsustainable. Eventually, Sandile sued for peace, while claiming not to be defeated.

"Sandile had learnt from Maqoma that suing for peace while still in a stronger position affords tremendous negotiating powers."

Phila re-read the pages he had written, but they didn't satisfy him. He gazed out at the sea and its sunlit waves.

'The thing was this.' Maqoma sat down on the chair next to Phila. 'No matter how many redcoats you killed, more came from the sea. They were like a hydra with numerous heads. Unlike them, we had no power to cross the sea, neither did we have friends far away to fight our wars. The white government called for peace talks. We met with them – under the leadership of Cox, if I'm not mistaken. Three friendly cheers rose from our warriors to signal that talks were beginning in peaceful terms. We sat, myself in front, followed by Xhonxo, Anta and Casa, Nqeno's albino son. Thyali was dead by then. Nqeno was himself minding the rest of the warriors, ready to come to our assistance whenever we needed it. There were a lot of our councillors around, watching for any strange behaviour from the side of the British.

'The British are cunning. They sent, with their negotiating team, my sister Nongwane to persuade me to surrender. I was very glad to see my mother's child. Then she had the cheek to lecture me on what protracted war would mean for our people. I, who was living daily with it, whose home was the wilderness and the canyons, like a wild beast, while she was comfortable on the warm couches of her newly found religion in the missions. Warden read the terms of peace from the Governor's letter to us. We were to surrender Sandile and his mother, Suthu, to live under British protection. We were to give up our firearms, powder, and any KhoiKhoi deserters that might be with us. We were to move out of the Chumie

(Tyumi), Amathole, Keiskamma, Ntaba kaNdoda and Buffalo Mountain fastnesses to the foothill plains near the Nyati River, with our women and children. Basically, we were expected to surrender all our traditional homelands. Warden and Shepstone, who were interpreting, would show us the country we were to reside in and its boundaries. The land we were given went from the Kabousie to the Kei, including the Gunube area. After paying close attention to the terms, I made bold to answer. To say I was seething would be an understatement, but I was careful to control my tone so as not to give undue offence.

'"That is not peace you are offering but surrender, as if we were defeated. Is it a character of men who are after peace to propose impossible stipulations as peaceful terms? We will only settle for peace that is honourable." I stopped. Our men grumbled their compliance. I looked at my choleric brother, Anti, to see if he was with me. I knew if trouble came it would be from his direction. His expression satisfied me. I could see even he was praying that I would lower my tone. Cox's brow furrowed with studious application from the weight of my words. Truth be told, I knew that we were all tired of war but I was not prepared to negotiate slavery as peace for my people. So I continued.

'"When at Gaga the other day you proposed to terminate war. You said it was the wish of the Governor to forget the past. You mentioned his willingness to give up anger of things gone by, things mentioned in his paper. Now, what firearms do you want from us? If there's to be peace between our nations, what are you going to do with the firearms? Why must peace be maintained by only yourselves being armed? Who appointed you policemen of the country? The KhoiKhoi were born in this country. I have no power of handing and not handing them to anybody. They are their own people by right. And as for Sandile, he's our chief. Do you now want to separate us from our chiefs? You want us to move to strange lands. Who will tend the graves of our forefathers here then?" I pointed to the rising ground east of Mkhubiso where my father, Ngqika, was buried. "Many of our forefathers are buried here, and that land" – I pointed to the Baviaans River– "that is the garden land that has fed our nation since time immemorial. Today you say it is yours to settle. We didn't quarrel with you when by the hand of Somerset you deprived us of our motherland. We moved away from Gaga, Mankazana, and so forth, where you saw fit to settle your farmers and Mfengus. You confiscated our cattle and distributed them to the Boers that helped you fight us. We were aggrieved in our hearts but we moved on, with our hearts aching in our throats.

Yet now, in turn, you do not grant us the courtesy of remaining where we wish with whom we wish. Every place we move you covet. And for that matter" – and this time I pointed to those I had heard had been part of the delegation that had murdered Hintsa – "why did you assassinate King Hintsa? Was it not enough that you had already stripped him of everything, and encouraged amaMfengu to rise against him? You had to murder him too? Where is this peace to be found if no justice is meted to us? Why has your government not brought Smith to justice, he who was the killer of our king? Instead we've heard that Smith has been promoted to figure the Indians after us.

'You create enmity against the black nation, though they're blood relatives. Do you think bullets are stronger than blood?"

'Warden interrupted me. "The Governor will continue military operations against you if you don't accept these terms, and give your land to the Mfengus."

'I interjected impatiently: "Let it not be said I'm the one who put obstacles in the way of peace. We, too, want to go and plough our fields, the fields you destroyed in inhumane maliciousness. It's already way past planting time. You know our stand. Thus we shall have you to thank when you advise the Governor to better counsel as I'm sure he does not make any major decisions without first consulting his generals. We want to go back to our land and live in peace. It is cold out there in the mountains. We do not want to live like wild animals as your acquisition of our land has forced us to live. But if we are forced, we will have no choice but to remain there until better terms for peace are found between our nations; terms that testify to the fact that no one won this war. These peace terms you've placed before us are treading on our entrails.

'"Should the Governor give our land away to the Mfengus, we'd not give them peace to sit anywhere. They'd have to take their muskets along when they went to plough the land. If we cannot live in peace in this land, no one will. We'll tow and bury it under our own ruins. And you, too, will be forced to plough your fields and dig your graves with your bayonets."

'I halted, seeing all sides were now alarmed, realising that my remonstrance was sounding like a declaration of war. I didn't care. By then in fact I was dancing with rage. The British officers held their breath in contempt and angry expectation.

'Taking up my hat, I called for my horse. I rose in my stirrups and before I brought the whip down, I said: "I'm sure you know our stance by now!" And I galloped away. When the ram's horn was blown my men followed me. The white people must have imagined my audacity was leaning on something. Little did they know it was just a bluff. In any case we had nothing to lose, our rope had been stretched to breaking point. Cox pursued us with vague intentions. Just before we got to the fastness of Ngqika's Kop I saw they made to spend the night at the mission station near the river, so I sent scouts to ask the intentions of their patrol. He sent back his answer, saying peace could only be accomplished if we agreed to the Governor's terms. It remained clear to me that their peaceful terms included our enslavement.

'The skirmishes and retaliations between us got worse. Warden came with the Governor's answer accompanied by that megalomaniac bag of ordure Smith, whose dolichocephalic features, thick vomers, and serpent-green eyes lurking under his bristling brows made me want to puke. With his parvenu love of pomp, Smith was nearly always in his coat of mail, metal greaves and so on. He wore double-soled shiny knee-boots with his grey trousers stuffed into them, and, that day, a buckskin coat trimmed with fur over his red devil's coat. But under all that you could see a man afraid to die like most of us, perhaps more so because of all of his pomposity.

'It was the last time I saw him before he came, a few years later, even more pompous, if that were possible, having recently been appointed Governor.

'On that occasion Suthu, acting as regent of amaNgqika, according to them, accompanied them. She came with her so-called principal chiefs, Vena, Guyana and Hasslas. Seeing her on such close terms with the killers of Hintsa made her abhorrent in our eyes.

'The British came escorted by eight dragoons to show their might. On our side we were guarded by two thousand warriors, most armed with firearms, which was something that put the fear of the devil in them. Not very far in the distance were about four thousand more men. These were our foot warriors, mostly amaGcaleka Kreli had sent at my request, forming a line on a nearby slope, ready to attack on my signal.

'The beetle-browed Smith started with his old bravura and melodrama. He cursed us as "remorseless and relentless savages" he was ready to "teach a lesson until we cried out for mercy". His characteristic splenetic, capricious and tyrannical temperament was at its worst that day. His unpleasant, sneering manner was also, no doubt, to convince himself of his own importance. My expression was stern, remote and distant, which concerned Warden, my friend. I knew by Smith's anger that he was involuntarily bearing tidings that were favourable towards us. He tried to make a rare show of our chiefs but was reined in by his companions. He started his speech by trying to make us aware, in his vainglorious, posturing manner and with the gimmicky peacocking of a narcissist, revealing only how hard he was trying to impress on everyone his own importance and the vulgar greatness of the government he served. He ended up making himself a cynosure by rounding everything to his own glory. How I scorned the pretentiousness of that man.

'Listening to Smith was an ordeal but I did it in forced politeness. I had never been able to breathe easy in the company of that man. His two-facedness was the worst: mingling threats with flattery, twirling and chewing his whiskers; those tomcat glinting eyes of his.

'"Children of great Ngika! You know when your father died, his last words were for you to be the friends of the English and live with them in peace. You forgot his injunctions and made war with the colony, which is still prepared to come to you with every desire to help and remove the difficulties under which you labour. The Governor would have gladly pressed you against his heart had you been obedient to him like his children. Now I'm here. In one hand I hold peace, in another war. I feel that deeds await me of which your kaffir minds cannot comprehend. The Governor and I are good men. We feel for you and your children, and will be your fathers if you stop your insurgence and obey us. If you do not learn to give up your old order for the far better one we bring, you shall be subjugated by the torrential force of Her Majesty's government. We shall go on until you become Her Majesty's humble servants. Artillery shall achieve what persuasion fails. My ear is at the heart of your needs, if only you would let go of your barbaric nature and be civilised. Swear to me then that as of now you shall be sedulous in avoiding mischief towards the colony, and I shall bring the spectre of peace upon your land ..."

'He followed this speech with forced praises, poisoned by his malignity, now and then switching from assiduous truth to the wild ideas his demented mind produced, mingling disdain with generosity, and so on and so forth. He despised the nation whose well-being he sought for his own vanity. Smith was a garrulous and infernal bore. We suffered him for the expedience of peace.

'I knew he was a man with a firm grip on the sword-hilt so, wishing to set a tone for the other chiefs, I answered first.

'"We will be kaffir Englishmen."

'From what we had seen D'Urban do to the Mfengus, this was their design for us.

'Needs must be when the devil drives, I thought to myself. I had to think about the future of our nation. No need to condemn ourselves to famine and a battle we couldn't win when we could take a break, plough our fields and live to fight another day. Although trembling with wrath, the other chiefs were constrained to silence.

'Smith continued to read from his papers, now and then smacking his whip of rawhide against his boot, his left eye nervously twitching. "These papers, which you must agree to," he continued, "say: 'The children of Ngqika cry Mercy! Mercy! Mercy! We wish for peace and to become British subjects. We promise to give up our arms if the Governor wishes it, since as British subjects we belong to him. But since we've suffered so much we implore to keep them so as to defend ourselves from the Governor's enemies, and employ them to kill game for our support." Thus in such manner Smith made even their conceding to our demands sound like their generosity.

'When we agreed to the terms he shook our hand. But in his destructive mischief Smith could not resist constructing new obstacles to our peace. It rankled in his mind that the talks had gone amicably and without incident. Consequently, he pulled a wicked prank that nearly sent us straight into war again. Just as we were departing he ordered his dragoons to fire seven shots in the air. A metallic ring struck into the depths of my spirit when I heard those sounds. Shocked and startled, I was sure the British had led us into yet another trap. Fear mingled with anger within me as I jumped to my feet, ready to give my signal to war. Standing, I found I was shaking with anger like a blancmange. Warden leaned over to assure me that nothing was going on except Smith's sick mind overstepping itself. He, with Stretch, had pre-warned me not to play to Smith's tricks. The Governor, he had told me, wanted peace at almost any price. Afterwards he took Smith aside. When they came back Smith was ready to apologise to us for what he termed a misunderstanding, saying he had just intended to fire the salute of peace.

'"Are you a great chief, Macoma?" His lips twitched in a mirthless smile as he spoke.

'I wanted to floor him with my knobkerrie. I hated the way he pronounced my name, not caring to pronounce the click of "q" but substituting it with a "c". My smouldering resentment standing on its feet, I decided to moderate my answer.

'"I don't know," I replied. "Ask my people. Only the subjects can testify to the greatness of their ruler."

'"Well, they acknowledge you. I guess a rickety colt makes a good riding horse. Now let me tell you where you shall have your land. The Governor knows you've had no country to live in for a long time."

'"Were I to receive my land back the Governor would have my eternal gratitude and loyalty, as I myself am tired of being driven from mountain to mountain. I am made to drink from this river to the next river, hiding in that valley and the other. I'm getting on in years. It does not suit an old person to be without a place he calls home."

'Smith pointed from the source of Zingcuka to the confluence of Qoboqobo down to the hills of Burnshill indicating that this was the land that was to be mine. Nqeno was to have the land from Iqanda Hills along the high road of Debe to Beresford and the boundary north-east of the Kei. The truth is we never really knew what our boundaries were, because another governor or commander would come along the following morning when we had planted our fields and demand we vacate the land for white settlers. Hence I was not even slightly excited when Smith told us this. I knew tomorrow would come with different tidings. When Smith finished talking I offered him my hand, saying, Pish! and Tush! inside me. I still nursed a grudge against him in my heart for the insolent death of Hintsa.

'We both knew that our scrum was not over, hence our real trust with destiny came five years or so after, in Waterkloof. For now it was expediency that made me swallow my pride, and only colonial orders that made him behave amicably towards us. He hated our guts as much as we despised his low-born conniving guile. I've rarely seen a person whose rapacity was equalled only by his sanguinity.'

Nongqawuse and the Death of a Nation

"YOU WOKE TO AN EMPTY HOUSE TOO, did you?" said Martyana across the veranda as she came out, stretching.

"Yes. Do you know where they've gone to?" Phila, shutting his laptop, raised his head with a smile.

"Scuba diving. Arno left me a note. He's very good at it."

"I got a note too – to meet them at the river café. I just didn't have the energy for it. I'm still paying for my sins, and now it's way past lunchtime."

"That makes two of us!" They both laughed.

"I'm thinking, why I not check the *plat du jour* at the communal dining room. Wanna come with me?"

"Sure. It's a better plan than potjiekos leftovers while entertaining a pounding headache."

"Good! Perhaps we go for a walk later for our penance."

"Let me put on shoes."

"Mat told me something about you being a writer also. What are you writing about?" Martyana asked as they strolled together to the communal dining area.

"I am trying to document the history of the Eastern Cape region according to my Light." Phila made a short waving circle with his hands to indicate the area.

"And how's that coming?"

"Come with me to the village and perhaps measure for yourself?"

"*Wunderbar*! Good."

"Truth be told, though, I'm struggling to find my voice."

"What you wanna do?"

"Tell a story about a nation that was invaded into a crisis? Carry adventure and raise it to the level of moral parable? Look to self-discover? I don't know! Perhaps all the above."

276

"*Fabelhaft!*" She smiled at him. "You want a pie or something?"

"In the sky?"

"No," she laughed, pointing to the food display in the dining hall café. "*Lebensmittel!* Food!"

They bought a few items: yoghurt, cheese, ham, fresh bread, nuts and such, having decided to elevate their walk to a picnic at the river mouth.

"I think I live with guilt of apostasy. I was not here during the height of apartheid," Phila said when they hit the sand path away from the café.

"Where were you?"

"Germany."

"Oh ja. I heard last night. Whereabouts?

"And what were you doing there?"

"Frankfurt mostly. I was studying there. Then Berlin as an intern."

"Interesting. So you saw something of the country, you did some travelling while you were there?"

"Yes, by train – throughout Europe I travelled by train – and I saw something of the *Bundesländer.*

"I love Cologne and the Bavarian area generally."

"Train is best way to see the continent," Martyana agreed. "But you didn't visit my country? I'm offended."

"Well, the fog of Auschwitz kept me away. Had enough of that sort of thing. When I was sixteen I watched a documentary about Prague. Ever since then I had wanted to see those canals and that city's marvellous architecture; made me fall in love with the field I went on to study, but I've not been yet. I hope there's still time. Perhaps I could squeeze in Poland somewhere when next I go."

"Tell me when you go. I will be your travel mate.

"I love the Czech Rep."

"Mine is a permanent longing, *ga'agua.* Generally, I'm never satisfied where I am."

"Spirit of *furriner*?"

"I have a restless spirit, yes," Phila acknowledged with a sigh.

Phila felt strangely comfortable around Martyana and he found himself telling her more of his life story, more, in fact, than he had told Matswane in the time they had been together.

When they reached the river the sun had softened to a clear blue sky. Phila took his shoes off. The sand felt wet and sticky on his feet. A slender, agile boy with, of all things, a *keffiyeh* around his neck, who was looking after sheep on the adjacent hill, scrutinised them. Phila wondered how he could have gotten hold of a *keffiyeh*.

The hills fissured where they met the river. The tops of dongas bristled with tall grass. Goats, with clustered tits and bold balls, stood on their hind legs to reach the juicy foliage on thorny bushes. The heat on the river bank was muggy.

"So why Africa?" Phila asked Martyana.

She shrugged. "Opportunity presented itself. I like to see how other people live in the privacy of their own countries."

"Good for you!"

"Thanks!" She paused before continuing. "I can easily see South Africa being for me a second home."

"There are no second homes," said Phila.

"One is born where one is born, and one's spirit never really leaves, wherever else a person might live."

"That's a little, how do you say, harsh?"

Phila said nothing. He admired the fields around them before finding a spot for them to sit, in the shade of a willow tree. Hills framed the northern horizon with something that spoke to the soul.

"Do you know the story of Nonqawuse?" Phila asked when they were sitting comfortably.

Martyana looked at him enquiringly.

"The Xhosa prophetess who led the nation to the void by asking them to sacrifice all their kine to what she called the 'River People', who were coming to liberate them from the encroaching English."

"I think I read about this in one of our travel guides," Martyana said.

Phila gestured to the hills behind them. "Some say Nongqawuse and Nonkosi met some Russian sailors not very far from here. They say they extracted a promise from them to help the Xhosa fight the English, and bring better cattle, since theirs were dying from the rinderpest. Some say that the Russians were the so-called River People. It could be conjecture, and of course it's easy to be wise in retrospect, but there might be truth to it. The name Nomarussia is legend in the Xhosa villages around here. Everyone used to claim it for their first-born girls."

Phila told the story but not in detail. By the time he finished the sun was low in the sky and it was time to go back to their bungalows. They walked slowly, further exploring the subject of Xhosa historical displacement.

A surprise awaited them: two handwritten notes informing them that Matswane and Arno had left for Johannesburg – together. They had taken Matswane's car and left them the rented one.

Phila felt his insides clench tightly. He took beer and the remainder of the whiskey to the veranda. After the initial shock (and two shots), something like resigned abnegation set in. Something Virginia Woolf wrote about the sun yellowing the day with crops of darted fire crowded out the thoughts about Matswane that clogged his mind. He was sure Woolf wrote those words for the view he was looking at.

After about an hour Martyana came out of the bungalow next door, her flip-flops click-clacking on the cement. She smelled shower fresh. She didn't say anything, just took a swig from the whiskey bottle.

It was Phila who broke the silence. "I guess Arno found his destiny."

There was momentary silence before they both burst out laughing, somewhat surprised, somewhat confused, but altogether not too bothered.

"He's always been the one on the hunt," Martyana said. "I noticed that Africa boosted his ego."

"Perhaps he felt noticed here, even envied." Phila smiled a little as he said that.

"I guess." She uttered the words more in sympathy than anger. Phila adored her non-vindictive heart.

After a while, he said, "I feel hurt ..." He did not know how to finish.

"Jilted, you mean. But that is your male ego speaking." There was silence again and Martyana sat up straight and said: "But you and I, we have better things to talk about, yes, than *Scham* and flouted lovers?"

"You're right." Phila was impressed by Martyana's sangfroid. "No use chewing one's cabbage twice."

The nascent cacophony of night insects pronounced the falling dusk.

"How was the Xhosa prophecy supposed to be fulfilled?" Martyana asked, pouring another round for them. "You didn't finish the story."

"According to Nongqawuse, at the appointed day two suns would rise and appear in the sky. On that day the spirits of the ancestors would rise and fight for the Xhosas against the whites. But before all that could happen, the Xhosas had to show faith by slaughtering all their cattle, and burning all their crops. Not a blade of corn was to be left in the fields; not an ox lowing in the kraal. That so many people believed Nongqawuse, methinks, shows the extent of desperation in Xhosaland. You see, their cattle were already dying from a strange disease called the rinderpest, which made them fall, struggling for breath while frothing flakes of soapy foam from their mouths and nostrils. In no time, no matter how strong your cow was, it died. So Nongqawuse was preaching on fertile ground when she suggested this was the doing of the River People. 'They want us

279

to kill all our present livestock so they may replenish us with strong fatted kine. They say we should not plough nor sow our fields for a season until the prophecy is fulfilled.'

"As they say, a dog never bothers an unready bitch. The killing of affected animals made sense to stymie the disease. Most people ordered their tenders to hide unaffected stock on grazing mountain fields. But the word came that even those cattle were already affected and would soon be dying like flies. The convenience of Delphi is that it is never wrong. The prophecy, according to believers, didn't come true because of those who refused to meet the condition of killing their animals. Nongqawuse basically started a millennial movement that almost killed the nation."

Martyana extended her hand across the table to touch Phila's. He responded by closing his fingers over hers.

"Do you know anything about analeptic memory?" Phila asked in a sudden change of topic.

"Not really …?" Martyana replied.

Phila remained silent for a while, thinking about the best way to put what he wanted to say without scaring her off. Another reason he couldn't think properly was because he felt cataleptic. When he spoke again it was in a different, grittier voice.

'On the appointed day I woke with the red dawn to walk to the mountains. The autumnal azure on the ridge blended dreamingly with the rising sunlight. We expected glorious things to come as the day launched itself with virginal modesty. But there was nothing strange about it. I stood on the hill to watch the sun's first rays, hoping its rosy silence would simplify my confusion. I had brought some provisions, victuals and the white man's fiery water. My KhoiKhoi wife was with me, a sot, but well-mannered, and with a beauty that could steal the heart of a stone. As we sat on the hill, drinking the tears of Victoria, she started with her drunken giggles. Alcohol gave her appetites. My heart thumped. I felt morbid dread at the absence of herds straying in the fields, no laden grain. It dawned on me for the first time that something catastrophic was about to happen to our nation. There was a dearth of everything – orchards had no figs, no peaches, no pomegranates, no quinces. No prickly-pears hedging them. The sight gave me the creeps.

'Of course, only one sun rose. That was the harbinger of the first trouble. The rocks, married to the newly minted sun, had a hypnotic tinge. I took a *sopie* brandy before tackling the second hill. The climb made my brow perspire and my intestines clench. Three steep hills made for a complete mountain. The sun looked singularly bright from the mountaintop. It travelled its steady course, not pausing or stopping at high noon as expected. After it reached its apex it went down on its usual course with no fiery tricks or gambol as had been predicted. It showed no signs of strangeness. I looked at my wife. She showed no signs of concern in her tipsy state. My dog, obediently sitting at my feet, anticipated with keen eyes signs of pending activity in vain. I envied his ignorance. He was wiser for it. His whiskered face came alive now and then when I made for stretching of my legs, only to drop his pricked vulpine ears when he realised I was not aiming to do much beyond that.

'"Horrors will accompany the course of the sun today," I said to my wife. She gave a lascivious laugh, rotating her head in owlish circles. On hearing my voice the dog's wandering attention steadied into what seemed like intelligent consideration. He seemed to wrestle for a minute with my meaning, flapping his ears, then relaxing after satisfying himself it was beyond his comprehension. He must have thought I was promising the excitement of a hunt when we climbed the hills. His disappointment was palpable, but it meant little compared to mine. I was shaking.

'My wife took a deep sip from the brandy and sat at my feet, tucking her kaross away between her knees. A harsh frown puckered her forehead as she rearranged her hair. I was slightly annoyed that at a time like that she was concerned with the crinkly puff of her matted hair. I took it to be a sign of indefatigable vanity. I struggled in my mind to find a proper way to spend the senseless grind until the end of the day. The best thing for that time was to make love, or rather, unburden ourselves. Mental pressure went to my loins. With the goose-grass scrub as our bed, spurges prickling us and grating against her back and my knees, we tried flooding the shame of the day with sweaty lovemaking and the wind dancing on my back. We moved together, rising and falling in conserved tenderness until we had our fill. Her laughter tailed off into gasping convulsions. There was chattering of teeth; the squeezing out of breath; the quivering of lips to signify the coming intensity. It gave a sneeze relief. Unfortunately, the spilling of seed didn't staunch the pain in the heart.

'Lovemaking and liquor were things that always managed to take my mind off brooding, but not that day. I sat on a boulder feeling hollow and defeated with my hands on my head. A female smell in my hands compounded the haze of melancholy. A developing ulcer in my stomach stirred a sense of despair. There was a pain of loss in my breathing. No one has enough strength to keep the finger pressed on the wound when one's life is slowly ebbing.

'A hawk circled in the sky; marmots whistled in the hollows. Fatigue invaded the body. Horror hung in the air, threateningly in deathly sultriness. When I am under pressure I have a need for solitariness. I moved away from my wife, putting about three trees' distance between us. It felt as if everything was failing me that day. If a man sees truth in the morning, he may die in the evening without regret. Suddenly it felt like a good day to die. I spent the next hours with feelings of mystification and edifying insights, my mind saturated like a steaming jungle of thoughts. As the sun began to dip behind the mountains, and shades of evening widened, I called to my wife. "Come collect our stuff. Let's be gone to our people. The time of reckoning has come."

'As we descended the mountain we saw hideous and leaden smoke coming out of every hearth in our villages. The skies had become ashy with clouds. I wanted to hear a sheaf of village news but none was forthcoming. People were all hiding in their houses. Others had fled the coming wrath of hunger to other parts of the land. By the time we entered our enclosure people were already gathered outside demanding an explanation for the non-visit from the River People and the sun's failure to stop at noon. I suppose, as their chief, I owed them an explanation, but I was too weary. I surveyed them for a moment before speaking in a soft voice, delaying and measuring my words. "Neither rest nor peace do I get from you people." I then proceeded to my sleeping quarters where I spent the next two moons looking at the thatch from the inside, hardly eating anything.

'After two moons I made bold to visit our villages, to assess for myself the actual damage done by the deliberate famine. Death hung in sorrow and woeful atmosphere. The air was saturated with the reek of putrefying flesh. Old men sat around their houses, some even eating their blankets; wilting and crumbling with loss of spirit. When you went too close they grabbed you by the tail of your blanket, enquiring if Nxele or the River People, or the ancestors had come yet. Nothing you told them altered their minds still conjured by the illusions of Nongqawuse. It is amazing how stubborn a convinced mind can be.

'Young men paced back and forth between huts and kraals, hanging their heads. The wailing of children replaced birdsong. The whole scene raked me over the coals. I was emotionally stymied. I don't know which was worse, the heavily brocaded wails, the shrieking and tumulus panic of women, or the granite-like deadening silence of middle-aged men.

'When it became clear Nongqawuse had devastated the nation into famine, loss of hope followed. Things got worse. I saw an old lady repose in silence while dogs devoured her rotten leg. I saw a young woman cook, nonchalantly and quietly, a dead foetus from her womb. One man walked, trance-like, over a cliff, falling onto jagged rocks. Nobody even winced; instead boys and dogs raced each other to claim the carcass down below for food. Horses and donkeys competed for the thatch grass on the roofs of the houses. Before long, their mouths bloody, foaming, from trying to eat cactus where there was nothing else to eat, they had all been slaughtered and consumed. Rodents as large as hares screamed for the oozing ankles of the living, and were in turn hunted for food by young boys.

'Within a few months things fell on disaster. Hardship protracted by hunger reduced us to extreme passive distress. It was common to see people gaunt and wild-eyed from want of food. Flies drank their fill from the blood-flecked saliva running from the corners of starving people's mouths. Terrible problems of indigestion became common, as a result of people eating tree bark as a substitute for bread; it also induced hallucinations born of delirium tremens. When food supplements such as nettles, dog-meat, and rodent flesh were no longer obtainable people moved about like ghosts, wasting away. It was not rare to see people fighting with spent strength over white ant nests. Some dropped by the wayside where they lay, exhausted, feeble hands trying to clasp and tear up blades of grass. Some cooked their goatskin blankets, strops, and so forth, but hunger would not be averted. We had no seed to plant anything. Unburied skeletons lay scattered all over village roads.

'Many times I had watched people reveal the courageous side of their nature during times of pressure, like when we were at war. During famine it is not so. Hungry people behave like animals – hyenas and crows.

'Only the devil could have been satisfied with the way events turned out that season.

'It was reported that Governor Grey was pleased with the way things had turned out, because it meant more human labour for white farmers.'

Phila stopped talking. While he saw that he had shocked Martyana into silence – perhaps from his words as much as his voice, he couldn't tell – she looked perplexed.

"What the fuck was that?" she asked.

"Me acting out from analeptic memory."

"You're a good actor. How does it work?"

"It comes from longing," Phila said simply. "It enables one to cross borders of consciousness."

"Interesting ..." Martyana frowned, concentrating on his face.

"I'm not sure what to call it – flood of ancestral memory or analeptic memory – but I've decided to embrace rather than fight it."

"That is a tragic, tragic story."

"Before famine took its dreadful toll," Phila went on in his normal voice, "word circulated from Nongqawuse that non-believers had delayed the day for the coming of the River People because of partial or no fulfilment of requirements. It said the non-believers were the stumbling block to Nongqawuse's prophecies. People formed what was termed 'patriotic parties' to persecute non-believers. These parties murdered and confiscated the cattle of non-believers wherever it was possible. Chief Maqoma wanted to drive people to desperation and, subsequently, war with the colonial government. Most of the non-believers exacerbated their lot by seeking protection from white missionaries. They flocked to colonial levees and missionary establishments. To save them from the wrath of the believers, who chose to put the blame for the failure of the prophecy on them, the colonial government took them under their protection. The British government saw the likes of Maqoma and the other chiefs who supported Nongqawuse's prophecies as a menace to peace. They wanted to make an example of them.

"Maqoma was identified as one of the ringleaders of the believers in the absence of the likes of Mhlakaza, who was already incarcerated. Even Nongqawuse and her chief collaborators were put under house arrest. Maqoma was arrested for specious allegations of killing one of the non-believers through the hands of their war party.

"Governor Grey put the last nail on the destruction of the Xhosa nation by refusing them any food donations. Instead he instructed them to go and work on white farms as hired workers, virtually slaves, on the land they had owned not very long before, tending for white people and Mfengus. The Mfengu now were the new black master race; the Xhosas were the new slaves. Proud Xhosas crossed rivers to chase ostriches for diamond stones; some found work on the diamond mines in Kimberley and, later, in the gold mines on the Witwatersrand.

"After a mock legal trial – Maqoma was first tried in King William's Town by what he called 'striplings who grew before me only yesterday, donning long black gowns and powdered periwigs, calling themselves magistrates' – the accused were sent to the higher courts in Cape Town. After the hypocritical formalities, Maqoma and other chiefs were stripped of their royal clothes and made to stand before courts like common criminals and highwaymen. Maqoma was of the opinion they desired to have him done legally to death. Specious witnesses supported the court's evidence and were themselves supported by the court's bribes.

"Thus Maqoma and other Xhosa chiefs were taken to be tried in Cape Town before being sentenced to the leper colony – Robben Island today."

❀

Martyana and Phila enjoyed a final coffee together at the airport in East London a couple of days later. Martyana was flying to Johannesburg, where she would catch a connecting flight to Munich.

Coffee Bay had been their last resort stop before she and Arno were due to head back to Germany.

"Do you think we will ever see each other again?" Martyana asked.

"I don't see why not. After all, getting dumped at the same time creates a deep bond between two people." They laughed softly. "If I feel, when you're gone, I cannot live my life without you, I'll come seek you. But I need to sort my life out first. It'd be unfair to invite someone into it at the moment; it's too messy."

"And if I come visit South Africa again, I should look you up in Cape Town?" she asked, more solemnly than she might have intended. "What will you do there?"

"Truth be told, I don't know. Sit down somewhere long enough to collect my thoughts and make something out of all of that has happened in my life since coming back to the country. Perhaps get a job in the municipality or an architectural firm or something; find my place in the world? Something like that. The rest I shall discover as I go."

"I hear Cape Town is a beautiful city."

"I suppose – but I am looking more for peace than beauty at present."

"If I may, to satisfy my curiosity, or mend my pride ... These past two days ... why didn't we have sex?"

Phila smiled. He had been asking himself the same question, without getting a satisfactory answer. "I can only speak for myself. I wanted to make love to you, but I also wanted it to be more than just a jilted thing."

"Or a holiday to remember in Africa thing, in my case," she said.

"Besides," Phila added, "I am a little tired of grabbing onto things without really knowing myself. It has gotten stale for me. I need to show better respect to others by presenting a known, more composite self to them. Otherwise I am just gonna keep making the same mistakes and never mature. Let's deal with what is fractured inside first. So if I end up in a monastery you shall constantly be in my prayers." They both laughed.

"For that I would begrudge God!" said Martyana.

They were calling her flight. She stood up to kiss Phila before going to join the boarding queue. After they had stamped her passport she came back to give him a long hug and a last kiss. It was not vigorous but enough to raise her colour and was deeply felt by both.

"I hope to be buying your book at a bookshop near me soon," Martyana said.

"I hope so too."

Phila walked out of the terminal to the parking lot. Somehow he felt he was taking a big stride towards his future. He was anxious to see what was on the other side.

It is said, in Africa, that at dusk the purity and beauty of God's creation makes the devil so mad with envy that he weeps blood. "What the devil does not realise," Phila's grandma would say, "is that even his anger and envy add lustre to the beauty of God's creations. How do you fight that, the one who uses even your wickedness to advance the cause of beauty and goodness?"

As he drove away from the airport Phila realised that he was weeping. Destiny disguises itself with trifling tidbits, he thought; no wonder it is so easy for most of us to miss it. Negotiating the traffic, he was already thinking how best to commit things Maqoma had told him to writing, to turn his notes and his thoughts into a structured whole. And thinking about Maqoma brought with it thoughts about Mandela, Sobukwe and all the others who had spent lonely hours surrounded by water on islands of human misery, and those who had perished on those islands of exile and sorrow – from Gyara off the Attica in the Aegean, to the *katorga* in the frozen Siberian gulags. He thought about the last days of Napoleon and John, the beloved apostle, almost blind in Patmos where he came back with a brilliant script of mystical rendering of the life of Jesus, the Christ. What could be more profound than the realisation that in the beginning was love, indomitable and indefatigable love?

Over the car radio Bob Dylan moaned: *I hear the ancient footsteps like the motion of the sea ...*

2017

Decluttering

Phila looked at his watch and realised he had been standing at the window of his Hout Bay home for well over an hour, looking out as evening swept down the mountain. He went to the bathroom, picked up his razor to shave, and looked steadily at the face in the mirror with dust of age growing it into his father's. It almost pleased him that its furrowing forehead etched the ineffable melancholic dignity he loved about his father's face. "Stop being a spectator to your life," he told the face in the mirror. "And stop putting so much emphasis on the life of your mind. Live."

While planning his nineteen-second shower – because Cape Town was under the severest drought strain that threatened the city with what was being called Day Zero (taps running dry to make it the first modern city to run out of water) – he went to his computer to answer Martyana's email. He had chosen to postpone his reply, wanting to think properly about her proposal on his way home from the office. He decided to agree to the suggestion of their visit to Cape Town. She had told Phila that her nine-year-old son was looking forward "to being in Africa".

Martyana and Phila had kept up a sporadic correspondence since they'd last seen each other at the East London airport over a decade ago. This was the first time she had dropped strong hints of wanting to take their relationship to the next level. This was what had thrown Phila into a little confusion. He had been waiting for it for so long, now that it was happening it made him dizzy with excitement.

Martyana had become a well known fine artist, "prestigious" was how the newspapers Phila read put it, and had had several major solo exhibitions in different central European cities. Most of the pieces Phila told her he liked, when she gave him a sneak preview, she sent to him, so he'd learnt to moderate his compliments to avoid acting as though he was dropping hints. His favourite was a black township youth in a melancholic pose. Phila had told her it reminded him of his favourite Pemba painting. Though almost a reproduction of Pemba's in posture and on the outlines, Martyana had introduced conflict on the boy's face. She gave the face grave lines of expression, almost grim, with a scornful lift of one eyebrow, while suffusing the straight one with marks of tenderness. The major communication was in the calm of the eyes, like a fortress against the storm. The slight tilt of the head gave the impression of a contemplative air from a buttressed conscience. The face was Phila's. She titled the portrait IMPREGNABLE WILL.

Hi there!
Kafka was of the opinion that written kisses don't arrive at their destinations because they get drunk up by ghosts along the way.
What did he know, couch traveller that he was?
I will be honoured to host the two of you.
I think we might be happy still.
Perhaps we can find love to last both our lifetimes? One thing I ask is that we aim to connect by the language of the soul. Everything else we shall learn as we go.
Keep well,
Phila

Phila never re-read his emails anymore before sending them. When he did they always sounded like gibberish and he ending up deleting them altogether. He hit the Send button before he changed his mind and waited as the bar gyrated before the yellow Sent message came.

He was sending it to his future life, his heart was telling him.

Feeling fresh after his shower, he went back and started typing.

The first time I met you I recognised you from the image of you formed in my spirit.

Phila's mind was still on Martyana. He was tempted to send a follow-up email, because he felt he hadn't properly communicated his sense of excitement. Instead he decided to tidy up things with the Maqoma business.

CHAPTER 1
FIRE NEXT TIME
I, Maqoma, son of Ngqika, prince of amaRharhabe and the tribal shoot of amaXhosa – I am incarcerated on this island of lepers by the British, for resisting their encroachment on our land. I am too weary and old to

be angry; too old to nurse grievances, even against white people, despite the fact that they were the architects of my doom, and of my nation's catastrophes. I have rheumatism, which makes it difficult for me to gad about this accursed island. All my pleasures in this life have faded. I eagerly await Qamata to send the wagon that will join me with my ancestors.

When my sister was learning how to read and write at missionary schools I taunted her because I saw it as a waste of time, a prolegomena to action that never goes anywhere. Luckily she didn't pay attention to me, and later she taught me. Now, after my life has been stripped of everything dear to me, it is the pen I'm picking from its ashes.

When the overriding flatness of these cursed waters invokes tragedy in my spirit I like to watch the behaviour of birds from early morning until evening. The coast disappears into a grey mist of sea and a stretch of fierce mountains that dominate the horizon. These flats are wind scrubbed. When the winds blow, the sliding drizzle makes it difficult to tell where the path ends and the void begins. All you hear is crashing bellows and the indecisive honks of birds. The air smells of rain; it has an odour of mustiness from guano. The sea boils when it rains here.

Sometimes I wake in the middle of the night with a taste of bile in my mouth, not sure whether I'm dreaming or awake. I see leaping flames in the direction of the white man's city. I sit morose, suspecting the flames are soon going to leap in our direction. Those distant fires have preternatural strength, and become as tall as mountains sometimes. Strange, strange things happen in this accursed place. If I don't die soon I shall die of longing to die.

I look at the chasm of my life and try to tell what I see and remember without glossing over the ugly parts. Anyone who listens to my words will see how the cruel rowels were dug into my flanks.

I've lived long and hard enough to have my own view of things. I've no respect for men who use religion to avoid the truth of their failings; who take refuge in pious thoughts and feelings to avoid the real labours of love; who employ false images of holiness to avoid encounters with Dal'ubomi. I know it to be *a fearful thing to fall into the hands of the living God*. I've been forsaken, completely cut off from those I love – and those I despise – in order to meditate on my life. I don't know which group to thank; the one that brought me evil, or the one that brought me love. Often people come promising one thing, only to leave you with the other. The saddest thing is to be implicated in another man's disorders and confusion. I thank them all, whatever their motives. This place has become like a desert where I can't hide from the truth. I've been made to encounter my shadowy side; contradictions of my own age with the light of truth. If anything, this place has brought me to the condition of an inner peace that is open to the experience of truth, and the incomprehensible principle of life we adopt different names to refer to. As a result, I now understand the saying that the places of our haplessness are also where we become open to possibilities of our greater selves.

Every ship I see on the shore uproots my hope, only to dash it when no news comes for me. The full force of my misery has overtaken me.

When I think about those with whom I travelled this bitter earth of hard stones, tears fall from my eyes. There were also from the white race the likes of Khula. The founder of the white Afrikaner tribe in our land. *Awu!* The egret that came out of the sea when no one expected. The wild animal of the blue ocean. Sleep well, my friend, your memory vindicates your race in my eyes. Blind fortune, with your insatiable purse: *Mhlaba uya fihla!*

Give ear, my people. The sun is descending on the limb of Phalo. The smoke is rising dimly in your desolate vales. Pick up your kerries and bucklers and charge! The gaunt hyenas are devouring your lambs with their ravenous maws. People were those of Nxele's stature who preferred the belly of the hundred sea beasts than to serf for white people.

Hark!

Take your heads away from your knees. Shriek and squall, you women of our land, your sons are skulking like dogs. The lengthening shadows are drearily falling over the land of Phalo:

For England hath spoken in her tyrannous mood,
And the edict is written in African blood!

When our history arrives at the present of our progeny, the horn of Africa shall rise again. Wake me then to watch the star of Phalo take its place around the skies of things human …

Phila walked out to the balcony to soak up the sensual whore Hout Bay became during summer evenings: the élan dusk from the receding sun; the dazzling way the Sentinel, the tilting mountain, arrests, midway, its totter into the sea; the rosy dust of Chapman's Peak Drive, all staring at the mirror surface of the bay. It made him feel wanted, part of something greater. He needed to be outdoors.

He put on his takkies and went on the gad. The artificial strobe of the harbour lights made everything look staged. A whiff of salt air souped the fish stench the closer he got to the fish processing factory. By the time he got to the Fish-On-The-Rocks shop at the harbour his lungs were fluffed like the devil's pillows. Shadows had stretched to the sea. The gaggle of gulls tormented the scavenging bergies at the dustbins of the rocky beach.

Phila placed his order of fish and chips before proceeding to sit at an outside table, carefully nodding to a young coloured lady – that peculiar pinpoint between black and white that apartheid insisted existed to drive division between black South Africans. He thought to encourage camaraderie with the gesture, but was ignored with unspoken emphasis. She hunched her shoulders before snorting her nose. Phila, feeling embarrassed, cleared his throat to repress emotions before turning his eyes away to fake indifference. The background of billowing waves and the brumous pewter light took care of the rest.

Grasping our lives inseparably separate!

He caught sight of his face in the window. He rubbed the shine off it, turning to the distance to avoid the need of agreeing with the young lady's disinterest. She must have been twenty-four or something. Phila was on the older side of forty. His sister had sent him flowers the previous day, and a virtual birthday message, the stuff you get from the internet about useless facts. This one said his birth month had five Fridays, five Saturdays and five Sundays that year, something that apparently only occurs once in eight hundred and twenty years. The Chinese called it the year of a 'money bag', something to do with feng shui. Phila liked feng shui, because it was about the arrangement of things in space. But his sister spoilt the whole thing by instructing him to pass the birthday message on to eight more people if he wanted the luck, and to avoid misfortune. Of course he didn't pass the bloody message on.

His number had to be called three times before he realised it was his, and that his order was ready. The eyes of the lady cashier were trained on him with unspoken irritation as he collected his order.

"Here we go, sir, fried yellowtail with chips, no salt or vinegar." The waitress was professional in hiding her irritation.

"Thank you," Phila reciprocated, using his customary politeness as both armour and weapon.

Outside the gulls were still screaming – *I miss you like rain,* or such things poets tell about. Phila turned his back to the clapping sea as he sat down to eat. He now wished he had ordered grilled fish with salad, to make himself more interesting and sophisticated. It would have taken longer too, giving him time for his musings. Everyone interesting is supposed to be a vegan these days, he thought to himself. Apparently it's a sign one has a conscience. He had discovered this on a date one of his colleagues had set up for him with a Cameroonian palaeoanthropologist. She had spent the entire evening dissing the stupidity and ignorance of black South Africans, correcting his pronunciation of French, English and even Xhosa words. She had talked incessantly and impatiently. And had a habit of uttering a long disinterested "Indeeeed!" to show disinterest whenever Phila said anything beyond two sentences.

"Even hominids knew it was barbaric to eat flesh," she'd said, crinkling her brow, making it clear with a termagant tone what she thought of Phila's pork ribs order.

"Indeeeed!" answered Phila in a failed attempt at ironic parody. She took it as an invitation to explain.

"We discovered that at least two of their species ate only bark, palm, fruit, shrubs and herbs."

"How do you discover what hominids ate if they are extinct?" Phila interjected sarcastically.

"From the stuff we scraped from their teeth, silly. You can tell a lot by examining the plaque deposited on one's teeth." She asked if she could examine Phila's plaque deposits sometime. "That would tell me a lot about your diet, and how you can change it to improve your health." Phila lost his appetite after that. He also discovered that his only interest in her now was the fact that she was born in Yaoundé where his people were supposedly to have originated in the eighth century. Somehow the association was not worth the remote ancestral connections. When she again went on her diatribe about how black South Africans had a violent contempt for other Africans – making it clear that she was only interested in white men, "British preferably" – Phila went Dutch on her with a rude departure. He wondered why she had agreed to the date. Perhaps as a favour to a friend; or, worse, not to pass up the opportunity to spite a black South African, seeing that she regarded them all as lazy, ignorant, gluttonous, unclean, and barbarously cruel and xenophobic. This had amused Phila, because these were some of the words and phrases, almost word for word, the white settlers had used to describe the Xhosas when they called them kaffirs more than a century ago.

No one imagined us.

The jog up Chapman's Peak was arduous, as usual, and made impossible by the rudeness of lycra-clad cyclists who acted as if they owned the road. After finishing the Old Fireman House hill Phila decided to sit on the public bench, overlooking the plunging coastline, the hulking rocky cliffs and the bay. The departing day, with crimson light, left behind a trembling brown air. The ocean had three colour rings, turquoise towards the shore with dirty milk scrim on the edge, blue and then deeper blue into the deep.

After a while, seated on the bench he felt the symptoms by then he understood very well, was even egging them on because it had been a very long time – a decade or so – since he had heard Maqoma's voice and he had missed him.

'*The glory of the one who moves all things, penetrates the universe, and glows in one region more, in another less...*'

'*Camagu!*' Phila interjected with the Xhosa phrase of respectful granting permission in humility, what the Christians would call Mary's fiat.

'My, my! How have we grown?' Maqoma exclaimed in satisfaction as he sat next to Phila on the bench, handing him some of the apricots he was eating. 'I thought you'd love these. They're ripe as the sun.' They kept quiet while Phila processed if their mutual love for apricots was coincidental or preordained. 'I came to see if you remember it is our meeting anniversary from lands far away from here.'

'Indeed I do, although I would be lying to claim credit for the similar setting I've just now noticed.' Phila was unable to hide his excitement in seeing Maqoma.

'That was my doing...'

'A shoe of my own stitching...'

They spoke in unison, which prompted their laughter. After a while Phila spoke.

'In fact, even the ring of mountains reminds me of your area also, except here, unlike Nkonkobe, the mountains gird the sea instead of the valleys like the Winterberg do to your Kat River valleys. And the sighs of the sea, singing on its chains, if the Welsh poet is to be believed, is something my soul will never tire of in a hundred lifetimes.'

'Was it not you who once told me that there's nothing like the love of a woman to make a poet out of all of us?' teased Maqoma.

'I'm not sure I understand you?' Phila played hard fuss.

'Is not your Polish woman coming next moon?'

'I thought you said you were gonna quit spying on me?'

'I did. I came along it when reading something I thought was about me.' They both kept silence, which Maqoma broke after a minute. 'Were you not supposed to write a book or something?'

'Well, life got to me. But I'm on it.'

'I knew you would once you knew she was coming.'

'Wait a minute? Are you responsible for that?'

'Not really. I told you we can't make you do anything you don't want to do anyway. But I've met your beautiful daughters who are yearning to be born.'

Both men fell silent. Then, before Phila could formulate in words what he wanted to say, Maqoma changed the topic. 'I see you've managed to turn your exile here into a pilgrimage?' he said with a warm smile.

'I learnt from the best. You're not the only who has been hanging out with ancient bards, druids and healers.' Silence hung between them again.

Then, 'Is your journey complete?' Phila asked. 'Have you reunited with your loved –'

'The journey I am on does not end, not even with eschaton. For it is learning to see through the eye of divine reality. Not even eternity is enough for that lesson. But please, continue reading my friend Dante. From him you'll gain a spark of things to come in your journey towards Paradiso. It'll be good practice for you to see things through the divine reality also. Whatever I say at this stage will be inadequate to gain you further understanding; the next task is now yours, it must come from within you. But I understand what you're trying to ask.' Maqoma trained his eye on the ocean before continuing. 'You can almost see the island from here, the home of my mortal remains.'

'I thought your remains were transferred to Ntab' kaNdoda?'

'You thought that? I wanted you to take me to the land once familiar to me. My remains are still here, surrounded by the pounding ocean. Not that it matters, but they dug up the wrong bones. Perhaps had I had you then I could have asked you to tell them that – maybe they would have believed you.'

'What?' asked Phila. 'What are you telling me? Is that why you didn't join me on what all these years I have believed to be your gravesite?'

Maqoma gave Phila a mischievous look, but said nothing.

'They've even built a monument to you there recently!'

'Nothing wrong with that. After all, it is part of the land I grew up on.'

'Well, anyway, I didn't even like the monument ...' Phila said, prompting another burst of laughter from both of them. 'And it has serious structural problems. In all likelihood it won't be long before it collapses.'

'Perhaps we can hasten its destruction?' said Maqoma with another mischievous smile.

After a while, with the return of solemnity Phila outed what they both knew was the reason for the visit.

'I have to go to Robben Island, don't I?' he said.

'Is that why you came back?'

'Not entirely – but partly.'

'A dead man would be here had you not showed up on the bus that day in Port Elizabeth, the day I got the news of my father's death,' Phila said. 'Is something else bad about to happen to me?'

'I don't believe so, but we had to take caution. I don't know if you're familiar with the Kabbalistic concept of Gilgul?'

'As in reincarnation?'

'It is not reincarnation per se. You're thinking of Bardo, which is Buddhist. Sometimes a soul, fresh from purgatorial purification, discovers a neglected duty. If this is crucial to the historical course of those still on earth the soul is allowed passage back to earth. They can then attach themselves to the living soul that would best serve their purpose of correcting the neglect, especially if this is also a soul feeling unequal to the task of their own journey. The process must be mutually beneficial. The Kabbalah religion calls this process "making a Tikkun", a ratification.' Maqoma stopped to assess Phila's reaction.

'I think your spirit had already explained this to mine. I am glad anyway to have a vocabulary for it.'

'Of course, I am giving you a simplified version. One day, when we both sit with our ancestors we shall talk some more. For now, I need also to show you my actual grave on the island.'

'I think I am gonna be uncontrollably angry if I go there. It has, in my mind, become a symbol of everything wrong with the political history of this country.'

'I'll be there with you. In fact, I'll organise a cloud of witnesses for you as my parting gift, a party of martyrs whose blood irrigated your freedom. Then you shall see that you're not on your own. Perhaps then you'll understand why we need to linger a while in these lands. There's more work to be done here, more lost souls wandering about seeking their rest, who died abhorrent slave deaths toiling these vineyards, felling trees from these woods and such things your generation has now forgotten. Keep listening to the land. The landscapes retain the memory of the departed. Beside your blood it is what you have in common with ages that came before you. The landscapes retain the ghost of the disposed and silently sing out their grief. This is why in the sigh of the sea you taste the breath of ghosts. And the mountains are like unmarked graves. Do not be afraid to take plunge on the depth of the abyss, because sooner or later you shall emerge on the side where you meet anew the stranger that is yourself.'

After a momentary silence Phila looked around but Maqoma had disappeared again. He felt rather sad the visit was so short after so many years. He stood up to continue his jog. He hated the jog downhill more because of its demands on his knees. As he jogged his mind turned back to his university years. Lecturers at the school of architecture had told them to expect a future filled with creativity since they were training to be God's assistants in wasting space, "sculpturing space to create a sense of surprise", they termed it. Things never really turned out that glossy for Phila. He'd been living in Cape Town for over a decade and for the most part he'd found himself designing government schools and clinics, or dull community halls in townships, whose facades needed to merge with their matchbox houses; now and again he designed a township church, with an extremely low budget. Nearly always, though, the emphasis had been on utility over aesthetics. If things got interesting it would be to redesign old industrial towship buildings into shopping centres. On these, the emphasis was on durability, since the developers took for granted that they would be vandalised. Or making them functional to the client's needs for conference, workshop and warehouse or parking garage facilities.

On top of this, his job made him a suspect. Architecture and property development were still a white man's domain in his country. A black man was not supposed to be good at them unless he was cheating at something. It irritated them that they could not really find what Phila cheated on but it was assumed to be hidden somewhere. Or that he was an affirmative action product.

When he'd first come to Cape Town he had worked for the city municipality before joining a renowned architectural firm whose rich clients were drawn from Camps Bay, Clifton or Constantia. His boss, a good Scottish bloke in his early fifties, required "black cultural background" to enhance what he called the "clownish Tuscany briefs" his rich clients demanded. Working for rich private clients was exactly what Phila had vowed never to do; his interest had never been in real estate. Rather his calling was in environmentally friendly and innovative social housing and other public spaces.

He was fascinated by technology and interested in communication through architecture. He thought he had learnt some experimental ideas and clever tweaks suited for his country's environment. Early on in his studies, he had found himself drawn to architects like Frank Gehry (his thesis had been about Gehry's work), who seemed to have found a way of introducing motion into architecture. The first time he saw the Guggenheim Museum of Art in Bilbao it blew his mind. It was then he realised buildings could convey emotion and movement. Since then his architectural design studies came from the natural world, things like beehives and termite nests, which Phila thought provided effective and perfect designs for stadiums, malls and public social housing. He belonged to the modern architectural movement that wanted to move away from conventional city council buildings into something that required vision and creativity, making ideas exist through solid materials. His frustrations and disappointment with his city job was his inability to break through the stubborn bureaucracy of mayoral committees, who seemed to regard him only as a pawn to check the black tokenism box. When he realised that even where possibilities did exist to create great public spaces, like parks, the politicians were always in the pockets of private billionaires, whose new money-making fad was to underwrite and sponsor public spaces for profit, he gave up.

When Phila started at the architectural firm the junior staff were not comfortable being assigned to him. They automatically assumed he was an affirmative action appointment, which meant they would have to do all the work. He quickly picked up nuances in their actions, voices, the way they tried not to be pinned down with him when giving briefs, their incessant nodding to make sure he understood. Even clients, including decent ones, almost without fail, became crestfallen when they were assigned him as their chief architect. Sometimes the prejudice became open and the firm would have to assign another person if they wanted to keep the client. And this was not only limited to white people – black people as well had no confidence in his skills. They assumed he was a charlatan, or a front. Signs of the lack of confidence in him from whites ranged from speaking too loud during briefs, asking the same questions over and over again, making sure he understood the brief, or coming to his office on a daily basis to check on progress. Blacks would wink a secret understanding that communicated that they understood he was just a window doll of white business and so was going with the flow. All preferred even the junior staff, so long as they were white.

"I'm sure he gets enough BEE briefs," one client said. "I want someone who is going to give me optimal value for my money." BEE, the government programme of black economic empowerment, was constantly used to whip black professionals in that sense, suggesting all contracts they got were through corruption or political connections to the ruling party. Initially his boss, who was now his partner, felt so embarrassed he wanted to reject the project briefs where such incidents occurred.

"Were I to concern myself with or be upset with the personal beliefs of every moron we work for we would never get any job," was how Phila played down the effects of those awkward moments to his partner. Phila had decided a long time ago to be philosophical about such things. He interpreted the need to be acknowledged for the work he did as just another trick of vanity. The rub was that he ended up doing the work anyway since the briefs to the junior partners always ended up on his desk one way or the other. He had more experience, a better work ethic. This, of course, didn't stop him sometimes resenting his colleagues for being white. He became angry watching them leave in their Maseratis, as early as 4:30pm, to yet another new expensive nightclub, while he remained behind to burn the midnight oil, doing the work they'd get all the credit for from the clients. He resented their smug attitude, disguised as flattery, when they dropped briefings on his desk. "Boss! Could you take a look at this for me?" Yet when he asked them to remain behind, to burn the midnight oil alongside him, they ended up being in his way, with their constant talking about their nightlife achievements. It distracted Phila, who required silence to think. Alone at the office, especially in the early evenings, was when he was in his element.

When he got home Phila sat at his desk to try and pick up where he had left off with the Maqoma manuscript. He realised he still required silence and solitude to think. For some reason, perhaps because of the rough seas they'd been experiencing around the Cape recently, he'd been thinking about shipwrecks. How white-skinned Xhosas, even chieftesses, survived shipwrecks on African coasts. When their ships came to take them home they refused, choosing to remain Xhosa, some even founding clans that were given chieftess status by Tshiwo, the grandson of Nkosiyamntu, the Mnguni chief whose people the KhoiKhoi named amaXhosa because they regarded them as angry men. Phila wondered about the internal lives of Xhosa people in the nineteenth century, especially those who were at the confrontational forefront with the British: Maqoma, with whom the confrontation was violent; Tiyo Soga, with whom it was religious; and the likes of S.E.K. Mqhayi, with whom it was intellectual.

Fleas Swallowing Elephants

MOVING IN TWISTS AND TURNS AROUND the carnival atmosphere of excited tourists, mostly American and Chinese, Phila went to stand in the stern after boarding the ferry at the Waterfront. The early morning breeze stung his face. The whiff of brine maced his nose. Hands on his waist, he turned to look at the landscape of Cape Town. Old lady Hoerikwaggo puffed on her pipe, meaning Umlindi craved company that morning, hence the white cloth laid over majestic Table Mountain.

The ferry – named *Makana* – was dwarfed by a cruise liner docked next to it, named after the then Queen of Britain. The ironies of history, thought Phila, leaning on the rail and looking down into the water. He wondered how many of his companions on this boat knew a single fact about the person it was named after. Probably not a single one, local or foreign. He adjusted the weight of history he carried on his back.

As the ferry plied across the line, unbidden thoughts of slave journeys to distant lands came to Phila. How some chose the ocean floor over the prospect of slavery in foreign lands, throwing themselves off the ships in droves sometimes. Some believed, in desperation, that the River People would see them through their African villages after being swallowed by the sea. Talk about harsh times breeding desperate wishes and cruel fates that were the midwives of the modern era, Phila thought to himself.

Nxele, the Makana the ferry is named after, himself drowned in these very waters, when the whale boat he escaped on from Robben Island capsized. Those who could swim survived, but Nxele drowned, leaving behind a despairing nation whose last hope of freedom and self-sustenance drowned with him.

What thoughts come to drowning men as the water floods their lungs, pondered Phila. What language do drowning people speak? The fate of Virginia Woolf also trespassed on his mind.

Matched by the seasick dizziness, a mental vacancy dogged Phila into sleep. He felt drawn out of a meditative mind stance into a trance as sleep's dark energy nuzzled him.

In the eye of his sleep the hum of the engines evolved into the moans and groans of a ship's timber. The seawater turned into dark molasses as the ship bounced about in the swell. A broken image of a trembling moon shone through the waters. A whale-oil lamp illuminated the ship's cabin. He heard strange noises, rats scurrying between the walls and the hull as the bloodcurdling roars of violent wind assaulted the ship. Shouts bolted through in confusion, incoherent cries about the Cape of Storms and the spirit of Gama about to bury everything into the floor of the ocean.

After twenty minutes or so the ship stabilised and, Phila, still in his sleep, again heard the steady rhythm of the swishing of oars. Now he could smell a bitter-sweet smoke scent, a smell he had grown to associate with Maqoma. The ship sailed along dikes and edges of lagoons. Blue-grey mountains folded along the littoral of surf-strewn boulders as they moved towards a familiar landscape. Momentarily he recognised it as Hout Bay in a grainy morning light of invading mist. Where Chapman's Peak Drive now snaked were only woods. The land became thickly forested as it climbed into a mountain. Next they passed rims of spectacular gorges at the bottom of which lay the seething sea. Flood paths along the mountains ran to the precipices. As they sailed past an undeveloped Llandudno towards Camps Bay, he recognised the boulders and Sandy Bay beach where German tourists came to be in the nude. Still in his sleep, Phila stood up to try and get a closer look, but discovered his movements were restrained. When he tried to take a step he heard a strange noise, like the clanking of chains. He looked down at his feet, and then at the six or so men also chained beside him. A stone came into his heart.

What's going on, he asked himself quietly.

Grey stone houses frowned down on the sea like isolated sentries, growing whiter and bigger as they moved along, smoke rolling out of their roof pipes. They arrived in a chaotic place, a naval dock or something. It all looked like a dream from a Belloise harbour painting of New York docks, bar the snow. A cold crystal air blew cold dampness. Those men not carrying things up and down from the ships stood around fire braziers, bundled up like sheep, and occasionally hanging their hands to catch the heat. The place was noisy and dirty under the bandage of grey mist.

They were ordered to disembark on this busy wharf and directed to walk to the promenade, passing sweaty stevedores, some with matted beards, loading and unloading cargo from the holds of vessels. Somebody kept saying something about Darling Street as the formless mist hived them into the muddy streets. The serenade from the twisting branches of tree sentries on the street brought apprehension to Phila's soul. They came upon a site of shops and chapels jutting to the sky in a riot of different patterns. Greenmarket Square. This he had managed to work out on his own, finally realising, too, that he was in the Cape Town of an earlier century. Around them a crowd grew, jostling, curious, trying to get closer. Looks of disgust darted on them.

There was a fountain in the centre of the square. Phila cupped his cuffed hands for a drink to slake his thirst and bathe his sweaty face. As he bent he felt a sharp sting on his back. The lash from a sjambok made of hippopotamus will tear brutally into a man's skin.

"Who taught you to pollute your master's fountains? That fountain is not for kaffir needs!" a man in a brown frock, a tonsure band on his wetly sunburnt head, hollered at him. As prisoners they were paraded through the town centre where trade and barter was in riot. The language was inelegant rabble to Phila but he somehow understood all its meaning. This is a scene from *The Divine Comedy*, he thought, as he dragged on. Merchants, petitioners, jugglers and fire-eaters, clerics and whores; musicians playing on stringed instruments, thirsting for applause and hungry for tips; brigands and smugglers, peddlers and knaves, pimps and panders. All ogled the prisoners with alarmed interest. In the crowded streets were netted butcher booths selling all sorts of meats: mutton, beef, chicken and goat carcasses still dressed in their fur at the tail ends for ease of identification. Bloated scaly fish hung from strings in front of fishermen's smelly stalls. Fruit and vegetables, most of which he could not identify, decked the tables.

A caged monkey, with puffs of white hair on its cheeks, surveyed its lost position, chittering and wiggling its tail before calming down in stunned resignation in seeing Phila, who felt deep affinity with the animal. For a moment the monkey halted to give Phila more of an attentive look, before continuing with its squeaking. Phila realised the monkey had found him out but had decided to play along.

On the corner of the square a white man raved about injustices of slavery, looking as much of a lunatic as those pointing and laughing at him. As the prisoners passed by they saw the man being escorted away by government officials, who accused him of rabble rousing. People gambled away their earnings in dark corners, some fighting like rams next to troops

301

of caged slaves, to the chagrin of scratching curs and gaunt scavenging cats. Wagoners, with whips as long as the masts of ships, fastened cattle with lariat, their wagons swerving dangerously to avoid boozed clerks on the streets. Clergymen, with long tail-coats and tall stove-pipe hats, preached in booming voices, words bursting out of their mouths like balls of fire, bringing tears to the eyes of some listeners. Singing females, pregnant, probably with the seeds of those same reverend preachers, happy-clapped their hands with heads tilted to the skies. Freed slaves and immigrant costermongers lined the pavements selling bottles of tonics, bitters, liniments and soaps.

The prison Phila and others were taken to was situated in the town's centre. It looked more like soldiers' barracks and smelled of human filth. A pestilent mix of unwashed men, smoke from the braziers, a permanent stench from the horse dung and chicken droppings clung to the prison walls where they were kept locked for four nights. A blustering wind whistled all night long, bringing with it rattling rain. Shingling and sighs of the distant sea sent notes of despair to the heart as Phila tried in vain to sleep. Everyone inside clung to their own skin, driving away fear by remembering and telling to each other legends of their lands. The food, not enough to feed a grasshopper, was a mere chitterling soup with floating chickpeas and black bread before noon. Eventually they were taken to a court building, where judges and magistrates in black suits and white neck-cloths argued their fates. During breaks and after hours, legal vultures – attorneys, lawyers, interpreters and judges – continued their arguments augmented by tots of peach brandy outside the court buildings. Spectators openly placed bets on court verdicts. Even inside the courtroom, unruly spectators interrupted the proceedings with whistling and turning over of tables and chairs when the judgment went against their bets. Some even threw old tobacco quids and stubs to signify their betting losses or wins.

After hearing evidence, and that of the prosecutors, the swellhead brassneck judge, whose ugliness was arresting – yellowing eyes, double-chinned, a busy Adam's apple, uneven teeth and a pale dyspeptic face – gave his verdict.

Rolling his eyes and stuttering in an affected tone, he pronounced: "The evidence against you, Macoma, is overwhelming." He wiped his grey handlebar moustache. "Her Majesty's government has tried by all civil means possible to provide you and your people with protection under her benign hand. She offered you protectorates, where you could learn more civilised ways of doing things, and how to save your soul from perdition.

You were free to go there like other kaffirs whenever you chose to, but you refused, choosing to make yourself a nuisance to Her Majesty's subjects, your superiors and masters. You chose to be a cacodemon to Her Majesty's government." He chewed his tobacco with an occasional drop of his head under the table to spit.

"You're indefatigable in your paganism and a bad influence on other kaffirs. You lead them astray by your bad influences and the overwhelming trust they place on you. It's become clear to Her Majesty's government that all remonstrance of civilisation has been defeated in your beastly breast by your barbaric base instincts. Therefore she has no alternative but to remove you, together with the chiefs accompanying you, whom I'm certain are under your belligerent influence, from society. Her Majesty's government can no longer stomach your unregenerate influence, thus she's taking you away, for the good of the rest of your people. It would appear as if whenever you're in your village you let out the demon of your fever into the fray to disturb the peace. If you're bent on living like a barbarian you shall do so in isolation, away from other innocent kaffirs. It is therefore incumbent upon me to follow the verdict of our lower courts in Frontierland by sentencing you to life imprisonment on Robben Island, coming out only when fleas swallow elephants. There you shall have enough time to contemplate your mischievous behaviour against Her Majesty's government, and be a warning to those who wish to follow your bad example.

"From what I've just heard, you've killed enough men to stock three graveyards because of your opposition to civilisation. Most disgusting to me is that your frenzy didn't stop with your animal kind, but you had the temerity to raid and kill white people also. For this your crime is not only deplorable to Her Majesty's court alone, but an abomination in the eyes of the Almighty who, in His unfathomable wisdom, has seen right to give superior intelligence and wisdom to white people while leaving the black race with only animal intelligence and instinct. We shall therefore put as much space as possible between you and the civilisation you're so averse to. With any luck you might even cultivate an acquaintance with the Lord's grace, and be purged of your savage manners. If you have nothing to say for yourself, you're all dismissed."

The judge bent down to take a swig from the flask he kept inside his jacket pocket, coming up and wiping his mouth with the back of his hand.

Phila felt someone take a stronger hold on him, making him stand. He was about to protest, thinking it was just Maqoma, when he realised they were legion: brown, yellow, white faces – all of them looking at him in anticipation. He was confused as to what to say or do. He felt his knees buckle. Then Maqoma was there, extending a hand to him, and Phila stood up, firm and tall. The courtroom was filled with the dead, men and women, all silently cheering Phila on with eagerness in their eyes. Phila knew none of these people and yet he knew every one of them.

Something forceful moved through Phila, burning like coal on his lips. He fought the flicker of panic when he sensed this might be the last time he spoke as a free man, or even alive, in front of an audience. When he spoke his voice was not his own.

"Let it never be said," he began, pausing as the packed courtroom gasped audibly. "Let it never be said that words were extinguished in my mouth when the need arose." Some people slapped their hands over their mouths in disbelief. They never expected a kaffir to address a white man's court of law with such familiarity, let alone with anger in his voice and fire in his eyes.

"I, sir, will try to invite you into the assembly under my skull, even if it costs me my life.

"I have cherished the idea of a free society, of universal justice, fighting against both white and black domination. All my life I've been against the notion of power serving only the needs of the strong, and condemning the weak and the poor.

"I've lived my life hard as an axe and kind as the rain. There's nothing I will be sorry to leave behind here when I depart. You fertilise your language with hypocrisy and call it civilisation. I've often found many savages under the cloth of your civilisation. You tell me that we were free to choose, yet we're not allowed to choose against the choices your government makes for us. Let your words be your judge.

"The only freedom we ever had, since the white man came to our land, was that of submission, perdition or resistance. I chose resistance! I chose to face the fire of your cannons knowing very well it would bring me to perdition or complete freedom.

"I grew up before the pestilence of white people coming to our land. Then our land was out-gloried only by the stars. There was an implausibility of wildebeest and a dazzle of zebras everywhere. Hardly fifty full cycles since you came all these have disappeared from our land. And you insist yours are civilised ways, though you are not able to coexist with anything, not with animals or people who don't look like you, without wishing to exterminate them.

304

"My memory might be slightly dimmed by time; it is now old as the hills. But, though memory decays, I remember in my youth roaming freely on our land without fear of white people's papers, guns and cannons. That is etched on my mind and will not be extinguished until I gain it again. It seems now it has brought me to my early grave.

"Strange you should call stony non-arable land 'protectorates'. I'll never accept your protection even if it bought me five lives in your robe-wearing, sheep-eating days. You may think in your mind that this will end here, with my silence and permanent exile, but it shall not.

"The spirit of the Xhosa people is indomitable, incorrigible and independent. It will rise again, perhaps not in my lifetime, which you're determined to shorten, but, like a flooding river on its way to the sea, it will rise. The Xhosa people can never be bondsmen forever. It is against their nature. We're more than proud people. We're the native spirit of this land. Without us this land loses its soul, and with us in bondage the land is in shackles.

"Do what your pink mind prefers with me, but know you shall never silence me. The spirit of Phalo, passing through these veins, will be reborn in every black man's heart. Will you close the wombs of our women? Unless you can manage that you're fighting a losing battle. I shall rise again, this time more powerful and multitudinous, because I shall live in each and every black person you murder by your unjust laws; every black person that inhabits this land. And then this land will erupt. The plots you cut by cunning among yourselves shall go back to the rightful owners of the land. The houses you build shall be the inheritance of the children of this land. Our bones you whiten shall fertilise the roe that will rise against your injustices."

There was a move from the side of the courtroom, soldiers lining up. Phila stopped them with a look of daggers.

"You have poisoned our atmosphere with the spirit of greed and harsh opportunism – what you call enterprise. But this is not the last you will hear from the house of Phalo. Isolate or kill me all you want, but it shall be significant when I'm laid underground ..."

The redcoats came to shackle them and take them back to prison before he could finish.

※

Pitchforked from sleep by the announcement from the guide of their

305

arrival on Robben Island, Phila felt nauseous and disorientated. As he stepped onto the dock he found that he was trembling.

The wind had lost its teeth. A hushed holding-in of things enveloped the island.

Tourists moved ahead eagerly and gathered around the guide who was narrating a bowdlerised historical version of the island. It filled him with a desire to let out a scream, in Baldwinian manner. Phila held back from the tourist crowd, adjusting the weight of history on his back. Then he lost them to go beyond the quarries where he had learnt the native chiefs' graves were situated. He found he was still not alone. Generations of freedom fighters marched through the dreaming fields of his mind as he walked the quarry fields of the island, where the likes of Mandela had toiled during their prison stay. A whisper came to his ear as he changed his saunter into a canter:

I, Maqoma, the cacodemon. I, Makhanda, the numinous. I, Moturu, the patient crocodile. I, Harry the Strandloper. I, Malagasy, the slippery leopard; I, Autshumato, the glue of the San; I, Langalibalele, the thick-skinned rhino; I, Mandela, Sisulu, Sobukwe. I, Phila Sobanzi.

Endnote

MAQOMA WAS ARRESTED IN 1857 and taken to prison in Grahamstown with his wife and a toddler son. He was charged with inciting the murder of a minor chief, Fusani, who was accused of being a colonial spy. The trial was by court-martial in Fort Hare. Maqoma was, naturally, found guilty of counselling and advising the 'eating up' of Fusani. This was contrived into a capital offence, and so death was the sentence. Governor George Grey commuted the sentence to twenty years of hard labour on Robben Island. Maqoma was subsequently relieved of hard labour in consideration of his age – he was over sixty. The rest of the Xhosa chiefs followed him to Robben Island in a similar fashion. The idea was to break the Xhosa tribal system.

On 19 December 1857 Maqoma was put on board a ship at Port Elizabeth to be transported to Cape Town. His wife and toddler son were with him, as were two other Tembu chiefs who had been found guilty of supposedly robbing white farms. Huge crowds of white people and newspaper reporters congregated on the docks in PE to watch the famous Maqoma, the "cacodemon", being taken to jail. He kept quiet and paid no attention to the commotion, unlike the other chiefs who were still protesting their innocence. One reporter commented that, "His dark eyes hadn't lost their frightening deep stare." Wearing chains "heavy enough for a ship's cable", eating apricots and smoking his pipe, Maqoma leaned over the side of the steamer. He sat calmly, indifferent to it all, in tune with the insouciance of the hills and the lassitude of the sea. It would seem most of what was happening to his life then inhabited only the fringes of his soul. His real life was no longer there, even though his physical body was still shackled. The journalists interpreted this as a sign of madness and contempt for the rules of common sense. They said he had a madman's stare. It could just as easily have been interpreted as the mystical stare of the religious.

Maqoma was released from Robben Island in 1869. He went back to the Eastern Cape and quietly settled on his beloved land at the foot of the Waterkloof mountains, in the valleys belted by the Kat River. He joined his son Tini, who owned land and farmed with grains in the area, his production even surpassing that of the white farmers. Tini was educated by Anglican missionaries at Zonnebloem College in Cape Town. He was never allowed to visit his father on Robben Island.

In 1871 a detachment of the Cape Mounted Rifles, Maqoma's sworn enemies, surrounded the farm, evicted Maqoma and his family and accompanied him to King Williams Town, where he was "to stand trial for his crimes". When no trial was forthcoming, he returned to establish himself and his family in the Waterkloof area. On 27 November 1871, he was again rounded up by soldiers for "trespassing'" and imprisoned in Ngqengqe (Fort Beaufort). Without any specific charge or trial, the magistrate there simply ordered him to be incarcerated on Robben Island. Along with a few chiefs and brigands for human company, he was deposited among the ruins of the huts he and the others had occupied the first time they were held on the island. There was no longer the opportunity to pursue the subsistence farming they had before.

He subsequently died on 7 September 1873 and was buried without any ceremony in an unmarked grave, in the same way as many of the others incarcerated on Robben Island. There's no way of telling for sure if the bones that were exhumed and reburied on Ntaba kaNdoda were his.

Perhaps it doesn't matter in the bigger scheme of things, except that Xhosas are particular about the remains of their kings and loved ones. Hence that wound on top of King Hintsa's severed head still festers in the Xhosa national psyche. By their own doing, the face of Maqoma hounded the British for more than the hundred years they were at war with the Xhosas.

Those who visited Maqoma in his final years overwhelmingly recount how he had fallen silent, refusing to speak with anyone and hardly eating anything. This book is intended to lend him a voice again, before we all meet in the greater silence.

Acknowledgements

I OFFER MY GRATITUDE TO THE AFRICAN continent, her land, her resilient people, the rivers and the sea, whose reverberations brings us news from the ancient of times.

None can write about the frontier history in South Africa without coming across Noel Mostert's seminal work *Frontiers: The Epic of South Africa's Creation and the Tragedy of the Xhosa People*. Scholars like Jeff Peires and Jeff Opland are indispensable pathfinders on the written history of amaXhosa. But the book that first sparked my interest was *Maqoma: The Legend of a Great Xhosa Warrior* by Timothy J Stapleton – I'm glad it has been reissued by Amava Books.

The numerous journals of missionaries and soldiers of the time greatly assisted me, especially with nuances of the era. S.E.K. Mqhayi, both his literary and journalistic writings, was a companion who helped me with the tone of Xhosa oral history and storytelling. He is my companion still. I have also spent many fireside chats with numerous Xhosa elders in the Eastern Cape, especially where Jong'Umsobomvu lived.

I cannot name all of the people by name here, but all their words, somehow, form the bloodstream of this book. In two lifetimes I can never repay the debt I owe to all of them. I hope, in us, the spirit of our ancestors raises the horn of Africa.

I would like to thank also my family who bore the brunt of my neglect while I was obsessing over this book; my wife, Helen, in particular for covering for my failures in raising our kids. I hope one day we will all find it worth the sacrifice and effort.